T0060226

# NEVER WAVE GOODBYE

A NOVEL OF SUSPENSE

DOUG MAGEE

A TOUCHSTONE BOOK
Published by Simon & Schuster
New York London Toronto Sydney

Touchstone
A Division of Simon & Schuster, Inc.
1230 Avenue of the Americas
New York, NY 10020



First Touchstone hardcover edition June 2010



*Designed by Akasha Archer*

Manufactured in the United States of America

10 9 8 7 6 5 4 3 2 1

Library of Congress Cataloging-in-Publication Data is available.

Magee, Doug.
Never wave good-bye : a novel / by Doug Magee.
p. cm.
1. Missing children—Fiction. I. Title.
PS3613.A3425N48 2010
813'.6—dc22
2010010085

ISBN 978-1-4391-5398-7

ISBN 978-1-4391-6009-1 (ebook)

For Mary
*Jeg elsker deg*

Hope is the thing with feathers
That perches in the soul,
And sings the tune without the words,
And never stops at all,

And sweetest in the gale is heard;
And sore must be the storm
That could abash the little bird
That kept so many warm.

*Emily Dickinson*

Truth is not the result of an effort, the end of the road. It is here and now, in the very longing and search for it. You do not see it because you look too far away from yourself, outside your innermost being.

*Nisargadatta Maharaj*

# NEVER WAVE GOODBYE

# One

It wasn't a routine event, something so normal and habitual that she was lulled to sleep by dozens of previous repetitions. She couldn't make that excuse. It was, in fact, a once-in-a-lifetime occurrence. And yet she had imagined the moments so often, rehearsed them, picked through so many possible problems and solutions to the problems, that when it finally did come time to put Sarah on the camp van, send her only daughter off for the first time in her life, it was as if she had done it many times before.

And when what she imagined actually happened, without any problems, the coincidence of her imagination and reality lent those whole few minutes of goodbye an even greater authenticity. She wasn't duped so much by a clever individual as she was by her own expectations. We see what we want to see. Magicians and con artists know this about us. We are blind and trusting at the same time. We trust our interpretations of what we see because to do otherwise would paralyze us. We are all blind. This was her mantra in the dark times, the words keeping the scalding guilt of those days from burning through to the bone. There had been every indication that what she saw was real. She never thought to question.

Perhaps if David had been there, one of them would have questioned, would have stepped back and said, "Wait a minute." But it hadn't worked out that way. Lena had been left alone to get things organized, calm fears, put Sarah on the bus, and say goodbye. An hour earlier, without warning, David had come out of the bedroom and said he would have to miss the send-off, that he had just gotten a call on his cell phone, that he would have to go in to work for a few hours.

"Something's come up and they need me."

Lena doubted this was true. David's calls from work, at least any she could remember, came on the landline. And it was Saturday and he was officially on vacation for the next two weeks. Plus his job, truth be told, was not so important that he would need to leave an event like Sarah's first departure for camp to deal with some work problem. Lena was about to question the call, the need to leave, when she saw the way David couldn't hold her gaze, and she wondered if the whole situation was just too much for him, that he feared the goodbye, feared, perhaps, the time alone with her after Sarah was gone. She let the lie slide.

David found Sarah in her bedroom and told her he had to leave. She wasn't bothered by this, he was happy to see, and gave him a hug before he asked for one.

"You get to email, right?" he asked as they held the hug.

"I think so, but it's something like once a week. Linda says the computers suck. At least they did last year."

"Well, take good notes so you can tell us all about it when you get back."

David kissed her on the forehead and smiled down at his nine-year-old. A sudden rush of incompleteness, of things not said or done, came over him. This wonder, who had gone from a bloody bundle of flesh to a bright-eyed young girl in no time, was only an hour away from her first solo trip out into the world. Weren't there warnings he should be giving her? Shouldn't there be some definite "I love you," one that didn't have the usual singsong, everyday, taken-for-granted tone, one that Sarah would hear and could carry with her for the two weeks she would be away? He had always planned to one day give his daughter a précis at least of his accumulated wisdom, the life lessons he had gathered. Shouldn't he have done that by now? But the look on Sarah's face, the one he and Lena always associated with a sort of tacit declaration of independence, stopped him. He realized that any utterance like "Watch out for snakes" would be met with a "Duh." He had nothing more to say.

He backed up, waved a goodbye, and she waved back. He turned and took his tall frame through the doorway. Lena was working through a checklist in the dining room. Since deciding not to challenge David on the phone call from work, she had been preparing herself for a frosty goodbye with him, a little piece of mutual dissembling, something they had become very good at in recent years. David didn't disappoint. He was almost out the front door, a good fifteen feet away from Lena, before he said anything. He held up his cell phone.

"If there's any problem, call me on the cell. I may not be at my desk."

"Right," Lena answered, wanting to jab in something like, "You sure aren't going to be at your desk." But she just gave him the usual half smile and knew that would send him out the door.

Lena looked at the grandfather clock in the living room and realized she was a little behind schedule. The van was supposed to come at nine. The camp had said that they were the first on the route, and so Lena wanted to be ready at least by ten of nine. It was eight twenty-five when she put down her list and headed for Sarah's room.

Sarah was on her computer, staring at some postage-stamp-sized grainy video. Lena saw that she had laid out clothes and a couple of books on the bed. Without saying anything to Sarah, she scooped these up and went to her own bedroom, hers and David's, and began packing Sarah's suitcase. Like David she wondered if she should have some words of wisdom for Sarah's departure, but big mother-daughter speeches weren't part of their relationship. Lena decided to make the goodbye as low-key as possible.

Sarah appeared in the bedroom door. She looked a little lost, maybe scared.

"What's up, honey?" Lena kept packing, not wanting to seem too concerned.

"I just remembered. One of the first things they do is make you take a swim test. Linda said it's, like, real cold and you have to float at the end."

"You're a good swimmer."

"No, I'm not. And I can't float. You've gotta be fat to float."

Lena laughed at this and went to her.

"Take it from a professional, that has no basis in fact. And, uh, I can float. Do you think I'm fat?"

"No."

"It has to do with bone density. If your bones are dense it makes it harder to float. I think you probably have the same bone density Dad and I have, so the likelihood is that you can be a good floater."

"Thanks for the lecture."

"No charge. Are you all set? What shoes are you wearing?"

"These," Sarah said pointing to the sneakers she had on, new ones. "And I know what you're going to say. 'They're new. You'll get them all dirty.' Right?"

"Well, yeah. That makes sense."

"But I'm just going to wear them on the bus and I'll change into my cleats when we get there."

Lena made a quick decision not to wade into the cleats waters again. Sarah, a better-than-average soccer player, had been torn between a soccer camp her Sprout League coach had been heavily promoting among his players and Camp Arno, the all-purpose sleepaway in the Catskills her friend Linda had gone to the year before, one that didn't have a soccer program at all. After she made her decision to go to Camp Arno, Sarah went through a long period of the nine-year-old camper's version of buyer's remorse and vowed to wear her cleats all the time she was in camp. Lena had tried to point out that hiking, in particular, would be a tough, perhaps dangerous slog in cleats. But she had long ago stopped trying to win that battle.

Sarah turned and left, and Lena stood there for a minute watching her young daughter go down the hall. Because Sarah had always moved gracefully, Lena had hoped Sarah's early dance lessons might have stuck instead of soccer. While others in the tutu set looked wooden and struggling, Sarah made the space around her float as she moved through the elementary steps. Lena, who didn't consider herself graceful at all, mourned a lost opportunity when Sarah had said she didn't want to go back to Miss Threadgill's "stupid" dance school and David had backed her. How nice it would have been, Lena thought, to be sending Sarah off to a ballet camp instead of either a soccer camp or Arno. But Lena was not the sort of parent who imposed her own wishes or thwarted ambitions on her daughter. Sarah was Sarah, and Lena was determined to support her in whatever direction she might take in life.

"They're here," Sarah called from the living room. Lena wasn't sure what Sarah was referring to at first but quickly realized the bus must be in the driveway. She went to the bedroom window and saw the blue van with the Camp Arno logo on the side. Lena called back to Sarah.

"Tell them we'll—" She stopped when Sarah came into the bedroom.

"No, Mom. You tell them." Sarah looked as if a lot of confidence had drained from her in the past few minutes. Lena put a comforting hand on her shoulder on her way out of the bedroom.

"Zip up that suitcase and . . . Let me think."

She went to the front door, opened it, and stood on the small front porch. A curly-headed young man, probably a college student, had opened the driver's side door and was getting out. Lena waved at him.

"Hi! We'll be right out!"

He waved acknowledgment and Lena went back in the house. Sarah was dragging her suitcase into the living room, a good sign, Lena thought. Lena checked the grandfather clock and saw that it was only twenty of nine. At least they're punctual, Lena said to herself as she went to the dining room table and picked up her checklist.

The next few minutes were devoted to that slip of paper: pillow, towels, sleeping bag, dopp kit ("What's a dopp kit?" "Oh, that's what Dad calls it. You know, with your toothbrush and soap and stuff."), hat, sunscreen, bug spray, flashlight, soccer ball, preaddressed postcards, and summer reading books, all stuffed into the new duffel. Lena kept checking out the driveway and saw the college student leaning against the front of the van, seemingly not worried about them.

Then it was time to haul the suitcase and the duffel outside. Lena grabbed the heavier suitcase and was about to tell Sarah to pick up the duffel when she saw Sarah's chin crinkle and tears form in her eyes. Lena gave her a small hug.

"Things are going to be fine, honey. Linda will be there with you. And it's just for two weeks."

"I wish I was going to soccer camp," Sarah managed, as she brushed away the tears. But she picked up the duffel and, true to her independent nature, led Lena out the front door.

The college student gave Sarah a big smile, held out his hand to her, and introduced himself as J.D. He wore a polo shirt with the camp logo on it that Lena thought was a bit too tight for his padded frame. He took the duffel and went to the back of the van. Lena followed and was pleased to see that the van was immaculate inside. Once the suitcase was in the back and the doors closed, Lena held out her hand to J.D.

"I'm Lena, Sarah's mother."

"Hi. J.D. Nice to meet you. I need you to sign some papers."

They moved toward the front of the van, and Sarah shadowed Lena as they walked. J.D. pulled a clipboard from the front seat and handed it to Lena with a pen.

"You need to sign the bottom of the first page, page three, and the last page."

Lena skimmed the pages, seeing it was the usual waivers and consent forms. "I didn't know I'd need my lawyer today."

J.D. laughed and then noticed that Sarah was hanging back. He moved to her.

"Was that a soccer ball I felt in your duffel?"

"Yes."

"You play, huh?"

"Yes."

"Well, you're going to have a ball, no pun intended, at Arno, then."

"How come? They don't have soccer." Sarah was confused but expectant too. J.D. hesitated a bit, then grinned as if he were revealing a secret.

"I know, the brochure didn't say anything about it, but they cleared a new field down by the lake last fall and they've decided to make a soccer field out of it."

Sarah looked at Lena, who was listening as she read and signed.

"Mom, you hear?"

"That's great," she answered, handing the clipboard back to J.D. When she saw Sarah's joy at the news, she also wanted to give J.D. a big thanks for bringing up the topic. This was going to make the goodbye that was around the corner a lot easier.

And it did. J.D. opened the side door, Sarah hopped in, Lena helped her with the shoulder seat belt, used the opportunity for a final hug, and spoke to her from only inches away.

"I love you, honey. See you in two weeks."

"I love you, Mom."

Lena thought she saw more tears, but she backed out and J.D. slid the door shut quickly. He held out his hand and gave Lena a look that said, "She'll be fine."

"Nice meeting you, Mrs. Trainor."

"Thank you. Have a good two weeks. And, uh, do you want me to call the Rostenkowskis and tell them you're going to be early?"

J.D. looked at his watch and shook his head.

"No, I think I'll be right on time. But we'll wait if we have to."

He smiled again before he got in the van. This time Lena noticed what she thought was a tobacco stain on one of his front teeth. It always bothered her to see young people who smoked. But it was a small glitch in her assessment of J.D. She had already formed the sentence she would use to describe him to David. "Sarah's in capable hands."

The reflections off the van windows kept Lena from seeing Sarah clearly as the van backed up, turned out into the street, then pulled ahead. For a brief moment Lena had the urge to run after the van. Why? She couldn't say. Was it the loss of control? She had prepared well, solved all the minor problems, and the goodbye had gone like clockwork. But now Sarah was out of sight, hurtling, Lena thought, into some outer space. Through tear-fuzzed eyes Lena watched the pristine calm of the Westchester street settle as the van drove out of sight. She wiped her tears and chastised herself for being so sentimental. Look at this clearly, she thought. Be proud of Sarah. She had hopped in the van with a stranger and left without theatrics, a credit to herself and her parents. Sarah, as J.D.'s look had told her, was going to be just fine.

Over her coffee and bagel during the next fifteen minutes, however, Lena wondered if she and David were going to be fine. His pulling out at the last minute had not been a real confidence builder. There wasn't any talk of separation or divorce but there hadn't been much talk of any kind between them for quite a while. They had been warm and loving in the years they had tried to give Sarah a sibling. But after they had made the decision not to "go techno" (Lena's phrase), i.e., the *in vitro* route, something had changed in the relationship—nothing tectonic, nothing the outside world would even be aware of, but a heart shift for both of them nevertheless.

Lena wasn't exactly going to make a checklist of things she and David needed to talk about, but she was going to approach the two weeks the way she would approach a problem in her oncology practice: the marriage had a cancer of sorts, something was wrong, they needed to describe the symptoms and find the causes in order to be healthy again. She would never use that metaphor directly, but her thinking went that way. Symptoms: sporadic, unhappy sex, avoiding time together, sharing little about anything not having to do with Sarah. Causes: David's job dissatisfaction . . .

She was stuck on this cause. He had been in investment banking in the city when they met and had hated it. When they moved out to Pelham, he hated it even more because of the commute, and so he found a well-paying job in the marketing department of the Dell regional headquarters. He mastered the job's basics in the first week, was promoted twice in the first year, and then began to itch for something more. Lena had urged him to look for another job, but he seemed stuck. The job gave him time with Sarah, he would say, the pay couldn't be beat, he didn't want to commute again, and the benefits were great. Lena thought the two weeks they had now would be a good time to broach the subject of his quitting altogether, finding something more satisfying, something creative even.

They didn't exactly need the money. Lena had been in her practice at Mount Sinai for five years. She and her partners had arranged a very lucrative deal with the hospital that had allowed Lena and David a bit of a financial cushion. David could take a year or two off and it wouldn't kill their bottom line, ruin their savings. She wanted David to be happy. That would be chemo to the cancer.

She was lost in these thoughts when the doorbell rang. She didn't know who it was ringing, but as she ran through some possibilities—the mailman needed something signed, a lawn care company looking for work—she hoped it wasn't Janet Rostenkowski. Janet was Sarah's friend Linda's mother, a perfectly nice but dishwater dull woman Lena had been forced to be friends with by virtue of their daughters' friendship. Janet and her husband taught at Pelham High School and had little to talk about except kids and things that were happening in the school. And money woes. Lena dreaded the times when Janet would drop Linda off at the house and stop in for a chat. She hoped this wasn't one of them, though with their daughters just off to camp together, it would be an ideal time in Janet's mind for such a kaffeeklatsch.

But it wasn't Janet standing on the front doorstep. It was a young woman with a trim athletic build, a lovely tan on smooth skin, sparkling eyes, and pretty, blond-streaked hair. She was upbeat and smiling.

"Hi. Is Sarah ready?"

Lena looked from the young woman to the driveway. There she saw a van, different from the Camp Arno van, green instead of blue, a different make, but it too had the Camp Arno logo on the side. Lena was confused for a second but then recovered.

"Uh, no. They already picked her up."

The young woman was not ready for this. Lena noticed that she had on the same type of shirt J.D. had worn and she carried a walkie-talkie in her right hand. She tried to smile through her confusion.

"Um, who picked her up?"

"J.D. The other counselor. I guess he was a counselor. He had a van like yours."

Now the young woman couldn't conceal her confusion. She put the walkie-talkie to her mouth, looking back at the van, and spoke to the driver. Lena could now see him through the windshield.

"Was there somebody else supposed to pick up Sarah Trainor?"

"No" came squawking through the walkie-talkie.

"Do you know a J.D. from camp?" the young woman asked.

"No. Why?"

"Well, um, Sarah's mother says a J.D. somebody came in a camp van to pick up Sarah."

This time there was no response from the walkie-talkie. Instead the driver's door opened and an older man with graying hair, the tan of someone who's been outside a lot, and a very purposeful gait came walking toward the house. Lena would never forget the seconds of that walk, of the way his stride and knit eyebrows made him look like a walking question mark, of what his even coming out of the van and toward them meant. The world was suddenly missing pieces. Things were floating that should have been anchored. Lena's ordered, scientific world was dissolving. What's the question here? Where's the problem? What can be tested? The man kept walking toward the house. Lena's heart beat hard in her chest. You're the dream, she thought. J.D. was the reality. Please. Go away.

Suddenly nothing in the world could be trusted. Was she really standing at her front door like this, with these people? Had she actually strapped Sarah into a van only a half hour ago? Was David gone somewhere or was he in the house? Who was she?

The man had reached her and was making a concerted effort not to seem confused, to be in control. He was asking questions in a calm voice, and Lena was answering them as best she could. But there was a horrible, drumbeat voice inside her that blotted out all the words the two of them were exchanging. Over and over it pounded. She couldn't fight it. The man talked. She talked. The blond girl's eyes went wide with apprehension. There were no anchors. Nothing was real.

Where on earth was Sarah?

# Two

If J.D. was a fake, an illusion almost, then Sarah was lost in an unreal world. That couldn't be. Lena hung on to the "this is all a big mistake" belief as long as she could. But slowly, with the two strangers inside her house unable to unravel the mystery, she had to give in. J.D. wasn't from the camp. J.D. had duped her. J.D. had taken Sarah with him, and they weren't going to the camp.

David didn't answer his cell phone. Lena had a tumble of words she was going to deliver when he picked up, but when she got his voicemail, she didn't know what to say. The situation was still a confused thing happening in the house, the voices speaking to her all distant and hard to understand. She managed only the basics.

"David. There's a problem with Sarah, with camp. Call me."

She thought about calling his work number but she was certain now he wasn't there. Why wasn't he answering his cell, though? Had he gone into the city and been in the subway? There was coverage everywhere else she could think of. Had his battery died? Would it be hours before they got in touch? She wanted to talk to him now.

She was calling from her cell in the bedroom. The gray-haired man and the young woman were using the landline to "straighten this thing out." Lena went back to the kitchen to see what they knew now, but she had no hope they would have figured out something so mysterious so quickly. The looks on their faces confirmed her suspicion. They seemed lost. The young woman was on the edge of tears. The gray-haired man was on the phone, not talking, waiting for someone on the other end of the line. He then listened, grunted, and hung up.

"They're all down at the front gate doing registration. There's a junior counselor in the office, but he doesn't know anything."

"Can't you call the front gate? Doesn't somebody have a cell?" Lena asked as she moved into the kitchen.

"There's no cell coverage at the camp."

"Well, have the junior counselor go get somebody."

"He's doing that. They have this number."

Lena was stiffening now, a reaction to the resignation she was seeing in the two people in front of her. She'd been in consultations when certain doctors, faced with a flurry of results and evidence, tucked their heads like turtles, and she would have to be the one to get everyone moving toward a diagnosis.

"We need to call the police. Sorry, what is your name?"

"I'm Winston and this is Kerry," he said. "Let's wait a minute before we call the police. This could be some simple mistake."

"What kind of mistake? You said you didn't know a J.D. and there wasn't any other van."

"That I know of. It's a big camp. You said it seemed brand-new. Maybe they bought something, didn't tell us, got schedules mixed up. I was out on a canoe trip most of last week. Maybe I got the wrong info. I wouldn't want to go running off to the police and find it was a simple mistake."

"Kidnapped. What if she's been kidnapped?" Lena said the word for the first time out loud though it had been poised to leap out of her mouth ever since Winston walked toward the house.

"I can't believe—," Winston started and was stopped by the phone ringing. At Lena's nod he answered. "Hello . . . It's me, Rich. You get the message? . . . No, she said it had the camp logo on the side and the guy had papers with the camp logo too. Waivers, sounds just like ours . . . Yeah. Right here." He turned to Lena and held out the phone. "He'd like to speak to you." Lena took the phone.

"Hello. This is Lena Trainor. Who's this?"

"I'm Rich Carlone, Mrs. Trainor. I'm sorry about this. Can you describe the man who, uh, picked up, uh, Sarah?"

"He looked like a college student. About maybe five ten, curly-haired, a little overweight, and he wore a shirt just like these people are wearing here with me. And . . . he had tobacco stains on his teeth, on a tooth, in front."

"We don't hire smokers."

"How was I supposed to know that!" Lena shot back, feeling herself losing control now. The image of the van driving away down the street was replaying over and over in her head and all this talk was keeping her from running after her baby.

"You're not. I'm sorry." Carlone sounded confused. Lena pushed.

"Is there any chance this guy had anything to do with the camp? Has there been some sort of mix-up?"

There was silence on the line, as if Carlone were really thinking through the question. "No."

"Then we have to call the police."

"Yes. But—"

"But what?"

"Can you let my drivers go? They have to pick up other kids. You can have the police call me if they need information."

"If? Who else are they going to ask for information?"

"Right. Right. Sorry. But my drivers don't know anything."

"Okay." She listened to Carlone's further apologies, handed the phone to Winston, heard him get instructions, and shared a look with Kerry. When Winston got off the phone, Kerry spoke up.

"Why don't I stay with Mrs. Trainor?"

Winston agreed but Lena imagined being alone in the crisis would be preferable to having to deal with this cheerleader.

"Thanks, but my husband will be home any minute. You go along with . . ." She had forgotten the gray-haired man's name again.

"Winston," he filled in. "Are you sure?"

"Yes. Any minute."

"Should we wait until you call the police?"

Lena was wondering if maybe that was a good idea when the phone rang. Winston instinctively reached for the receiver but then handed it to Lena. Lena got a wary "hello" out.

It was Janet Rostenkowski, and as usual she just launched into the reason for her call.

"Hi, Lena. Sarah wanted me to call you. She forgot her fleece and so we lent her one of Linda's. She didn't want you to see her fleece at home and worry she was going to be cold. How are—"

"She was there, the van?" Lena rushed her words, not knowing what question to ask first.

"Yup. They're off. Two happy campers. I wondered—"

"A blue van? A guy named J.D.?"

"I didn't get his name. Phil talked to him first. Seemed nice. Uh, why?"

"He's not from the camp. The real drivers are here, with me."

Janet was silent for a long time. The line buzzed as if she were walking with a mobile phone. "I don't understand. What are you saying?"

"The guy who picked up Linda and Sarah wasn't from the camp. They don't know anything about him."

"The van was from the camp. It had the logo on the side."

"I know. He must have done that himself. And the forms. He had you sign forms?"

Janet didn't answer and Lena could hear her talking to Phil, telling him what Lena had just told her. Phil got on the phone.

"Lena. It's Phil. What's up?"

"I think the girls have been kidnapped."

"Kidnapped? By whom?"

"The guy who picked them up. He said his name was J.D., right?"

"Yes, but, I, uh, knew him. From last year." Phil said this haltingly.

"You knew him?"

"Well, come to think of it, he said he remembered me from last year. He said he was a junior counselor then. I didn't really remember him."

"The real drivers are here now, with me."

"Shit." The word was completely out of character for the buttoned-up Phil. "I signed . . . the forms were the same as last year."

"When did they leave?"

"I don't know. I went out to the garden . . . Janet, when did they leave?"

Lena could hear Janet in the background. Her voice seemed to be coming through tears. Phil spoke into the phone again.

"Maybe a half an hour, forty-five minutes ago, Janet thinks."

"I'm calling the police."

"Yes. You've got the real drivers with you?"

"Yes."

"Any others they're supposed to pick up?"

"I think so," Lena said, suddenly realizing that other parents should be alerted. She turned to Winston. "You have others you're supposed to pick up?"

"Yeah. Out in the van. I've got the list out in the van."

"How many?"

"Three more, I think."

"Get it. Get the list," Lena barked, kicking herself for not thinking of the other parents sooner. Hadn't J.D. said he had other pickups? Kerry dashed out of the kitchen. Then Lena spoke into the phone again.

"Phil, I'm going to hang up and call the police. Then we'll call the other parents. Or maybe we'll do that first."

"Is David there?"

"No, he's uh, at work."

"Oh. Look. We'll come over, be with you."

"You don't have to—"

"We'll be there." He hung up. Lena hung up as well, forgetting Winston was still in the kitchen. When she turned and saw him standing there, a hangdog look on his face, nothing to offer, she was startled at first, then frustrated. She couldn't remember his goddamn name.

# Three

There were two other families hit by the same lightning that hit the Trainors and Rostenkowskis. One was named Walker and they lived in one of the tonier neighborhoods in Larchmont, near the water. The wife had already gone to work after putting her son Franklin on the van with J.D. Winston, who was doing the calling while Lena got in touch with the police, reached the mother at the First Presbyterian Church and found out she was the senior minister there. The fourth family was named Williams and lived in White Plains. Their son Tommy was the last one to board the van. When the father, Mike, a contractor whose trucks were ubiquitous in Westchester County, heard what had happened, he had all his crews searching for the van within minutes.

Lena had gone into the bedroom to call the police. She had to go through a couple of layers of command at the station house before she got a captain who could comprehend what she was telling him.

"So did the guy like grab your daughter and throw her into the van?"

"No," Lena started. This was the third time she had told the story.

"He pretended that he was from the camp. My daughter was being picked up to go to camp. He pretended he was the driver. He had me sign papers and then he left."

"And you're saying he wasn't from the camp?"

"Right. About a half hour later the real drivers showed up. They're here now."

Winston, on cue, came to the bedroom door, got Lena's attention, and held up two fingers.

"And they don't know anything about this other driver?"

"No. It's not just my daughter. He took my daughter's friend from her house and two others, I think."

Winston nodded that this was right. The captain cleared his throat.

"Were they here in Pelham too?"

"I don't know. Let me put the driver on."

Lena gave Winston the phone and listened as he detailed the families involved for the captain. Then Winston listened for a while, nodding, and hung up. Lena didn't want to let go of the captain.

"What? What did he say?"

"We have to call the Westchester County Sheriff's office. He says it's their jurisdiction because the other families are in different townships."

"Jesus, can't he call them?"

Winston gave her a blank look, and Lena decided that she was wasting time trying to figure out why the police couldn't call the sheriff's office. She took the phone and paged through the book of emergency numbers the city had sent out, found the sheriff's office number, and began another climb up the chain of command there.

The first sheriff's cruiser arrived in the driveway about ten minutes later, and the officer who came to the door was fairly well briefed on what had happened. He was a man in his forties, with a starter potbelly and a large nose. His name tag said Norman. As Lena began to give him details, she caught a hint of skepticism from the officer, as if the story wasn't smooth enough. She could see herself while she was talking and realized how farfetched the whole thing sounded in the retelling. Not so much her end of the story, but that of the kidnapper, the lengths to which he must have gone to effect the kidnapping. Thank heavens, she thought, that she wasn't the only one who had been duped by this scheme. The biggest contractor in the county had let his son leave with the bogus driver too.

Officer Norman had turned his questioning to Winston when his radio crackled and he answered. Lena, who had gone into the kitchen, couldn't decipher the squawk that followed but, expecting news, went back in the living room. Norman told the radio operator that he "copied," then turned to Lena.

"They found the van."

"With the kids?"

"No. Empty except for some of their gear. They're checking the registration now."

"Where?"

"In a little cul-de-sac in White Plains. They must have had a switch planned. That van was way too identifiable." It seemed like Norman's skepticism had diminished. He began to ask about possible suspects, people who might know the pickup routine. Lena knew nothing and Winston said he'd have to check with the camp. Norman said somebody from the sheriff's office was probably already on the way out there.

Then there was a knock on the front door and the Rostenkowskis came in without waiting for Lena to answer. Janet looked horrible. She was a plain woman to begin with, one whose looks got a boost from a small amount of makeup, but now, without makeup and clearly having cried a lot since getting the news, her face looked like a fright mask. Lena was surprised by this. Janet was always composed, too composed.

Phil, coming in behind Janet, was seething and looked like he wanted to punch something, anything. He was tall and gaunt with eyes that bulged normally, and an Adam's apple that bounced when he talked. Lena had rarely seen him without some sort of cheap sports coat, even on the weekends. But he was wearing only a short-sleeved blue shirt now.

Janet went to Lena, ignoring the others in the room.

"It's our fault. We pushed the camp. I'm so sorry. It's our fault."

Lena and everyone else could see this was a piece of theater. Linda had had a terrific time at Camp Arno the year before, Lena and David were impressed with the change in Linda after she came back, and Sarah had made the decision to go to Camp Arno instead of soccer camp completely on her own. Lena brought her into a hug, the first sincere one the two women had ever shared.

"No. It's nobody's fault . . . You know there were two other families hit, don't you?"

"What?" Phil yipped, looking from Lena to Norman to Winston.

And they began to fill the Rostenkowskis in on the news about the families and the van. As they were doing so, Lena suddenly remembered that David wasn't there. When she had been absorbed in the calls to the cops, she hadn't missed him, but now, looking at the Rostenkowskis, she felt his absence. Where was he?

This question was followed by a thought so devastating that she had to sit down. How many times had she heard that when horrible things happen to children, the police almost always suspect the parents first? In one of her rotations in medical school she had been involved in a case in which a boy brought to her with multiple stab wounds was eventually found to be the victim of his father's rage. What were the police going to think about David and her? Were they going to suspect them first? Lena knew this was ludicrous. You don't kidnap your own child. But where was David? And why had he left under such a phony excuse? And why hadn't he called back? It wasn't that she suspected David, but that she could see how someone unfamiliar with him, with his love for Sarah, might raise an eyebrow at the circumstances.

Lena was drawn back into the conversation by a question from Norman, one that seemed to have plumbed Lena's thoughts.

"And where is your husband, Mrs. Trainor?"

"What?" she stalled, weighing the possible answers.

"Your husband? You are married? He does live here?"

"Yes. Oh, yes. He's, uh, at work."

"Was he here when the van came, the first van?"

"Um, no. He got called in early this morning." Lena felt Janet's eyes on her but didn't look over.

"And you've called him. He's aware?"

"Yes."

Lena thought it best to keep everything clean, even if she was stretching the truth. Something might be going on with David, but it didn't have anything to do with the kidnapping, and it would only detract the police from the real investigation. She looked over at Janet and Phil. She hadn't fooled them. They could see the dissembling behind Lena's assurance. Maybe, she thought, Norman could too. She always got angry with people in books and films who didn't tell the truth, who covered for others, and here she was doing the same, perhaps. But that was melodramatic thinking. She had told David's voicemail that there was a problem. She had told the truth.

Norman got another squawk on his radio and said, "The detectives are here." He nodded toward the driveway and they could see an unmarked police car stopped, a heavyset older man and a thirtyish woman, short and petite, get out of the car and walk toward the front door. "It's Auggie Martin. You're in good hands."

Martin and the woman were barely in the door when the phone rang. Lena started for the kitchen, but Norman stopped her with an upraised hand. He spoke to Martin.

"Auggie. You want her to answer?"

Martin came toward them, nodded a hello to Lena, and addressed her.

"You okay? You prepared if it's them?"

Lena wasn't but she tried not to show it.

"Uh, yes, but what . . . anything special?"

"Listen, don't commit to anything, try to keep them on the line, we've already got a tracer on the phone, don't yell at them. Got it?"

Lena nodded yes and picked up the phone on the fourth ring, just before the answering machine would have clicked in. It was David.

"Hi. What's up? Sorry I didn't get back to you sooner. I left my phone on my desk."

"Just a minute." Lena turned to the others and said, "It's David." They started to turn away and Lena went back to the phone. She spoke softly, hoping no one would hear her. "Where are you?"

"I told you. At work. What's up?"

"You've got to come home. Sarah's been kidnapped."

"What?"

"The driver who came to pick her up was . . . was a phony. He got Linda and two other kids too." Lena turned as she said this to see if people were listening to her. Norman was, staring, his antennae up.

"What are you talking about?"

"Just come home. I'll explain it all . . . There are police here. And the media's on the way."

"Kidnapped? Like . . . ?"

"David, yes."

David said nothing but didn't hang up. Such silence wasn't foreign to Lena. It was a silence born of shock and the inability to make sense of information. For her it was as if she had just said "metastasized," explained the word, and given the patient quiet time to put it all together. She waited, with David on the other end of the line, in the same way. Let him speak first.

"I'll be right home."

They hung up and Lena went back in the living room. No one was sitting. Janet and Phil were in a huddle with Martin and the young woman. Martin saw Lena come back, turned, and walked to her. As he did, Lena looked over his shoulder, out the front window, and saw a news van cruise past the house. She was still staring at this when Martin reached her with his hand out.

"Dr. Trainor, I'm Detective Martin."

Lena took his hand and wondered how he knew she was a doctor. He smiled and held her hand a little longer than necessary. From afar, when he was in the driveway, he had looked pudgy and predictable, a graying, red-faced cop. But up close now, with warm incandescent light from the kitchen doorway bathing his face, his soft blue eyes centered his features, and Lena felt as if she knew him, as if they'd been friends for a long time.

"I'd like to introduce you to my partner, Detective Salerno." The young woman moved beside Martin and held out her hand as well. She seemed nervous, and young, but the thin-lipped smile of reassurance she gave Lena was genuine.

"Denise. Please call me Denise. I'm sorry this has happened to you."

"Thank you." Lena knew this was a formality but she was comforted by the passive voice. It had happened to her. She had done nothing but see that her daughter got off to camp. Safely. Everything had gone off as she had imagined it would. She had checked the van. She had helped with Sarah's seat belt. She had . . . Facing the detectives, she was batting away an attack of guilty thoughts as if they were buzzing gnats. But Denise's words had helped.

Martin turned and addressed the Rostenkowskis as well as Lena.

"Why don't we all sit down and start." He turned to Lena. "Is your husband on the way?"

"Yes."

"Do you want us to wait for him?"

"Yes. I would like that. He's at work. He's only ten minutes away." After this was out of her mouth, Lena remembered that she didn't know where David was and didn't know how long it would take him to get home.

"Sure, we'll wait," Martin responded. "Wish I lived only ten minutes from work." He said this and waited. Lena wondered if she was supposed to respond in some way. "You wouldn't have any coffee, would you?"

"Oh, yes, sorry. I made a small pot earlier. Let me make some more."

"Don't fuss. We can always send out."

"No. It's no problem."

Lena started back for the kitchen and Janet caught up with her, saying she would help. Janet seemed to have gained some composure. Her face looked less rubbery and strained. But she was still wound very tight. As Lena dumped the old grounds, Janet spoke to her in a low voice.

"What do we do about the press?"

Lena was well aware that people under stress do odd things, have strange thoughts, try to deflect the central cause of the stress. She assumed this is what Janet was doing. Who cared about the press now? Their kids were gone. What were they going to do about that? What could they do?

"I don't know. Let the police handle it."

"But you always see the parents. I couldn't say anything in front of cameras."

"You won't have to." Lena was starting to get annoyed.

"But I'm the mother."

Janet had always struck Lena as self-centered, someone who thought she was the only one with problems, problems that others needed to hear about at length. She had been in a very serious car accident, not her fault, some five years earlier. She had broken many bones and spent almost a year in the hospital. Lena hadn't known her before the accident and so didn't know what effect it had had on her outlook, but in the time Lena had known her, Janet's life seemed pinned in one way or another to the accident. Janet referred to it often, and the many times she mentioned her money woes, the cause was always the medical bills they were still paying off.

Lena busied herself making the coffee, not responding to Janet's worry. Then she wondered about the Rostenkowskis' other child, a high school junior.

"Where's Paul?"

"He's home. He's supposed to go to Montana tomorrow. His friend's grandparents live there, on a ranch. We thought it would be good for him to see the West. And we thought we'd get two weeks to ourselves."

Lena was through talking. She wanted only two things then: she wanted David to get home, and she wanted to listen to the detective with the soft blue eyes in the living room. She had already invested him with some magical powers, some way he could use his radio and his skill and some unseen network to find Sarah and bring her back. She asked Janet to take cups into the living room and stood staring at the dripping coffee while she waited for the sound of David's voice.

When the coffee was finished, David still hadn't arrived. Phil and Janet had questions they couldn't hold back, about the press, about the other families. Martin answered them as best he could, sipped his coffee, and quietly took control.

"Why don't we start?" Lena said finally. "David must have been held up on the Hutchinson River Parkway."

"I avoid the Hutch like the plague this time of day. Okay." Martin put his cup down and stood. "Folks, obviously we don't have any experience with this type of thing. To tell you the truth, I've never done a kidnapping. Twenty-four years in this business and I've never had a kidnapping. I'll be reaching out to people who have, but I wanted to let you know how green I am."

Lena was impressed. Martin's confession worked to convince her of his competence.

Martin opened a pad and flipped through some notes.

"The van. You know they found the van. I say 'they' because we didn't find it. You may know one of the other victims of this crime is Mike Williams. You've seen his trucks all over, I'm sure. The red ones with the white letters? He had 'em all fan out as soon as he found out what had happened, and one of his crews spotted the van. That was some smart thinkin' on his part. I doubt we would have found it that fast."

"Not fast enough." All looked at Phil, who stared straight ahead, not accusing anyone in what he was saying.

"Right, of course. Now, the kids all had suitcases and duffels. I guess that was what the camp wanted, right?" The three parents nodded their heads yes. "Well, the suitcases were in the van, opened, and it looked like some clothes might have been taken out. We'll have you inventory all that. But there were only two duffel bags. We guess they stuffed some basics in the two duffels."

Janet, hearing details like these, sniffled. Lena wondered what sort of force J.D. must have used to get Sarah to do something like that, take her clothes out of the suitcase and stuff them in a common duffel. Sarah, Lena knew, might resist such an order. Did J.D. have to grab her by the arm, make her do it?

"We imagine this guy who picked up your children had an accomplice, someone who was waiting for him up in White Plains. We don't have any way of knowing what the other car, if there was one, looked like. Our people are out there now trying to see if there were any witnesses, but I think that's going to be a long shot."

"Where was the van found?" Lena asked the question before she even thought about doing so.

"Off of two eighty-seven, there's an industrial park on the left near the first White Plains exit. It was behind there, a little dirt road where they're going to start excavating next year. Way out of sight of the road, any of the buildings in the park."

Lena hardly heard the answer. She had asked the question just to hear Martin talk. She was becoming dependent on his voice now. He knew things. He was going to make everything better.

"Okay now . . ." He stopped when the front door opened.

David, who had gone through the police cars out front, the news trucks, and who had passed a couple of words with an officer on the lawn, still looked shocked to see his living room filled with people. Lena got up and went to him quickly. She wanted to be near him at least. She wanted to touch him.

"Sorry. I, uh, there was traffic on the Hutch." He put his arm around Lena's shoulders. Martin came toward him.

"Your wife guessed that. Mr. Trainor, I'm Detective Martin." David removed his arm from Lena's shoulders and shook hands. "And this is Detective . . ." He looked around for Salerno. She was in the kitchen on the phone. "Okay. Well, my partner, Detective Salerno. If you don't mind I'm just going to continue and we can fill you in later."

"No, but. I just can't believe this. I mean, the guy just waltzes up the driveway and you let the kids go with him?" He looked at the Rostenkowskis as he said this, but Lena could tell she was the real object of the accusation. The room went deathly quiet. Lena had all she could do to keep from screaming back at him, asking where he had gone, why he wasn't there to help her see J.D. was a phony. Martin's blessed voice broke the silence.

"I don't think we can blame anybody in this room, Mr. Trainor. Looks like you all crossed paths with a real slick Willy. You didn't do anything wrong. Let's get down to the business of finding your kids, okay?"

Lena hoped David heard this. Did he have any idea what she was going through? She kept staring at him, wanting eye contact, wanting a connection. Please, David, Lena thought, I was blinded by my expectations. We all were. I let Sarah go like a balloon I forgot to tie to my wrist. I could die from guilt. Help me. Our little girl is out there somewhere. Please.

But David was staring blankly at Martin, studiously avoiding Lena's gaze, and Lena understood that he might be in worse shape than she was. At least she had been there to face J.D., to be duped. At least she had seen Sarah leave. Lena had that one ragged, ironic saving grace. David didn't. He might have to live with the consequences of his absence for the rest of his life.

# Four

J.D. didn't say much on the ride from Sarah's house to Linda's. He made one cell phone call while he was driving, and Sarah knew this was illegal. But it was a fast call in which J.D. only grunted yes and no and hung up. Sarah could see only a corona of curly hair over the headrest on his seat and an occasional glimpse from him through the rearview mirror.

"Are you comfortable back there?" he asked as they neared Linda's house. Sarah nodded and said she was.

Sarah was glad to see Linda when they got to her house, even though Linda was mad about something. Sarah stayed in the van as J.D. got out and helped Mr. Rostenkowski with Linda's suitcase and duffel (Sarah always called Linda's parents by their last name). Mrs. Rostenkowski came out of the house then, carrying a fleece for Linda, and Linda turned back and yelled something at her mother.

Then J.D. opened the side door and Linda got in. Linda hadn't gone through the growth spurt Sarah had gone through. She was small and dark-haired, often nervous about little things. But she and Sarah saw eye to eye on the major stuff, including homework (they didn't mind it), boys (they didn't need to be silly in front of them), and soccer (Linda was pretty good as well). Linda, who often had spats with her mother, was steaming now. Before Sarah could say anything, Mrs. Rostenkowski was at the van door, holding out the fleece.

"Take this, Linda. Now."

"I don't need it! I've got a sweater and a sweatshirt and it doesn't get that cold up there."

"You never know. Take it."

Then Mr. Rostenkowski was at the door. He took the fleece.

"I'm packing it for you," he said to Linda, and went to the back of the van.

Mrs. Rostenkowski looked to Sarah for help.

"I bet you've got a fleece as well as a sweatshirt, Sarah."

Sarah saw her fleece on top of the blanket chest in her room. In her haste Lena hadn't picked it up. Sarah shook her head no.

"No, I forgot it."

"See?" Linda said, sitting next to Sarah.

"I see nothing," Janet shot back. "I'll get her one of yours."

She headed for the house and Phil trailed behind her, stopping halfway, not sure where to place himself in the argument. Linda fumed next to Sarah.

"She always does this. Tell her you don't want the fleece."

"I can't. I was supposed to bring one."

Suddenly J.D., his face only a foot away from them, leaning in the side door, whispered conspiratorially.

"No big deal, huh? You don't have to wear them if you don't want to. Hi, Linda. I'm J.D."

"Hi. But it's so stupid."

"We had a little cold snap last week. Some rain too. You get your sweatshirt wet, what are you going to do?"

Linda puffed out a sigh, then turned to J.D. "You're new."

"Yup, first year. This is your second, right?"

"Yeah."

"Well, then you can show me how to get there." He made this sound serious enough that Linda looked over at him and scowled until he broke into a grin. Then he saw Mrs. Rostenkowski come out with the other fleece and give it to Mr. Rostenkowski, and both come toward the van. J.D. backed out of the side door, grabbing the clipboard from the front seat as he did. Mrs. Rostenkowski was softer as she came to the side door.

"Did we put the postcards in the suitcase?"

"Yes. I did."

"Good. At least one this year, okay?" Linda only nodded to this. She could hear something in her mother's voice that told her her mother was going to cry. She didn't want to be embarrassed in front of Sarah.

"I'll be okay, Mom."

"I know." Mrs. Rostenkowski stepped into the van, gave Linda a peck on the cheek, and stepped back. She did have tears in her eyes, but she wasn't crying. J.D. and Mr. Rostenkowski finished the form-signing and J.D. came around to the side door.

"All set here? Ready to go?"

Mrs. Rostenkowski didn't look at him, didn't say anything, so Linda spoke up.

"Yup."

And J.D. slid the door shut. Linda, mildly embarrassed by her mother, said nothing for a while. Sarah looked out and saw Mr. Rostenkowski standing a ways off, on the lawn. It's the mothers who say goodbye, Sarah thought. The fathers go to work or stand back. She wondered why that should be so.

# Five

For a detective going through his first kidnapping, Martin was remarkably assured and knowledgeable, Lena thought as she listened to him school them on how to handle a phone call from the kidnapper.

"Like I told Mrs. Trainor earlier, don't commit to anything. Say you're going to have to think about it. Whoever it is talking to you will say you've got to commit now, might threaten doing something to the kids, something like that. Keep reminding yourself that the kids, alive and well, are his only assets. He's not going to do anything to them until he gets his money."

Lena liked the fact that he was talking about a specific. The image of the van driving off into some vague nowhere was driving her nuts. She longed for a phone call from the kidnappers.

Detective Salerno got off the phone in the kitchen and came into the living room. Martin could see she had news.

"What's up?"

"The van was stolen from a new car lot in Clifton, New Jersey, two days ago. The PD there said it was a pretty clean snatch—broke into the office, took the keys. And like we expected, it's been wiped, no prints up front, but a couple of hair samples."

Martin nodded and turned to the parents. "Mum's the word on this stuff, right? We don't want the bad guys to know what we know."

"Do you think this is some kind of ring or something?" Phil asked.

"Not likely. Most often you get a couple of numbskulls who think they can make a bundle just by snatching a kid; they get the snatching done—that's the easy part—and then they haven't a clue what to do next. That's why the phone call is so important. They may sound like they've got everything worked out, but they're probably just fishing."

David looked over at Lena. She felt his eyes on her and she looked back. He seemed changed, as if the shock had worn off, the information had been absorbed, the guilt tamped down, and he was now dealing with the particulars in the way they all were.

Martin looked outside, at the growing news presence. "Looks like the troops are movin' in here. Westchester's where folks come to keep their kids safe from the city. Big story. Expect politicians to show up and get their mugs in front of the camera." He turned back to the Rostenkowskis. "Why don't I take you out through that crush out there. You should be home waitin' for the call."

Lena felt her stomach sink. Martin was her lifeline and now he was leaving. Janet turned to Lena as she stood to leave.

"I'm so sorry, Lena."

"It's good the girls are together," Lena heard herself say, but she didn't know what that meant. What could possibly be good about this?

Everybody but David and Lena filed out with the detectives and the Rostenkowskis. Officer Norman came to Lena as he was leaving, held out his hand, and Lena shook it.

"I'm sorry this has happened to you, ma'am," he said, his voice low and even. But his eyes said many other things, reminders that he knew Lena hadn't been completely truthful with him. Lena thanked him and tucked away the image of that look for future reference. She was going to tell the absolute truth from now on.

The door shut, and David and Lena were alone with each other.

"There were probably clues, weren't there?" David blurted out as if he'd been holding the question for long minutes.

"Clues?"

"Things you, we, Janet, Phil, the others could have picked up on."

"No."

"No?"

"No, David. Jesus. It was just like we expected it to be."

"I'm not accusing you."

"Yes, you are. You're Monday-morning-quarterbacking the whole thing."

"No, but I bet if you think about it, there were signs."

"He had tobacco stains on his front teeth."

"Well . . ."

"Oh, for chrissake, David. He was kind and attentive. He noticed Sarah had a soccer ball, he asked her about soccer, he . . ."

"He what?"

"He told her she was going to like the soccer program."

"Arno doesn't have a soccer program."

"I know. Sarah said that to him. He said there was a new one this year."

David could tell, from the slow delivery of this last, that he had won his point, that Lena had conceded to herself at least that there might have been a clue to the disguise in this seeming lack of knowledge about the camp. But he didn't want to pile on.

"Let's check the camp materials. Maybe we missed something about a new—"

"No!" Lena said sharply. "What difference does it make? Was I ever going to say, 'Aha, you don't know about the soccer program! You're a phony. You're probably here to kidnap my daughter. Police! Police!'?"

Tears spilled over the rims of her eyelids now, but she fought a cry. She wanted to draw a line. She wanted to say to David that she was going to refuse to blame herself, to shoulder some sort of guilt. Martin was right. None of them were to blame. And if David had his own reasons for wanting to point a finger, then he would have to deal with them on his own. Lena turned toward the window.

A glimpse of the increased number of news vans in the street, the confusion there, slammed home a truth for Lena. Her problem, Sarah's abduction, couldn't be pared down to some sort of basic elements. When she had imagined being alone with David after Sarah left, she had hoped they would zero in on a few specifics, things about their marriage they could work on. But now the thing that was bulldozing through her life was something large and out in the world, something intangible and yet piercing, something she couldn't get a handle on because there was no real data—something David certainly couldn't help her with. All her training was about narrowing, eliminating variables, burrowing into the central cause of some illness. But there were no symptoms here, no test results. Her quest for answers would have to open out wide and the prospect of that global search terrified her.

David said something she didn't catch, and as she was turning to him, the phone rang. They froze.

"Get Martin," Lena said, assuming, without thinking, that she would answer.

"You. I'll get it."

But Lena was already on her way to the phone. She wasn't thinking about who should answer, who should go outside; she was thinking about Sarah. In her mind it wasn't the kidnapper calling, even though she expected to speak to him, but it was a connection to Sarah. Those rings were calling her to come get some answers, to talk to someone who was with her daughter now. She grabbed the handset as David, realizing there was no sense in arguing who should answer, flew out the front door.

"Hello."

Instead of a stranger's voice, one of the most familiar voices in Lena's life—sonorous, manly, and loving—came through the line.

"Hey, honey. I lost track of time. Wanted to give Sarahbell a little send-off call. Did I miss her?"

Lena, caught off guard, broke into tears. Her father, used to the interruptions of international phone calls, thought he heard something like crying, but thought too it might have been just something on the line.

"Dad . . ."

"What, honey?" Now he could hear the tears.

"Dad, Sarah's been kidnapped."

Just getting this out made Sarah cry harder, and her father's confused "What?" was lost to her.

The front door opened and Martin came through with David trailing. Thinking Lena was talking to the kidnapper, Martin scowled at the crying but approached Lena gently, mouthing a question. "It's them?"

Lena couldn't speak. She motioned to David and handed him the handset. He took it, looking from Martin to Lena. Finally Lena was able to get a word out.

"Dad."

David took a breath, relieved at first, then tensing at the prospect of talking to his father-in-law.

"Richard, it's David."

"David, what's going on?"

"I don't know what Lena told you but—"

"She said something about kidnapping."

David swallowed and licked his lips, getting ready to talk, fearing he would have to say he wasn't home when his daughter was . . . "Sarah and three other kids. A guy posed as the driver from the camp. Camp Arno. Remember she was—"

"That's why I was calling to say . . . Posed? What?"

"We don't know much. It all seemed legitimate. He, uh, looked like a real counseler, had a van, had papers. But he wasn't from the camp."

"He had an ID?"

"Yeah." David didn't want to sound indecisive, didn't want to open any line of questioning that might reveal he had been absent.

"Let me talk to Lena."

"Sure."

Lena had recovered enough to talk. Martin had realized who was on the line and had moved away.

"Dad."

"Honey. Jesus Christ. I'm having trouble imagining all this. Cops?"

"Yeah, they're all here."

"You know the other kids?"

"Linda. You've heard Sarah talk about Linda."

"Yeah."

"We don't know the other two."

"What the hell? What do they want?"

"We don't know. I thought you were one of them calling."

"Goddamn." The line went silent for a long few seconds. "Fuck. I can't believe this is real."

"I know."

"Jesus, honey. I'll come."

Lena waited to respond. She knew the offer was sincere, but she knew too that it was impossible, that her father would be arrested as soon as his plane landed.

"No, there's nothing you can do."

"Jesus." There was a long pause. Lena could imagine her father's sharp, handsome, olive-skinned features crinkling in tears, but when he spoke, his voice was steady, almost defiant. "They don't know what they've got on their hands. Sarah's gonna give 'em hell."

This opened more tears for Lena. He was right. Lena had been thinking of the vulnerability of her daughter, the danger she was in, and she had lost sight of something so many people said about Sarah, how tough-minded she was, how independent and confident. These were qualities she'd always thought had come from her father, from his fearlessness.

She needed that fearlessness now. With every minute the problem was ballooning dangerously out of control. Martin was going to leave. There had been no phone call. David didn't have any answers. Even if her father had been able to come, what could he do? The horror of Sarah out there somewhere, a speck in a vast landscape of unknowing, froze Lena. There was nothing to hold on to. She was slipping away. She was talking to her father, looking at her husband, but she was utterly lost.

# Six

Sarah and Linda were chattering away when the van pulled into a long, elegant driveway leading to a large, white, clapboard house, a lawn behind it sloping down to the bay. When the two girls did look up, they both omigodded at the size and splendor of the place, then laughed at their own surprise.

J.D. went through the same routine he had gone through with Sarah and Linda. He met the mother, an African-American woman in her forties wearing the collar and suit jacket of a Presbyterian minister, carried a suitcase and a duffel out to the van, put them in back, and took out the clipboard.

When Linda saw the spindly light-skinned boy come out of the house behind his mother, she whispered to Sarah that she knew him from last year.

"His name's Franklin. He was in my theater class. He didn't want them to call him Frank. He read all the time."

And in fact he was carrying a book as he walked toward the van. He stopped and waited for his mother to finish signing the papers.

Sarah noted once again that there was no father around. Then through the open window she heard the woman speaking to J.D.

". . . on a plane coming back from Berlin . . ."

She turned to her son and they bowed their heads together. The woman spoke with her eyes closed, then opened them and gave Franklin a somewhat perfunctory hug. J.D. opened the side door, and Franklin stepped in. He said nothing to the girls and took a seat behind them. As they went back out the long driveway, Sarah turned and saw Franklin already reading.

The last house they stopped at was a big one as well, with lush landscaping and, Sarah could see, a full array of sports facilities out back—a basketball court, a swimming pool, and a tennis court. She wondered why anyone would have to go to camp if he had all that in his back yard.

At this house both parents came out with their son; two of his siblings, a four-year-old girl and a teenage boy, followed as well. Linda was jabbering away about something, but Sarah wasn't listening. She was transfixed by the happy scene out the front window of the van. The son, whose name they would learn was Tommy, was hugging everybody in turn. When he came to his mother, a woman with bright black eyes and Hispanic or Indian features, she wrapped him in a long hug, stroked his hair, kissed him on the top of the head, and then wiped some tears from her eyes. Tommy's father, a burly, round-faced man who looked to be a little older than his wife, lifted Tommy off the ground in their hug, twirled him around in a little rough play, and set him down gently. Tommy practically ran to the van, and when he got in, he smiled at both the girls, saying "Hi," before sitting in the back with Franklin.

As they left Tommy's house, he waved vigorously at his family, his big brother coming to the side window and knocking on it, his little sister, engulfed in her father's big arms, waving, his mother smiling through tears. Tommy kept waving until they turned onto the street and were out of sight of the house. Then Tommy turned to Franklin.

"Hi, I'm Tommy."

Franklin looked up from his book. "Hi."

Sarah wanted to turn back and introduce herself, but Linda was still jabbering on. Finally Sarah turned and caught Tommy's eye. He smiled.

"I'm Sarah and this is Linda."

"Hi," he said, but he was less exuberant now, a little catch in his voice. He had his mother's eyes but not her complexion. He was quite striking. "Have you been to the camp before?" he asked Sarah. Sarah was about to say something when Franklin, thinking the question was directed at him, spoke up.

"Yes. This will be my third year. It's adequate."

Franklin went back to his book. Tommy and Sarah exchanged a look, and Sarah almost laughed out loud when Tommy made a face that questioned the word "adequate."

The van was on the crowded, noisy route 287 now and the four kids rode in silence for a while. J.D. kept checking on them in the rearview mirror. Then he spoke up.

"What do you say, Linda? Is this where I turn off?"

Linda giggled. "I don't know."

"I'll give it a try," J.D. said, smiling. He pulled the van into the right lane and started down the off-ramp. Franklin's voice, sharp and directed, surprised the kids.

"This is definitely not the way. We need to take two eighty-seven all the way to the Tappan Zee and then north."

J.D. looked at him in the rearview. He smiled but there was concern behind that smile.

"You're right, Franklin. But we're not going directly to the camp. We have something special for you kids today, a little side trip."

"What sort of side trip?" Franklin was sitting forward now, his book closed.

"You'll see. It's a little surprise. We're going to have you take a few of your things with you and go on an explore before we get to the camp."

"Do our parents know about this?"

"Of course. We came up with it last night, in staff meeting, and we've emailed them all this morning."

Franklin stopped his questioning, but the others, hearing Franklin's implicit doubts, became skeptical themselves. Linda looked at Sarah and then spoke.

"We didn't do that last year."

"Nope. Brand-new. But you took day trips last year, right?"

"Yes."

"Hikes and stuff like that?"

"Yes."

"Well, we figured that instead of going all the way to the camp, then turning around and going back out tomorrow, we'd have you get your first trip in before you got to the camp. More efficient that way."

Tommy seemed satisfied and piped up. "So where are we going?"

"That's a secret. Mr. Everett made me promise not to tell."

"Who's Mr. Everett?" Sarah asked, catching something in the way J.D. was presenting this that she didn't like.

"He's another counselor. He's an expert on wilderness living."

"What's that?" Linda asked.

Franklin answered before J.D. could speak. "Survival training. You learn to eat found food, make temporary shelters, stuff like that." Then he directed a question at J.D. "But isn't that a course just for senior campers?"

"Used to be, but they've modified it for you all."

As he said this, J.D. pulled the van off the road, which was a service road running behind some low, flat office buildings, and they bumped down an unpaved dirt road. Dust rose up and Sarah noticed that the van was getting hot. The road veered left, and as they made it around the bend, the kids could see a shiny silver SUV parked at a dead end a hundred yards away. When they approached, a man in his sixties, wearing a Camp Arno polo shirt, stepped out of the SUV. He had a full head of hair, not all of which was gray, and sported a substantial paunch. When the van stopped and he came to the driver's side window, he flashed a pleasing, dentured smile as he reached in and shook J.D.'s hand.

"How're you doing? Everything all right?"

"Great. Got a nice bunch of kids here all set for an adventure."

The man looked at the back seats.

"I'll say. Hi, guys. I'm Mr. Everett. You all ready for some fun?"

The kids mumbled their yeses. J.D. spoke as he got out of the van.

"Okay. I want you to grab the warmest clothes you have, get a toothbrush and soap if you have it, and put everything in two duffels. Girls, you share one duffel. Boys, you share the other. Come on. Move quick. We want to get as much of this in during daylight as we can."

The kids were a little too surprised by this to complain. They filed out of the van when Mr. Everett opened the side door and started to do as they were told. Mr. Everett helped them, got their names straight, told Franklin he couldn't take his book with him, that this was going to be "primitive" camping, and then herded the kids toward the SUV, helping them with the duffels.

"What about our stuff?" Linda asked.

"J.D.'s going to take it on to Arno. It'll be there when you arrive."

When the kids were in the SUV and strapped in, J.D. addressed them through a side window. His tone wasn't as carefree as it had been.

"Now Mr. Everett is in charge on this special trip. It's very important that you listen to him and do everything he says. The woods can be a lot of fun. But they can be dangerous too if you don't know what you're doing. Mr. Everett is an expert on the woods. Listen to him and you'll have a great time."

Sarah felt constrained now. The seat belt seemed tight. She had never liked this sort of grown-up speech. Her grandfather had always told her, joking sometimes, to "question authority." But she somehow got the impression from J.D. that this was no time for questions. This was a time for obedience. She kept quiet, but she didn't like it.

Mr. Everett started the engine. J.D. mumbled a question. "You sure you don't want to tell me where?"

Mr. Everett shook his head no. "Discipline, son. We don't deviate one inch, got it?" J.D. nodded. "And something small like, like not smoking around here, not droppin' a butt they might find—make sure you stick to that or everything could go to hell." He added a grin to this but there was no warmth in it. J.D. looked back at the kids to see if they'd gotten any of this, convinced himself they hadn't, and returned the empty smile as Mr. Everett backed up and pulled away.

He stood there in the heat and the dust until the SUV was out of sight. Then he quickly stripped off his Camp Arno shirt, pulled a "Nascar Rocks!" T-shirt out of his backpack, used the Camp Arno shirt to wipe every surface of the van, pulled out a cell phone, dialed a number, said only, "Done," hung up, and walked into the scrub pines past the dead end.

# Seven

Detective Martin returned a half an hour after he had left and said that he thought he should be there in case a call came in. David had the feeling they were being watched by this too-friendly cop. Lena practically hugged him when he came in the door. In short order Martin got both Lena and David talking about themselves.

"I was raised in Sweden," Lena opened, finding any kind of talk helpful. "I went to Penn, Johns Hopkins for med school, New York for my residency."

"Sweden? You're Swiss?"

"You mean Swedish?"

"Yeah. I get those two mixed up."

"No. I mean I have dual citizenship. My parents are both American. My father was in the army, about to be shipped to Vietnam. He applied for CO status, was denied, fled to Canada, and then got asylum in Sweden. He wasn't eligible for Carter's amnesty program. He can't return. My mother was his college sweetheart. She went to live there a year before I was born. They named me Lena so I would fit in in school."

Martin twitched at this and Lena thought maybe he was a veteran himself. He looked a little younger than her father.

"Yeah. War," he said finally, but didn't elaborate. "He get to see his granddaughter?"

"We go at least twice a year. Sarah and my dad are very close."

"Lucky. My kid's out in California. Thirty-two. He's married to windsurfing. How the hell'm I gonna get a grandchild like that?"

Lena didn't get a chance to respond. Martin's cell phone sounded, he listened, and stood.

"Rostenkowski's got an email. Let's see if you got one too."

All three of them went in the bedroom and Lena flashed through her hospital account and her practice account but found nothing. In her Yahoo mail, however, she found a funny-looking address that was in Polish or some other Eastern European language. There was no subject line. And the only content was a twenty-point type message in red that said, "STAY TUNED. THEY ARE ALL RITE."

As they all stared at the screen, Lena remembered that she had used her office account to register Sarah for camp, that the Yahoo account was one she used just for online purchases and such. She told Martin this and he shrugged.

"Real privacy's an antique," he said. His cell phone rang and he answered, telling Salerno about the message, hearing that all the families had the same one. "We've got to call in the FBI geeks now," he said both into the phone and to Lena and David.

As Martin talked with Salerno and then made other calls, wandering out of the room, David got on the computer and checked his two accounts. There was nothing unusual there. Except for the misspelling, Lena had thought the message was a positive sign. They were going to use the computer. That's where she could find Sarah now. Her thoughts raced ahead.

"How much equity do you think we have in the house?"

The question caught David off guard. "Not as much as six months ago. I'd say, hundred and fifty, two hundred."

"Do you think Bill would consider a loan?"

"For this, of course."

Bill was David's older brother. He'd stayed in Oklahoma, not gone away to school, joined forces with a wildcatter and made a fortune, and had retired at forty-one.

Lena didn't say anything more and left the room. David turned back to the computer and, making sure Lena was gone, checked a third email account. There was a message there, but not from a kidnapper.

The unique nature of the kidnapping made it an instant hit on the internet. Had Lena checked her Yahoo account only five minutes later, she would have seen the story as the lead on the Yahoo home page. Many of the news accounts began with a variant of "A parent's worst nightmare, times four, is unfolding in Westchester County north of New York City." Bloggers and comments on the blogs were beginning to fill up with pity, clucking, outrage, and plenty of confusion. Descriptions of the kids and even school pictures (which Lena and David at least had not supplied) were popping up on sites.

In the living room Martin was talking to someone Lena assumed was from the FBI. She was surprised when she looked at the grandfather clock and saw that it was only two twenty. It seemed like so much more time had elapsed. She went into the bathroom, sat on the toilet without lifting the cover, and closed her eyes. She wanted to drill down, become a diagnostician again, use this slim thread of an email to anchor her problem solving, but her thoughts wouldn't stay tethered. The word *where* repeated and grew, amplifying, it seemed, in the echoey bathroom, even though she was saying nothing. She could be anywhere, Lena thought. The uncertainty nearly made her gag.

David knocked on the bathroom door and asked if she was all right. She said she was.

"One of the other parents is going to be on TV in a minute," he said.

Lena got up, looked at herself in the mirror, saw that her face was reasonably well put together, and went out into the living room. David was standing with Martin, the TV tuned to a local news station. A reporter in front of a large house, with the waters of the bay behind it, was speaking to an anchor in the studio, telling him they were going to have a live statement any minute now.

"We understand the statement will be given by John Walker, who is an executive vice president in the international banking division of Citibank. We understand that Mr. Walker was not home this morning when his son Franklin was picked up by the camp van, abducted that is. He, Mr. Walker, was on a plane back from Berlin and was over the Atlantic when it—I think he's coming out now."

The camera left the reporter and found the podium set up in the driveway. Behind the podium, coming down the driveway from the house, Lena could see a tall, impeccably dressed black man, a woman in casual clerical dress, and a second woman, white, hyperkinetic, gesturing to the press—some sort of handler, it seemed. The man went to the microphones with experienced grace and waited until things settled.

"I'm going to make this brief and there will be no questions. My name is John Walker. Our son Franklin was taken from us under false pretenses this morning along with three other children intending to go to Camp Arno. This is an unconscionable act of cowardice by one or more individuals. We demand that the perpetrators of this crime release the children immediately. We have had one brief message from the kidnappers, by email. We ask citizens throughout the county to come forward with any information they might have concerning the whereabouts of our children. Thank you."

Reporters hurled questions at him, but he turned quickly and strode back up the driveway. David stared at the TV set, watching Walker's back receding.

Martin, who had been on the phone the whole time, growled into the receiver, turning away from Lena and David.

"I don't care who she's friends with, get the Citibank PR twat out of the house and tell her not to come back until we say so." He listened for a while longer, then hung up, giving Lena an apologetic look.

"Sorry. That was a breach. I'll have to talk to this Walker later. We're going to go over there in an hour or so. All the parents."

"What for?" David's tone was sharp, almost defiant.

"Well, we want to get everybody in the same room. You're all in this together."

"No, we're not. This Walker guy's not in it with us."

"That was a mistake."

David pressed. "A mistake on whose part? His, yours? You want to get us all in a room for sort of a group interrogation, isn't that right?"

"Nobody's saying—"

"Bullshit. You always look at the parents first, the relatives, friends, in a kidnapping."

"It's a place to start, yes, but—"

"So, what do you know?"

"David." Lena was baffled by David's attitude. Why was he going after the man with the soft blue eyes, the savior.

"It's only been a few hours. We don't know much."

"Turn on your computer. Walker's division at Citibank is in trouble. He himself has been under scrutiny by some regulatory agency. Maybe he needs a diversion, one that gives him a large dose of sympathy."

"We'll certainly check out—"

"Or Mike Williams, the hotshot contractor. How'd he find that van so quickly? A lot of people are asking that question."

"He's got a lot of employees."

"And he's got a housing market that's tanking."

Martin signaled that he'd had enough. "I'll be back to pick you up in a half an hour or so. No talking to the press, and frankly, Mr. Trainor, I'd turn that computer off if I were you."

He left before David could respond. Lena closed the door behind him and turned a chilly eye on David.

"Who cares who did it?"

"What do you mean?"

"I mean I want to know where Sarah is. I want her back."

"So do I."

"Then concentrate on that. Forget the goddamn bloggers or whatever."

"How am I supposed to do that, concentrate on Sarah—meditate or some shit?"

"Yes. Anything but play junior detective."

Lena couldn't stand it anymore. She moved quickly out of the living room, went into the bedroom, saw the computer on the desk screaming at her, and angrily shut it down.

When they walked out of the house with Martin later, the harsh heat of the day had become a moist, fragrant twilight. It was the sort of summer evening Lena loved, especially on the street where they lived. They were leaving for the Walker house at about the same time she usually arrived home from work, and often when she would get out of the car, she would take a minute or two just to absorb the leafy calm of the neighborhood.

But there was the opposite of calm now. Even though the press had been kept back, held off by yellow tape, their lenses and shouted questions made Lena feel even more like a target. They got in the back of Martin's car, Martin sat in front with a driver, and the car inched its way through a clutch of press, some even running along with the car.

Seeing the neighborhood, the world outside the house, gave Lena that sinking, lost, hopeless feeling again, the feeling that the problem was too wide for her, that there was no way to narrow it down. Sarah had traveled this street with J.D. and again she felt as if Sarah had been rocketed into space. Lena struggled against the panic of these thoughts.

As the car headed farther down the block, David pointed to something outside and Lena looked to see a neighbor, someone she'd seen around but whose name she didn't know, standing at the edge of his driveway, holding up a digital camera, taking a picture of the car. More than the professionals in front of the house, this amateur made her feel the nausea of being a victim celebrity, a rider in a doomed motorcade, the neighbor a Zapruder of sorts. She willed herself not to look out the window.

# Eight

Chase Collins had arrived at the hospital around noon and made his presence known in the hours before his shift ended. He wanted to make sure that his time card hours would be backed up by fellow workers who remembered his being there that afternoon. When news of the odd, four-kid kidnapping buzzed through the laundry, Chase had lots to say about it. He gave his immediate supervisor a very graphic description of what he would do to the kidnappers if he ever found them, a description he knew she would remember if she was ever asked about Chase's being in the hospital that day.

But he wasn't all that worried about anybody connecting him to the abduction. He was just being cautious. He had peeled the professional wig off as he walked away from the abandoned van, and his near-shoulder-length hair would keep him from any sort of detection by those he had encountered as J.D. He actually fantasized about walking up to one of the victims, like the big contractor who said, "Call me Mike," talking with him, maybe offering advice, calling him Mike, and walking away without being recognized.

As for his not being around in the four hours he was collecting the kids and dropping off the van, there was no chance anyone would remember that. He worked in the hospital laundry and there was never any work to be done in the morning. In fact, when he got back to his department, there was no work for him until one thirty. He was home free.

As soon as his shift was over, Chase went to the fourth floor of the annex, a phony package under his arm in case anyone saw him there, went to the deserted wing of the floor, used the key he'd had made for the tiny office at the end of the hall, and let himself in. The place was, as always, spotless and windowless, a flat-screen monitor and keyboard on a brown formica desktop, his command station. He sat, eager to see if the programmed message had gone out. It had, right on time, complete with the deliberately misspelled "RITE"—his idea, one his father thought was uneccessary. He was happy to see too that his long, hard labors to cover his tracks electronically had paid off as well. The server reports showed that several attempts had been made to trace the source of the message but had failed.

He scheduled the second message and once again had his doubts about the wisdom of this part of the scheme. He didn't know why his father had insisted on inserting this in the plan when they could have easily gone straight to the ransom. Chase thought it had something to do with information relayed to them from their client, but he didn't know what that information was.

Before he closed down the computer, he wiped out all traces of his time there and, as the middlemen had instructed, reformatted the hard drive on the desk, set up a new user account with another hospital employee's ID, and turned the whole system off completely. Now he would be able to send the final message from his home computer.

When he left the annex and went to his car in the parking lot, the sun was low, just dipping below the trees, and hot for that time of night. He figured his father and the kids should have reached their destination, wherever that was. He was ecstatic. He wanted to pump his fist and do cartwheels and shout for joy. But he didn't want to call attention to himself. So, silently, he kept replaying his piece of theater from the morning. The whole operation had depended on him transforming himself, acting, becoming J.D., the kind, helpful, sincere, upbeat camp counselor. He based his character on a nice-guy gym coach he had had in middle school. The wig, with its sort of happy-go-lucky curls, was close to the hairstyle the coach sported. Chase saw himself hopping in and out of the van, calming parents' anxieties, having the parents see him work well with their kids.

He got in his car and started home. As he drove through the New Jersey evening, he had a vision of where this might all lead. He had talent. That much was clear from the morning's success. He had always suspected he could act, but now he could really see himself doing it. He imagined a movie camera right there in the front seat with him, a director and crew riding along, hanging on his performance.

"Don't worry, babe, I got everything covered," he said out loud, a snippet of a scene he thought was right for the moment. "Don't worry, babe." He stayed in this character for the rest of the ride home and only dropped it when he went in the back door of his house and his two-and-a-half-year-old daughter, Jennifer, came running from the living room to greet him.

# Nine

They had to go through another gauntlet of press in order to get into the Walker driveway. There were other cars parked in front of the porticoed front door, and Martin said that they were the last to arrive. A Larchmont policeman stood by the door and let them in when they climbed the steps to the porch. Lena had the feeling they were being let into some inner sanctum, that they were members of an exclusive club. The door opened to a foyer, a wide spiral staircase beyond, the living room to the right, a formal dining room to the left. The couples were seated on facing couches and easy chairs in the living room. Sheila Walker, still in her clerical garb, came to meet them. She introduced herself simply as Sheila and said she was sorry to be meeting them under these circumstances. Her husband, John, came up behind her. He was taller than he had seemed on television. He had clear, caramel skin and cautious eyes, ones that spoke of reserve and judgment, the kind that David had always been wary of in his professional life. Walker seemed rehearsed, especially as he shook hands with Lena and David and ushered them into the room.

John made the introductions as if he were the host of a business meeting.

"You know the Rostenkowskis, I understand. And this is Mr. and Mrs. Williams. It was Mr. Williams's crew that found the van."

Mike Williams came toward them, hand out, his gaze direct, spending time with Lena as he shook her hand, then with David as he shook his.

"I'm Mike. Sorry we're all involved in this." He turned and his wife came forward. "This is Porfira." She seemed shy but her voice, lightly accented, was engaging, affable.

"Call me Po. Everybody does."

Lena tried to remember what David had said about Williams. He seemed the soul of warmth and confidence to her. She looked over at David, at his blank-faced reserve. He couldn't hide the fact that he thought one or more of the parents in the room had set up the kidnapping. Lena looked at the group and found this a stretch at best.

There followed a couple of minutes of finding seats, settling, asking if the Trainors wanted coffee, calling a woman Lena assumed was a cook or housekeeper, a woman with an island accent, to bring more coffee, and then a time when Martin took the floor. He was seated on a chair next to the couch. Mike was the nearest to him on the couch. Lena was catty-corner from the two of them. As Martin began to speak, Lena's gaze drifted to Mike. He and she were about the same age, she figured, though it was hard to tell. There was a boyishness to his looks, and yet a bit of salt and pepper in his hair. He wore jeans and a polo shirt with his company's logo on the breast. Lena watched him listening and thought you could tell a lot about people from the way they absorb words and ideas. Mike seemed thoughtful and considerate, open, willing to take in all Martin was saying and evaluate it.

He looked up suddenly and his eyes went directly to Lena, as if he knew she was staring at him. For some reason she didn't mind being caught like this. She didn't look away. Mike gave her a nodding smile and held her gaze. "Everything's going to be all right," his look seemed to say, and it was only after Lena got this message that she looked back at Martin.

"We've sent a team out to the camp to see what they know, but we don't expect to get much there. We figure whoever used the camp as a pretense for the abduction musta covered their tracks. But you never know. I'm always amazed how sloppy criminals can be."

John Walker, who seemed to have a restless impatience with the whole gathering, snorted and moved in his chair. "Well, I don't see the sloppiness so far. That was a pretty precise operation. If my timeline's right, they picked up the Williams boy about the same time, maybe even later than the real drivers showed up at the Trainors'. If Mrs. Trainor and the drivers had been able to register the deceit a few minutes earlier, Mr. Williams's crew might have nabbed the kidnappers instead of just an empty van."

"I don't think—," Mike began but Lena cut him off.

"Are you saying I was, what, slow, negligent?"

"No, I'm sorry. I didn't mean that. I just meant the timing of the whole thing seemed well calculated. Sorry."

Martin stood up to reclaim control.

"Right. I've said this to the Trainors and the Rostenkowskis but let me put a fine point on it. This whole damn scheme worked because none of you had any reason to doubt that the driver who came to your door was from the camp. He looked like a duck, walked like a duck, and so you had to assume he was the real deal."

"I should have said something," Mike said, looking down at the rug. "I wondered why a camp in New York State would register their vehicle in New Jersey, why they would still have dealer's plates on. I answered the question for myself, said they probably just bought the thing, hadn't had a chance to register it in New York, the dealer let 'em use it for the pickups, something they're not supposed to do, and let it slide. But boy, I wished I'd asked. I wonder if that little shit would have cracked."

Mike's open, sunny face was clouded now with a scowl. Po put her hand on his thigh and rubbed it lovingly, as if she'd heard this before and was again telling him it was all right. Phil broke the silence.

"I don't think he would have cracked. He was young and all, but I've seen liars like him at that age. He was very smooth, with us, with the kids. In fact he was very good with the kids. Right, Janet?"

Janet nodded. David couldn't help himself.

"You talk about it being smooth and all and what a good liar he was, but it looks to me like whoever's behind this shit knew a hell of a lot about the kids, about us."

"I agree," John Walker said. "What are you saying?"

"Just that, I don't know, how'd that happen?"

There was a subtext of accusation in David's question, but nobody wanted to address it. Martin was about to continue when Sheila Walker's voice, the one she perhaps used from the pulpit, stopped him.

"I'm sorry, but I'm uncomfortable with this language. I know it's common parlance and it's on television and all, but I would ask that you refrain here. Words like the one you used upset me normally, and under these circumstances they are doubly difficult. I hope you understand."

Mike made a quick apology; David nodded his second to that. Martin made a note to keep the salt out of his own language, and then he continued.

"Well, what can you tell us about the camp that might be relevant? Did anybody, for instance, push you to have the kids picked up rather than, say, take them up there yourselves?"

Nobody seemed to want to answer that.

"Okay, so nobody got the bum's rush on this pickup? We can't say that so and so from the camp called and told you it would be a great idea if your kid was driven to the camp by one of their staff."

"I think the brochure says it's sometimes easier for first-time campers to say goodbye at home and drive away," Lena started, tearing a little, then continuing, "drive away rather than have the parents be the ones to drive away at camp."

"No," Janet said. "It wasn't the brochure. I was the one who said that. We had had a difficult time with Linda the first time we dropped her off. I was the one who told you that." Lena was surprised to hear Janet, who was always blaming others, take responsibility.

"Franklin made the decision himself," John said. "He makes his own arrangements in cases like this. He asked if we were willing to spend the extra fifty dollars for the ride."

The other parents absorbed this and compared their own children to Franklin's behavior. Lena could feel David's reaction without looking at him. He was probably building up a nice little head of dislike for John Walker, she thought.

"Let's talk about the schedule of the pickups," Martin said, sitting back down. He consulted a notebook. "Was the order of the pickup ever changed once it was established?" This drew something of a blank from all of them. Janet looked at Lena.

"They just gave us each a time, I think, and when I found out they were picking up Sarah before Linda, I think I asked you if you wanted that reversed, right, Lena? Or did I just think that and not say anything? I thought it might be easier for Sarah if Linda was on the bus when she got picked up."

"I don't remember you saying anything." Lena in fact had wondered about switching things, but only a day or so before the pickup, and she didn't think there was time to talk to the camp about it.

Then suddenly Lena's thoughts went dead and something inchoate but present and threatening arose in her. Her grandmother's face leaped at her, then receded, the shock lingering. What was that? What happened? Lena breathed hard, then shook off the vision or whatever it was. She looked around. Only Mike Williams seemed to have noticed her sudden change. What was that?

Various people had been coming in the house during the meeting, mostly uniformed officers. The overweight female and the Hispanic male who came in as Martin was finishing this last were different, didn't have uniforms, and carried themselves with a smoother authority. Martin turned, conferred with them *sotto voce,* and then introduced them to the group as "our friends from the FBI." Lena, distracted, didn't catch their names. The two waved briefly and were directed to the Walker's computer.

Martin then continued to talk about the camp, to ask questions about their policies, why the parents had chosen the camp, if there was any hint of financial problems, if they remembered any counselors from the year before who might have been privy to inside information and would want to use it in such a horrible way. David thought Martin was being contradictory, beginning by saying that they didn't suspect the camp, then asking all sorts of questions about the camp. David thought this must be some sort of investigatory trick.

Lena kept looking back at Mike and Po. They didn't say much to each other, didn't touch all that often, but Lena could tell they were together in this crisis, that they had lines of communication that were rope strong. David was to Lena's right, sitting a little higher in an arm chair, and she felt as if he were miles away. Other than his attitude toward the Walkers, she couldn't tell what he was thinking. It had been a long time since she had the confidence that she knew what was going on in David's mind, that he cared what was going on in hers. She looked at a table clock. It was nearly four. Had Sarah not been abducted, would she and David have been beginning to bridge the gap between them now? She ached for that lost possibility.

Martin finished with his list of questions and asked if there was anything else anyone had to talk about. Phil asked about ransom money. Lena thought this was in character, given that the Rostenkowskis were constantly concerned with finances, bargains, rising prices.

"Are we supposed to pay the money or do we refuse or what?"

"Let's put that one on the back burner. I don't know what's gonna happen, what the abductors are going to demand, what the feds want to do. But whatever, if they come to you, don't go to the media. That's the first rule."

Everyone realized that John Walker was the target of this admonition. He shifted in his chair and began.

"I'm sorry, but I have obligations to stockholders and the bank. I'm on the board of several reputable organizations as well. At least for my part, I have to manage the news in this crisis. My company is more than willing to share our resources with all of you. I hope you understand my position, however."

"And I hope you understand, that your company understands, that this matter is being handled by the sheriff of Westchester County and the FBI. Any moves your PR people take need to be cleared with us first." Martin put a point on this with a small slap of his knee.

"I'm sure they will do that."

"Well, they didn't a little while ago with that statement of yours."

"My apologies. I will make certain that doesn't happen again."

Lena didn't quite believe the sincerity of John's quick retreat. Working with cancer patients from all walks of life and social strata, she'd become adept at figuring out which patients would follow a treatment regimen and which ones said they would but most likely wouldn't. She would put John, an executive not used to being told what to do, in this second category. David caught her eye as if he knew what she was thinking. "See," his look seemed to be saying, "this guy could have set the whole thing up." Lena looked down. At least she had an idea of what was going through David's mind.

They ended the meeting agreeing to meet the next morning, until Sheila reminded them it was Sunday and she had her ministerial duties. They moved the meeting back to the afternoon, and Martin said he "sure as hell hoped it wasn't necessary."

There was small talk as they gathered in the foyer waiting for police cars to be readied, the way for them cleared. The Rostenkowskis were just about out the door, shaking hands with the Walkers, when the Hispanic FBI agent came from the dining room and spoke in a low whisper to Martin. Martin raised his voice immediately.

"Hold it. Come on back. Looks like you got another email. This way."

They followed him into a study that had three different computers on three different desks. The FBI agents were huddled over one. The parents gathered around a second one and began reading. After a while Mike broke the silence.

"What is this shit?" he asked, apologizing to Sheila immediately.

"We're going to have to see if this is authentic," Martin said, scowling down through his reading glasses.

The Hispanic FBI agent spoke up, coming to them. "I don't think there's any doubt it's authentic. Your accounts have all been filtered."

"Filtered or not, that's a joke. That's not real," John responded, turning to Sheila, who was glaring at the message, breathing hard.

Lena didn't quite understand it the first time and read it again.

*FIRST STEP. TOMORROW MORNING, AT THE ELEVEN O'CLOCK SERVICE AT THE FIRST PRESBITERIAN CHURCH IN LARCHMONT YOU WILL TAKE UP A COLLECTION FOR THE CHURCH BUILDING FUND. YOU MUST RAISE AT LEAST $25 THOU AT THAT SERVICE AND PROVE IT IN ORDER TO GO ON TO THE SECOND STEP. I'M SERIOUS.*

Nobody standing there believed that the message was anything more than a cruel hoax that had made it through the filters, whatever they were. But it was a very effective one. Instead of asking for something for himself, the hoaxer had asked for a charitable contribution. And in pinpointing Sheila's church he had attempted to sprinkle some suspicion on one of the victims. Actually his barb had been felt by another member of the group around the laptop. Mike Williams's construction company was in line to build the new wing of the church once the capital campaign was complete.

"That's one for the record books," Martin said. He looked at Sheila. "I take it you've got a building fund."

Sheila was wound tight and spoke through thin lips. "I don't think this is funny. I can't believe it's for real. Yes, we have a building fund."

"You wouldn't mind an extra twenty-five thousand, would you?"

"What do you mean?" Sheila asked, a steely core evident.

"I mean we're obviously dealing with some sort of sick joker here, but that sick joker may very well have your kids. This isn't like paying ransom. What can it hurt to pass the hat?"

"We'll never get twenty-five thousand that way."

"Yes, we will," John said in something of an end-of-discussion voice. Sheila knew him well enough to stop there. The others took their cue from Sheila.

The group moved toward the front door silently. What sort of person not only kidnaps your kid but then yanks the rug out from under your expectations, throws you for a loop, doubles the uncertainty, and deepens the anxiety for the fate of your child? they asked themselves as they filed out of the house. Lena found herself next to Mike going down the walk to the police cars. They had to stop as a car was pulled up, and Lena felt she wanted to hear something from him, as if they'd just come out of a twisty, complicated film or play and she wanted his take on it. Perhaps sensing this, or more likely from his own sense of disorientation, he turned to her, and caught her gaze.

"Give me a fuckin' blueprint. I hate this."

Lena understood. Someone else had been forced from their normal way of approaching the world by this abduction. Someone else was going to have to find a new way to learn, solve, persevere without the data, road maps, and training he had always relied on. Lena nodded her agreement, pleased he felt comfortable swearing in front of her.

Detective Martin joined Lena and David in the car just as they were about to pull away from the Walkers. After they had gone a block or two, he turned, able only to see Lena fully.

"The FBI wants to take a look at your computers, if you don't mind."

Lena nodded her okay, but David spoke up. "Why? They're monitoring them through the servers, aren't they?"

"I don't know. I don't know about those goddam things," Martin said, unable to see David's face.

"Well, I do. I work in the computer industry and I'm not all that crazy about the government snooping around in my computer. Shouldn't they get a search warrant?"

Martin let this sit, his silence amplifying the suspect nature of the complaint. Lena gave David a look, but he continued.

"You think Walker and his goddam bank are going to let them poke around in his computer? I doubt it."

"I think they already have—," Martin started, but David cut him off, relenting and protesting at the same time.

"That family," he growled, looking out the window as he spoke. "What the hell were they doing sending their snooty little kid to Arno anyway? If that kid is anything like the way his father describes him, Sarah's going to have a fit. And Mrs. Minister there, what, you can't say 'shit' in front of her? I mean as soon as she said that, I wanted to scream obscenities. Our kids have been kidnapped, for chrissake. We can't drop a few *shits* or *fucks*?"

He huffed, unable to look at Lena. Martin turned to her and spoke as much with his soft blue eyes as with his words.

"They're not going to take the computers away. You can sit with them if you want." Again Lena nodded her authorization. David said no more.

They were nearing the Trainor house when Lena caught a glimpse of a backyard swimming pool, spotlit in the growing dark, no one swimming in it. Lena looked at the scene until the house blocked her view. Then, for the first time since the abduction, Lena took hold of an image of Sarah that didn't have to do with the van or J.D. or the departure. It was an image from earlier in the summer, when they had gone to a pool party for one of the members of Lena's practice who was moving away. Sarah had met a couple of new kids and they were diving off the small board at the deep end of the pool. Lena was sitting with the wife of the departing member of the practice and looked over to see Sarah frog-kick herself up and grab ahold of the springy diving board. Lena was about to say something, tell her to watch out for divers, to be careful, but as she was thinking this, Sarah turned to her, craning around her extended arms, and flashed her the happiest smile Lena had ever seen from her daughter. Sarah's vitality then was stunning, her lean biceps framing her pure features. Lena had the sense Sarah could pull herself up beyond the diving board, could with one swift, graceful movement launch herself into the space above, the clouds and blue sky overhead. And as the second or two of that smile passed, Lena and Sarah were one and the same, mother and daughter, each an extension of the other, together.

The glow of this memory faded quickly as they approached the house and the car inched again through the crush of press. Now Lena felt her separation from Sarah deeply. The thought of going into the house and Sarah's not being there tore at her as she got out of the car, deflecting the hurled questions, as she and David were walking with Martin up the sidewalk. Sarah had to be in the house. With every step Lena convinced herself that Sarah *was* in the house, found, safe, waiting for them. She almost said something to David as she hurried past Martin in order to be the first to see her daughter. Her brain told her over and over this couldn't be, but the blood pumping from her now fast-beating heart washed all that reasoning away. Sarah was there. She was sure of it. She wrenched the front door open and threw herself into the darkness of the living room.

# Ten

Mr. Everett was quiet as they traveled up the New York State Thruway. At first he had had the kids play a game with him. He had given each of them a number and whenever he called out their number, that kid had to slouch down in his or her seat. Sarah had asked why they had to do this, and Mr. Everett answered that it was fun. Then he called her number. After a while though, when the traffic thinned out near Albany, Mr. Everett stopped the game and drove without speaking much.

Above Albany, on the Northway, the SUV went through a quick, violent thunderstorm, one of those hard, heavy rains that obliterate any real view of the road. Several bolts of lightning lit up the highway as the wipers slapped furiously at the cascading water. Mr. Everett leaned forward, slowing the car, working to stay on the road. The kids tensed. Tommy jumped when a semi, gushing water from its wheels, passed them. He breathed hard and turned to catch Linda's frightened eyes looking at him. Neither said anything but they didn't have to.

The rain stopped as suddenly as it began and they were back in sunshine a half a mile later. Mr. Everett sat back and turned off the wipers.

Five minutes later something spooked him, and he called out, "One, three, four!" Franklin, Tommy, and Linda took a second to remember what that meant, then slouched down in their seats. Sarah watched Mr. Everett's eyes in the rearview mirror as he kept looking at a car about to pass them. When it did, Sarah saw that it was a police car of some sort, a state trooper probably.

As he told the kids they could sit back up, Mr. Everett caught Sarah's look in the rearview mirror.

"What's up, there, Sarah? You look worried."

"Why aren't we going to the camp?"

"We are, but not right away. This is a special trip. You guys are lucky."

Franklin's voice wobbled as he spoke. "I'm sure my parents didn't sign up for this."

"No, of course not. None of your parents did. This is a surprise. I think somebody has gotten in touch with them and told them about it already." He grinned broadly now, checking the kids in the rearview, laughing to himself.

"I have to use the bathroom," Tommy said. Mr. Everett didn't seem to hear him. Sarah spoke up.

"Tommy has to use the bathroom."

"You have to use the bathroom?" Mr. Everett scowled back at him through the rearview mirror.

"Yes."

"Okay, good. About a half an hour. Can you wait?"

"I don't know."

"I'm sure you can." This was more a command than a statement. The kids gave each other furtive looks. They'd all encountered this tone before in strict teachers. But they weren't in a classroom now; the bell wasn't going to ring; they didn't know where to turn. Sarah looked out at the cars passing them in the other direction. She wanted to be in one of those, not headed north with Mr. Everett.

They took an exit off the Northway and started to follow a two-lane road into the woods. The sun was still high and the terrain outside the SUV looked hot and baked. The air conditioning inside the car was very chilly. Sarah had thought about asking Mr. Everett to turn it down, but after he had brushed off Tommy's request, she didn't want to risk a similar response.

After a few miles on the two-lane, they turned onto a gravel road that climbed steeply for several miles. Dust swirled behind them. The few houses on the road were squat, older ranch houses, set back from the road. They looked almost uninhabited. When the road finally crested, the kids could see briefly the tall peaks of the Adirondacks in the distance. Then the road plunged back down into deep woods and for a long while they were riding in the shadows of the trees. Mr. Everett slammed on the brakes when he missed a turn, backed up, and pulled the SUV into a little grassy area that didn't look anything like a road. He went ahead about a hundred yards and stopped. The kids followed his every move as he got out of the car, went back toward the road, and started scuffing the grass with his feet, obliterating the tire marks the SUV had made.

When he got back in the driver's seat, Tommy surprised the other kids by speaking up.

"I really have to go to the bathroom."

"Oh, right. Be just a few minutes."

There was no road ahead, just a grassy path through saplings and underbrush. After a bumpy, rolling mile of this, Mr. Everett turned the SUV right and parked it under a canopy of dense pine branches.

"Okay, everybody out."

The kids obeyed slowly. Linda was about to whisper something to Sarah, but Mr. Everett opened the side door first.

"Come on out. We've got to spray you."

When the kids were outside, Mr. Everett told them to cover their eyes and he began to spray them head to foot with bug spray. Tommy reminded him he had to go to the bathroom, and Mr. Everett told him to go off in the woods. This was a new concept for Tommy, but after a while he went behind a clump of bushes and peed. The girls could hear the peeing and were embarrassed. Mr. Everett saw this.

"Hey, girls. You're in the woods now." And they wondered what they were going to do when they had to pee.

Then Mr. Everett told them all to get the two duffels and follow him. He shouldered a large pack and started up a barely distinguishable path through the pines. Sarah picked up one of the duffels. Tommy took the other.

Mr. Everett hadn't gone far when he looked back to see Tommy, Sarah, and Linda following him, Franklin standing back by the SUV.

"Hey, Franklin, come on."

Franklin didn't move. He shook his head no. Mr. Everett went back to him.

"What's the matter?"

"I don't think we should be doing this. I need my parents' permission."

"We've got that. You don't think the camp would let you take this trip without their permission, do you?"

"But they didn't say anything about it."

Mr. Everett got a little impatient. "Look, I told you. Everything's all right." He took a cell phone out of his backpack as he spoke. "When we get up to the cabin, we'll have coverage and you can call your parents. How about that?"

Franklin looked from Mr. Everett to the other kids. They all seemed like they were going to follow him. Franklin certainly didn't want to stay behind. Mr. Everett held up the cell phone for emphasis. Franklin relented.

"Good boy," Mr. Everett said as he clapped him on the back and escorted him toward the others. "Good boys and girls. Come on. We've got a little hike and then we'll be at the cabin."

"What's at the cabin?" Sarah asked as they all began to walk again.

"Nature. Wilderness. I've got some food stored up there too. What do you like to eat?" Nobody said anything for a little while. Then Tommy piped up.

"Pop-Tarts."

"Well, we don't have any of those. You need a toaster."

"No, you don't," Tommy shot back. "I eat 'em cold."

Mr. Everett stopped and glared at this mini-insurrection. "They ain't good for you and we don't have any. So let's just shut up about that, okay?" He turned and marched up ahead. Tommy's little chest heaved up and down as the others gave him sympathetic looks.

The trail started up a rocky incline and everybody was too busy climbing to talk. After a while the path leveled off and they reached an open area with a view of some of the nearby mountains. Mr. Everett stopped and took off his backpack. He took in a big, exaggerated breath of air and threw his head back.

"Smell that, kids? Beautiful up here, isn't it?" They stood, tired from the climb, and said nothing. Mr. Everett turned to them scowling. "I said, 'Beautiful up here, isn't it?'" And the kids nodded their agreement.

Mr. Everett then pulled a length of rope and four sleeping masks out of his backpack. He gave one mask to each of the kids.

"Now, the cabin we're going to is a secret one, and so I'm required to have you wear these for the last part of the trip. Go ahead, put them on."

"How can we walk with these on?" Sarah asked.

"See this rope? You'll all hang on to the rope and I'll guide you. It'll be fun."

The kids obeyed slowly. Tommy and Linda had the duffels and had trouble latching onto the rope. But soon they were all making their way down the trail, Mr. Everett in the lead, the kids each with one hand on the rope. Sarah remembered little trips she used to take in day care where all the kids would be tethered to the teacher with a rope like this one. But this was different. They didn't blindfold you in day care.

After a few hundred feet Mr. Everett had them go around in a circle, go left, then go right, then back up, moves clearly intended to disorient them. As they began to walk in a straight line again, Tommy, at the end of the rope, thinking about a story of kids lost in the woods, brought the duffel to his rope hand, opened the top, fished down into the duffel, found a sock, and dropped it. Mr. Everett's voice made him jump.

"Yessir. You're lucky campers."

The kids stumbled a lot but managed to make the rest of the hike without falling. Mr. Everett praised them for this. Sarah heard crickets in the grass and felt the sun beating down on them. She no longer felt the shadows of the trees. Then Mr. Everett had them turn around several times again and stopped them.

"Okay, troops, we're here. You can take off the masks."

When they did they saw they were in a small clearing, surrounded by pines and brush. A tumbled-down shack made of weathered boards squatted near the edge of the clearing. A funny little stand-alone hut, an outhouse, was behind the shack.

Linda started to cry, and Mr. Everett's tone sharpened.

"What? What's the problem?"

"I don't like this. I want to go back."

"Go back? C'mere."

He took Linda's arm and moved her toward the shack. The door opened without a lock and he half shoved Linda inside, motioning for the others to join them.

"See. It's nice and cozy in here."

Sarah followed Tommy into the shack and smelled the musty wood. She could see little until her eyes adjusted. Then in the dimness she saw the space was divided into two rooms, a sink in the corner of the first room, next to it a small counter and a large cooler. Through the door to the other room she could see single bed mattresses on the floor. Linda continued to cry. Sarah went to her and put an arm around her.

"I don't like this," Linda sniffled to Sarah through tears.

Mr. Everett was about to say something to Linda when Franklin spoke up.

"You said we could call our parents from here."

"Did I? I think I said maybe. But no matter what, we'll have to go over to the pond. That's where you get coverage. You wanna see the pond?"

Linda's crying slowed. She imagined a pond with houses on it like her grandmother's house on a pond in Connecticut. Mr. Everett took his cell phone out of his pack and motioned for them to follow him. He smiled to himself as the little file of kids and he walked toward the pond. He had done it. He had gotten the kids safely away from any inquisitive eyes. There hadn't been any major rebellion. Back in

Westchester the plan was probably humming along. He could relax a little. Then he remembered something. He stopped the group.

"Wait a minute. I'll be right back."

He went back in the shack. The kids looked at each other. Tommy spoke first.

"Do you think he's really from the camp?"

"No." Franklin was emphatic, angry.

Sarah and Linda looked at each other. They didn't want to believe this. If he wasn't from the camp, where was he from? His voice turned their heads.

"Over here, smile."

He was holding a digital camera, using it on video mode. In the bright sun he couldn't see much on the LCD screen. But he could see they weren't smiling. He figured that was okay, better to have them look unhappy when their parents and the world saw the clip. He adjusted his angle so that the background was completely nondescript. Just generic woods. He pressed the video button and panned over the kids. When he was finished he reviewed the results. They were perfect. The kids looked well taken care of but sullen, and as far as identifying marks were concerned, there were none. These squinting little campers, he said to himself, could be anywhere.

# Eleven

It was nearly one in the morning when the two FBI agents left the house. They had spent several hours going through the computers, with David hovering as they worked. He could tell they weren't doing a very thorough investigation, didn't seem to know that much about how to search a hard drive or follow up on deletions. He wondered if they were there to examine the computers or if that was just an excuse, if they were really there to gauge the temperature in the house, feel the mood, see if they could smell guilt. A couple of times David decided to help them, show them some tricks, just to keep them from thinking he had anything to hide. They never found his third email account, however, and he never steered them toward it.

Lena, who had spent the hours in the living room and then the kitchen, saw the agents out as they left. She still hadn't gotten their names down, willfully preferring Detective Martin over the two. As they left she stepped out into the night, hoping David, who had opened a bottle of wine and gone through most of it, wouldn't follow, wouldn't want to talk, might just go to sleep. The news vans had left and the street was empty except for a sheriff's patrol car, parked quietly at the curb, the dome light on, two officers sitting there. They exchanged words with the FBI agents as they left, got in their car, and drove off.

Cicadas in a bush to the right of the house churned up their scratchy music. Lena stared out at the driveway. The flurried goodbye of the morning, the one that had seemed so normal and perfect, floated up in front of her. In the hours she had been by herself, while the agents examined the computers, she had fought those images of farewell, pushed against the second-guessing, told herself that she wasn't alone, that the solid, open-faced Mike had let his child be taken away as well. Over and over again she took her thoughts to a higher plane, to an examination of how the mind's anticipation can lead it to mistakes and misapprehensions. But trying to philosophize in this situation was like leaping over slippery stones to ford a treacherous river. Standing on the front lawn, facing the scene of the crime, she couldn't keep the particulars of the abduction at bay: Sarah's wide eyes as J.D. told them about the soccer program, the smell of the new van, the clunk of the van door as it closed.

Then it happened again. As if it were a physical presence, Lena's grandmother's face rushed at her out of the dark. Lena took a step back. The face talked. The face was in Lena's childhood kitchen. Her grandmother was making cookies, talking to Lena. Her mother's mother—Noonie, the kids called her—a strong-willed, independent spirit who would visit Sweden every year. Lena must have been close to Sarah's age now, nine or so, hanging on her grandmother's every word.

"You listen to your Noonie now; never use margarine, always butter, got it?" Or something like that. She was always giving advice, laying down rules. She smiled as she took the ball of dough in her sinewy hands and shaped it. "And this year, if you come to the airport, I don't want you waving goodbye like you did last year." Why, young Lena must have asked, or her look must have said the same. "Why? Maybe they don't teach you right in this country, but where I come from, if you want to see someone again, if you want them to come back, you don't wave 'em off like they were flies you wanted to get rid of. No sir. Listen to me, Lena. Never wave goodbye to someone you love. Got it?"

In the darkness on the front porch Lena could hardly breathe. Had she waved goodbye to Sarah? In all the details of the parting that had been pounding in her head all day there wasn't a memory one way or another. That moment was a blank. But Lena could remember being at the airport in Stockholm as Noonie walked toward the jetway and her mother, Sally, saying, "Wave goodbye, Lena," and Lena refusing, telling her what Noonie had said, and her mother dismissing the admonition with a laugh. But Lena couldn't dismiss it, and she couldn't remember what she'd done only hours earlier. She looked out at the driveway but it was dark and empty and held no clues. Suddenly the warm night became chilly and she went back inside.

David was in the kitchen, draining the wine bottle. He asked if she wanted some and she declined. He told her about what the agents did and didn't find. He said he was tired and he was going to bed. She knew he was asking her to follow but she couldn't. Sleep, while Sarah was gone, seemed unimaginable. David looked hurt and went to her, glass in hand, his face a cliché of concern, it seemed to Lena.

"We'll get through this," he said, in a wine-mellowed near whisper Lena couldn't stand. She shook her head and walked away. David waited a while and Lena imagined him behind her, swaying a little maybe, his eyelids drooping. Then he left the kitchen.

The night outside the patio doors was dark and deathly still. Then, from the street, came muffled male laughter. She imagined it was the cops under their dome light, for whom this was just an ordinary shift. She instinctively looked over at the clock on the microwave and realized it was already eight o'clock in the morning in Sweden. She could call.

Lena's mother, Sally, answered the phone and was immediately worried, thinking the call was news of some sort. When Lena told her there was no news, Sally then asked a flurry of questions about how Lena was doing. As Lena answered she teared up at her mother's concern. Sally had always been a paragon of caring. She had finished college and rushed to her boyfriend Richard's side in Sweden, after he had made the difficult decision to go AWOL. Throughout her time there, throughout Lena's life, Sally had ministered to all sorts of troubled people, from other deserters in the country, to the mentally ill, as a social worker, to her daughters in their difficult years, and most recently to a large community of Arab immigrants who had settled in their suburb of

Stockholm. It was her mother's dedication to others that had led Lena into medicine, but that dedication also had made Lena feel at times inadequate. Sally's selflessness simply could not be matched.

"We've had two communications from the . . . abductors," Lena said, wanting to talk about the facts of the case rather than her own feelings.

" 'The fucking bastards,' Dad's been calling them. Yes, we know."

"Know what?"

"About the communications."

"They haven't been released to the press, Mom."

"It's all over the internet, honey. Haven't you seen it?"

"No. I couldn't get on . . . How much is out there?"

"Tons. This has been a very big story in Europe. There was video of you and David going into the big house in Larchmont."

"They make it seem like we've got to keep everything hush-hush here."

Sally slipped into Swedish, something she did when she wanted to have a private conversation with the girls. Richard had struggled with the language, never really becoming fluent, and relied on English and some French to get by.

"I want you to tell your father in no uncertain terms that he can't go to be with you. He's driving Sylvie and me crazy. We are making plans to fly tomorrow if nothing is resolved, and he says he's coming too."

Lena responded in English. "What good would that do? He'd be in prison in no time."

"He's talking about going to Canada and sneaking across the border."

"Let me talk to him."

"I will, but you want Sylvie and me to come, don't you?"

Lena didn't really know how to answer that question. Yes, she wanted them, but if they came that would mean Sarah had been missing another day or two. She recoiled at this thought.

"Of course, but they're going to find Sarah soon."

Sally went back to English. "Is there some break?"

"No, but you can't hide four kids very long."

Sally's silence told Lena she wasn't convincing. "We'll get

reservations and then call you to see if you want us. How's David doing?"

"He's, uh, torn up. None of us know what to do."

"I can imagine. Here's Dad. I love you, honey. Sylvie sends her love too. This is just horrible. We're with you."

Lena wanted to ask her mother about what her grandmother had said, but she doubted Sally would even remember. She had been pacing in the kitchen with the handset, but now she had to go to the living room and sit on the couch. She suddenly felt drained. Her father's voice was strong and animated. She could imagine he was fueled by the pitch-black coffee he loved.

"Lena, hi. Anything new?"

"No, it seems like you know more than we do over here."

"What's this nonsense with the building fund?"

"We don't know. One of the other parents is—"

"The minister of the church. I know. But what are these fucking bastards trying to do? Add insult to injury? Jesus."

"It's strange, Dad."

"What about the wig?"

"What wig?"

"A sanitation worker at one of the office buildings near where they dumped the van found a curly-haired wig. You didn't hear about this?"

"No."

"They think it might have been worn by the . . . by the . . . fuck, I can't even think about him without wanting to rip something apart."

"Dad?"

"What?"

"You can't come here."

Richard didn't answer for a few seconds. Lena heard his breath through the line and remembered that he had had a bout of angina a year earlier.

"Well, if they don't find her soon, I don't know how I'm going to stay away."

"You are on a list. If you try to enter the country, you'll be in a brig before you know it."

"Honey, where there's a will, there's a way. You let me worry about that."

"Dad."

"What are the other parents like?"

Lena answered his deflecting question with some brushstroke portraits of the others. When she got to Mike and Po Williams, she said that Mike reminded her of "you, Dad."

"Ornery son of a bitch?"

"Yeah, right. Junkyard dog." This was something of a joke between them. Richard was a puppy, but compared to his wife and the gentle way she dealt with the girls, he characterized his rougher style of parenting as harsh. Lena's retort, as always, was her way of saying he was full of shit.

"Boy, I wish I was right there to give you a hug, honey."

"Me too, Dad. I've gotta go or I'm going to start crying. Will you email me some of that news you're getting over there, the one about the wig?"

"Sure, send it right along." He didn't want to hang up. "We've got some money over here, you know. And Sylvie's minting it these days. You just tell us what you need. Okay?"

"Yeah, Dad." Lena didn't want to think about a detail like that. She wasn't denying that a ransom was in the future, but she wanted to know, to really know first that Sarah was okay and was coming home. Then she would be willing to give every cent she had or ever would have.

They finally hung up and Lena lay down on the couch. The call had anchored her, as she had hoped it would, reminding her of the real and solid world she had grown up in. The day just past seemed tolerable now in memory, the uncertain future less horrifying. She could imagine sleep. It wouldn't be a dereliction of duty. It would be good. She wouldn't have to think about whether she had waved goodbye or not. There were others around the globe who were keeping watch. The terror of the word *where* receded. She could let her heavy limbs and her misfiring brain take her into a realm in which no one was missing and all were together, all were one. All were one.

# Twelve

A crack of thunder signaled a drenching rain to come for Westchester County. The storm, blowing in from the Hudson Valley to the northwest, promised to be quick and vicious, one that might wreak havoc with tree limbs and power lines. Among the victims of the abduction, it would pound the Williams's house first. Mike, who had been up since three in the morning, was just returning from a drive around the county. He hadn't really been searching for the kids. He simply needed to get out of the house, to be active. As he pulled his company pickup into the driveway, his older son, Jack, was rolling his motorcycle into the garage ahead of the rain.

Mike spent a moment watching this simple act. Jack was an athlete, all-county in football and basketball, all-state as a shortstop in baseball. Po had hated the idea of him having a motorcycle, but after he saved his own money for one, Mike talked her into letting him have it, arguing that he was a skilled driver, very coordinated, and would be able to handle any situation. Now, with Tommy gone, Mike wondered if he'd want Jack to ever ride that motorcycle again. Mike knew Tommy was going to be back soon, but he knew too that having him away like this had changed him. His tall, muscular son got the machine in out of the rain and turned back to see why his dad wasn't getting out of the car. Mike stared through the windshield and Jack, frozen by this stare, had the eerie feeling that his father was much farther away than just down the driveway. What was his father thinking?

The first big raindrops plunked against the windows of Sheila Walker's study moments later. She had slept there, on the couch, up and down all night. Early the previous evening she had had a long conversation with Tom Adams, the assistant minister at First Presbyterian, and had assured him that she was up to delivering her scheduled sermon. But now, after hours of trying to put words to paper, she wasn't sure she could do it. Tom said he would be standing in the wings in case "things weren't possible," but Sheila couldn't imagine abandoning the pulpit. She thought about God putting words into Abraham's mouth when he felt he couldn't possibly speak. She wondered if she could do something she'd never done before, deliver a sermon without a complete text in front of her. In divinity school, as an exercise in a homiletics class, she had delivered a sermon from notes, and it had been a disaster, one that had made her scrupulous about sermon preparation ever after. Now, she thought, maybe the only way to bring God's word to the congregation, on what was promising to be a slate gray washout of a morning, was to just open up her mouth and hope. She bowed her head in prayer.

Even though the house was being rattled by thunder, and lightning was dancing in through the windows, Phil Rostenkowski had trouble waking Janet. She had taken a sleeping pill at midnight after she found her heart racing so badly she thought it would come out of her chest. Now she was in some groggy underworld and Phil had to shake her, to tell her that he had just had a call from Detective Martin, who was coming by soon to show them a wig that had been found. Janet suddenly went from deep sleep to frightened, disoriented consciousness. A clap of thunder made her scream, and Phil sat on the bed and held her. It was the first time they had embraced like this in a long time. He was holding a different Janet. She was more than words now, more than money worries, more than checklists. She was his wife again.

Lena smelled the coffee brewing in the kitchen before she heard the downpour outside. She knew something dark and bad had happened to her recently, but in the seconds before she was fully awake, she couldn't remember what that was. The coffee smelled good, and the fact it was brewing meant that David was up, that he was still here, that nothing had happened to him. It felt like she had been hurt somehow, injured maybe, as if she'd lost a limb. Loss, yes, that was it. Loss.

And then, full blown, she solved the mystery in an instant, and the horror of the abduction filled her once again. A rush of wind-driven rain tattooed the bay window and made Lena imagine Sarah outside in a drenching storm or in some inadequate old building. Now the coffee smelled horrible and the dry warmth of the house was hideous, a luxurious protection against the elements that her daughter might not have.

Lena sat up, hating herself for having fallen asleep on watch, for letting her guard down, for briefly forgetting. She stood and took a couple of steps, not knowing where she was going. She stopped and could see a slice of the kitchen from where she stood. David's bare shoulder was visible near the window over the sink. He was stirring his coffee. A crack of thunder made him jerk his body around. But Lena absorbed the sound as if she'd been prepared for it. Nothing, she thought to herself, could take her away from thoughts of Sarah now.

The pond wasn't anything like Linda had imagined it. It was much smaller than the one her grandmother lived on, there were no houses on it, the shoreline was weed-choked and murky, and a small dock thrusting out over the water was wobbly. The water itself looked black and impenetrable.

"Isn't this great," Mr. Everett crowed, throwing his arms wide, knowing that the children behind him were wary and in no mood for celebration. He turned to them. "This was my swimming hole when I was growing up. Anybody want to take a dip?"

Silence greeted the question. Sarah, who had been worried when she saw the water, and who was still clinging to the hope that Mr. Everett was indeed from the camp, now froze at the thought that perhaps this was where she would have to take her swimming test.

Before anyone could think, Mr. Everett scooped up Tommy, clutched him under his arm like a loaf of bread, and chugged down the dock. Tommy kicked but he was held tight.

"You want a dip there, don't you, Tommy?"

"No! No!"

But Mr. Everett went to the end of the dock and made a swinging motion with the struggling Tommy, as if he was going to throw him in. Then Mr. Everett nearly lost control of Tommy and half threw him back on the dock. Tommy scrambled to his feet.

"Jesus! Don't do that," Mr. Everett growled.

Tommy went back to the kids while Mr. Everett stewed. Franklin found his voice before the others did.

"Do we get to call our parents now?" he asked, unable to disguise his fear.

Mr. Everett turned to the water as if he hadn't heard, but then he turned back, for dramatic effect.

"Here's how it's going to work, kids. The camp has set up this little adventure for you guys, but they haven't told me exactly how long we're going to be out here. Could be just overnight, or maybe a couple of days. Anyhoo . . . they won't know how long until they get a call, sort of, from your parents. And when they get that call, then I can, uh, let you be in contact. You understand?"

The kids looked at each other. Mr. Everett pulled the cell phone out of his jeans pocket, opened it, and took a hard look, moving it around to be able to view the screen. Through the looks the kids gave each other, they tacitly decided to have Franklin speak for them again.

"No. I don't understand. Why can't I call my parents?"

"'Cause I said so," Mr. Everett flashed at them, tired of his own little game. "Now move back there and keep quiet. I'll be back in a minute."

He dialed a number as he walked back out on the creaky dock, stopped when the call went through, and spoke low. The kids couldn't hear what he was saying, though all were straining to pick out the words. After a couple of sentences, Mr. Everett snapped the phone shut and turned back, striding down the dock with a big grin on his face, obviously pleased about something. When he reached the kids, his voice was softer than it had been.

"Okay. How about we go back and get something to eat, set up the beds?"

He didn't wait for an answer and started off through the tall grass toward the cabin. The kids followed slowly. Then Mr. Everett stopped and turned to them once again.

"First lesson here in our outdoor adventure. The snakes you see around here? They ain't poisonous. I don't want to see you jumping and screaming if you see a snake, got it? 'Cause jumping and screaming around in the woods can get you hurt. First of all you might twist an ankle or something. Second off you might attract bear." He let this last sit for a while before continuing. "Bear ain't no big problem. Most of 'em's black bear up here and unless you leave some food out, they don't want nothin' to do with you. But if you're jumping around and screamin' and say they got cubs with 'em, they might take that wrong and attack. Now, we all got that?"

The kids certainly did get that, along with the big grin Mr. Everett added to the end of his last sentence. Something was way off now, Sarah knew. The effect on her had been the one Mr. Everett had hoped for: she was frightened, she wanted to run, but she felt as if she were in the jaws of a trap, that leaving sight of Mr. Everett was much more dangerous than staying with him. In his clever way he had become her protector. The other kids made similar calculations. When Mr. Everett turned and began tramping back to the shack, they did not hesitate to follow.

When night came to the clearing, it came quickly, the dark of the surrounding woods seeming to rise up to the purpling sky, soon forming a dome of star-speckled black. Mr. Everett had made hot dogs and beans, heating them over a propane burner in the shack. He had made the kids take their paper plates outside to eat, sitting on some chair-sized boulders that were strewn around the clearing. He talked about the Iroquois who used to roam the Adirondacks, and he pointed out some of the constellations he could remember. Tommy was the only one who ate the soggy canned beans that soaked through the paper plates. The hot dogs tasted miserable in the kids' mouths. A loon's plaintive, anguished coo made Linda jump, but Mr. Everett reveled in the sound, saying it was a reminder of his boyhood. A riot of cicada song filled the space around the shack.

They went back inside after Mr. Everett used the flashlight to make sure no one had dropped bits of their hot dog. He said the bears could be attracted by the smallest morsel. When they were in the shack he opened a chest and pulled out several old, scratchy blankets. He told them they would need these for cover when it got colder later. He made them all rinse their hands and faces in the sink, telling them that the water coming out of the faucet was the most natural in the world, true spring water.

He got them situated on the mattresses in the second room. When he swept the flashlight around at the four, he saw the frightened looks in the direct glare of the beam, as if he were doing a head count in a prison.

"Don't worry, kids, we'll have fun tomorrow. We'll do a hike. What do you say to that?" Nobody responded. Mr. Everett moved the light from one face to the next. "I said, isn't that cool, a hike?" Taking their cue the kids mumbled about how good a hike sounded to them.

He left the door open and they could see him only fifteen feet from where they lay. They wanted to talk to each other but they didn't dare. Mr. Everett moved around in the other room and soon lit a small kerosene lamp. The yellow flame danced, throwing spidery shadows on the wall in the kids' room.

The light soon had a hypnotic effect and Tommy and Linda drifted off to sleep. Sarah, after seeing Linda's eyes close for good, rolled over and saw Franklin nearby staring at her. He said nothing, mouthed no words, but spoke volumes. "We are in deep trouble," his look said. "One of us has to stay awake." Working in tandem, the two managed to keep a spotty watch all night.

In one of her waking hours, Sarah saw the glow of a strange light coming from the corner of the other room. She got up on all fours, leaned over Linda, and craned her neck to see around the door jamb. The light was coming from a laptop. Mr. Everett was hunched over the small table on which the laptop rested, his digital camera connected to the computer, his features lit from below by the screen. As if he felt Sarah's eyes, he looked slowly over at her. She didn't look away. The distant, affectless look he gave her made the hair on the back of her neck stand up, but she couldn't tell if he was actually looking at her, if he could see her shadowy presence outside the glare of the computer, or if he was looking into some deep, unknowable future and trying to understand its indecipherable message.

# Thirteen

The FBI was now fully in charge of the investigation, but Martin continued to do legwork for them. Early in the morning he came to the house to show Lena and David the wig that had been found the previous evening. He had pictures of an officer who was close to the description of J.D. wearing the wig. The officer looked so ridiculous under the jumble of curls, Lena couldn't say with any certainty that the wig was the one J.D. used, if indeed he used one at all. In all the images of him she carried, none betrayed a hairpiece. Martin said that there had been long strands of hair stuck to the inside of the wig, that it could have been worn by a woman, and that they were doing tests.

When Martin asked if they were planning to go to the church service, Lena said she didn't know. David nodded to this. Lena asked if any of the other parents were going and if they really thought they could raise the necessary money. Martin let out a long sigh.

"The Rostenkowskis aren't going to go. You may have talked to her this morning. She had a real bad night. He's afraid she's on the edge, called me to say so on the Q.T. an hour ago. The Williamses are going but not taking their little girl. And Mr. Walker's going. He's going to donate the twenty-five grand to the building fund. I guess he carries that much in pocket change."

David and Lena looked at each other, then both looked down at the floor.

"I can't go," David said finally, shaking his head. "It's going to be a circus."

"We're not letting press anywhere near the church. We're bringing people in the back way, by Culpepper Road."

"It's still going to be a circus inside. You know the emails we got are all over the internet. Lena's father knew about the wig before we did. This is fucked up."

"I'm going to go," Lena said, looking at Martin even when David shifted his glance to her. "I'm not religious but I . . . I would like to go." She had made her decision impulsively, not wanting to spend hours in the house alone with David.

"I really can't do it, Lena," David implored, as if they were making the decision together.

"That's fine. I don't mind going by myself." If Martin hadn't been there, David would have pressed, would have asked how it would look for her to go and him not to. But as it was, he had to sit and stay with his decision. He felt sandbagged, as if Lena had let him speak his mind and now was punishing him for it. He was close to the truth in this.

Martin had three stuffed flipbooks of mug shots and Lena went through them all over the next half hour. She didn't see any face that resembled J.D.'s but she admitted to Martin that after the first book and a half she could no longer remember much about what the abductor looked like. Martin told her that was normal. He closed the books, said someone would be back to pick her up about ten thirty. A hole in the clouds drifted over the house and the living room was suddenly flooded with glancing sunlight. They all looked out the window and only then noticed that the news vans and their antennae were gathering again. Martin took out his cell phone, dialed a number, asked if there was any special reason the "goddamn press" were congregating again. He got an answer, snapped the phone shut, and turned to David and Lena, who, he could see, wanted to know what he heard.

"Slow news day," he said.

After Martin left, David wanted to talk about Lena's decision, but she said she was in no mood to talk. She feared that any conversation with David now would lead her to ask him why he wasn't home when Sarah left, and she wasn't ready for that. She took a shower and allowed herself to be soothed by the water. She put on the small amount of makeup she wore for work, not wanting to seem as if she were gussying up in any way. She chose a pantsuit to wear to the service and then looked at herself in the full-length mirror in the bedroom. She looked no different from the way she usually did, and that bothered her. She felt she had been changed completely in the past twenty-four hours, and yet here was her image hardly altered. How could that be?

She went in the kitchen and started to make an egg for her breakfast, but when she looked at the congealing yellow mass in the frying pan, she completely lost her appetite. She even felt as if she might throw up and went into the bathroom, but the feeling passed. She knew she was going to have to push herself to eat soon.

She called the Rostenkowskis and got Paul first. He quickly put his father on and Lena asked about Janet.

"She's not doing too well," Phil said. "She had a rough night." He didn't seem to want to give details.

"Is there anything I can do?"

"No, I don't . . ." He stopped, didn't say any more and must have handed the phone to Janet. Janet's voice was weak, barely audible.

"Lena?"

"Hi. Bad night, huh?"

"I can't take this. I don't know what I'm going to do. I took a sleeping pill last night, but I woke up even more anxious."

"Do you want a sedative or a Xanax? I can call the pharmacy."

"Maybe." She paused and Lena was about to say she could take care of the prescription when Janet let loose a rush of words. "There were supposed to be two. I looked it up. Last night. In the emails from the camp it says clearly that there would be two counselors in the van. Why didn't we realize something was wrong when there was only one?"

"I don't think it would have done any good."

"Why? We would have caught him."

"He would have had an answer. He was very clever. He had the whole thing planned out perfectly. Plus he knew we wouldn't be thinking about things like that. I don't know about you, but I was much more concerned with what was going on with Sarah than with the driver. Janet, you can't let yourself take the blame. None of us did anything wrong."

"Everything's driving me crazy. I can't stop myself from taking the blame. The guilt. It's killing me. It's like this itch, or like when I was healing in the hospital and I had constant pain; it won't go away and there's nothing I can do to stop it." Lena could hear tears in all this.

"Let me get you something to help. Which pharmacy do you use?"

Janet told her and Lena was about to hang up when Janet added something out of the blue.

"I don't trust that contractor. I can't put my finger on it, but I don't like the way he looks. And his wife. It's like she's hiding something. You know what I mean."

Lena neither agreed nor disagreed, said she had to leave and got off the phone. She thought about the conversation later when she was being driven to the church service. Janet had talked only about her own pain, her own guilt. Not a word about Linda. And then she tried to paint the Williamses in dark colors. People don't step out of character when they are hit with something like a kidnapping, Lena thought.

The church was one of the oldest in Larchmont, a plain barn of a worship center with vaulted ceilings, polished wood beams, ten stained glass windows depicting scenes from the life of Jesus, and a plain, barely elevated altar with a pulpit to one side. Lena came into the foyer and realized that she was completely ignorant of the protocol. David was the one with the church experience. He'd grown up Baptist and had been forced to go to church every Sunday and Wednesday night until he graduated from high school. Lena had attended a teen group in a Lutheran church in Sweden, but that was more a social gathering. All around her there were congregants who chatted easily with each other. Then a greeter, a man with white hair and a patrician demeanor, came to her and thrust out his hand. He welcomed her and handed her a bulletin, but then moved on to the Williamses as they came in the door. He didn't spend much time with them either, his manner perfunctory. Mike caught Lena's eye and came to her.

"We're Catholic. You know the steps here?"

"No, I don't. I see there are ushers in there who will take you to a seat."

"You want to go in with us? We'll stumble through it together."

Lena nodded and thanked him with a smile. Po and Jack came, and Mike introduced his son to Lena. Mike told his son that Lena was a doctor, and then turned to Lena and told her Jack was thinking about medicine. Lena mumbled something like "nice" and saw that the boy was a little embarrassed. But he had his father's ease and said that would be after his baseball career. His mother gave him a little playful punch. Lena thought that gesture was one of the more beautiful moments of parenting she'd ever seen. What was Janet talking about? This was the perfect family.

They were seated near the front. The church was about three-quarters full. As Lena slid into her place in the pew and settled, a woman's voice behind her came close and whispered.

"We're all so very sorry for you. We're glad you're here."

Lena turned and acknowledged this with a nod. She avoided eye contact with anyone around her by burying her nose in the bulletin. She saw no mention of the collection there but reasoned that the bulletin had been printed before the abduction, before the email from the kidnappers. Further evidence of this was that the sermon title for the day, by Rev. Walker, was "Joyous Days of Summer." Lena was pretty sure that wouldn't be the day's homily.

John Walker came down the aisle and stopped at practically every pew to shake hands, accept parishioners' concerns, to be hugged and clapped on the back. When he came to Mike, sitting on the aisle, he made a show of camraderie, which Mike reciprocated graciously. He sat in what was probably his normal place, on the aisle of the first pew, bowed his head and remained like that for a long few minutes. He lifted his head when the organ introduction for the processional hymn sounded, and he and the rest of the congregation stood.

Rather than feeling like an outsider in what followed, Lena was drawn into the formalized ritual of the service, the choir filing in from the back of the church, dividing at the altar and moving to separate sides of the church to reach their special pews, the movement of ushers and deacons who undertook various functions that weren't all that clear to her.

But all these habitual movements couldn't mask the tension that filled the sanctuary when Sheila entered and sat on the altar with the assistant minister. Lena, as well as everyone else, wondered how she was going to be able to go through with the service. Lena hadn't passed more than a couple of words with Sheila, had found her distant and off-putting in the meeting the day before, but that didn't stop her from feeling for her in the position she was in, her work in a very public arena, work she obviously felt she had to carry on with no matter what. Lena had imagined a day when she might have to go back to Mount Sinai with Sarah still missing, but that was one-on-one work, nothing like Sheila's standing in front of a congregation.

Tom Adams, the assistant minister, undertook the call to worship, the Old Testament reading, the announcement of hymns, and the prayer of confession. After a doxology, which left the Williamses and Lena standing mute while all around them sang the familiar prayer, Adams told the congregation to be seated. He gestured to the back of the church and the ushers strode to the altar and spread out in front of the assistant minister. He took collection plates from a stand and handed one to each usher. He then addressed the congregation.

"Today's offering will be a special one for the building fund. As you know, we have reached almost half of our goal of two million dollars. We ask that you give generously. Because this is a building fund collection, we will divulge the amount of the collection immediately after it is tallied."

Lena blushed. She had been unprepared for this, even though the collection was the only reason she was there. She saw John Walker put a check in the collection plate and she realized she didn't have her checkbook, didn't have much cash. She fished in her purse and found two twenties and three ones. She took out the twenties. Mike took the plate from the usher and passed it to Po, who passed it to Lena. As she put her twenties in, she saw a salad of colored checks and many zeros in the amount lines. She felt horrible. She bowed her head in embarrassment.

When the ushers returned, as the congregation sang, the head usher went to Tom Adams and handed him a slip of paper. Adams collected the plates and bowed his head. He said a prayer of thanks and after the "amen," looked up at the expectant congregation, most of whom certainly knew the stakes.

"Praise be to you all and your generosity. We have today raised forty-eight thousand dollars to the glory of God."

Lena jumped when the congregation broke into applause. Tears came to her eyes as the clapping continued and seemed to be a wall of defiant sound striking back at the kidnappers and their obnoxious email. She felt a hand on her shoulder coming from behind her. She felt the warmth of the place and the people. A phrase from her long-ago brush with Lutherans came back to her. She was lifted up.

When the clapping settled, and the buzz around the sanctuary quieted, all eyes went to Sheila. She seemed shrunken now, the high-backed chair engulfing her. She was staring out at John, not moving at first, rooted where she was, it seemed, not gathering strength. Then she took a deep breath, stood, and went to the pulpit without text or notes in her hand. She asked the congregation to bow their heads in prayer and intoned the ritual, "May the words of my mouth and the meditations of my heart be acceptable in thy sight, oh Lord." The congregation added the amen. It took Sheila a good fifteen seconds to compose herself enough to speak.

"I miss my son, Franklin, more than I can possibly say. Twenty-four hours ago I put him on a van, certain that he was safe and I would see him again in two weeks. Now I don't know where he is. I don't know who is taking care of him if, indeed, anyone is. I can't bear to imagine what is happening to him, and to Tommy and Linda and Sarah. Since the first minute we knew what had happened, how we had been tricked, I prayed all I was hearing was a bad dream. But I am here and all this is too real. Today, ironically enough, I was scheduled to preach about the joys of summer and how the memory of those joys can foster hope in our lives. I still feel that I want to say something about hope, but not what I had originally intended."

She stopped and stood still, as if waiting for something, not fidgeting, not concerned about the extended silence.

Lena felt David beside her, though nothing had changed in the pew. She could feel his restlessness at a moment like this. She was glad he wasn't there. Sheila finally found her voice and began again.

"I will never use the word *hope* again without realizing that it is antithetical to my faith. Throughout my life I have used the word countless thousands of times and given many great comfort when I did use it. Certainly the word gave me great comfort many, many times. But now I know something I'd never known before. Hope and fear are simply two sides of the same coin, and that coin has nothing to do with true faith. In the early hours of Franklin's abduction I said over and over to myself, to John, to many of you, 'I hope my boy will be brought back to me soon.' And as deeply as I possibly could, I feared that something horrible would happen to him, death not being the worst of my imaginings. And I prayed, of course. And it was in the answer to those prayers that my life was changed irrevocably. Hope, I was led to understand, was, like fear, an anxiety about the future. And I saw that if I was hoping for an outcome, I was doubting my God and his perfection. Abraham, I realized, didn't take Isaac to the mountain hoping God would send him a revised message about what he had been told to do. His faith in God would not allow such shallow anxiety. He had such deep and abiding faith that he trusted his God to stay his own hand should that be God's wish, or to let him proceed with his horrible task, if that alternately was God's demand. It wasn't hope that kept the knife from Isaac's throat. It was the most profound faith imaginable.

"I no longer hope that Franklin will be returned to us safely. I have put my complete faith in the God whom I have served my entire life.

Should Franklin not be returned to us, should something happen, I will grieve until my dying day. I will miss my bookish, overly serious soul mate of a son with every breath I take. But we are now and forever will be united in faith, and the only way I can ever lose my wonderful son is to let that faith wither in hope and fear. I have been taken by the hand and led to this place. With the other hand I grasp you all, and John, and Franklin's delicate bones, and ask you to follow, to find the deepest faith in your hearts, and to trust that faith unto eternity."

Sheila turned and walked back out the door she had come in through. Suddenly the ritual of the service dissolved. Tom Adams seemed at a loss but he stood there for a few long seconds before he skipped the final hymn, raised his hands, closed his eyes, and intoned, "The Lord be with you. May he lift up the light of his countenance upon you and give you peace. Amen." The congregation, which usually broke into chatter as they left the pews, stood stunned and said nothing.

# Fourteen

As they walked out of church, Mike came close and spoke to Lena.

"Must be a Protestant thing. I didn't get that. I'm supposed to stop hoping?"

Lena nodded in agreement, but she was feeling less resistant to Sheila's sermon, more envious of her solution to their shared, horrible problem. For a brief moment Lena thought she might be able to grasp that most unscientific thing Sheila was talking about. But when she went through the flung-open doors into the bright morning sun, even the faint connection she had with Sheila's faith vanished.

Detective Martin surprised her by coming up the steps and greeting her and the Williamses. He pulled them to the side.

"There's been another email. It's a video of the kids. They all seem to be safe." He looked at Mike. "You'll probably want to see it at home."

Mike seemed to bristle. "Why are you here?"

"To take Lena back. To give you some warning of—"

"No. What does this mean? The video. What aren't you telling us?"

"Nothing, Mike. Trust me. It's a video, that's it. Don't read too much into this."

"I want to read, period. What does the FBI tell you, huh? You get a video like this, it means something's happened to the kids? What the fuck's hidden here?"

Martin was about to reply when John Walker, just getting off a cell phone call, came to them.

"I hear there's a video. What's up?"

"Where did you hear that?" Martin asked. John didn't seem like he was going to answer. "Look. This just came in. The FBI's doing all they can to examine it. Go home. Look it over. We'll be in touch. Lena, I'll take you home."

Lena started to follow Martin but she felt there was something more she needed to say to Mike. He had put a dent in her polished opinion of Martin. She felt almost as if she needed to defend the detective. She looked Mike in the eye. "I don't think they're out to fool us."

"I hope not," he said, emphasizing the "hope," but letting Lena know he was wary.

As David, along with Martin, led Lena into the bedroom, David was jabbering all sorts of qualifiers about what she was about to see. Lena stopped him.

"Let me see it, David." Lena was certain now she was about to see her daughter lying somewhere, eyes closed. She dropped into the shock-proof, ice-in-the-veins mode she had learned to will herself into in med school when she was forced to see the mangled bodies of the dead.

David clicked the mouse and instead of dead children lying somewhere, she saw four very much alive bodies, their faces squinting in dappled sunshine, framed by the saturated greens of some nondescript woods. As her eyes adjusted to the jerkiness of the image, she found Sarah, slightly in front of the others, and to the left, not speaking.

"Sarah!"

Lena felt her daughter's presence now and was calling to her.

Tommy said something inaudible on the tape, Sarah turned to him, and then the video winked off abruptly. Lena waited for more. In the brief few seconds of the video she had been drawn into the screen and now she was being ripped apart from it, from Sarah.

"The FBI said they have people in a digital imaging lab in Washington who are going over this with a fine-tooth comb. They've already talked to botanists, and they say the background could be anywhere from your backyard to the Canadian Rockies and beyond. It gives us no information, in other words." Martin was much more subdued and sensitive than he had been before. Lena took note of this changed behavior, the kid gloves treatment, and became even more anxious. She asked to see the video again.

Watching the kidnappers' video over and over, Lena took heart in seeing some of the same natural grace in her daughter's movements in the clearing that she remembered from their home videos. But each viewing deepened her anger. She could imagine someone behind the camera, to whom the kids for a few seconds seemed to be reacting. The four were standing lumped together unnaturally, too close to each other, Lena thought, huddling perhaps. They weren't overtly scared, but they weren't in the loose configuration nine- and ten-year-olds adopt when they are together.

It wasn't until Martin, standing behind her, mentioned the time and date stamp that Lena was aware of the numbers in the upper-right-hand corner.

"We're trying to correlate weather patterns in the area, sunshine and such, with the time of the video, the angle of the sun, that sort of thing. It's a long shot but now that we're more than twenty-four hours in, it's the best we can do."

"What does twenty-four hours have to do with it?" David asked.

"Well, it's just a loose time frame." Martin had slipped and was reluctant to explain that chances of finding kidnap victims without the abductors giving them up diminished greatly after the first day. But he didn't have to say this. Lena and David understood and shared their understanding through a look.

Lena moved her gaze to the computer monitor. The stupid flat screen just stared back at her like some idiot with nothing to offer but a wide-mouth grin. It brought her no closer to Sarah. It was not the solution she desperately sought. She was inches away from smashing the piece of machinery when she willed herself to get up and leave.

The video itself had not been released to the press, nor had the kidnappers sent it to the media or posted it, but it was all over the internet by one o'clock in the afternoon. There were already commentators spewing their revenge fantasies, opportunistic pundits ostensibly taking the families' side in the crisis, coming to their aid, but only, of course, hyping themselves. The politicians who couldn't get into the houses were nevertheless omnipresent in the media with their opinions, prayers, and self-aggrandizing calls for action.

Lena was surprised that by four o'clock in the afternoon none of the parents, including John Walker, had made a public statement about the video. Janet had called around three thirty to thank Lena for the prescription, to say the Xanax was helping, and to say that she didn't think the kids on the video looked too "distressed." That thought hadn't even crossed Lena's mind. She had simply assumed the kids *were* "distressed" and that anything that seemed to run counter to that was either due to the lie of the two-dimensional image or the kids' abilities to mask their fears.

During the afternoon Lena felt heavy-limbed and near sleep, as if she might be coming down with something. She popped some vitamin C but didn't think whatever bug was on the horizon would be stopped by the tablets. She lay on a chaise in the back yard, fighting sleep but dozing occasionally, a picture of which, taken from very far away by a stringer for the *Post*, was in the paper and on the internet the next day. In it Lena looked as if she were relaxing and more than one commentator thought it shocking that the mother of a kidnapped child could be sunning herself in the back yard while her daughter suffered. The image was, of course, a horrible lie. Lena had been near panic as she lay there, trying once again to remember if she had waved goodbye to her daughter, if maybe Sarah had waved goodbye to her.

Lena heard David on the phone a lot during the afternoon. She didn't know all the people he was calling and didn't feel she needed to. He wasn't being furtive. He talked to his brother in Oklahoma and to a golf buddy, Lena knew for sure, but other than that, she didn't know and didn't care. His words to all were similar, however. He was "baffled," and he didn't "have a clue" who could have brought all this about. He took solace in the fact that Sarah was a "trooper" and said he thought the video showed she was holding up. He mentioned to some that others were talking about forming some sort of search "posse," but that all sounded vague and hollow. He was talking, Lena could tell, to keep from thinking, maybe even to keep from feeling.

Detective Martin had been gone for a long stretch and returned about five, with the two FBI agents. Lena met them at the front door and could tell something was different with Martin. He couldn't hold her gaze now. He reintroduced the agents and this time Lena, feeling she might need them, remembered their names; the Hispanic was Domingo and the overweight female was Newmark.

Martin asked to see David alone. David, who had just come into the living room, phone to his ear, heard this and asked why. Martin said there were some questions they had of him that were better asked without Lena. Lena didn't like the sound of this at all, but David told the person on the other end of the line that he had to hang up and went into the bedroom with Martin and Domingo. Newmark stayed with Lena. Lena tried to find out what was going on, but Newmark only opened her palms and shrugged.

As soon as they sat down, David on the bed, Martin and Domingo in chairs, Domingo took over. He asked David to tell him what he had already told Martin, where he was when Sarah was abducted. David repeated that he had been at work. Domingo sighed, stroked his bristly mustache and used a short pause to tell David he didn't believe him.

"You're not under oath or anything, Mr. Trainor, but I would caution you to be accurate in what you're telling us."

"No. I got a call, and I went in."

"To Dell?"

"Right."

"Mr. Trainor, we're aware that you were let go by Dell thirteen days ago."

David absorbed this, looking from Martin to Domingo. "Right, but . . . there were some things I had to clean up, a project that wasn't finished, and they called me in to work on it."

"The company has no record of that, and no one in your former division knows anything about a call to you or you going in to work yesterday. We would like you to be candid with us."

David took a deep breath, again looked from Martin to Domingo, saw that he was caught, and nodded.

"I didn't want my wife to know I'd been fired. She still doesn't know. I'd, uh, been applying for other jobs and I, uh, got a call yesterday morning from one of them. They asked for a breakfast meeting. They said they wanted an immediate hire and that I had to take that meeting or lose the job. I couldn't tell Lena where I was going."

"Who were you meeting with?" Martin asked. Domingo seemed miffed that Martin had interrupted.

"Her name was Sands. Tricia Sands. She's at the Kraft Foods headquarters in Rye."

"Do you have her number?"

"Uh, yeah. Somewhere. I have her card."

"Did she call you from work?"

"From work? I don't know. She just said to meet and I met her."

"Where?"

"A coffee shop in Tuckahoe. I can't remember the name."

Domingo cleared his throat, a signal to Martin to back off, and asked the next question himself.

"Did you call Miss Sands back after she called you?"

"No. I don't think so. I mean I met her but . . ."

"Mr. Trainor. When we examined your computer, you allowed us access to your cell phone records, do you remember that?"

"Yes." David's shoulders slumped but his expression remained impassive.

"You did get a call from Miss Sands yesterday. She was calling from her home. It wasn't the first time she had called you."

"No. Right. She and I have exchanged a number of calls about this job."

"Going back to before you were, uh, let go. Dozens of calls to her home and cell phone."

"Um, really? I may have been looking—"

"Let's cut the bullshit, Mr. Trainor. We can go talk to Miss Sands about this, but it would probably be better if you cleared things up."

David took his time, thinking, looking down at the rug, his fingers tenting in front of his face. When he looked up, he appeared to be calm and ready to talk.

"You don't think this has anything to do with Sarah, with her disappearance, do you?"

"We don't know," Domingo said. "We don't know what 'this' is."

"It sounds like you could guess. I've been having an affair with Tricia for about four months. It's one of the reasons I got canned. My boss found out about it. He's one holier-than-thou sonofabitch. He said he couldn't have people with low moral values working for him. He said he wouldn't expose me, but he would fire me. Tricia and I met by accident in a bar in Dallas. We were both there for conferences, different conferences. After I got fired, Tricia started getting insistent about things. You know, about the marriage. She knew Sarah was going to be away, and she wanted to see me. I told her Lena and I were going to be spending the two weeks together. She—Tricia—called yesterday morning and threatened to tell Lena about us. I had to go meet her. I was with her when I got the call."

"When your voicemail got the call."

"Right. We were in the middle of things and I didn't hear it ring."

"Where were you, uh, in the middle of things?" Domingo asked.

"Where? Oh, I thought you . . . the Holiday Inn in Yonkers. It was under her name."

"Did she seem different, nervous, anything out of the ordinary?"

"I don't know. Like I say, she was insistent. Why, I mean—?"

"She got you out of here at a crucial time. She might have had something to do with the abduction."

David shook his head but Domingo had planted a seed.

"We're going to have to talk to Miss Sands," Domingo said.

"And Lena?"

"We'll see."

David turned to Martin to plead with him.

"Look, I realize I fucked up here. But do you have to tell Lena about the affair? Now, I mean. You know how horrible this is for her, for both of us. She and I have been distant for a while. That's probably why I . . . Anyway. Can we shelve it for now?"

"Mr. Trainor, as I see it, that's your business, for now," Martin said, not waiting for Domingo to answer. "If we find something about this that impacts our present investigation, the abduction of your daughter, then we will have to speak to Lena and others about this. But as far as we know right now, this is a private matter between you and your wife."

"Or not between us."

"Right."

"Well, she's gonna want to know why I'm being questioned separately here."

"Once again, that's your business," Martin replied, his voice stern and his tone scolding. "If you had told us the truth from the beginning, we wouldn't have had to question you this way."

"Yes, I . . ."

"And we'll do everything we can to keep this quiet. But these goddam computers have a way of passing shit around and we can't control that."

David thanked the cops with a look. Domingo made his point about Tricia more explicit, wondering if she might want to harm David by kidnapping his child.

"No, she couldn't possibly have pulled this off," he said, trying to remember what she had been like a day ago.

"And Lena?" Domingo asked. "Is there anything about Lena's behavior recently that might indicate she was planning this kidnapping?"

David looked from Domingo to Martin, saw that this was a real question and snapped. "No! Jesus. What the fuck? I can see why you might suspect me because I lied to you. But for chrissake, Lena's a saint. Have you seen what this has done to her?"

"Frankly, Mr. Trainor," Domingo shot back, prepared. "We've noticed that she has been pretty composed. Normally—"

"She's a doctor! She deals with crises every day. She is torn up, I can tell you that. Just because she doesn't cry her eyes out or curl up in a ball doesn't mean she's not hurting. Christ."

Instead of getting apologetic words from the two cops, David got looks that told him his defense of Lena might be suspect to them, that they might think that he protesteth too much. He didn't care. Part of his own confusion about the marriage dissolved with Domingo's question about Lena. He loved her quiet strength and he wasn't going to have some goddamn cop attack her for that.

They found Lena and Newmark in the kitchen. The twenty minutes or so that David was in the bedroom had been agonizing for Lena. While she and Newmark were exchanging banalities, Lena was trying to imagine what the other agents needed to be talking about only with David. She asked Newmark directly a second time why they were separated, and the gum-chewing agent said she didn't know. At first Lena wondered if there was a break in the case, something grisly, something they didn't think she could take, and so isolated her. But she hadn't displayed any histrionics yet and so, she reasoned, they couldn't be worried about her reaction.

After declining coffee, the three cops left and the house belonged to David and Lena. Lena fixed him with a look that said, "Tell me all," and David knew he had no choice but to launch into his story.

"I lied about going to work yesterday. I—"

"I thought so. Where—?"

"Let me finish. I lied about going to work. There was no work to go to. I was fired about two weeks ago."

Lena was so unprepared for this that she made him repeat what he had said. Then she turned away to try to make sense of the revelation. David spoke to her back.

"I wanted to land another job before I told you. I was ashamed. I got a call asking me to go to a breakfast meeting yesterday. It, it meant they wanted me and I felt I had to go, even though Sarah was leaving. I'm sorry, honey. I shouldn't have gone. I should have told you the truth. And I really should have told the cops the truth."

"But . . ." Lena was trying to catch up, the news far from her imaginings. "But why did you . . . how . . . were they having layoffs or something?"

"Not really. It was Crocker. He and I never saw eye to eye. The department made some mistakes and he just found an excuse to can me."

"Couldn't you protest that?"

"Probably, but why?"

"I don't know. Why couldn't you tell me?"

"I told you. I was ashamed."

"Ashamed!" Lena yelled, surprising herself by the level of vehemence she'd reached so quickly. "You left me and Sarah to go to a job interview and you didn't have the decency to tell us the truth?" She felt the rush of this anger and realized it was the result of twenty-four hours of restraint. But she didn't want to stop it.

"I thought I was being—"

"Did you get the job?"

"What?"

*"Did you get it?"*

"I . . . I don't know. I don't think so. It was . . ." He trailed off when Lena turned away from him again, her anger now coming out in short, choppy breaths.

"I'm sorry," David said weakly, wanting now to go to Lena and hold her, make that connection for the first time since the abduction. When she turned to him again, eyes glistening, he saw his opening. He moved closer. She stayed where she was. "I was going to tell you as soon as I got a new job."

"Jesus, David. I don't want you to get a new job. I was going to tell you that when—after—when we got to talk. Jesus."

David felt hot tears coming now. He moved instinctively toward his wife, and she let him embrace her. For both of them there was a moment of shock. This is David, Lena thought. The David who had been gone for months, years, the David who had made her laugh, shown her life outside her practice, coached her through a difficult labor, the touching, vulnerable man she had loved almost from the moment she'd been introduced to him. Lena couldn't stop the tears now and buried her face in David's chest.

David felt the tattered lies and numbing anxieties of the past few months lift away in the press of Lena's face and body. He wanted to finish his confession, to bring Tricia to the fore and rid himself of that burden as well. But he knew that would heal nothing at this point, that there were news vans outside their windows, that their daughter was in great danger who knew where, and that his stupid affair would only be gasoline to a flame. He wanted to make a good decision, instead of the stupid ones he'd been making for months.

Lena pulled back, wiping her eyes, then looked up. She didn't say anything, but David understood the tacit reconciliation in the look. He kissed her forehead and remembered with a suddenly heavy heart that he had kissed Sarah goodbye in the same way. He ached for his daughter now with a pure sense of loss, one not clouded by anger and guilt.

"I want her back so badly," he murmured, as much to himself as to Lena. Lena sighed heavily and pulled away again, fearing an unstoppable flood of tears.

They stood apart long enough for all that had happened in the last few minutes to settle. But as David stood motionless, staring at a wood grain pattern on the kitchen table, Tricia Sands entered his thoughts. He had left her on the motel room bed, after telling her Sarah had been kidnapped. He had been so completely addled by Lena's phone call, her news, that he had completely forgotten Tricia's reaction. But now, after the looks and questions Domingo and Martin had given him, he remembered pieces of those moments when he was rushing out the door. Tricia had questioned him when he said Sarah had been kidnapped, but now as he remembered it, the disbelief she showed didn't seem the startled sort you might expect in the circumstances. As he was dressing, she had raised herself to a kneeling position on the bed, not covering herself, the cant of her hips and the openness of her breasts and pubic hair almost an invitation for him to return to their lovemaking. Shouldn't she have been shocked? David thought. Was she prepared for this news? Of course he knew he had told the cops the truth when he said she couldn't pull off something as intricate as what J.D. had pulled off. But she certainly had a motive and the timing of her threatening call was perfect. Maybe she had friends who had friends who could snatch Sarah and, what, teach David a lesson about not leaving his marriage?

And then there had been silence from Tricia, no email of concern, no voicemail. David had been grateful for that at first, but now he wondered if the lack of communication might be some sort of clue. Nobody seemed to know where to look for Sarah. Did he have an avenue to pursue? And if he did, would he have to confess all to Lena first? He looked again into Lena's warm hazel eyes, seeing her anew as the woman who had taught him what love meant. If Tricia was behind the kidnapping, then David was responsible for the deep pain Lena was going through now. The thought froze him, though he did his best to cover it with a half smile.

Lena, registering only the smile and the feeling of having her head again on David's chest, trailed her fingers over his arm and reached up and kissed him. All wasn't healed, she thought, but they'd dressed the wound.

# Fifteen

Sarah woke to the far-off caw of a crow. The dawn light filtered into the shack through a scrim of fog that swathed the greasy windows. The crow's call was sharp and startled, as if it had been rousted by someone and was flying away. Sarah imagined her mother and father were the ones who scared up the crow, tramping up the trail, coming to get her. When, out of the corner of her eye, she saw a face appear in the window, she was sure it was one of her parents.

She turned to see Mr. Everett peering in, shading his eyes so he could see through the glass. He didn't say anything and moved away from the window. Sarah, coming back to the reality of her situation, looked around at the three other kids sleeping on the mattresses. Franklin was awake, eyes open, but still with his head on the bunched-up blanket, not moving. He had taken the last watch and was still at it. Linda was tangled up in her blanket, her hand near her sleeping face, its thumb out as if she were ready to suck. Tommy lay sprawled on his stomach, arms out wide, legs spread, making a face-down angel on the stained mattress.

Sarah heard Mr. Everett come in the shack and start to make

breakfast. She thought about the last breakfast she had had, at home, with her father at the table, her mother moving in and out of the kitchen as she got things ready for camp.

"Why don't you sit down," David had said to Lena when she came back in the kitchen, but Lena hadn't answered. David had smiled over at Sarah, but Sarah could tell he was anxious about something. She could always tell that about him, the way his voice receded, the way his silliness stopped.

"Did you remember to get extra flashlight batteries?" Lena had asked. David looked at her, knowing that she knew he had forgotten.

"No, but I can run out and—"

"There's no time."

"Sure there is. It'll just take—"

Sarah had interrupted the two of them. "They have them at the canteen if I run out."

Sarah remembered now that Lena had given her an odd look. What was it? Was she mad because Sarah had solved David's problem? Or was it something else? It was hard to tell these days with her parents. When she was alone with either of them, things were as they'd always been. But when she was with them both together, there were odd moments, such as this one.

Sarah's memory was halted by Mr. Everett coming to the door between the two rooms of the shack and telling the kids to get up. Tommy, startled by the voice, rolled over quickly, blinking, rubbing his eyes. Linda still didn't move. Franklin sat up. Sarah shook Linda awake as Mr. Everett spoke.

"Things are on track, kids," he said, staying a respectful distance away from the door as the kids started to rouse themselves. "You can roll up those blankets. I don't think we'll need 'em tonight."

"How come?" Tommy asked expectantly.

"Well, I don't think we'll be stayin' here tonight."

He didn't allow time for questions and walked back to something sizzling in a pan on the burner.

The kids gave each other looks but didn't say anything. Sarah heard the crow again, closer now. This time she didn't think it meant her parents were coming to rescue her.

The fog had burned off by the time the kids had finished the eggs and bacon breakfast Mr. Everett had given them. He had talked almost constantly during the meal, which was once again eaten outside.

"This is a great country we live in, kids. But it don't reward a man with ideas. A man gets himself born into money, he don't have to think a day in his life. He just shows up. Someone like me, kind of a brainiac, somebody who knows how things tick an' can solve problems, somebody who's got inventions and innovations behind him, he don't get nothing. He—"

"Are we going to be leaving soon?" Franklin interrupted. Mr. Everett scowled but answered evenly.

"I think so. Soon's I get the signal."

Before they had gone to bed the night before, Mr. Everett had given them a tour of the outhouse. Linda had peered in at the rough wooden seat and the little roll of toilet paper that looked like it had spent several seasons propped on a bent nail and said she would never go in there. But when breakfast was finished and she could hold it no longer, she asked Sarah to go with her to the outhouse, to stand guard.

This started a trend of sorts and soon all four kids had used the rough-hewn facility. When Mr. Everett asked facetiously if the outhouse wasn't a lot better than "some namby-pamby toilet," Tommy said yes, "because you don't have to flush." The other kids weren't so positive. But the exchange had lightened the group up some. Mr. Everett was talking about their leaving, and that gave the kids hope that this odd and troubling detour would soon be over, they'd be back at either the camp or their homes, and they'd be safe again.

Mr. Everett was so bouyant that he packed up a lunch and took them on a hike. They went down a little ravine, over a brook, up the other side of the ravine, and found a trail that led to a peak with a great view of the Adirondacks. The wind up there was cool. The sun heated the flat stones, and the lunch of bologna sandwiches, chips, and Gatorade tasted good after the hike.

Mr. Everett opened his cell phone and saw that he didn't have a signal. That put a little dent in his good mood. The kids saw the shift. But Mr. Everett then lectured them on the vagaries of cell phone coverage, reminding himself in the process that he could get a signal at the pond for sure. They were starting back down the trail when Linda tripped over an exposed root and fell forward, putting a long gash in her thigh just above the knee and a large brush burn below her elbow. She cried hard as she examined the injuries, sitting where she landed. Sarah tried to calm her. The boys stood back, helpless. Then Mr. Everett, who had been some yards ahead of them, came back and looked at the damage.

"Get up. Let's see if you can walk."

Still crying, Linda stood with Sarah and Mr. Everett's help. The gash was sending a rivulet of blood down over Linda's kneecap. Mr. Everett daubed at it with a napkin, his mood darkening even more as he did.

"Why didn't you look where you were going? You're in the woods, missy. I told you you've got to be careful."

In her pain and tears Linda was suddenly defiant. "No, you didn't! You didn't say anything about being careful!"

Mr. Everett slapped her face once, a convincing slap that jolted Linda and made the others step back. Sarah gathered herself first.

"Don't do that!"

"I'll do whatever I damn please and you'll do what I say. Now let's get going. Move!"

He pushed and herded them down the trail, treating Linda roughly when she hobbled some on her injured leg. He spent the hike back in a foul mood, spewing his thoughts on children who talk back, the state of parenting today, and how he was going to be "fucking glad to get rid of you." If the kids had been wary before, they were now on the edge of open fear. Walking in single file, they couldn't see each other except when they turned around. But after Mr. Everett had caught Tommy turning around to look at Franklin and had given him a tongue-lashing for doing so, the kids kept their eyes straight ahead.

When they crossed the brook again, Mr. Everett stopped and pretended he didn't know the way to the shack.

"Anybody know which way we go here?" The kids looked at the brush and trees on the slope in front of them but no one spoke. Mr. Everett snorted and walked to his left. "Good. Now you know you ain't gonna make it out of here without me, right?" He didn't wait for a response as he tromped ahead.

When they reached the shack again, it was midafternoon and the sun was hot in the clearing. The shack was still cool and the tired kids flopped on the mattresses.

"That's right," Mr. Everett said. "Get a nap. It'll—" He stopped because he had seen something out the window. He turned back to the kids and, eyes blazing, said, "You stay on those mattresses, right there, until I get back. You got it?"

The kids all nodded and he left. None of them dared leave their mattress.

Once outside the shack Mr. Everett took giant steps across the clearing to meet the lone, female hiker he had seen come into the clearing. She was in her twenties, short but obviously in good shape, hefting a full pack, wearing a ball cap. Mr. Everett turned on the charm.

"Hey, how're you doing?"

She had a fine smile. "Good, good. Great day."

"I'll say. What brings you up here?"

"Doing a few days in the woods, clear my head. Actually I'm a little lost."

"Lost?"

"I mean, not like lost lost. I'm from around here. Grew up in these woods. Just it's a tricky part of the woods and I thought . . . Never seen this shack before. It yours?"

"No. I take care of it for a guy in New York. You alone?"

"Yeah," she said and smiled again. "I know. What's a woman doing alone in these woods? Don't worry. I can take care of myself. Done two tours in Iraq. Can't throw me anything here I can't handle."

Mr. Everett's mind was fogging now. Could she see the kids back at the shack? Was there any evidence of them around? "How long you been out?"

"Since yesterday morning. Camped on Potter's Ridge last night. Got my ass soaked in the afternoon. It felt great. I love the rain after two fucking years of that sand shit."

"Where're you stayin' tonight?" Mr. Everett blurted out, not giving a shit about her love of the rain.

"I don't know. What would you think if I pitched my tent over there? I wouldn't bother you."

"No. Can't. Guy down in New York doesn't want any trespassing."

"How'd he know?"

"He drops in unexpectedly. He saw you here, he'd have a shit fit and I'd be out of a job. No, that won't work."

The woman was a little curious about this lack of wilderness etiquette, and her look said so. "Any good sites you could direct me to?"

"There's plenty. You go down this way, through them birches over there, the ones that make a gate like, follow that down for a while, and there's some good ones about a mile away, near a stream."

"Hmm," she said, looking. "I know that's not the direction I want to go. That's not heading back toward the road. But a stream'd be good. And I promised myself I'd just follow my nose out here."

"Yeah. Those are good ones down there." He stood, as if he was seeing her off. She got the message.

"Okay. Thanks." She gave a quick look back at the shack, turned, and went through the two arching birches.

Mr. Everett waited until she was gone, then headed back toward the shack, replaying the encounter in his head. It didn't sit well on second viewing. The little cunt was too sure of herself. Had she been hanging out, watching the shack, seen the kids? He turned and followed the woman. He watched her recede down a small incline, hating the sight of her. What was she doing out here? Trying to mess things up? Lost, my ass. She had something up her sleeve.

He moved forward, slipping some on the leafy ground. When he got within fifty yards and she still hadn't heard him, he picked up a palm-sized stone from the ground and hid it behind his back. Then he called to her.

"Excuse me." She turned as he approached. She had that same goddamn fresh-faced smile. That smile had to be wiped off. "Maybe we can work something out."

They were a few feet apart now. "No, it's okay. I understand. No big deal. I'll just—"

He had caught her so off guard that he was able to get a full swing in and land it on the left side of her face. He felt the cheekbone there crack and teeth and blood spilled out of her mouth. But she didn't go down. And she didn't run. Suddenly furious, she hurled herself at him. The added weight of the backpack helped her knock Mr. Everett back several feet, and she kicked viciously at his shins.

Mr. Everett took another swing, but she blocked it with her forearm. She had tipped forward, though, and Mr. Everett was able to grab the bar of her pack frame, draw her toward him, and deliver a short heavy pummel to the top of her ball cap. She dropped to his feet like a supplicant and stayed there, not moving.

Breathing hard, Mr. Everett tipped her back over, struck her three more times and then gave up out of exhaustion. She was slumped, suspended from the pack frame, inert. Mr. Everett couldn't think. His hand and the rock were dripping blood. There was blood on his T-shirt. He was going to have to bury her. Or maybe not.

Then he thought about the kids and whirled, as if they might be above him on the incline watching. They weren't. He scrambled up the hill, not looking back. He had to stop to catch his breath.

"Jesus Christ," he said out loud, lost to his surroundings. "Why did she do that? I'm just about done here. She couldn't let me work?" He looked again at his bloody hand. It seemed to belong to somebody else. His vision was blurring. "Nobody comes up here." He tried to slow his breathing, talk himself down. "The op's a success. The ransom note's goin' out. I take the kids down early. I call Chase and take the kids down early. No prob. Middleman never has to know. Home free."

He wasn't breathing hard when he went back in the shack, but his vision was fuzzing. He got his cell phone, called out to the kids, and told them to follow him. He didn't want them to find that body.

The kids hadn't seen a thing. By the time Tommy had screwed up enough courage to look out the window, the clearing was empty. Only minutes later Mr. Everett came back into the shack and told them to follow him. They were far behind him as he charged down the path.

At the pond the hot sun made the air ripe with marshy smells. Mr. Everett was on the dock, kneeling, washing his hands.

"Stay there," he commanded, having a hard time getting off his knees. "I'm gonna make a call and then we're going to get out of here." The kids were wrinkling their noses at the odor, but Mr. Everett was having a harder time. His breath became labored as he walked over the bone-dry, uneven planks.

He was turned away from them again as he made his call. They could hear his voice swoop up and then fade away. He was gesturing with his free hand but seemed to be pressing the phone harder to his ear, his left elbow digging into his ribs. The kids saw something strange in this and were transfixed.

He hadn't finished the call when he turned around violently, almost tipping himself off the dock, shouting into the phone, "Something wrong . . ." His free hand now went to his chest and tore at his T-shirt. Then his phone hand flew out; the cell phone helicoptered out over the water and landed with a plunk fifteen yards into the pond. Mr. Everett pitched forward like a defensive lineman, his upper body close to the dock as his legs churned, both hands now clutching at his chest. Then he crash-landed on the rotting wood, cracking a plank with his fall-driven head. His arms stayed pinned under his chest and his legs flopped fishlike a couple of times before they settled, akimbo. After that, he didn't move.

Linda had been the only one to laugh at the bizarre spectacle, but once he was still, she, like the others, was dumbstruck. They waited for a long time, for him to get up, to bounce up, even, like clowns they had seen who did bellyflops, remained in the sawdust for a long time, and then came up smiling. But Mr. Everett never came up. The weak ripples that radiated from the cell phone's plop into the pond reached the dock posts. The stillness around the pond was deep. Finally Sarah broke the silence, yelling.

"Mr. Everett!"

Her voice echoed and accentuated the eeriness of the moment.

"He's knocked out," Tommy whispered, as if saying it out loud might wake him.

The other kids hoped Tommy was right. He had to wake up to get them home. Sarah yelled again.

"Mr. Everett!" and the others followed suit. But the body didn't move, a lump on his exposed forehead was turning purplish, and his arms stayed stuck under his chest.

"Heart attack," Franklin said finally.

The others absorbed this. Tommy knew his grandfather in Costa Rica had had a heart attack, but he was still alive. Linda had always had the mistaken impression that a heart attack was something the heart did to other people. Sarah remembered something about heart attacks from health ed but couldn't remember if that was the one that sent a clot to the brain or the one that shut down the arteries. She did remember a video on CPR and, as she looked at the inert body lying in the sun, couldn't remember anything but pounding on the chest of the victim.

Without saying anything to each other, the four moved toward the dock, calling Mr. Everett's name now and then.

"We're supposed to blow into his mouth," Franklin said with some authority, though none of them could imagine doing this.

They tread the creaking boards lightly. Sarah was in the lead, and when she stepped on the board Mr. Everett's head had cracked, it broke further and she jumped back. Mr. Everett's body moved some as his head burrowed deeper into the cracked board. They stood still for a long while, unsure of the wood under their feet, not knowing what to do with Mr. Everett.

Then with Sarah directing them, they took positions on the side of the body and prepared to roll Mr. Everett over. When they lifted him, his head lolled toward them and a ghastly mass of bluish, scraped skin and a gaping mouth loomed up at Linda. She screamed and let go and the others dropped the body as well.

"He's dead! He's dead!" Linda screamed as she ran off the dock. Franklin took a closer look and confirmed the death with a nod. Sarah moved back quickly and Franklin followed her.

Tommy hestitated. He was staring. From his angle he could see only a bit of Mr. Everett's face, a part that still retained its flesh color. His grandfather hadn't died from his heart attack. Maybe Mr. Everett was just unconscious. He remembered a story about how his grandmother had brought his grandfather back to life when he had his heart attack by praying to her favorite saint. But Tommy didn't know what saint it was and he didn't know the prayer. So he simply stood there over the dead body of Mr. Everett and prayed to his grandmother for help.

# Sixteen

Chase Collins heard his father end their phone call abruptly. It sounded like he was saying there was something wrong with the connection, but that didn't matter. They had finished. Chase had his marching orders. All he had to do now was to send the third message, and unless the parents were complete idiots, the whole thing would be over soon.

Chase's father would have killed him if he knew that Chase took the call standing with curious onlookers across the street from David and Lena Trainor's house. He had been there for a couple of hours with his daughter, Jennifer, in tow. He was supposed to take Jennifer to a park while his wife, Helene, took their four-year-old, Hector, to a birthday party, but once he got in the car and thought about what great cover Jennifer would provide, he was across the George Washington Bridge in no time.

Standing across the street from the scene of his triumph the day before was a thrill at first. He replayed his dialogue, the ease with which he had gained the girl's confidence, his looks of assurance to the woman, the drive off down the street. He wished he could have had the whole thing on tape. That would have made a great reel to get acting work out in Hollywood.

He chatted up a cop who was standing between the onlookers and the press. "Excuse me, Officer. They got any clue who did this?"

"Don't know. And if I did, I couldn't tell you."

"But, I mean, I heard it was some guy come right up, pretend to be from the camp, waltz right away with the kid. That right?"

"Yup."

"Jesus. I mean, they couldn't tell?"

"Guy musta been good."

Chase was about to leave after he heard that review of his work. What more could you ask? Jennifer, who had no idea what they were doing there, wound around his legs singing some song to herself. A fiftyish woman standing next to Chase nodded down toward Jennifer.

"I remember when Sarah was that age."

Chase didn't connect the name immediately. He and his father had always talked about Target 1, Target 2, etc. "Are you a neighbor?" he asked.

The woman pointed to a house down the street. "We've been here thirty years. This is just the worst. That little girl meant everything to them. I understand she was trying to have another but couldn't. Imagine, a doctor, and they couldn't get it to work." Chase nodded to this and the woman continued. "A lot like yours there, you know? Happy little girl. Cute."

Five minutes later the call came through from Chase's dad. Chase was glad to get it. He suddenly wanted the whole thing to be over with, wanted to get the kids back home. After the call he picked up Jennifer and walked down the street to his car. She did one of her flops, draping herself over his shoulder as if she were asleep. Chase had always loved carrying her like that. Hector, his son, had never flopped when he was that age, always sat up, alert. Jennifer just succumbed to the ride and Chase felt closest to her when she did so.

Driving home he wondered what he had been like in his father's arms when he was Jennifer's age. Maybe his father hadn't held him at all. He didn't know, had never seen any pictures of himself being held. Ever since he could remember, his father was all business, always deep in some idea, some plan, some scheme. His father had worked for years pumping gas at a Mobil station in Tenafly, but he was no schmoozer. He asked "How much?," filled the tanks, took the money or ran the credit card, and that was it. "My mind's on other things," he would tell Chase.

His father believed that life had conspired against him, that his academic career (he barely made it out of high school) had been torpedoed by nincompoop teachers, and because his brilliance had been overlooked, he had been forced to sign up for the army. There his schemes for restructuring the command he was in were greeted with derision by all. He was one of those rare soldiers asked to quit five months into his term of service. Bitter and unappreciated, he alienated people left and right, and when Chase was thirteen, his mother had walked away from the marriage, taking Chase's older brother with her. Chase had put his foot down. He wanted to stay with his father.

Chase had always believed in his Dad, tagged along with him on his quixotic adventures, feeling that someday they were going to strike gold of some sort. Just because things didn't pan out—the electric bicycle never worked, the portable swamp drainer weighed too much for even three or four men to transport, etc.—didn't mean Chase lost admiration for the man who had always entranced him with his grandiose plans. Even when Chase married and started his own family, he spent a lot of time with his father, listening to him for hours on end. Helene, Chase's wife, didn't understand the attraction but reasoned it was just an abnormally tight father-son bond.

Chase didn't quite believe his father when he came to Chase and told him he'd been hired by a middleman to carry out a kidnapping. Chase protested the illegality of the whole thing, said it was out of his father's areas of expertise, but when his father started to detail what he was going to do, the very brazenness of it, the genius of it really, drew Chase in, just as schemes, such as one to game the state lottery, had drawn him in in the past. Playing on the parents' expectations of the ride to camp, taking the kids far away, working through densely encrypted computer networks, having shadowy, foreign middlemen orchestrate the ransom, keeping the whole thing nonviolent was, in his father's telling, a stroke of genius and completely in the realm of the possible. Chase took a day to think about it and then decided to accept his father's offer to be the one to make the actual snatch.

When Chase and Jennifer got home, Chase went right to the computer in the little sewing room Helene worked in and began to send the third and final message to the parents. They had decided he would do this one from home so as not to risk being seen at the hospital computer. The encryption would prevent anyone from identifying the computer, his father had told him, but even if they did, the whole thing was rigged so it would look like someone had hijacked Chase's computer from afar.

As per his father's orders, the encryption protocol was not anywhere to be found on his computer but was written out and encoded in a small loose-leaf notebook. Chase had carefully hidden the notebook under the false bottom of one of the dresser drawers. This was, he knew, an extremely conservative measure. Helene was not the snoopy type, not at all suspicious, and never in a million years would look for anything in his drawers. But even if she found it, he could easily finesse any questions. Helene thought Chase was perfect, a brilliant man and a loving father, and never questioned his reasoning.

The protocol required some time. Because it was undertaken over several different servers in a number of different time zones, there were often waits between steps. He was down to the last step in the protocol, the one that would make his IP address as inscrutable as those used by the CIA. Once this piece of code was linked to the chain of server and client conversation, there was virtually nothing anyone could do to identify his computer as part of the chain. As he was about to effect this piece, Jennifer came in the room.

"Annabelle's hu't," she said, holding up her rag doll and showing Chase the doll's ripped arm.

"I'll look at it in a minute, Jen."

"No, now."

She started toward Chase. All he could imagine was her screwing up the delicate operation he was about to complete. He got up, picked her up, and took her into the hall.

"Stay here, Jen, and I'll come and help you with Annabelle."

"Now."

Chase turned and went back into the room. Jennifer followed, still holding up the doll. Chase snapped.

"Get out, Jen. Now!"

The force of the command surprised her and tears came immediately. They heard a car door slam outside and Jennifer realized it was Helene coming home. She went screaming out of the room, yelling for her mother.

Chase's heart raced. Helene was home early. He could probably just shut the door and she wouldn't question what he was doing in there, but Jennifer was caterwauling and he would have to explain that. He turned back to the protocol. He found his place in the notebook and tried to concentrate on it. Helene was in the house now. He could hear her talking to Jennifer. Hector was yapping about something too. Chase looked at the screen, assured himself he had everything ready to go, and took a deep breath. As he had done throughout his work with the computer on this job, he started to count to ten before he hit send. At the count of seven he heard Helene's steps near the door. He hit send.

"What's this with Jen?" Helene asked as she opened the door. Chase put himself between her and the computer monitor.

"Nothing. I'm just working on something here and she wouldn't wait. Can you give me a second?"

"Sure." Helene turned and walked out.

Chase turned back to the computer. A "message sent" sign blinked there and Chase felt fulfilled. His work was done. He surprised himself when the first thing he thought about was Target 1, Sarah, running up her driveway to her parents. Only after that did he think about the money he would be "inheriting" soon.

He was about to close the notebook and put it away when an asterisk caught his eye. It was at the end of a line of coded gibberish that he had inputted in the final step of the encryption. But he couldn't remember inputting that asterisk. He went quickly back over the encryption in his mind, hoping he was wrong. He wasn't. He had missed an asterisk.

Chase turned back to the screen. What could be done? Was there time to stop the message? He flashed around the site, looking in the delete bin, then flipping through his notebook. He kept coming back to the "message sent" screen and his heart raced. Dad. He had to get in touch with his father. He grabbed his cell phone and started to dial. He concentrated on the rings. Then his father's terse "Leave a message" voicemail came on and Chase whispered firmly, "Big problem, Dad. Call as soon as you get this."

His mind raced now. He knew how fast messages flew around the world, even heavily encrypted ones like his. Would the four other layers of encryption be enough? Panic was spiraling up from his stomach to his throat. If he destroyed the computer, would that protect him? Helene. What would she say if he destroyed the computer? Should he bring her into the whole thing? He roller-coastered from certainty that everything was still all right to the black knowledge that the FBI might already be on his trail. After a few minutes all the uncertainty boiled down to one question. Should he run?

# Seventeen

Lena and David were at different computers when the email came in. Lena was in Sarah's room, killing time scrolling through emails, hardly reading the "sorry's" and the "I can't imagine what you're going through's." When Lena saw the now-familiar odd email address pop up, she screamed and David came running. The phone rang at the same time.

"It's from them" Lena said. "Get the phone."

David got a peek at the email before he left. "One million . . ."

Lena read the email quickly. "WIRE TRANSFER ONE MILLION USD IN THE FOLLOWING ACCOUNT AND YOUR CHILDRENS WILL BE RELEASED IMMEDIATELY." Then it gave account numbers, routing numbers, and some other details about a bank in the Cayman Islands.

David came back in the room. "It's Martin. He wants to make sure we got the email."

"Ask him if it's a million each or all together."

David did this. Martin thought it was a million total. David listened for a while and hung up.

"They're picking us up in an hour. We're all going to a meeting with the federal prosecutor at the Hilton in Scarsdale."

Lena barely heard this. The letters and the numbers in the email danced in front of her like a good news chorus line. There wasn't the ugly violence of letters pasted on paper that you see in movies or hear about from other kidnappings, words clipped from magazines. This one looked like a very simple, businesslike transaction. She was rapturous at the solidity of the demand. This was data, this was concrete. Nothing uncertain about this at all. Send off some money, get Sarah back. It was physical now for Lena. Sarah was coming home. She could feel Sarah's body again.

David, hunching over Lena to read, scowled at the screen. "I don't get it. Even if it's offshore, you can't protect an account like that. We send the money and the FBI just clamps down on the guy who has the account. You think this is real? Is this some kind of joke?"

Lena hadn't even considered the possibility.

"They wouldn't be having a meeting if it was a joke."

"Yeah, but . . . maybe I should call him back."

"No, we'll find out at the meeting." Lena really wanted this to be an authentic communication now. She didn't want to have her excitement dented by some suspicions about this as a hoax. She didn't think she could stand that.

Suddenly she was hungry. Her body needed fuel for what lay ahead. She went in the kitchen, but the only thing that she could find was granola. She ate a bowl. David had a beer. They both spent the next hour fidgety as cats. They pulled out financial records, bank statements, mortgage papers. If Martin was right about the million being an amount they all had to raise together, then each family would have to come up with a quarter of that. After a few minutes of calculations they realized they could come up with at least that much, if not more, but they didn't know how soon.

The media was in full carnival mode outside the Scarsdale Hilton. State troopers directed traffic, and the cars carrying the parents drove up to the entrance to the hotel as if they were part of an international summit. David and Lena were ushered into the lobby and whisked to the back elevators. Phil and Janet Rostenkowski were there, waiting. Janet looked as if the past twenty-four hours had added a decade to her life. Phil stood close beside her but he seemed lost, only able to nod at David and Lena. Lena went to Janet, trying to give her a hug.

"Hi," Lena started. "How're you doing?"

Janet shook her head no but couldn't say anything. Lena wondered about having offered her the prescription. She was obviously on something. Her eyes were rheumy and unfocused.

As the elevator doors opened, Mike and Po Williams came toward them. Mike was the polar opposite of Janet—alert, upbeat, energized. Lena thought that he must have reacted to the ransom note the way she did. Nobody said anything as they got in the elevator but Lena could feel Mike's positive presence and smiled over at him. He smiled back.

When they reached the top floor, the doors opened and a state trooper in a Smokey the Bear hat gestured for them to go to the left. A double door at the end of the hall opened onto a glass-walled banquet hall. Out the windows they could see the tops of trees and a cloudless sunset over Westchester County. Lena suddenly remembered that she had attended the bar mitzvah of the son of one of her colleagues there. The bar mitzvah had some comic book theme and the party ended with the kids dousing each other with that string-in-a-can stuff.

A woman who appeared to be in her forties but was making an obvious effort to look ten years younger approached them from the crowd of people standing around a horseshoe-shaped table in the center of the room. She had lacquered hair, a face glistening with makeup, and was wearing a low-cut top under her suitjacket, one that highlighted an impressive pair of breasts. "Hi, I'm Lynn Witherspoon," she said shaking hands, expecting all to know who she was. "Please have a seat." She turned to the room. "Can we get started now?" Lena figured she was sort of like an event planner for the meeting.

But when they sat around the table, with the families aligned on one side and Martin, Domingo, Newmark, and some men in suits sitting on the other, Witherspoon stood up and addressed them all.

"On behalf of the United States Attorney for the Southern District of New York, I want to welcome you all. I'm sorry we're here under these circumstances but—"

"Excuse me. Who are you?" Mike asked.

Witherspoon seemed a little hurt by the question. "I'm the assistant federal prosecutor in charge of the case. I thought . . . Well, do we all know each other?" There was some silence, so she went around and named everyone in the room. Something about the too-chipper twang of her voice grated in Lena's ear.

"One thing right off the bat," she said then. "The bad guys might have slipped up with their last note. I can't tell you specifics, but the computer guys tell me they might have good news soon."

"We can understand computer guys," David said with bite.

"I'm sure but, well, not now." She wasn't rattled. "The ransom note. First of all, the FBI, working with Interpol, has determined this to be coming from the same source as the last two. So if those two were authentic, and we have no reason to doubt they were, given that the video came through the same encryption system, we can assume this one is too. The bank account referred to in the note is a real one, we know that much. We do not know who the account belongs to, and unless things change in the years ahead, we may never know. This type of account is the most private in the world. We have never seen an arrangement like this used in a kidnapping before, but frankly I'm surprised we haven't. Once the money goes into this account, it's as if it disappeared off the face of the earth. It—"

"Not true." John didn't look up as he broke in. "There are ways to extract the information."

Witherspoon was ready for this. "That's for diplomatic channels, Mr. Walker. I'm talking about other ways. We can't involve ourselves in illegalities. If the safety of those children depended on knowing the holder of that account, we might contemplate the extreme and very damaging methods you're suggesting. But it doesn't and we won't. For the purposes of this meeting we are assuming that if a decision is made to pay the ransom, the money will be lost."

"Until you catch the bastards," Mike said.

"Maybe, but even then we couldn't be sure we could get it back. I won't go into all the details, but we're dealing with a very shadowy world here."

Lena didn't care about shadowy worlds or money lost. She didn't see why John was slowing things by talking about finding out who owned the account. She just wanted to pay her money and get Sarah back. Why would anyone want to slow that down?

Witherspoon pulled on her suit jacket, giving her breasts even more prominence, as if to emphasize what she was about to say. "About the ransom itself. Experience has taught that meeting kidnappers' demands does not necessarily increase the probability of abductee recovery. So the FBI discourages the payment of any such demands."

The parents were caught by surprise. Mike was the first to recover from the shock.

"What do you mean, 'discourages'?"

"It means the FBI will not be willing to participate in the payment of any ransom until all other avenues have been exhausted."

David's voice, strong and angry, made Lena jump. "What other avenues?"

"Capturing the bad guys, Mr. Trainor. Look, folks, I know how this sounds to you. It seems like a simple equation. You pay the money, you get your children back. But kidnappers don't always play by the rules of logic or fair play. This is not just a simple exchange of commodities. Their biggest risk is the money drop, and once they have navigated that risk, once they're sailing off to who knows where, they have little incentive to follow through on their end of the bargain."

"But they have to!" Janet's anguished voice sliced into Witherspoon's even cadence.

"No, they don't, and that's just the point. Once the drop is made, they are under no obligation whatsoever."

"Well, what the hell's the alternative?" Mike was getting hot under the collar now, his face a deep red.

"Before I answer that, let me have Agent Domingo fill you in on the latest in the investigation."

Domingo stood up as if he were going to go to a blackboard, but he only rubbed his hands together before he started to speak.

"Briefly, here's what's happening. In their communiqué this afternoon the abductors left the back door open on the originating computer. I don't know all the tech stuff, but the computer geeks are zeroing in on that computer now.

"Once we get close on that front, we have other information to triangulate with it. As you know, we have a wig we believe this J.D. wore. We believe that wig was bought at a store only thirty miles or so from where the van was stolen. The paint on the Camp Arno sign on the side of the van came from a batch that was partially sold in areas near that same New Jersey location. So eventually, we hope, all this information will come together in a perfect storm sort of way, and we'll have a suspect."

Lena chafed at the hesitancy of this. Domingo seemed to be drifting from the hard facts Lena felt were now in play. "What's 'eventually'? Can you put a number on it?" she asked with a hint of annoyance.

"No. No, we can't. But I can tell you we're talking about days, not weeks."

"Days?" David spat out, as if the thought were sour milk. "How about hours? We're past the twenty-four-hour period now. Isn't that when the FBI says things begin to deteriorate in a kidnapping? Aren't we—"

"Frankly, that twenty-four-hour figure is television. They use that to pump up their dramas. Yes, the first day is important, but we've had recoveries weeks and even months after the abduction."

Lena's heart beat heavily in her chest. She couldn't imagine another night without knowing where Sarah was. She had fully expected to sign some papers at this meeting, take out a loan, have the money organized somehow, then wired, and walk out of the meeting making plans to meet Sarah when she was released. Now this agent was telling her she might have to wait weeks or months. She knew she would never be able to do that.

John Walker could barely contain his anger. "Are you, you two here, saying that we're supposed to wait for the FBI to try to find the computer the notes came from before we pay the ransom?"

"Essentially, yes," Witherspoon said, clicking her fingernails on the table in front of her as if she needed to get on to some other meeting.

"Well, essentially, my wife and I are not going to stand for that." John looked around at the other parents. "Finding a computer is not the same as finding a suspect, not these days. Hell, I can pirate another computer myself. You find the computer and whoever has it, some granny or some ten-year-old, and they don't know anything about any ransom note because some clever kidnapper has hacked into their computer. And if you do find a suspect, who's to say you find the kids at the same time?"

"Wiring money to the Caymans is not going to get you any closer to the kids, Mr. Walker," Witherspoon shot back, stiffening at his insubordination. "If we didn't have solid leads, didn't know anything about these guys, their location, the IP address, we might allow the ransom to be paid. But under these circumstances—"

"Wait a minute." It was a new voice, an accented one, and all looked at Po Williams. She was leaning forward and her dark eyes were flashing as she spit out her question. "What do you mean, you allow? That letter came to me, to us. If we decide to pay the ransom, how are you going to stop us?" She didn't have to pound the table to make the force of her anger felt around the horseshoe and the rest of the room.

"Well, we have ways of enforcing our policies, but we hope it doesn't come to that." Witherspoon was unflappable.

"What ways?" This came from two or three people at the same time.

"There's extortion and there's complicity in extortion."

John Walker did pound the table. "So you're going to charge us with complicity if we pay the ransom?"

"We might. But once again, we hope it doesn't come down to that. Listen. This is the first time any of you have had to deal with a kidnapping. We have a long history with abduction and many experiences to draw on. We urge you to trust those who have been through this before."

"Which one of you had their kid stolen?" Mike's open face was pinched and accusatory now.

Witherspoon was ready for this. "That's just the point, Mr. Williams. None of us are in that category. We don't have the horrible emotional weight of this on our shoulders. You do. And the love you have for your children might not always lead to the best decisions for them in a case like this. That's why you need to trust professionals who are and will remain dispassionately dedicated to getting your kids back safely."

Lena suddenly no longer wanted to be around Witherspoon and Domingo and their groups. "Can we have a break here and the parents can get together and talk?" she asked.

"Of course. We actually have a room over here set aside for you. I understand there's a light supper in there too." Witherspoon looked at an aide and he nodded yes. Lena had the feeling they had prepared for the angry reaction, and that the law enforcers were two or three moves ahead of the parents. As they stood, David looked over at Lena with a tacit question. "Are we together on this?" his eyes asked. Lena answered by briefly rubbing his back.

"Citibank is prepared to loan any amount needed at zero percent interest," John began when the parents were in the room, standing around the cold cuts platters.

"We can't afford even that," Phil said quietly. "We're schoolteachers. We're just getting by, and we still have medical bills. I don't see how we can borrow two hundred fifty thousand dollars. I don't know what we're going to do."

"Look," John started, obviously ready for this. "Trust me. There will be ways to get that money back. Witherspoon's being very conservative here."

"I don't know," Janet said. "That's a lot of money." Lena felt a little wave of nausea listening to this. She couldn't believe Janet was still putting money ahead of everything else.

Mike scratched his head and ran his fingers through his bushy hair.

"I don't have a fingernail's worth of faith in the FBI, but I just want to make sure we're doing things right. I want Tommy back with every fiber of my being, but wanting and thinking straight don't always go hand in hand."

"We're not going to wait weeks," David said, not even looking at Lena.

"Me neither," Mike replied. "But things move fast in the computer age. Who knows what the next few hours are going to bring?"

"It could take longer than a few hours for a wire transfer to go through," John said. "These kidnappers might not know that. They might get jittery."

The thought of the kidnappers being anxious gave everyone pause. The last thing any of them wanted to imagine was some kidnapper not thinking straight, being spooked into some fatal mistake with the kids. Janet stirred a cup of coffee. "We don't have the money, so I don't know what to say. But I wish we could get this over with."

Janet, Lena realized, was saying that the group should pay quickly but that she herself couldn't pay. That sort of thinking was typical for Phil and Janet. Lena felt David's eyes on her and looked over at him. He was probably having the same thought, but he looked to be impatient with the whole discussion. John's voice turned both their heads.

"I think it's time to talk logistics. First of all the money, then the transfer. The money. What have we got?"

Po looked at Mike for confirmation and then spoke. "We're prepared to put in our quarter of the ransom and also half of the Rostenkowski's amount." Phil and Janet looked down at the floor but didn't protest. "If they want it, that is," Po added.

"Thank you," Janet said quietly. "We will need it."

"I think we can cover the other half as well as our own," John said.

The group waited for Lena and David. David pursed his lips. He didn't know what to say. But Lena did.

"I don't like this. I know there are differences here. I know that some of us have more money than others. But when it comes to our kids, we're all equal. This isn't about money or going into debt. This is about doing something to get our children back. I think we should all shoulder the same burden, even if it's more difficult for some of us than for others."

Janet shot Lena a surprised look, as if she'd been betrayed. Phil shook his head almost imperceptibly. The others felt the tension. Lena didn't back down. She hadn't really prepared her thoughts. She had spoken from some deep place of feeling. Sheila Walker, perhaps used to these sorts of situations, found a way out of the dilemma. She looked at her husband.

"Can we guarantee the return of the money?"

John thought for a second. "Guarantee? Not unless we get cooperation from the FBI, the Justice department, the—"

"I'm not talking about that. Can you and I guarantee the return?" Sheila could show surprising backbone when she needed to.

"I suppose so. Over time."

"So. We'll each assume equal financial responsibility. John will do everything he can to get the money returned. And in the event he doesn't, we are offering an insurance policy for all of you. Does that suit everyone?"

No one answered Sheila's question directly, but there was a tacit agreement all around. Janet and Phil, offered a no-interest loan that someone else was guaranteeing to pay back, had no recourse but to accept the deal. Mike moved things along by asking about the transfer. John briefed them on the particulars and they all agreed to schedule one to begin at noon the next morning. John had already arranged for the details to be handled by his bank and handed out information about the loans, if needed, and the account that would be used in the transfer.

"What about the legalities?" David asked after looking over the paper.

"To hell with that," Mike practically shouted. "She wants to charge some victims of a kidnapping with, what was it, complicity in extortion, she'll have one hell of a PR problem on her hands. I say we go back in there and tell her what we're going to do."

Which is what they did, not realizing that their plan to delay the payment until noon of the next day was exactly what Witherspoon had hoped for. She had, in a very clever way, manipulated the group.

Lena only began to realize this when she and the other parents stood behind Witherspoon an hour later, outside the hotel, as she faced the cameras and dodged all the questions about the investigation and a possible ransom. Watching her bring the heckling press into line, getting them to accept the meager information she was giving them, made Lena remember that she had gone into the meeting wanting to send the money off immediately, and yet here she was endorsing a plan to delay the payment by almost sixteen hours.

Sixteen hours. Eleven or twelve of them at night. What will be happening to Sarah in those sixteen hours? Is she somewhere where she can tell the difference between night and day, or is she in a hole somewhere? What will she eat? Will she be cold? Has she been crying? What can I do for her? The swirl of the press conference, the words, the camera flashes, the lights receded and a throat-clutching dread gripped Lena. She reached for David's arm and grasped his shirt. He turned to her, but she didn't look back. She was going to have to endure the press conference, the ride home, the long, long night. She felt light-headed, almost sick. She didn't want to give in to the anxiety, but here she was heading in that direction. She looked over at the other parents standing behind Witherspoon. Po seemed calm and had her hand looped through Mike's arm. The growl that had been just under the surface of Mike's features earlier was gone. Janet was hanging on Witherspoon's every word and seemed oddly satisfied with the way things were going. John had dropped his normally imperious demeanor and looked to be aware of the cameras when they were on him. No one seemed as sickened by the delay, by the media theater they were in as Lena. She felt another small wave of nausea and fought it as she pulled harder on David's sleeve.

Lena's tug pulled David out of his thinking. He felt as if he had just signed on to a deal he didn't understand fully. John had pushed them all into a complicated bank transfer and assured them, literally he claimed, that they would get their money back. David knew enough from his days in investment banking to know such guarantees were often tissue thin. Why the push on John's part? How was it that the kidnappers had chosen a method of ransom payment that fit so neatly into John's professional world? If this were a game of Clue, David thought, he would have already circled John's name as the suspect.

David saw a TV cameraman panning the families standing behind Witherspoon. He wondered if one day soon that footage would be used, and when the pan came to John, it would freeze-frame and some announcer would tell the sordid story of a banker who, for some twisted motive, had his only child kidnapped.

# Eighteen

The shock of Mr. Everett's death gripped the kids for the rest of the afternoon. They found some sandwiches in the cooler, but when they went out on the rocks to eat them, no one had much of an appetite. Linda put hers back in the plastic bag after only one bite and put it down in a crevice, telling herself she'd eat it later. Black flies bore down on the sweaty kids and as they chewed and tried to talk, they swatted the nasty biters.

At one point they convinced themselves that Mr. Everett might not be dead. Franklin suggested they all go back and check on him, and they trooped off with renewed optimism. But the body hadn't moved at all. Franklin was elected to make a close inspection, and when he got to within five feet of Mr. Everett's now bluish head, he stopped. He leaned over from there and shaded his eyes from the lowered sun.

Suddenly a crow, black and glistening, with a huge wingspan, swooped down from a nearby tree and dive-bombed the body. Franklin stumbled back and slipped off the dock into the shallow, murky water. The others screamed and started to go to his aid. But Franklin scrambled awkwardly back onto the dock and raced away from Mr. Everett, his pant legs covered with muck, his sneakers sopped.

They went back to the shack quickly. Once there, once Franklin had gotten a lot of the dried muck off his pants, the knowledge that they were now alone settled in. Sarah first gave it voice.

"We have to get out of here. We have to get help."

Still feeling that Mr. Everett would somehow rise from the dead, the group posted Tommy outside the shack door to watch for any signs of him as Franklin took Mr. Everett's laptop from his backpack and turned it on. The screen lit up and the operating system booted, but then they were asked for a password. They tried names and letters close to Mr. Everett, but nothing worked. As they were thinking about what to do, Tommy called from outside. Not knowing what he was saying, Franklin slammed the laptop closed, shoved it into the backpack, and they all went outside as casually as they could.

"Look," Tommy said, pointing. "Over there. I saw the bushes move."

As they looked the bushes moved again, they could hear a couple of thumps. Then the flank of a deer became visible. Linda, not knowing what it was, gasped. At her gasp the deer lifted its head and they could all see the sleek lines of a doe, staring at them now. She stayed motionless for a long minute, as did the kids. Then, scaring them, she bounded off back into the woods.

They sat on the rocks outside the shack until Franklin remembered that in his haste he hadn't turned off the laptop. He went back and did so, and while he was putting the laptop back in Mr. Everett's backpack, he found a three-ringed notebook in another pocket of the pack. Franklin brought the notebook out to the rocks and they all puzzled over it.

Most of the pages were written normally with phone numbers and addresses, some information about the SUV, and a diary of sorts, one with odd, aphorisitic scribblings, like "Time has come today but the clock is broke." Then there were several pages that seemed to be in code, nonsensical words written with a strange alphabet. Sarah mumbled something about a book she'd read where the words were scrambled like those and you just had to figure out what letters on the page referred to what letters in the real alphabet. But after fifteen minutes of trying, they couldn't figure out the formula.

When the sunlight became a lacy soft haze through the trees surrounding the clearing and the air cooled, the kids began to examine their options. Sarah refined her earlier remarks.

"We need to find the way out, down to the place where he put the blindfolds on us. Then we just have to follow the trail."

"There were a lot of different trails," Franklin countered. "We're going to get lost."

"I don't want to get lost," Linda said, shivering. "I think we should stay here until they find us."

"Who's going to find us?" Sarah asked, and this sobering thought sent all of them into their little private worlds of anxiety. Tommy broke the quiet.

"I left a trail, sort of. I dropped a sock down there when we stopped so I'd know I was on the right trail going back."

"Just one sock?" Sarah asked, and when Tommy nodded, the others realized that one sock wasn't going to do them that much good.

Franklin picked up the notebook again and studied the coded pages. A moving cloud of small darting bugs hovered nearby. Evening calm was settling over the clearing, but it was anything but calming for the kids. Linda said she wanted to go back in the shack, that she was scared. Sarah came down on her quickly.

"Don't say that, Linda. Even if you are. Don't say that. None of us should. It just makes us more scared."

"But I can't help it. I am scared."

"We all are too, right?" She looked at the boys. They were less inclined to acknowledge their fear, but their faces said plenty. "See? So let's just figure out how to get back."

"Well, we can't walk," Linda said, trying to assert herself after Sarah's little tongue-lashing. "We don't know which way to start and we don't know which trails to take. And there are bears out there. You heard Mr. Everett."

Neither Sarah nor the boys had an answer for this last. But while Sarah had to tacitly agree with Linda, she chafed at the lack of anything to do to save themselves. She stomped off to the edge of the clearing, in part to think, in part to show the others that she wasn't as worried about the woods as Linda was.

The cicadas were raising a buzz, a chattering wall that seemed to challenge Sarah's bravery. Sarah didn't turn back right away and to the remaining kids it was as if she were being swallowed by the racket. But then a low, far-off grumble cut into the cicada sound. Sarah coming back to the group, looked up and pointed. They all looked up to see an airliner, glinting in the setting sunlight, a tiny floating crucifix leaving a snow-white contrail that was hard to connect with the noise it was producing. They watched this very normal occurrence, as if it were something unique in history, until it disappeared into the peach haze of the western sky. They all longed to be on that plane. But instead they went back into the shack as if they were prisoners told to return to their cells. They closed the door tight against the eerie darkness that was rising up in the clearing. Linda felt safer inside and didn't give a thought to the remains of her sandwich that she'd left on the rock.

# Nineteen

It had been several hours since they returned from the meeting and during those hours Lena had prowled the house, obsessively checking emails, turning the television on and off, on and off, glancing at the clock as if she were a death row inmate in his last hours.

When her father, Richard, had called, saying he wanted to talk just to keep from going crazy, Lena understood. He said he had been out in his back yard, unable to move, unable to go to sleep. He said Lena's mother and sister had not yet decided if they were going to go to the States, "and I haven't counted a trip out yet." Lena told him that there wasn't anything to do, that the FBI claimed that they were zeroing in on the computer that sent the ransom note and that was the only possible search at the time.

"I keep thinking about the time your mom and I lost Sarah for a few minutes in Stockholm. She was fine. We were wrecks."

Lena could smell Sweden in the summer, the long bright nights of June and July. She saw Sarah, in her parents' back yard, ready for bed in summer pajamas, wearing the sleeping mask Sally had given her. Sarah giggled as she bumped around the back yard. Lena had always hated to wear a sleeping mask and she had always struggled to find the joy in the unknown and the unseen that Sarah had found on that summer night.

Lena asked her father about her sister. Sylvie had sent one email but hadn't called. Lena was grateful for this. Sylvie would, Lena knew, in one way or another make her, Lena, feel guilty as hell for the kidnapping.

"She's in Madrid on business tonight, I think. She's thinking of you, Lena. In her own way."

After Lena hung up from the call, she was even more fidgety. David suggested a game of Scrabble and this sounded like the most absurd thing Lena had ever heard. The clock was hardly moving. David asked if she was hungry and Lena decided cooking something would be an activity at least, would take up some time.

She made an omelet, had one bite, and dumped the rest. David offered wine and she decided to force herself to have a glass. It was a rosso, one she and David liked a lot, but it hung in her mouth like a sandy sock. She took another swallow, though, because the alcohol warmed her and slowed her some.

"Let's go to bed," David said, as he poured her a second glass.

Lena looked at him quickly to see if this was some sort of invitation. He returned the look steadily, indicating he only meant what he said, nothing more. Lena was flooded with desire for the swathing bedsheets and David's body nearby, but the stabbing guilt of that comfort when Sarah was on her own, in danger, yanked her back from nodding yes. She took another mouthful of the wine.

Fifteen minutes later the world had slowed enough that Lena was able to get her clothes off and get in bed. David was closing down the house. Lena could hear some chatter from the skeleton news crews hanging around in the street. Her eyes closed.

Movement in the room surprised her and she opened her eyes quickly. David, near the closet, was undressing, down to his boxers. He saw that he had startled Lena.

"Sorry, I thought you were asleep."

"No. Just closing my eyes."

David had peeled off his boxers now and stood naked as he talked to her. His body was long and thin, still in good shape. He moved to pull back the covers, and the light fell on his penis. It was smallish in its resting state, and Lena had always found it aesthetically pleasing like that. She wasn't aroused by the glimpse she had of it now, but she could imagine taking it in her mouth simply to connect. He looked down at her, scratching his pubic hair lightly, pulling on his scrotum the way he often did. The normalcy of this drew Lena to him, but he kept his distance as he lay next to her, lightly touching her shoulder and kissing her cheek. This was enough, she thought.

Then Lena felt full. Not in the sense of fullness after a meal, but as if she had accomplished something. This was in such contrast to the emptiness of the past two days, the hollow, fearful, frozen-blood feeling that gripped her in those times when she really understood that her daughter had been taken from her and might be gone forever. Lying there she puzzled over the fullness but didn't fight it. She had some sense that Sarah was a part of whatever she was feeling. Were she and her daughter becoming one in a different way now that Sarah was so far away? She was on the cusp of sleep and the strange fullness clashed with the hard numbers, hours and dollars, ahead. She saw the gray-haired camp counselor walking from the van toward the house, and she slammed her eyes closed against this horror.

Mike and Po Williams made love the way they often did when the love-making was not about desire or passion but about being together. Mike eased his soft erection into Po but stayed still as he caressed her neck with his lips. Po spoke in Spanish, knowing Mike would not understand all she was saying but that he would understand the sentiments whenever she used the word *manito*. It was what she lovingly called her sons. Mike kissed Po's small breasts. He stroked up and down Po's body, reassuring with his hands, until his erection left him altogether and he pulled out and rolled to his side of the bed. Po put her head on his arm and couldn't stop the tears. Mike brushed her hair from her forehead.

Several minutes later Mike remembered that he had bought Mets tickets for the Friday after Tommy was to return from camp. Those tickets were all for Tommy's sake. Mike had been a lifelong Yankees fan, but Po's relatives, huge Mets fans, had indoctrinated Tommy at an early age, and Mike always took him to one Mets game a year. Lying in bed, Mike fought the images of him and Tommy in the seats, Tommy with his glove, ready for a foul ball, eyes shining with the spectacle of it all. But he lost the battle. He looked at the bedside clock and thought to himself that it was late, that the kids should definitely have been back by now.

"Where do you think you're going?" Janet had caught her son Paul, earphones on, about to head out the front door. He turned to her.

"I can't go out?"

"Of course not. What are people going to think?"

"Think? I'm not going to a party. I'm just going to meet some friends, hang out."

"That's worse." Janet turned and started to walk away.

"What's worse about it? I'm going."

Janet turned back to him quickly, taking a threatening step forward. "No, you're not. You're in this house until this mess is over with."

"What?"

"You heard me. Show some respect for us."

"For you? What about me? I didn't kidnap Linda. I'm not the criminal here. Jesus Christ."

"Don't take the Lord's name in vain. You're staying in. Got it?"

"What if this goes on for years? What if they never find her? Have I got to stay in forever?"

"Don't be ridiculous."

"Well, what about it?"

Janet pursed her lips, fighting tears. "They're going to find them. Soon." She couldn't hold her son's gaze, turned, and stomped down the hall.

• • •

John Walker got off the phone and stood up. But he didn't move for a long minute, and Sheila, sitting at her computer in the study, looked over at him.

"Who was that?" she asked.

John seemed distracted. "Marshall, uh, Rogovin. Head of Citibank global IT security."

"What did he say?"

"He said he was on the case. I authorized him to work on it. FBI computers can't handle the kind of stuff ours can. It's all technical. Something about nodal fingerprints. Something . . ."

"John," Sheila said, turning to him. "Is everything all right?"

"Yeah. But something just struck me."

"What?"

"I'm tainted."

"Tainted? Is that what this guy said?"

"No, but I've seen it from the other side. You know how paranoid execs are about their safety. You know what they have to do in South America, Asia, all over. Nobody's going to say anything to me directly. Everybody's going to be polite and sympathetic, but I know what they're thinking."

"What?"

"I couldn't protect my own son."

Sheila got up and went to him. She could tell he didn't want a hug, wanted to just stay with his own thoughts. But she took his hand in hers for reassurance. He didn't resist.

"I didn't think of that," John said.

"Didn't think of it when?"

"Before. Before this happened."

"How could you have?" Sheila was confused. She looked at John but he was staring off into space, thinking thoughts he wasn't about to share.

Lena's dream was about Janet Rostenkowski and Sarah. When she woke in the middle of the night, that was all she could remember. She was sweating. David was sound asleep. She could see a small patch of black sky out the window above her head. It was flecked with stars and there was something vertiginous about this, as if Lena were being sucked up into the vastness of space. She sat up. David groaned but still slept. Lena swung her legs over the side of the bed but didn't get up.

Suddenly it was no longer early Monday morning but days, maybe months later, and Sarah was still missing. Lena could feel the panic of this viscerally, her skin now soaked. She willed herself back to the present and ran through a checklist; she could not have avoided being duped, they had done all they could since Sarah had left, there had been emails and a video, they were going to pay the ransom in six and a half hours, Sarah was going to be coming home.

But then she thought of a patient several years ago, a woman whose name slipped her now, but whose case popped up as if it had been part of a Google search. The woman had cancer of the throat and had listed herself as a lifelong smoker. But one day she confessed to Lena that she had never smoked, that she put that down because she couldn't face what she thought was the real reason for her cancer: extended, chronic, unstoppable grief. In her thirties, the single mother of a teenage daughter, the woman had experienced the tragedy of having her daughter leave the house to take a bus to an afterschool job and never return. No trace of the teenager had ever been found. The woman felt that the constant ache of this loss had eaten into her tissue and formed the cancer.

In bed now, Lena turned away from this horror of a memory. She didn't have the strength to get out of bed. She flopped back down on her already soaked pillow. She couldn't imagine never seeing Sarah again. But that possibility loomed. Had she waved goodbye? Was Noonie right? She didn't know who she was praying to, but she was praying to have these black thoughts go away forever.

# Twenty

Chase couldn't keep his panic disguised from Helene. He had come out of the bedroom after he had made his initial attempts to halt the not fully encrypted email, and his very presence, jittery and disoriented, sent the placid afternoon into a tailspin. Helene, who was huddling with Jennifer over the wounded Annabelle, came to him.

"What's wrong?"

Chase couldn't answer, couldn't talk. He needed to think, but the kind of thinking he needed to do he'd only done with his father. "I'm fucked" kept pounding in his head, wiping out any other thought or phrase. Finally he got a grip.

"Patient at the hospital. Woman I've gotten to know. Died."

"Aw, I'm sorry to hear that."

Helene tried to soothe him with a hug, but "I'm fucked" came up on the soundtrack again and he couldn't be soothed.

"I'm going outside," he said, pulling away, gripping his cell phone.

He went down the driveway, thinking he might get in the car and go somewhere, but he was suddenly afraid that he might just leave for good, flee, and he knew that wasn't the right choice. He took the sidewalk instead.

A block away from his house he dialed his father's number. Their phones were both coded, so he didn't worry about making the call. He did wonder what sort of message he should leave if his father didn't pick up: "I'm fucked," "Trouble, Dad," "I need to speak to you." He couldn't decide. He prayed his father would answer. But he didn't, and the instant voicemail greeting he got told him his father had either turned off the cell or was out of range. When the tone sounded, Chase spoke without rehearsal.

"Something's wrong, Dad. Call me."

He hung up, started back toward his house, realized he wasn't ready to face Helene yet, and walked the other way. Fleeing with the family was an option, but he knew he couldn't do that without his father's approval. And that would only worsen things anyway, making him a clear suspect to the FBI and a fugitive to boot. He could alert the middleman, but he was only supposed to do that if he sensed imminent arrest. A coded call to the middleman, which was all he could do, would trigger an immediate shutdown of the operation, loss of any reward, and who knows what as far as the kids were concerned. So, at least now, that wasn't a card he could play.

Then his thinking began to clear a little more. He remembered being on the front porch with his father in the early stages of their planning. Helene had brought dessert out to them after a dinner on a warm spring night. She had lingered for a while, interrupting the talk the two were having. When she went inside, Chase's father had whispered that one of the best shields Chase had was the normalcy of his home life and the fact that Helene was in the dark.

"This thing's foolproof," he continued, still whispering, "But if for some reason some genius gets through all the encryption, which will never happen, if they come to your door, you're still golden. Helene, with those eyes, the kids, is gonna make 'em feel stupid for coming to your door. And then when they take a look at your computer, they're gonna find nothin'. Don't panic, 'cause it's gonna look just like somebody hijacked your computer and you and your lovely wife and kids are just dupes. Now you got that?"

Chase remembered this as he was halfway around the block. A lawn sprinkler system came on automatically and Chase took this as a sign of sorts, an exclamation point to the thought. He didn't have to flee, he didn't have to do anything abnormal, he just had to sit tight and wait. And if they came to his door, he'd just remember his dad sitting there with strawberry shortcake on a plate on his lap, telling him to be cool. And he would be cool. He didn't know how fast these things might work. He began to worry that the FBI might already be at his door and become suspicious if Helene were to say something like "Oh, he had a problem and went for a walk." He hurried home.

Late at night, with the kids in bed, Chase was staring at a reality show on TV, cell phone in hand, dying to have his father call. Helene came into the room, fresh out of the shower and sat next to him, wearing only a towel. Chase knew what this meant, but he couldn't imagine foreplay in his state, much less the full meal. But he had almost never rejected one of Helene's advances, and he realized that to do so now might be something she'd think about if the FBI came.

So he went back into his acting mode and found himself into the fuck. Shit, he thought, I'm good at this. Why can't I just keep the performance rolling? Bring on the FBI. I'll loop my arm around Helene's shoulders, I'll lift the kids, I'll be really surprised when they tell me my computer was used for this operation. Fucking Oscar, here I come. Helene stroked his chest. He could play the part. He was sure of it.

# Twenty-one

As night came and the small kerosene lamp the kids had figured out how to light threw its eerie shadows on the walls of the shack, everything Mr. Everett had hoped the kids would fear and more flooded them. He may have been lying dead on the dock a half mile away, but he was buried in the imaginations of the kids in a way that was more devastating than his physical presence ever could have been.

Franklin worked against this horror by studying Mr. Everett's notebook over and over. Tommy attacked the problem directly, obsessively checking the windows, even though Linda had asked him to stop. Linda was certain that even if Mr. Everett was dead, he could rise and come to them all mangled and bloody. Sarah played games with herself, imagining that this was like the surprise birthday party her parents had given her once, that her father's absence at her departure was, as it had been with the surprise party, a way for him to sneak off and get things set up. She didn't say this out loud, though, knowing it was nonsense. Instead she mouthed brave words.

"I'm sure our parents have this figured out by now," she said, breaking a long silence.

"Figured what out?" Tommy asked, a sincere question that bubbled up from his continuing inability to understand just what they had been thrown into.

The silence that followed the question was revealing. It said that all the others were having trouble coming to grips with the exact nature of their predicament. Mr. Everett had said they were on a special Camp Arno outing. And the van had been a Camp Arno van. But they all realized that what Mr. Everett had told them was a lie. And yet he had also told them, just before his accident (the word they were using now because none of them really knew what a heart attack was) that they were going home and would be seeing their parents soon.

Finally Franklin, near the kerosene lamp, answered Tommy's question.

"We've been kidnapped."

The others didn't want to believe this.

"Shouldn't we be tied up or something?" Linda asked.

"You don't have to be," Sarah said, all of a sudden remembering something that had really scared her. "There was that boy who was kidnapped and lived with that man for, like, years. He wasn't tied up. He could even walk around the neighborhood."

"What boy?" Linda challenged, not wanting to think about even another night away from home.

"I don't know. It was on the news. And he got older and the man took another kid and that's when the two of them escaped."

At the mention of escape, all went into their private thoughts again. As if on cue, the kerosene in the lamp dried up and the wick guttered out. The kids pawed around in the very dim light coming through the windows, looking for a flashlight, but they couldn't find one. Franklin said they should all go into the other room and try to sleep. He sounded like a parent when he said this, and in fact he was imitating his own parents, comforting himself by doing so. The other kids must have found this a balm of some sort too because they obeyed.

None of them slept. In the inky black it was as if the walls of the shack had dissolved. They gave no protection from the dangers, real and imagined, that lay just outside the clearing. Every now and then one of the kids would shuffle around or make some small noise. "I'm here," the noises seemed to say. "Are you there?"

After about an hour a milky light began to come in through the windows. Tommy looked out and saw the beginnings of a moonrise in the east. Earlier in the summer he and his brother, Jack, had been home by themselves on a full-moon night and had played catch with a football, using just the moonlight. That had been a magical time for Tommy, first for getting such attention from his big brother, second for the delight in seeing the ball come toward him like a spiraling ghost. He thought maybe they should all go outside, that things would somehow be better out there.

As he was turning away from the window, movement out in the clearing popped up in the corner of his eye and he turned back. Looking at the scene fully, he didn't see any more movement for a while. Then he saw a large shape, silhouetted against the moonrise, lifting itself on the rocks.

"Hey," he whispered back to the others. "Look."

They came to the window but saw nothing as their eyes adjusted to the light outside. The shape didn't move for a long few minutes, and Tommy had to tell them a couple of times to wait. Then the shape rose again and now it was clearly discernible.

"Bear," Sarah said with a catch in her throat. Linda let out a squeak of surprise. The others were wide-eyed and rooted to their spots.

Then the bear turned around a couple of times, as if it were going to curl up and go to sleep. But instead it looked over at the shack, or at least seemed to. It was hard to tell in the half-light of the moon. When it started to walk toward the shack, however, there was no doubt what was happening. The kids ducked and huddled under the window.

The next few minutes were terrifying. Linda couldn't stop shivering, but they were all keeping quiet, straining to hear what was happening outside. The slap of paws on rock came to them and then faded. There were sounds they didn't recognize, either grunts or chewing. And then there was a sound that made them all jump, a loud dull scraping sound along the wall, as if the bear were bumping into the shack. The sound came closer and the kids moved back into the room, cowering. Then the top of the bear's back passed the window and Sarah gasped loudly.

The bear stopped, its hunched back still visible through the grimy window, the fur silhouetted against the deep blue sky. The kids were petrified now. The bear seemed to be sniffing their presence, gathering for an attack. It moved away from the window and made no sounds for a long few minutes. The silence was worse than the noises. Suddenly the walls of the cabin shook and a window in the other room shattered as the bear butted the fragile structure. Linda screamed and the others turned to quiet her. They waited for another attack, but it didn't come.

When silence fell again, they heard nothing outside. They waited, hardly able to breathe. But after several minutes of wired anticipation, they began to realize the bear had left. Or had he? The tension held for a long while until finally Franklin found his voice and said he thought the bear was gone. Linda started to cry softly.

"I left my sandwich out there," she sniffled. "It's my fault."

The next hour or so was pure misery for the kids. The imagined terrors outside the shack, outside the clearing, had become frighteningly real. The sheer size of the monster that had scraped against the walls of the shack, grunted, and slapped around the clearing sent them all into private hells. When they talked, in little fits and starts, their thoughts were choked, paralyzed, incoherent. Someone had to come and get them, Sarah thought, her brain fuzzed by hunger, fear, and a tiredness that made movement an effort. Someone had to come because they couldn't leave. They were trapped.

They were hauled into sleep by simple weariness. Sarah woke in the middle of the night but thought she was still in a dream. She heard the bear's return, his chuffing breath and clicking paws. She was in a dream, wasn't she? She let sleep take her again.

Franklin woke first, hours later, still exhausted. With the other kids asleep, he didn't have to pretend he wasn't scared anymore. He wanted his mother to come in the room the way she did on school mornings, sit on his bed, wake him gently by rubbing his back and saying a prayer for his well-being that day. Thinking about this brought tears to his eyes and his body shook with the full-out cry he had been trying to hold back for days. Then Sarah stirred and Franklin sniffed back his tears and rolled away from her.

He was cold and reached for one of the blankets. Cried out, Franklin felt his thinking clear and he remembered reading about mirror writing. Maybe Mr. Everett's notebook nonsense was mirror writing. Now he was dying for light to come so he could search for a mirror and test his hypothesis. Tommy mumbled something in his sleep. Franklin closed his eyes in prayer and asked the Lord to help him crack the code, get the password, and send for help.

# Twenty-two

As she woke, Lena was in free fall, untethered, dropping through space. She felt helpless, dizzy. She thought she might be sick. She got out of bed and made it as far as the door to Sarah's room. It wasn't nausea or vertigo. She wasn't in danger of toppling. She began to realize that the accumulated weight of days of uncertainty, days without facts and signposts, had hollowed her and left her vulnerable to the deep anxiety of nothingness.

She picked up Sarah's pillow and buried her face in the enveloping cushion of its softness. After a minute of soundless embrace, the panic subsided and Lena found herself breathing again. As she put the pillow down, Sarah was suddenly there, in the bed, ready to go to sleep. Lena recoiled from this illusion and left the room.

She went into the kitchen and started to make coffee. She put a bagel in the toaster oven, more out of duty than appetite, and then took a sip of her coffee. It tasted like a watery soup, almost papery on her tongue. She got the butter out of the refrigerator and smelled something on the shelves that was off, maybe rotten. The smell made her queasy. She buttered the bagel when it was toasted and brought it to the kitchen table. She remembered then that about forty-five hours earlier she had sat at that table, with coffee and a bagel, and the doorbell had rung. She could still hear that doorbell. Would she hear that for the rest of her life?

Then something gripped her stomach and she knew she was going to be sick. She got up quickly, went into the bathroom, and just barely got the door closed and the toilet seat up before a strong vomit poured from her mouth. A couple more retches followed before her stomach settled and she knew she was finished. She mopped up the toilet rim and the floor wondering if this sickness was the result of her earlier sense of free fall. But that feeling had passed completely. Maybe, she thought, she was coming down with something or perhaps had some food poisoning. She was about to take her temperature when she looked at herself in the medicine cabinet mirror. She stared and had the feeling her reflection was speaking to her, asking her to look deep inside herself.

Suddenly she knew that she wasn't sick, wasn't the victim of food poisoning. She opened the medicine cabinet and found the home pregnancy test kit. She hadn't used one of those test strips in well over a year. She took one out of the box without thinking, without anticipation. She was on autopilot as she sat on the toilet and peed onto the strip. She didn't really have to read it. She knew. When the positive plus sign popped up almost immediately, she stared at it until she heard David coming from the bedroom. She knew he would be heading straight for the bathroom as he always did. She dropped the strip into the toilet, stood, and flushed.

David knocked and pushed the door open a little.

"All right if I come in?"

"Yes." They were used to sharing the bathroom this way. David was in such a hurry to pee he didn't notice the look on Lena's face. She left the bathroom as David lifted the toilet seat.

Lena walked into the living room trying to absorb what she had just learned. She tried to remember the last time she and David had made love. There was a fumbling, drunken attempt only a couple of weeks ago, when they had come back from a party and the tensions and the distance they had been feeling for months were gone. But David couldn't maintain an erection and they just gave up in frustration. Then she remembered a morning a week or two before that when she woke to David caressing her breasts. She was still half asleep; David's hand felt warm and soothing and her body came alive. When he nudged her with his erection, she pulled him on top of her and he was inside, warm and hard, before she had even opened her legs wide. She remembered that she wanted him to stay like that, not to move, to just be connected. But she didn't say anything and she felt the pull of her own excitement start her moving. It had been so long since they had made love that her orgasm came quickly and David's came soon after. They didn't have time to savor the moment, though, because they heard Sarah's door open, and David left her and rolled to his side of the bed.

Was that it, then? It had to be. Had she missed a period and not even known it? She tried to think about her cycle, the days, but she had lost track recently, and she didn't know where she was, when she should have menstruated. I'm a doctor, she thought to herself, and I can't keep this stuff straight. She heard David leave the bathroom and go back into the bedroom. When would she tell him?

A rush of horrible thoughts hit her then. Would she have to go through this pregnancy not knowing where Sarah was? Would this new life somehow compete with Sarah for Lena's love? How did mothers of two children do it, separate their love? Lena became increasingly confused now, wondering if she should go through with the pregnancy at all, with the future such a blank. David was coming out of the bedroom. Could she keep this from him long enough to think clearly, to decide on a course of action? And finally, what had she done to deserve this fate, this minor medical miracle popping up now, with Sarah lost to her?

David came up behind her, put his hands on her shoulders, and kissed her neck. He hadn't done that in ages. It was as if he knew something. Had the test strip not flushed? No, she had seen it go down. She turned to him and they looked each other in the eye.

"How did you sleep?" he asked, clearly worried about what he was seeing in her face.

"Badly."

"What was that smell in the bathroom?"

"I was sick."

"Threw up?"

"Yes."

"What is it?"

"I don't know. Food poisoning. Nerves. I just want this thing over with."

"I know. You got coffee?"

Lena remembered the coffee and bagel on the kitchen table. She didn't think she could face them.

"I did. Go ahead. There's a bagel there. Have it. I'm still feeling nauseous." Maybe, she was hoping, David would see deeply into what she was telling him and realize that meant she was pregnant. But that was asking way too much when she herself almost missed the sign.

"Why don't you go back to bed? Have you checked the computer?"

"No. Maybe I will."

She started to leave for the bedroom, but David took her by the shoulders and held her gaze, almost forcing her not to look away.

"I feel horrible I didn't tell you about the job."

"It's okay. I understand."

David ached to say more, to get it all off his chest. But he disciplined himself.

"Get some more sleep. I'll let you know if anything comes up."

When she took her clothes off and got back in bed, she felt she might be sick again. But after a few minutes the questions about the pregnancy wisped away, all the feelings dissolved, and as had happened with Sarah, she knew instantly that she was attached forever to this new child. Guilty tears rolled down her cheeks. The hollow uncertainty she had woken with was replaced by a fullness beyond belief. She buried her face in the pillow and wept for joy.

David knew the number on his cell phone was familiar but at first he couldn't place it. Then he realized it was Tricia's number, that she had called at 11:24 the night before and that she hadn't left a message. He spent a few minutes debating whether he should call her or not. He went to the bedroom, nudged the door open, saw that Lena was asleep, and went back to the kitchen. He hit the send button and stepped out onto the patio. The morning was heating up quickly. The phone rang eight times before Tricia answered.

"David?"

"Hi. You called last night?"

"I did?"

"Caller ID. At eleven twenty-four."

"Jesus."

"What?"

"I was drunk. I had drinks with Sherry and no dinner and I came home and finished three-quarters of a bottle of wine. I passed out and slept on the couch. I just got up."

David waited. He felt the ball was still in her court. He didn't know what question to ask beyond the straightforward, "Did you have anything to do with Sarah's disappearance?" but he knew that would be useless. He thought he heard movement in the kitchen, whipped around and found it empty.

"You okay?" This sounded perfunctory coming from Tricia.

"No. Sarah's still gone. I won't be okay until she's back."

David thought he heard a sigh. "I saw a picture of your wife. Looks like she's taking this hard."

"What would you expect?"

"You're a strong man, David. You deserve a strong partner."

David wanted to kill. He wasn't a strong man. He'd let himself fall into the clutches of this obnoxious creature at the other end of the line. Had that fall led to Sarah's abduction? Hearing Tricia's boorish insensitivity made him ask himself the question again.

"David? Are you there? You know I'm right. You're going to get your kid back, but doesn't this show you you need a—"

"How do you know I'm going to get my kid back?"

Tricia said nothing.

"How do you know?"

"I just know. The cops that came to talk to me, you know. They said you'd get them back. You pay the ransom and then get them back, right?"

"What do you know about the ransom?"

"Jesus, David. Nothing. I have to go. Don't call me again until you're ready to trade up."

She hung up. David's phone hand swept outward, but he stopped himself before he let the phone fly. Self-recrimination clawed at him now, and vital investigation questions sprouted. Could Tricia have possibly set this whole thing up? How? He fast-forwarded through images of their time together; her dismissive gestures, her demands in bed, her ice-cold assessment of colleagues and even friends. He resisted giving himself the how-stupid-could-I-have-been tongue-lashings and tried to imagine this utterly self-involved woman going to great and horrible lengths to teach him a lesson about what sort of woman he needed as a partner. He couldn't fathom it but neither could he dismiss it. He would never call her back, but for now he knew he was still caught.

When, an hour later, David woke Lena and told her there was going to be a conference call in a few minutes, Lena had trouble figuring out what he was talking about. Her sleep had been very deep. Only slowly did she remember that Sarah was missing and that there were other families involved.

John Walker treated the call as if it were one of his business meetings. He introduced the parents to some officer at his bank who handled wire transfers. The only mention of the fact that the whole call was occasioned by an abduction came when the officer prefaced his remarks by saying how sorry he was the kidnapping had occurred. He then moved on to the details.

David was on the kitchen phone, Lena on the bedroom extension, still under the covers. Her mind wandered as she listened to the people talking, hoping David was listening for the two of them. He had said he would when he woke her. Lena realized that Sarah had now spent two nights without her in some place Lena didn't even want to try to imagine. Separated from the other parents on the conference call, Lena wondered if the kidnappers might have separated the kids in order to better hide them from scrutiny. They were going to pay the ransom as a group, but would they be getting their kids back as a group? What if the kids had been separated and one of their captors was more competent (she got stuck on that word for a minute; how could a monster like that be competent?) than the others? Or completely unsuited for the task? That thought set up a horrible situation for Lena in which she had to hope Sarah got the best treatment, meaning that one or more of the other kids wouldn't. Once you didn't lump all the kids together in your thinking, you had a competition of the worst order. Lena tried to bring her mind back to the conference call.

"Witherspoon is asking for more time," John was saying as Lena returned. "She says they are getting closer to what she calls 'a significant suspect.' I don't think we should wait. We put this in motion at noon and whoever is in charge of the account will not get definitive information from the bank until around three. If we put it off any more, with bank closings in the Caymans at five, we'll have to wait another night."

"No," Lena blurted out.

"Who was that?" John asked.

"Me. Lena. I don't want to wait another night. Please. Let's just put this through."

"Mike here. I agree. If the payment goes through at the same time they're nabbing their goddamn 'significant suspect,' then what's the problem?"

"Nothing other than losing the money," John answered. There was silence on the line. "So then, we go ahead with this at noon?"

John polled the group one by one and there were strong voices all around in support. Janet added a plaintive "I just want to get this over with" to her yes. Mike ended the call by saying that he and Po would be glad to have any of the parents stop by if they felt like being around the others. That invitation sounded great to Lena as she hung up. But when David came in from the kitchen, he said the last thing he wanted to do was be around the other parents waiting for news.

"Well, what else are we going to do?" Lena asked, getting up and getting dressed.

"I don't know."

"Don't say Scrabble."

"I won't."

Standing up made Lena nauseous again and she went to the bathroom. There wasn't much left to throw up. David followed and stood at the bathroom door.

"Think it's a flu or something?" he asked, without any indication that he could imagine "morning sickness" as the answer. Lena shook her head as she rinsed her mouth and began to brush her teeth. She looked at her face in the mirror, the same image that had made her realize she was pregnant earlier. There was no such revelation now. She was a woman with a toothbrush in her mouth, a missing child, a husband who was still too distant for her to trust with the most important information a couple can share, and a new life already growing wildly inside her. She felt as if the image in the mirror were being pulled in too many directions, a funhouse squiggle of a portrait, one that would burst apart with one small movement. She bit down hard on the bristles of the brush as if that could somehow hold things together.

# Twenty-three

An hour into his workday, with nothing much to do, Chase stepped outside the hospital to try again to reach his father. Again he got the voicemail. Chase repeated to himself what he'd been saying all morning, that he was ready to act his way through anything that might come up, but he wished he had some contact with the old man.

His dad's passion for this project had been great. It wasn't just the money, Chase knew. "That dough's the end of it all," he had told Chase early on. "It's the doin' I'm lookin' forward to. I wanna be in the middle of it, wanna have the kids under my thumb, have the parents by the balls, yankin' 'em this way and that, watchin' the machinery hum. An' I'll have the satisfaction of knowing it's all because of me. Me and you, that is."

Chase hoped his dad was enjoying the ride as much as he'd anticipated. And if it came to acting on Chase's part, he would be sorry his father couldn't watch him perform. He went back in the hospital renewed by the simple memory of the man who had always meant so much to him.

Forty-five minutes later the curtain rose for Chase. He thought the two men were salesmen at first. They had plain suits and one had a briefcase. They were coming from the direction of the basement elevator; salesmen who were familiar with the hospital often used the basement garage and walked through the laundry to get to the main elevators. So Chase ignored them until they addressed him, one holding out a badge in a wallet.

"Mr. Collins. I'm Agent Allen and this is Agent Toomey. We're with the FBI. We'd like to ask you some questions."

Allen was older, probably in his fifties, with thinning hair. Toomey was in his thirties, pale-skinned and blue-eyed but with thick, dark hair. The two reminded Chase of him and his father.

"FBI? What is this?"

"Your supervisor said we could use his office. If you come in there with us, we'll explain."

"Sure, but"—and this was something Chase had worked up when he planned for such a meeting at work—"I don't know anything about the administration of the hospital. I just do my work."

"This isn't about the hospital, Mr. Collins."

Chase did his best confused look and walked with the agents to his supervisor's office. He sat in his supervisor's chair and the agents sat across the desk from him. Chase liked the seating arrangement. It made it seem as if he were in charge, that he was interrogating them. But he knew he couldn't get too cocky, be too sure of himself. He wanted to project a little fear.

"Is this about taxes? 'Cause I did my own this year and—"

"This isn't about taxes," Toomey said. "That would be the IRS's responsibility. This is about a computer registered to you."

"Oh. I don't have a computer. We don't need them down here and—"

"At home. We're talking about a computer at home. Do you have more than one computer?"

"No. I have a cell phone. And a TiVo." Chase could see this played as he'd intended it to, naïve, trying to be helpful. He was sizing up the two men as he'd sized up the parents. The older guy would probably like the fact that Chase wasn't good with computers, could identify with that. The hairy one might want to know what a good family man Chase was. Allen took over.

"We're just interested in the computer. Are you the only operator?"

"Operator?"

"Are you the only one who uses it?"

"No, my wife does."

"Are there others who use it?"

"No."

"So then anything on your computer, on your hard drive, is yours or your wife's?"

"I guess so. I get those pop-ups, you know, click on the bull's-eye and win . . ." He stopped himself and did a pretty good job with a worried look. "I, um, Jesus. I go on some of those XX sites. Not the sleazy ones with kids or anything. You know, clean stuff. Is that . . . ?"

Toomey always took the attitude that a suspect was guilty until proven innocent. That way it was harder to miss a truly guilty interviewee. If some guy could hit you over the head with his innocence, if it was that obvious, then Toomey'd reluctantly let him go. But if it was only a little spot of innocent-sounding stuff here, another one there, then he stuck with his initial belief. This Collins guy was saying the right things, but he wasn't hitting Toomey over the head with anything that sounded genuine. He decided it was time for him to do the talking.

"We've traced some potentially criminal activity to your computer. We—"

"Criminal activity?"

"I won't specify. We have agents who are searching your house as we speak." Toomey waited for a reaction from Chase but he gave none. Toomey didn't quite know how to read this.

"My wife, uh . . ."

"Your wife what?"

"She doesn't know anything about the porn sites. I swear it's just, you know, normal."

"Your computer will be seized and examined off premises. As long as there is no criminal activity, your privacy will be maintained."

Chase looked down, worried, he thought, but not criminal worried.

He felt the performance was humming along beautifully. He was hoping they suspected him a little, though, because he had some wonderful stuff planned for when they came to tell him that his computer had been pirated by kidnappers.

Allen took over again. "We'd like you to come with us to our office. We have some further questions. You may call a lawyer to meet us there if you like."

"A lawyer. Do you think I need one?"

"That's up to you, Mr. Collins. The questions are routine."

"Well, I don't know any lawyers. Can you ask me one? And maybe I'll know if I need a lawyer or not."

"One what?"

"A question. One of the questions you're going to ask me."

"Your time card says you checked in here at eight twenty-eight on Saturday and left at four thirty-one. Were you in the building the whole time?"

"Yes. I have to be. I can get lunch in the cafeteria but I can't leave."

"And you didn't on Saturday?"

"No." Chase saw the agents were ending things there. "If that's the sort of questions, I don't see why I need a lawyer."

Toomey still had his doubts but they were melting fast. He was glad they had a computer in this case and they didn't have to come to a conclusion based on guesswork. This guy was hard to read. As they stood to leave, he tried to imagine how Chase was going to look with the wig on.

# Twenty-four

Sarah was awake just as light was coming into the clearing. She went to the window and scanned the edges of the surrounding woods. She could see the tattered remains of the sandwich bag Linda had left on the rock, but the clearing seemed calm otherwise. She had to pee badly. Franklin whispered to her.

"Do you see anything?"

"No."

He got up and went in the other room. He was fishing Mr. Everett's notebook out of the backpack when Sarah came out of the second room. She went to the door and opened it.

"What are you doing?" Franklin asked.

"I've got to pee."

In Franklin's family they used the word *urinate* but he didn't mind the vulgarity now. He had to pee too.

"I'll go with you and keep watch."

The grass in the clearing was wet with dew. A morning dove's coo, as soft as it was, made Sarah jump, but she hurried to the outhouse, endured the cold boards of the latrine, and was done in record time.

Franklin rushed in after her and by the time he came out, Tommy and Linda were shivering in line, waiting.

They found some packaged muffins in the bottom of the cooler and had those for breakfast. Franklin puzzled over the notebook. It didn't seem like the mirror writing he had remembered from the story he'd read. He searched in the backpack and the rest of the shack for a mirror but had no luck. The others, smacking their tongues on the dry muffins, listened to him as he moved around.

". . . and if it is mirror writing, then we'll have to figure out if any of it is the password. Then if we get the password . . ." His thinking seemed to stop there.

"What?" Linda asked.

"Well, we'll email our parents."

The kids were all thinking the same thing. Sarah said it first.

"I don't know my parents' addresses. Mom wrote them down. They're in my bag back at the car."

"Me too," said Linda. "I just have them in my computer address book."

Franklin scowled. "I only know the one for my mother at church. I don't know if she checks that one."

"I think I know my mother's," Tommy said, though he didn't seem too confident.

"Well, we haven't even got the password yet," Franklin said, looking around the shack. "What can we use as a mirror?"

They all looked for shiny surfaces but the rough-hewn shack yielded none.

"The window, outside," Sarah said. The others gave this thought, figuring in the fact that they would have to be out of the shack, vulnerable to whatever was out there. Sarah could see this. "I don't think bears come around in the daylight. We didn't see any yesterday, right?"

Images of the hulking mass outside their window the night before countered Sarah's observation. The others didn't want to gamble on a hunch. Franklin broke the impasse.

"It'll only be a few minutes. And we don't have any more food out. That's what the bear came for. The food."

With nervous, wary looks the four circled the shack until they found a window in shade, one that reflected the notebook well enough to read. Franklin held the notebook up, but the scribbling seemed even more impenetrable like that, the letters not resembling the alphabet.

"Turn it upside down," Tommy suggested.

That worked. It was a form of mirror writing that popped out once the notebook was upside down. The first page was headed by the word "Contacts," and that was followed by the names Chase, Marshall, Middleman, Gursy, and Farrow. But the writing opposite each name, instead of phone numbers, was a combination of numbers and letters, more code. Franklin turned the page. The heading here was "Sequence."

"What's 'sequence'?" Linda asked. The others didn't seem to know. There were dates and times below the heading, however, so Sarah took a guess.

"It's like the time things happen."

They read words like "van snatch," "paint van," "Trainor pickup," and "kid switch." Linda whispered her own last name aloud when she read, "Rosten." The others could see their own family names on the page. There was a moment of quiet then as the kids realized they had been targeted and stalked.

"He planned it all," Sarah said.

"What's that?" Tommy asked, pointing to a big, underlined word, "RANSOM."

"That's what they pay kidnappers," Franklin said slowly, the realization that someone was going to have to pay for them to be released dawning on him.

"Who pays them?" Tommy asked, genuinely confused.

"Our parents," Sarah answered. "Our parents have to pay them and then they let us go."

Their thoughts all turned to Mr. Everett. It was his notebook they were reading, but he was not there. He was probably still lying on the dock, dead. How could he release them if he was dead?

"There's more than one?" Tommy asked. "You said 'them.' There's others coming here?" No one answered his question.

Franklin, not wanting to think about this, turned the page. There was no heading on this page. The first line said, "Op. name," followed by "Arno." The second line said, "Op. Capt." followed by "Thinker." Other lines paired words the kids couldn't make too much sense of: "abducts," "recon," "mission duration," and "compensation."

The last page had a heading that said "Encrypt" and was filled with words and numbers that meant nothing to any of the kids. Franklin closed the notebook, dejected. They all headed back to the shack door. The sun was up fully now and very warm. Sarah didn't want to go back in the shack.

"Let's stay out here. If a bear comes, we can just run back into the house."

"That's not a house," Linda blurted out.

"I mean the cabin or whatever."

Sarah, Linda, and Franklin decided to stay out in the sunshine. Tommy was going to do so as well, but he wanted to get his hands on that laptop again. He had been itching to open the screen, feel the keyboard, and give some passwords a try. He had his father's genes for getting under the hood, and he'd always found computers to be as much about touch and feel as about some sort of abstraction. When his computer at home froze up, he didn't just sit there and think about it, he worked all the keys, turned it off and on again, sometimes even gave it a little bang with his fist.

Sarah looked at the ripped bag that had held Linda's sandwich. It was just a mess of torn plastic with bits of food stuff clinging to it. Linda, standing nearby, let out a little "yuk," and Sarah looked over. A huge mound of bear droppings sat on a patch of matted grass. Sarah and Linda moved away from both of these reminders and rejoined Franklin, who was sitting on another rock, still staring at the notebook, as if doing so might yield some clues. Then he looked up.

"I think we should go see what's happened to Mr. Everett," he said a little tentatively. "Maybe he has something in his wallet, a paper like, with the password on it."

"Maybe," Sarah responded, thinking now about the dangers a trip back to the pond would entail. "I wish we could get his cell phone."

"Yeah," Linda said. "Why did he throw it away?"

"He dropped it," Franklin replied.

"No, he didn't. I saw him throw it into the pond."

Franklin didn't contest this, still thinking about what Mr. Everett's pockets might yield. Tommy's voice from inside the shack caught them by surprise.

"Hey! C'mere."

Tommy was hunched over the laptop and when the others got around behind him, they could see that he had made it to the desktop.

"How did you do that?" Franklin asked.

" 'Thinker.' I used the word 'thinker' and it worked."

"Why did you use that?" Linda asked.

"That was in the notebook. I tried some other stuff but it didn't work."

"So, how do we do email?" Sarah asked. None of the kids knew. The icons on the desktop were unfamiliar to them. Tommy clicked on a couple. One brought them to a spreadsheet with a lot of dollar figures on it. One brought them to something that looked like an email program but asked for a password. "Thinker" didn't work with this one.

"This all looks weird," Franklin said. "I have a Mac."

"I think this is the internet one," Tommy said, clicking on the Internet Explorer icon. After a while a page came up that said, "The page you want could not be found," and explained that the page might have moved or the connection might have been broken. Then a little bubble popped up from the bottom bar on the screen and said, "wireless connection not found."

This was baffling to the kids but Franklin reasoned that, like the cell phone, if they moved it outside, they might be able to get a connection. So with both Franklin and Tommy holding the opened laptop, they went out to the rocks. The connection didn't work there either.

"The pond," Sarah said. Linda looked at her with pleading eyes, not wanting to go back there. Sarah didn't either, but it only made sense. "That's where Mr. Everett got his cell phone to work."

Still carrying the laptop like some sort of offering to the gods, the four made their way cautiously toward the pond. It was, from a distance, an odd scene; the vast wilderness of the Adirondacks in all its summer morning beauty, dotted with four young people bearing a piece of technology they hoped would lead them to their rescue. When they got to the pond, the scene became even more surreal. Mr. Everett lay where they had left him, but now two huge crows were pecking at any exposed flesh. They looked up when the kids arrived, but didn't fly off.

The shock of seeing this bloody scene stopped the four in their tracks. They were too stunned to say anything for a while. Then Linda, gagging on her words, broke the silence.

"They're eating him!"

Sarah turned from the carnage and stared at the laptop Tommy was holding. Then she remembered seeing Mr. Everett hunched over the piece of machinery in the eerie night light.

"Where's the thing sticking out of the side?" she asked, looking over the laptop carefully. Tommy joined her search, pushed what looked like the door to an empty port on the side of the laptop, and a small, flat antenna popped out. The screen changed immediately.

"Hey, there's a signal."

"Satellite," Franklin said without much authority as they gathered around the almost magical machine. They had a hard time seeing the screen in the bright daylight. But they could definitely see a home page with a familiar bar at the top. Then the question became what to do about it. Tommy knew how to get to his account on Yahoo, but when the Yahoo home page came up, he realized he didn't know his own password. "My brother set up the account and it just does the password automatically." Franklin said he used a Mac account but he too couldn't remember how to get there. They all seemed stumped by having shortcuts and automation on their home computers. Then Sarah had an idea.

"Facebook!" she shouted. "My mom's a friend. I can email her like that."

"Me too," Linda said.

They found the Facebook pages easily and started to write, but they didn't know what to say.

"Tell them we've been captured and we need help," Franklin started.

"Where are we?" Sarah asked, as Tommy put the laptop down on the ground and she began to type. Her question stumped them all.

"We're not near Camp Arno," Franklin said. "We went past Albania, I think."

"Albania? How do you spell that?"

Franklin was about to answer when a vicious caw from one of the crows split the air and made them jump. Both crows then unfurled their tremendous wingspans and flapped away. When she had composed herself, Sarah went back to typing and sent the email. Linda followed her and wrote almost exactly what Sarah had written.

They didn't know what more to do but didn't want to turn off the laptop, close it up. It was their lifeline. Then Franklin squinted in and saw a battery indicator. He knew what that was and could see that it was down quite a bit. He told the others, turned off the machine, and closed it.

The pond was still. They weren't close enough to Mr. Everett's body to see much of the gore, but they could get an idea of what the crows had done to him. They had solved a couple of problems and sent their messages out to those who could save them, but who knew if the messages would be picked up and if their parents could do anything about them if they did.

As they were walking back to the shack, Sarah realized Franklin had been off.

"It's not Albania. It's Albany. Albany is the capital of New York State," she said as she stopped walking. Franklin realized she was right.

"Well, but they'll understand. Won't they?"

No one knew but all hoped. They had to hope. They had to believe their parents could take the information they had given them, point to a map, say, "Oh, sure, that's where they are," and come and get them. It was morning, the sun felt good, but if their parents didn't act fast, it would be night again, and night meant the shadowy world beyond the clearing.

Sarah was enough of a realist to understand the odds of such a rescue. She remembered seeing the oceans of forest around them when they had taken their hike. She fought the tears she felt forming. Her mom was real smart and her dad was strong, a good hiker. They'd figure out a way to save her. She knew it. She just knew it.

# Twenty-five

David shut down the computer, left the bedroom, and found Lena in the back yard.

"There's a lot of shit on the internet. I'd stay away from it if I were you," David said, sitting, looking around to see if there were photographers lurking in the bushes. "The FBI will call if there's anything we need to see."

"What kind of shit?"

"Ugly stuff about us, about the kids, YouTube parodies. You name it. That goddamn Web is supposed to be a boon in situations like this, isn't it? Jesus. Every computer user in the world should be out there with the kids' pictures instead of inside swallowing all this garbage."

"I'll stay away from it," Lena said automatically, as if she'd hardly heard.

David had actually been plowing through the internet backwash trying to see if his affair had been discovered. His former boss wasn't the only one at Dell who knew about it. There was plenty of slanderous screeching in blogs and essays and comments, accusations of all sorts of criminal activity by the parents, conspiracy theories that had the parents setting up the whole kidnapping for their own gain, pitch-perfect Web nonsense, but nothing, David found, about his trysts with Tricia Sands. He wasn't elated by this, as if he were off the hook. He had resigned himself to a day when he would have to face his lovely, trusting wife and tell her what he had done. He didn't want that day to come while Sarah was missing, but as he trolled the Web pages, he almost hoped he had been exposed. He wanted to get that part of his life over with.

"Camp Arno's been shut down for the rest of the summer by all the howling." David said finally.

"Good."

"What?"

"I don't know. I hate that camp. I can't stand the thought of it. Why didn't we let Sarah have her way? Why didn't we let her go to soccer camp?"

"We did, Lena. She made the choice."

"Are you blaming her now?"

"What?"

Lena could feel herself drifting away from reason, but it felt good to do so.

"We maneuvered her into that decision, remember? Her heart was really set on soccer camp, but that was not a sleepaway, and you and I wanted these two weeks to ourselves. You remember that, don't you?"

"No. I remember being proud of our very independent young girl who weighed the pros and cons and chose Camp Arno."

"Bullshit, David. Why was she going to wear cleats at Camp Arno? Huh?"

"So she could have it both ways. She's nine, Lena."

Lena felt the toast in her stomach and worried she was going to be sick again. But the wave passed. She relented.

"Sorry. I think I'm going to go crazy here. What did they say, three? Is that when we should hear from them?"

"They said that was the earliest, if we send the money at noon."

Lena guessed it was about 11:30. She didn't want to think about time anymore."I'm going to go over to the Williamses this afternoon."

"Boy, I'm not doing that. Hang out with my fellow victims? No way."

"What else is there to do?"

David couldn't answer the question. Lena felt again that she had to get away from him. She went back in the house and felt a tug in her stomach when she saw the remains of a breakfast David had had. She left the kitchen and went into her bedroom. The computer sat in the corner like a menacing gargoyle now. She went to it and stared down at the keyboard and monitor. A Post-it fixed to the bottom of the computer, in Sarah's handwriting, had instructions for how Lena could become Sarah's friend on Facebook. Lena wondered if the garbage-mongers on the internet had hacked into Sarah's page and made mincemeat of it. She didn't have the heart to see. She looked outside and saw two men on a news crew tossing a Frisbee. The simple freedom of that game of catch sickened her. She flopped down on the bed and stared at the ceiling, trying to lose herself, trying to keep the vast expanse of the world beyond her walls from driving her crazy.

She had been in that near-catatonic state for fifteen minutes or so when the phone rang. She sat up quickly and answered.

"Hello."

"Mrs. Trainor. This is Lynn Witherspoon." Lena had to take a second to remember who Witherspoon was. Then she worried that there was bad news.

"Yes?"

"We are interrogating the owner of the computer used to send the emails you've been getting. I don't want to get your hopes up. He may have been duped by the real kidnappers. But we're going to try to photograph him with the wig on and we'd like you and the other parents who spoke with this J.D. to have a look at the picture."

"What do you mean you're going to try?"

"Well, he has the right to refuse that."

"Oh."

"But he's been cooperative so far, so we might have a photograph for you to look at soon. Are you planning to go to the Williamses?"

"We were just talking about that. I think I am."

"Well, could you wait until we get the picture to you? We want you to view it yourself, without any of the others around."

"Okay. How long?"

"We're not sure. And Mrs. Trainor, could I ask another favor of you?"

"Yes."

"Do you think you could get the other parents to hold up the ransom payment for a while?"

"Why?"

"It's a strategic thing. If we have indeed found J.D. and you make the payment but it goes to someone else, we may never catch that someone. But if you haven't made the payment and we can get this J.D. to talk, we can get the whole ring."

Lena had the same reaction to Witherspoon's grating voice she had had the day before. That, combined with her vagueness and her reasoning dotted with too many "ifs," made Lena balk.

"I think the group's mind is made up. I know mine is."

"I see. Okay. Well, we'll let you know if we get a picture. We'll email it to you. Bye."

When she hung up, Lena found David in the kitchen. He had heard the conversation. "Do you think you'll be able to identify him? Do you remember what he looked like?"

Lena couldn't answer those questions. Or rather she didn't want to answer them. She wanted to see the photograph. She felt certain she would know immediately. It wouldn't be a reasoned assessment. It would be emotional. The sight of J.D. she was sure would make her skin crawl. Then she would know.

Phil Rostenkowski took the call from Witherspoon. He had a splitting headache and could barely concentrate on what Witherspoon was telling him. He said that he and Janet would look at any photograph, but he was sure he wouldn't be able to identify J.D.

"Why is that, Mr. Rostenkowski?"

"We've talked about it. We just don't remember that much. We were more concerned with our daughter. Janet didn't even remember that he had curly hair. It was all a blur."

Witherspoon then asked about delaying the ransom, and Phil was emphatic about the payment going through as soon as possible. They hung up and Phil massaged his temples hard, hoping the vigorous rubbing would mask the pain. Janet had taken another pill to calm her and was lying down. Phil thought about doing the same, but he worried his thinking would be dulled by the drug. He needed to be on his toes, sharp.

He went into the bedroom. Janet was awake and opened her eyes when he came in the room.

"Who was that?" she asked.

"Witherspoon."

"What?"

They both heard Paul cough in the hallway and turned to see him coming to the bedroom.

"Who was that, Dad?" he asked.

"I was just telling Mom. The assistant federal prosecutor, Witherspoon." He turned back to Janet. "They have a suspect they're interrogating."

"Who?" Janet sat up, alert now.

"She didn't give a name. Just someone they were interrogating. That was her word, interrogating. They're going to try to take a picture of him with the wig on and send it to us."

"We can't identify him."

"I told her that. But she's going to send it anyway."

"Well, that's good news, isn't it?" Paul asked. Phil and Janet both nodded yes, though neither seemed excited. Phil put his fingers to his temples again. The headache was really killing him.

Sheila Walker was hesitant about her ability to match a photo to the J.D. who had taken her son away.

"I had a lot on my mind then—Franklin, a meeting I was about to attend. He seemed nice enough. That was all I was worried about.

Franklin needs understanding adults around him. The young man seemed understanding."

Witherspoon didn't even ask her about delaying the ransom. She already had two families fully behind the payment, and she knew the Walkers were adamant as well.

After Sheila hung up, she found John in the kitchen and gave him the substance of the call. They were about to discuss it when another call came in, this one from Marshall Rogovin, the Citibank IT head. He said he was calling John to give him a report on their investigation before they turned the results over to the FBI.

"Sorry I don't have better news for you, John. Our analysis seems to indicate that the IP address that sent the emails was pirated."

John knew what that meant but needed to be sure.

"Someone just wormed their way into the computer and used it to host their emails," he said. "So this computer they've got doesn't have anything to do with it?"

"Probably not. Probably picked a name out of the hat, somebody who didn't have much security. I'm sure the FBI will figure this out, if they haven't already."

"Okay. Thanks, Marshall. Have you got a name at the FBI you can forward this to?"

"Yeah. Will do. There's one other thing."

"What's that?"

"There was regular traffic through a third-party computer to an IP address in your parents' group."

"To all of us, right? The emails?"

"No, before that. To one. The Rostenkowskis. Maybe three or four dating back to May."

"What does that mean? They're involved?"

"No. This looks like the bad guys were testing the apparatus, trying to see if they could work the circuit. What it really means is that this is no fly-by-night operation. They had the scheme pretty well worked out."

"Oh. Sorry to hear that."

"And, John."

"Yes."

"We're going to stay on top of this now. We're considering it a bank matter, not just a personal one for you."

"How do you mean?"

"You know, it's my job to be paranoid. With this sophistication we have to assume that these kidnappers are not just a couple of beer drinkers sitting around planning to get a quick mil. And we also have to assume that making one of the victims the head of a global banking department in one of the world's largest banks was not random. We don't know what they might be getting into, but we've got to be very careful."

John didn't like Rogovin's tone. "What are you saying, Marshall?"

"I'm saying that to you this is a kidnapping. But we have to look at it from another angle. We have to assume it might be something different. We have to suspect it might be a ruse."

John didn't want to ask any other questions. He was beginning to see where he stood. It wasn't as if he couldn't be trusted. But for their own safety the bank would have to keep John at arm's length, distance themselves from one of their executives. That their executive might be missing a son was a tragedy. But the bank had responsibilities far beyond an executive and his son. They had depositors, investors, shareholders, and a board. And if someone was attacking them through some feint with an executive, well, that executive would have to be watched first and cut loose second. After a terse goodbye, John hung up. Again he had the same thought, Why didn't I think of this before?

# Twenty-six

The wig surprised Chase. He had been sitting with Toomey and Allen for fifteen or twenty minutes and had been doing what he thought was superb work, balancing innocence and naïveté with heart-felt, genuine talk about his kids. When they went into the guts of his computer and found that it had been "pirated," he knew this mix he was showing them would make sense. He wasn't some techie who should have figured out that criminal activity was being orchestrated from his computer.

But when Toomey left for a few minutes and returned with the wig in his hand, Chase slipped out of character for a moment, as if he had been in the middle of a performance and someone in the audience had sneezed loudly. He had dumped the wig right where his father had told him to. How had they found it? He managed to right himself quickly, but he didn't like the looks of this new development at all.

"Where were we?" he asked Allen.

"Computers at work."

"Oh, right. I don't have to use them. Like I said. The supervisors in my department use them to keep track of linen, to see if the outside suppliers are honest, that sort of thing. But I'm just a manual laborer, sort of, so I don't have to use the computer. I know mine at home. I can get around that one. But other than that, I'm kinda lost."

Toomey sat and put the wig on the table. Chase knew he had to say something about it. "Does that have anything to do with me?"

"It might," Toomey said, keeping his eyes on Chase. "You tell me."

"I thought it was a pelt when you brought it in. I was tryin' to figure what animal you got it from. You guys hunters?"

Toomey and Allen both shook their heads no.

"We'd like to take a picture of you with this on, if it's all right." Toomey said.

Chase gave out a little laugh. "You want me to wear this?"

"Yes."

"What does this have to do with a computer?"

"We're not sure. Maybe nothing. It's just sort of an experiment."

Chase realized the tone had changed. It was time for him to get serious. "Well, I don't know about that. This isn't like the questions you said you were going to ask. I don't want to get involved in something here."

"Involved in something?" Allen asked.

"Don't get me wrong. I'm not accusing you. But I've been reading a lot about these false convictions, how they convict some guy of a murder or something and then they test the DNA years later and find the guy's innocent. And it all goes back to something funny the cops did, or the prosecutor. And a picture . . . I don't know."

"You think we'd do something funny?" Toomey asked.

"Not on purpose. What are you going to do with the picture?"

"We're just going to show it to a few people."

"What people?"

"Can't really say."

Chase breathed an interior sigh of relief. He saw a way out. "Well, I'm sorry, but no. I won't do that. Not without a lawyer telling me it's okay."

"Do you have a lawyer?" Allen broke in.

"No. Never needed one, except when we closed on the house. But I don't even remember who he was."

"Well, how about we get you a yellow pages and you can find one?"

Chase laughed again. This was easier than he thought. "You don't expect me to get a lawyer out of the yellow pages, do you?"

"How do you plan to do it?"

"Let me call my wife. Her side of the family knows stuff like this."

Toomey and Allen stared at him, knowing they'd been bested. Chase could see the same and congratulated himself. He decided to take his victory one step further.

"You know what? I haven't got money for a lawyer. I can just refuse to put on this wig by myself, can't I?"

The two agents nodded a resigned yes. Chase fought off a smirk.

"Then that's what I want to do."

The grandfather clock said it was 12:04. Lena called to David, who was in the kitchen.

"Do we get a confirmation that the wire transfer went through?"

"I don't know. I'm sure the banker's on that one."

Lena fidgeted, wondering what she could do now, thinking the wig picture should be coming through sometime soon. Then she remembered she had said she would call the office periodically while on vacation. She dialed and got the receptionist, Mayra Sanchez, a very efficient young Dominican woman, who jumped when she realized it was Lena on the phone.

"Oh, Dr. Trainor. I'm so sorry to hear about Sarah. My God."

"Thank you, Mayra."

"Is there . . . is there . . . ?"

"News? No, not really. Just what you read."

"Is there anything we can do? We all came in this morning and we were, like, in shock."

"I know. No, there's nothing you can do."

"I'm praying, I can tell you that. My whole family too."

"Thank you."

"Did you want to speak to one of the other doctors?"

Lena didn't know what she wanted to do. Make a connection,

she guessed. Maybe this little moment with Mayra was enough. "No. Would you please just tell everybody that I thank them for their emails and that they can call me if there's an emergency? I'm okay for that."

"Sure." There wasn't much more to say, but Lena sensed Mayra didn't want to hang up. "Dr. Trainor?"

"Yes."

"I saw the drawing they had, you know, on TV and in the *Post*, the one of the guy who . . . who picked up Sarah."

"Yes."

"Well, there's this orderly who works in the surgical ICU. It looks just like him. Do you know who I'm talking about?"

"No. But you know the man in the drawing was wearing a wig. We don't know what he looks like without the wig."

"Oh. He was? A wig? I didn't know. Sorry."

"That's okay. Tell everybody I'll be in touch soon. Thanks. Bye."

The composite. Lena had forgotten about that. That had come sometime on Saturday. Detective Martin had given details to an artist, the artist had passed sketches around to the four parents by email, all had made their corrections, and he then sent the final drawing around. Lena thought about it the way she thought about all such drawings she'd ever seen: it was too generic, too masklike, and there just weren't enough distinguishing characteristics for someone to make an identification with a real human being. She had the thought on first seeing the final version that Sarah, who had good drawing skills, could have done a better job.

Lena went to the computer to look up the composite and to see if Witherspoon had sent the wig picture. The composite looked as vague as it had when she first saw it, and she clicked off quickly, not wanting to mess up her mental image of J.D. There was no email from Witherspoon. She sat staring at the screen, resisting the urge to poke around in the muck David said waited there.

But then she felt protective of Sarah; not seeing what was going on was letting the cyber world have its way with her daughter's plight. She Googled Sarah's name and was taken aback by the number of citations that came up instantly. She stared at these for a long time, feeling the way she did about Sarah's report cards. All these words, like the letter grades, weren't her Sarah, couldn't begin to sum up the complex, wonderful human being Lena loved. She scrolled down a couple of pages and the effect deepened. How dare all these people presume to have something to say about Sarah?

The search result pointing to Sarah's Facebook page had her picture along with it. The tiny image made Sarah look vulnerable despite her shining smile. Without thinking, Lena clicked on the citation and went to the site. She navigated to Sarah's page and was relieved to see that it hadn't been defaced. Lena teared up when she saw that she and David were Sarah's first two listed friends. The "friend's comments" section was, Lena could tell, filled to overflowing with reactions to the kidnapping by people Sarah actually knew and thousands she had no connection with whatsoever outside her notoriety. Lena didn't bother scrolling down the page. She just stared at it, trying to feel some enhanced connection to her daughter, but it didn't work. Sarah wasn't to be found among the pixels. Lena noticed that Sarah had last logged on on July 12. Lena remembered Sarah hunched over her computer just before she left, figuring that was the login referred to. The pain of that image of Sarah was too much. Lena shut down the computer.

David took the call from Witherspoon and hung up before Lena could even get on the extension.

"The goddamn suspect refuses to have his picture taken with the wig, and his computer was hijacked by the kidnappers."

"So, dead end?" Lena asked, turning from the sink with a glass of water.

"Right. They're letting him go. I'm glad we didn't wait a few more days to send the ransom."

Lena agreed and took a sip of her water. The talk of days made her shift her gaze to the tear-away calendar on the wall by the phone. Neither she nor David had bothered to tear off the pages during the crisis and it still read "Saturday, July 10." Lena went to the calendar now and tore off Saturday's and Sunday's pages, crumpling them forcefully and throwing them in the garbage.

David saw her do this and went to her.

"The ransom's going to bring her home, honey."

"When?" Lena shot back, as if David was withholding the date. She turned from him and stared at the wall, the calendar's big, black 12 almost pulsing in her vision. David reached for her, but she pulled away.

"No, David." She moved out of the kitchen and went into the bedroom. She didn't really want to be there either, but there was no place to go. She thought about turning the computer on, but there was nothing to look for now, no email from Witherspoon. She looked at the bedside clock. It was 12:24. In a half hour or so she could go to the Williamses and be calmed, she hoped, by Mike's presence. Together they would wait to hear. Three o'clock. She was hanging on that time. She feared that if they didn't hear from the kidnappers, she'd never be able to make it through another day.

The calendar came to her again and she realized the next day would be the thirteenth. She had no superstitions about the number but she now hated the thought of that day if it were to be one without Sarah. She looked over at the computer again. Again she replayed Sarah at her computer just before she left. Suddenly she was filled with a strange sensation, one she normally felt in her work when the ragged pieces of symptoms became the certainty of a diagnosis. What was causing this feeling? What was going on? There was something in the computer that was setting this off. What was it? She turned. David was coming down the hall. He would interrupt the attempt to discover what was going on. She had to hurry. What was it?

The date! Today was the twelfth, she mumbled to herself. What was . . . ? And then the little line on Sarah's Facebook page popped up in front of her. Last log-in July 12. Sarah had logged in today!

"Honey," David started, but Lena tore away from him and charged over to the computer. With David behind her asking questions, she got the poky machine booted and went to Sarah's page.

"She logged on today," she practically shouted, pointing to the line on the page. David was playing catch-up but got it quickly.

"Wait a minute, Lena. That might not be her. I'm sure they can hack those pages without any problem."

"Well, we should call Martin, do something, right?"

"The FBI monitors this, I think. They should know."

"Call them."

David hestitated, staring at the screen. Then he went and picked up the phone. Lena scanned the page as if it would come alive, as if Sarah would pop out from behind her picture and say, "Hi, Mom." That feeling grew and Lena remembered that when Sarah first set up the page, she and Lena communicated a couple of times through the friends' network. Lena tried to log on to the site but she had forgotten her password. What the fuck was it? Why did they have these goddamn passwords . . . Finally a combination worked and she was on her own bare page. She had an email. From Sarah!

"David!"

He had reached Domingo and was talking. He turned. Lena clicked on the email and it popped up.

*Mom,*

*A man took us to the woods not camp. The man is dead. His name is Mr. Ivrit. we saw a bear. I don't know where we are in the woods. we went past Albania. I help you can come and get us. I want to come home.*

*Sarah*

"Jesus, David," Lena said, turning to him. "It's an email from Sarah. Tell him I got an email—"

David held up his hand, listening. Then he spoke to Lena. "He knows. They saw it about an hour ago."

"What?"

Lena looked back at the email. It had been sent at 9:46 that morning.

"He says they're checking its authenticity." David was pacing behind Lena now. "Janet got one from Linda too."

Lena barely heard this. She hit the reply button and started to write a response. David, still on the phone, waved at Lena to get her attention.

"They don't want you to reply right away."

"What? Why?" Lena kept typing.

"They can't get a fix on the computer it came from. It might be a hoax."

"So?"

David was becoming the middleman in a conversation now. He listened, then relayed.

"Or the kidnappers are up to something. They want us to wait."

"That's Sarah. I'm sure that's Sarah."

"She said she's sure that's Sarah," David said into the phone. He listened, then spoke to Lena. "They said give them a couple of hours."

Lena shook her head no. She finished her reply and read it.

*Sarah,*

*We're so glad to hear from you. You need to tell us more about where you are. We'll come and get you. Are you okay? Are there other kids with you?*

*Love,*

*Mom*

David hung up and put a hand on her hand guiding the mouse.

"Lena. We could be doing damage here."

"It's Sarah, David. Read it. Can't you see?"

"How would she get a computer, get to use one?"

"The guy is dead. Maybe—"

"Lena, come on. Does that sound right to you? You're letting your emotions rule here. That's made up."

"So what?"

"Well, whoever did this is going to, I don't know, spread it around, get a big laugh at our expense."

Lena looked up at David. "Who gives a shit?" She shook off David's hand and hit send.

# Twenty-seven

The FBI drove Chase back to the hospital and dropped him at the emergency entrance. He called Helene and told her the interrogation was a big mistake, that someone had pirated their computer. She didn't seem all that worried and had to cut off the call to deal with a kid problem.

For a fleeting moment Chase imagined blowing off work, hopping in his car, heading back to Westchester, standing again in front of the Trainors' house, blending in, catching the show that he had, in part, created. He had, after all, aced his test with the FBI and there was no reason he shouldn't enjoy the fruits of that little victory. But as he was thinking this, a nondescript black Ford, with two men in the front seat, turned into the U-shaped driveway in front of the emergency entrance, cruised past, and went back out on the street. Chase came out of his triumph reverie long enough to imagine that the FBI might not have been beaten completely, might in fact have the nuts to follow him, and so he went in to work.

His performance in front of his supervisor and fellow workers was, he thought, quite good. "Once they found out my computer was hijacked by someone else, they were all, you know, 'Sorry, pal' and shit and bought me lunch," he told them. He could have gotten the rest of the day off but he decided to hang around, do some thinking. Helene was not going to be the toughest audience yet he still needed some time to prepare.

Chase caught a little bit of a television news broadcast later when he passed a patient's room. He heard something about an email from the kids but he figured that was just rumor, news guys trying to fill up their hours. On a smoke break he tried his father's number again, eager to tell him about how well he'd done. He didn't leave a message with the voicemail. He wondered where his father was. In their planning, Chase's father had adopted some CIA tactics he'd read about for their mission. One of those was for Chase not to know the location of the "sequestering."

"That way you can't make a slip and tell somebody where I am."

"I'm not going to make a slip, Dad. Trust me."

Chase's father had fixed him with a condescending, eyebrow-raised look. "We gotta go beyond trust, Chase. This here thing's like a precision engine. Any part comes a little unglued, the whole thing breaks down. I can't trust you're not going to make a slip. I gotta know you *can't* make a slip. Got me?"

Chase finished his smoke and felt his mood changing. What was it? He was thinking about the little girl, the first one he had picked up. She seemed like the confident, athletic type. He hoped his Jennifer would be like that when she grew up. His feelings were getting all mashed up now. Maybe he wasn't so crazy about being in the middle of the operation. He wanted those kids home, soon. When that happened, he'd go over to Westchester then, see the kids dropped off. That would really finish things. That would bring it all to an end.

He headed back into the hospital in deep thought. The automatic door sliding back with a hiss startled him. He stopped, realized what the sound and the movement were, told himself he had to be more aware of what was going on around him, and went back inside.

Word of the Facebook emails spread on the Web and then was picked up by the major media. Within an hour of Lena's opening Sarah's letter, the number of news vans outside the house had grown exponentially.

"You can't blame them" was David's sober assessment as he watched the frenzy out the front window. He didn't go into details, didn't say what was on his mind, that the picture of kidnapped kids in the woods, with a dead kidnapper and bears in the area, was high drama. But Lena knew what he was talking about.

Lena had been glued to the computer since she had sent her reply email. If they had been able to get one email out, they should be able to respond quickly, she kept saying to herself. But as the minutes, then an hour went by with no response, that hope turned into a sour fear. The details were too specific and led to dark, frightening images.

Detective Martin showed up at the door, and Lena could tell almost immediately that he had been sent by the FBI to keep an eye on her. But he had information, and he still had his comforting blue eyes. That was better than staring at her blank Facebook page.

"Here's what I know," he started, as Lena handed him a cup of coffee. "The Rostenkowski girl's email had the same information Sarah's did. So there's that. But it doesn't mean much." He pulled a notebook out of his jacket pocket and referred to it as they all sat at the kitchen table. "They got a bead on the computer both of them came from, something called an IP address, and it turns out it was a computer that was stolen about three months ago."

"Figures," David said.

"Doesn't it? This computer shit. Anyway, the FBI says the emails might help them with that suspect they had. There's a name similarity. That's all I can tell you, and you of course can't tell anyone else this, but they're bringin' the suspect back in for questioning."

"But where's Sarah?" Lena asked, knowing this was a stupid question.

Martin looked at her with compassion unusual for a man of his profession, as if he ached to be able to answer her question. "They've got an area," he began, and looked down at his notebook again. "They're assuming the 'Albania' in the email is Albany. So they're north of Albany. And there's a time and date stamp on the video the kidnappers sent, so they can sort of tell how far north they got. And there's the talk of . . . of bears. So, they figure the kids are in the Adirondacks. They've got an arc of about a hundred, a hundred and thirty miles they're looking at."

"In the Adirondacks," David said flatly, imagining the wilderness of that territory.

"In the Adirondacks," Martin repeated.

"So have they started to search there?" Lena's eyes blazed. David and Martin could see she was all coiled impatience, itching to race to Sarah.

"It's a big area, Lena," David said.

"I know that. Have they started searching?"

Martin shook his head. "I think they're getting things organized for tomorrow. I'm not sure about that."

Lena struggled to contain her anger. "The FBI didn't tell us we had an email and now they're dragging their feet on a search?"

"They're hoping to get something specific from this suspect," Martin said, knowing that wasn't going to be enough for Lena.

"Be reasonable on this, hon," David added. But that was fuel to the fire.

Lena rose quickly and went into the living room. The two men looked at each other, not knowing exactly what to do. Then they heard the front door open and slam shut.

Lena caught the reporters and cameramen completely off guard. When they saw her charge out of the house, pass her car, and head toward them, they scrambled to meet her, to set up cameras, to get microphones and recorders working. She stopped at the end of the driveway, fuming. David and Martin came quickly out of the house, run-walking to catch up. The reporters got their bearings and their shouted questions broke the neighborhood calm. Lena waved them off and waited until one of the reporters got the others to shut up. When she began, her voice was almost a growl.

"I'm not pleading for anything. I want our kids back. If you have anything to do with this horrible act, you stop it now and get our kids home. If you have any information, call the FBI. And to you, here, with your cameras and your microphones, make yourselves useful. Stop hanging out here and go look for my daughter!"

Only the most brash and obtuse reporters followed this with shouted questions as David turned Lena around and the two went back into the house. Martin stayed and tried, unsuccessfully, to get the media to not use the material they'd just gathered. Some seemed chastised, however, and a little later, up and down the street, one could hear reporters begin their stand-ups with sober variations on "A victim's mother scolded the press today as she . . ."

Back in the house Lena went to the computer but found only a brief email from Witherspoon's assistant to all the families asking them for patience. To Lena that was like asking her to age backward. She couldn't have summoned up an ounce of patience if her life depended on it. Sarah's email had put the anxiety of the past few days into a focused, vectored quest, and Lena felt the revving motor of that quest every second now.

Agents Toomey and Allen were waiting for Chase at his house when he arrived. Chase was able to demonstrate his family-man attributes in front of the agents, telling Helene everything would be all right, hoisting the kids. But he hadn't been able to get to the TV to see if there was some news. The agents wouldn't say why they were returning him for questioning.

They were silent on the trip down and deposited Chase in a small back room in the crowded regional headquarters. They left Chase to himself, and after a few minutes Witherspoon arrived, introduced herself, and sat down. She said that she was now investigating Chase's possible participation in a criminal act but that Chase was not under arrest. She asked if Chase wanted a lawyer.

Chase's first impulse was to say yes and delay the whole thing. But he liked the fact that this chesty woman was sitting across from him and he wanted to impress her, wanted to unleash one of his performances for her benefit. She held his gaze like a schoolteacher asking about homework. He'd always been good in those situations. He said he didn't want a lawyer.

His resolve held up even when Witherspoon brought in an assistant, a court reporter, and a tape recorder. These were just for show, Chase thought. He prepared himself for his upcoming role as Witherspoon rattled off some identifying information for the tape recorder. He would be once again innocent, surprised, naïve, maybe even shocked. But with

Witherspoon's first question after the preliminaries, he didn't need to feign either surprise or shock.

"May I call you Chase? Okay. Chase, is your father's name James Everett Collins?"

My father? What do you need to know about him for? I'm on stage, not him.

"Yes."

"And can you tell me the whereabouts of your father right now?"

For Witherspoon's part she could have stopped right there. Chase's face not only said that he, Chase, did know where his father was, but also answered the larger question of his involvement in the kidnapping. Witherspoon knew she was talking to J.D.

Chase held the surprised look, got a mental image of his father, and then recovered.

"Has something happened to him?"

"Perhaps. Do you know where he is now?"

"It's, what, Monday? He's probably at home. He's semi-retired, only works a couple of days a week."

"We tried his home. He's not there. When did you speak to him last?"

"I don't know. But if something's happened to him, I think you should tell me. Like, because—"

"Have you spoken to him since Saturday?"

"Uh, Saturday. No, I don't think so."

"You have not spoken to him today?"

"No."

Witherspoon had debated with herself and her staff about whether to go for the jugular early in the interview, but when she saw the initial look on the Chase's face, she didn't need to make a decision.

"We have reason to believe your father has died," she said.

Chase didn't respond for a while. This was either an exceedingly cruel tactic or the truth. Chase didn't want to think about the latter. That couldn't be. But, of course, he really hadn't talked to his father since Sunday and . . . "What makes you think that?"

"We have a communication from someone we believe was with him when he died."

"Who?"

"A child who was kidnapped two days ago."

This dovetailed too neatly with his Dad's cell phone silence. Chase couldn't hold his performance.

"I don't understand."

"I think you do. Did you once have the nickname 'J.D.' because of your fondness for Jack Daniels?"

"I don't drink like that anymore." Chase couldn't think. Dad dead?

"But that was your nickname."

"I don't know. People call me a lot of things. What does this have to do with my dad?"

"Maybe you can tell me."

"I can't tell you anything. I haven't spoken to my Dad since, I don't know, what did I say, Saturday?"

"You can't remember what you said?"

"I can't think of anything! You're telling me my Dad's dead! What do you expect!" The veins in Chase's neck were roped, his face red.

"I expect you to tell us how you and your father kidnapped four kids on their way to Camp Arno and where they are now," Witherspoon shot back, not matching Chase's high-volume pitch.

"Are you kidding?"

"Absolutely not."

Chase was breathing hard now, his thoughts going all rubbery, not holding up to the searing image of his father somewhere dead. He looked from Witherspoon to her stone-faced assistant, then to the pretty young court reporter with her fingers poised on the keys of her machine. He looked back at Witherspoon.

"Stop this. I want a lawyer."

# Twenty-eight

Lena was strung so tightly waiting for a return email from Sarah, she thought she might miscarry. She talked to herself, she jabbered to David, just to keep the tension at bay. Mike Williams's voice on the phone was a welcome antidote to her own wired nattering.

"Hi, Lena. It's Mike Williams. Just wanted to touch base."

"Hi. Thanks. This is, has been horrible."

"I can imagine. Po was sayin' she didn't know whether it would have been better or worse to get an email from Tommy."

"I don't know either. She seemed so close when I opened the email. But now, it's like she's drifted off."

Mike waited a few seconds to reply. "I hope this isn't offensive to you, but we were talking and we were saying, you know, Tommy can have quite an imagination sometimes. And when kids are out in the woods . . ." Lena wasn't put off. She hadn't thought of that.

"You mean they might . . . Sarah and Linda might have thought they saw a bear?"

"Or that this Mr. whatever his fucking name is isn't really dead.

Maybe he was asleep for a long time, the kids stole his laptop, and he woke up."

Lena didn't know which would be worse, the kids with a dead body in the middle of nowhere or with a live body and no way to email again. "I don't think Sarah would mistake sleep for death. She's not one of those imaginative kids. I'm afraid she's sort of a scientist, her mother's daughter."

"Not a bad thing at all," Mike said. Lena thought in another context that might be construed as some sort of flirting.

"But I keep thinking I wasn't scientific enough," Lena responded.

"How's that?"

"There were clues, I suppose. I'm trained to examine every bit of evidence, like shouldn't I have seen that he was wearing a wig?"

"He wasn't coming to you for a diagnosis, Lena. I've thought some of the same things. I'm not exactly trained, but I've had years of experience sifting the phonies from the genuines, the ones who can get the job done from the ones who are going to give you cost-overrun headaches out the wazoo. Hell, I hardly looked at the guy. I was so proud of my little bugger hopping up into that van, taking off by himself, I didn't have eyes for no one else."

Lena teared up at this. She'd always had a weakness for men who were so obviously in love with their children that they gave them little nicknames. Her dad had always called Sylvie "Runaround Sue" for her early hyperactivity. And he called Sarah "Sarahbell." David had called Sarah "Toodle" when she was little, but she couldn't remember him saying it recently.

"Lena," Mike said after a silence. "You okay?"

"Yeah. Yes. Thank you."

"Feel free to call, or come over. This goddamn fishbowl they got us in can get pretty upsetting."

"I know. I can't leave the computer."

"We can hook you up here. My boy Jack's a whiz with that stuff."

They hung up after a few more thank-yous and Lena stood in the kitchen staring out at the back yard.

"Who was that?" David had come in the kitchen.

"Mike Williams."

"News?"

"He wondered if the kids could have been imagining things," Lena said, pouring herself a cup of lukewarm coffee and taking it to the microwave.

"Who?"

"Mike."

"Oh. Making things up, you mean?"

"Yeah, sort of. Maybe they just thought they saw a bear and maybe this Mr. Ivrit was just asleep."

"I don't think Sarah would confuse sleep with death. Maybe some of the other kids but—"

"That's what I said. I think he was just trying to be helpful."

Whether it was the mention of Mike's concern, or something else, David had an urge to go to Lena and give her a hug. But she was standing there at the counter, arms folded in front of her, blowing on her coffee cup. He could imagine her rebuffing his attempt, something he didn't want to have to go through. Except for that one embrace, she had been in her own world in all this and for the time being David couldn't imagine some return to their old ways.

"He say anything about a blogger?"

"A blogger? No, what?"

"There's a blogger who calls himself NutsandBolts. The blog's a home improvement kind of thing but he says he knows Williams and he knows they have a big life insurance policy on their kids."

Lena scowled at this, upset with David. Mike's soothing voice was still in her ear.

"And the implication is he set up this kidnapping, he's going to have his kid killed for the life insurance? Jesus, David. That's loony."

"Well, I don't know. The guy says the economy has put a huge hole in Williams's business, and think about it, how'd his guys find that van so fast?"

"Old news. Didn't Martin tell you to stay away from that stuff?"

"You're being like a doctor who ignores a patient just because the patient got some information off the internet."

Lena didn't want to think about that. She wanted to think about why David was pulling the rug out from under her feet, casting aspersions on the man who'd been most helpful to her in the past three days.

"I bet there are blogs that say we have a witches' coven in the house and have the kids tied up down in the basement."

"It's not as crazy as it sounds."

"What? Us with a witches' coven?"

"No, Williams needing cash. He and his wife are awfully calm about this whole thing. And all their supposed togetherness. They don't seem broken up."

Lena heard this not as criticism but as jealousy. She put a hand on David's arm and looked into his eyes. She didn't need to say anything. Their old way of communicating kicked in, the shortcut that said, "Listen to what you're saying." But David didn't want to let it go.

"I don't know. He wants us all to come over to his house. What, does he want to keep an eye on us or something? And why does he call you?"

Lena looked over at the phone but she couldn't get Mike's voice back. There was no almost-flirting Mike anymore. There was only a contractor with an insurance policy on his kids.

As if on cue the phone rang. It wasn't Mike but somebody from Witherspoon's office asking David to stay on the line for a conference call. David told Lena and she went in the bedroom to pick up the other line. She felt her blood beating in her temples. She could hear voices and breathing as others on the line waited. Then John Walker spoke.

"Lena, are you there?"

"Yes."

"Thank you for saying what you said to the press. I'm a little constricted by my bank as to what I can say, but I sure felt what you expressed."

There were other voices saying the same thing, then Witherspoon came on the line and asked if everybody was there. They took a roll call and she started.

"I'm going to be talking to the press in a few minutes but I wanted to brief you all first. There's been a development." Lena could hear the anxious breaths on the other lines. "We are booking a suspect who we believe is J.D." She took a moment to let this sink in. "It's the same man, Chase Collins, who refused to be photographed with the wig on. His father's middle name is Everett, very close to the name in the girls' emails. His response to certain questions leads us to believe it was his father the girls were referring to."

Overlapping questions went flying through the lines, and Lena lost a lot of them. So did Witherspoon.

"Can you save those questions? I don't know much more. Perhaps we can meet tonight. We are not going to be able to question the suspect again until he has secured a lawyer. That might take hours."

"I'll question him," Mike growled.

"I understand your feelings. Let me add one thing here that I won't be saying to the press. There is a possibility Collins will not make a statement one way or another. That is his right. There is also the possibility, slight but you should be aware of it, that he himself does not know where the kids are being kept."

Lena could hear breaths drawn in at this.

"How could that be?" Janet blurted out, obviously distressed.

"We are seeing that this is a pretty sophisticated operation. Collins's only job might have been to pick up the kids and hand them off to his father, who took them to some unknown place. That would be something I might do if I were setting this up. He can then genuinely answer our question 'Where are the kids?' by saying, 'I don't know.' Sorry to leave you with this but I've got to go." Witherspoon made a quick exit.

There was silence for a while, then David surprised Lena with a declaration to all still on the line. "If we don't know anymore in the morning, I'm going to join a search party up there."

There was some support for this, then Po spoke softly.

"Lena, Janet, are you sure your return emails made it through to the girls' mailbox?"

Lena was floored. Something so simple and she hadn't even checked to see if the email had gone through. She hadn't requested one of the "read mail" things. What if she had been waiting all this time and the email to Sarah was just sitting in some cyber dead-letter office. John spoke up and helped calm Lena's fears.

"The FBI is monitoring the whole thing. I'm sure they'll know that it got to the right address."

None of them wanted to hang up, but eventually there was nothing more to say. Po this time invited them all to her house if they wanted to come, saying they could monitor emails from there. Lena was suddenly too exhausted to think about bucking the press and going anywhere. They all hung up after saying a round of goodbyes.

Lena and David met in the living room, where he was pacing, agitated.

"Did you mean that?" Lena asked.

"About going up there? Yes, I did. Another day sitting around waiting for them to get this asshole to talk would drive me nuts." He then went through a checklist, out loud, that included getting in touch with a friend from work who was a deer hunter and was always talking about the Adirondacks, calling his brother to see if he had advice, "provisioning," and deciding which car to take.

Lena looked at him as he paced. He had grown up in a hardscrabble section of Oklahoma and had spent some time in his youth outdoors. He had taken Sarah camping once, a sort of folly of a trip that was marred by poor equipment and torrential rains. But the comfortable, urban, Ivy League skin he had grown at Cornell had stayed with him over the years. Lena couldn't imagine him following trails in the dense wilderness of the Adirondacks. He needed to do something, however. She understood that. And she sort of envied him his freedom to leave the house, to light out in search of his daughter. But Lena couldn't imagine doing so. As irrational as it was, she felt she had to be home if and when Sarah came through the door. She would have to fold her into her arms and let her cry until she could cry no more. And she would have to be strong and prepare for the aftermath, for the months and years in which the slime and nettles of these past few days could be cleansed from her skin and her soul forever.

# Twenty-nine

Late in the afternoon the bright sunshine in the clearing was dulled by a layer of quickly thickening steel gray clouds. Franklin said that they should take the laptop back to the pond before it rained and see if there had been any response from the parents. No one wanted to leave the safety of the shack and the clearing, but they couldn't get a signal there and they knew they had to go back to that horrible place.

This time the crows flapped up vigorously when the kids arrived. Tommy looked around quickly, guessing that if they hadn't flown away when the kids arrived the first time, maybe there was something else, like a bear, that scared the crows away now. But he didn't see anything unusual.

It was easier to see the laptop screen in the cloudy light, but what they saw was dispiriting. The battery indicator was blinking now, a sign that the battery was dangerously low. Sarah worked as fast as she could and cried out when she got to her page and saw a letter from her mother. She began to tear up when she read it, but Franklin kept her on task. With time ticking they were all thinking of what to say, what they could remember. Finally they got this message out:

*Mom,*

*Weer in a shack. Weer near a pond. There are crows. We drove in a grey car and then walked up heer. Help us.*

They all agreed this was all they knew. Franklin said that wasn't the way you spelled *we're* but he didn't think they should take time to change it. Sarah was about to send it when Tommy had a thought.

"I dropped those socks. Should we put that in?"

Nobody knew, but the battery light was blinking faster now. Franklin made the decision.

"We have to send it now."

Sarah took a few seconds to get the track ball cursor to the send sign and clicked. They all watched the indicator spin, saying "sending." But before it stopped, the screen winked out and went blank.

"Do you think it made it?" Linda asked.

No one answered. They stared at the black screen as if a genie would somehow pop out and answer their questions. Practically all their lives they had been dependent on one sort of genie or another popping out of one sort of screen or another. Now nothing.

A low rumble of thunder to the west made them all turn their heads. The sky had darkened considerably and the gray clouds now looked charred and were building. Sarah tried to turn on the computer one more time, but it was dead. Franklin had an idea.

"Maybe he had a backup battery with him." They all knew what he was talking about. They had searched every nook and cranny of the shack, of Mr. Everett's backpack, even the now almost empty cooler for a battery pack, but they had found none. All looked back out at the corpse still sprawled on the dock.

"I don't think so," Linda said, her thought more revulsion than reason.

"We should at least look," Franklin said. Another growl from the clouds in the west put an exclamation point on this. "Before it rains."

"Where would it be?" Tommy asked. "His front pockets or back?"

Sarah looked at the laptop and the size of the battery. "Have to be his back."

"Good," Tommy said. "Because we can't turn him over."

Without hesitating Tommy walked toward the dock as the others hung back. He whispered what he knew of the rosary to himself. As he made his first steps onto the boards, he willed himself to look only at the back pockets of Mr. Everett's jeans. The closer he got, the more he had to restrict his vision. When he got close enough to see the back pockets clearly, he stopped. He turned and saw the others not yet on the dock. It didn't matter. He turned back and felt a little dizzy, as if he might fall into the water. He let this pass and then moved ahead. There was a bulge in both the left and the right back pocket. Tommy remembered how his father's wallet looked in his jeans, how there were worn white lines from the wallet always being in the same place. Mr. Everett's right back pocket had those same lines, so Tommy figured he only needed to pull out whatever was in the left pocket.

As he came close to the body, still zeroing in on the pockets, flies lifted up and buzzed around Mr. Everett. That stopped Tommy for a second, as did the bad smell, but he was determined now and he dove toward the left back pocket. When he got his fingers under the cloth, he felt something hard and rectangular and plastic. A battery! He squeezed his fingers around the object and yanked. Something that looked like a battery came halfway out of the pocket, but the jerking movement had thrown Tommy a little off balance. To right himself he stepped forward and his head went down. Mr. Everett's mangled, bloody, pecked face loomed in his vision as he did, and Tommy jumped back in horror.

Standing there panting, he could see the half-exposed battery. In a swift move he went for it, grabbing it clawlike and yanking so hard, Mr. Everett's stiff body rose and bounced on the planks. Battery in hand, Tommy turned and raced off the dock, into the group of three saucer-eyed kids. They moved back as he approached, as if he were tainted by his contact with Mr. Everett. But when he held out the recovered object, they moved closer for a look.

"It's not the right size," Sarah said.

"It's a cell phone battery," Franklin added.

Tommy looked down at the battery. They were right. Now, instead of being an agent of their salvation, the rectangle of plastic was a useless reminder of the man who had kidnapped them. He turned and hurled the battery into the pond.

As he did, the kids noticed that the water was being freckled with raindrops. They turned and started back toward the shack. A nearby crack of thunder split the air and Linda screamed.

"I hate thunder!"

This was news to Sarah. As the kids started to trot along the path and the drops whistled into the grasses around them, she tried to remember when she and Linda had ever been in a rainstorm before. She couldn't come up with a single incident.

When they were about a hundred yards from the shack, the rain came as if dropped from a bucket. They reached the door and tumbled into the now almost dark room. They were all soaked and panting. The drumming on the roof was so hard and steady they thought the boards would give in. Already leaks were streaming thin waterfalls of rain onto the floor. When Sarah moved Mr. Everett's backpack out of the way of one of these leaks, the others followed suit and began to push things away from the water. Tommy found a little red bucket in a darkened corner and put it under the most severe leak. Then they moved into the second room. Things there weren't as bad, but they had to move a mattress away from a steady march of drops. Soon their mattresses were banked against one wall, and the kids felt they had the leaks under control.

Suddenly the room was lit by a charged blue luminesence, and the world outside—the clearing, seen through the windows—was, for an instant, strobe-lit and spectacular. Before the kids had time to react to this, a sharp, power-packed wallop of thunder broke over the shack, shaking the structure and rattling the loosely glazed windows. Now they all either screamed or jumped and in an instant found themselves huddling on the banked mattresses, rain pounding the roof, the sound of the more muscular leaks in the next room adding a bass note to the rain, and the anticipation of another bolt of lightning and clap of thunder palpable.

When it came, the lightning was in the distance, more diffuse, and it took longer for the thunder to strike their ears. When the little screeches the noise had caused died down, Tommy pronounced his verdict, remembering a phrase his father had used.

"It's passed over."

Three o'clock came and went and there was no communication from the kidnappers, no indication the wire transfer had gone through, no email from Sarah, and, Lena could see on a weather map on her computer, a vicious thunderstorm sweeping across the area the FBI thought the kids were in. David, energized by his decision, had been packing for an hour or so, calling people in the Adirondacks who were organizing search parties, getting advice from his deer hunter friend.

When Detective Martin showed up about 5:30, he seemed almost like family to Lena. He said he had news, that he'd once again been sent by the FBI, and that he was supposed to "keep you tied down, Lena, after you get the news." His was such an affable manner that Lena wasn't upset by this little joke.

"Facebook has been monitoring Sarah's account and about an hour ago their servers picked up a message intended for Lena's account that originated at the IP address Sarah sent her last message from."

"We didn't get it," Lena said, breathing a little harder now.

"Neither did the server, whatever that is."

"It's the computer that transfers the outside email to the Facebook accounts," David said, still holding a flashlight he'd just brought up from the basement. "If the server didn't get it, how do they know it was sent?"

"Got me. I really don't know the technical shit. All I know is they picked up the computer that was sending it, it was the same one the girls had sent the earlier email on, but the email itself never made it through."

"What does that mean?" Lena asked.

"That means somebody, Sarah maybe, was trying to send a message but something at her end of the line cut it off." Martin seemed uneasy relaying this information.

"Something? Like what?"

"It could be a number of things. There could have been a power failure, say a battery went out. They are on some sort of newfangled

Wi-Fi, so it could have been some atmospheric interruption. Or it could have been human error—someone hit the wrong key, something like that. In any event we know she was trying to reach you again, that she still has the capability, probably, and that when the circumstances are right, she'll be back in touch."

"There's rain up there," Lena said.

"Right," Martin said. "And on the positive side, she tried to reach us. She must have gotten your email."

The three stood where they were in the living room. Then David spoke, looking at Lena.

"Mike might have been right."

"What do you mean?"

"Maybe this Everett wasn't dead. Maybe the kids were sneaking the laptop from him. Maybe he caught them just as Sarah was sending the email and he stopped it."

Martin saw the fear this brought to Lena's eyes. "Sounds a little Hollywood to me. The FBI guys say the connection that laptop's makin' out there in the woods is damn shaky. I'd go with somethin' like that."

A slanted rain began to send little oblique darts of water down the window panes. Lena could see the press out the front window starting to cover up equipment. David and Martin were running through other possibilities, but Lena could only see the dark side of the news. The line of communication had been open and now it was closed. Sarah was somewhere in a vast, unknown wilderness. Once again the problem became too big, too open, too uncertain. Lena felt her hope draining. She wondered if Sheila, with her deep faith, was riding out this period, not suffering the way she was. She wanted to stop herself but she couldn't. For perhaps the first time in the whole ordeal she imagined fully the possibility that she would never speak to Sarah again. She slumped into a chair as thunder sounded in the distance.

What could his father possibly have died of? Chase thought over and over waiting for the lawyer to come. Chase couldn't remember the last time his father had been sick. He always ate lean red meat. He was in good shape. Even with his paunch he could still do twenty chin-ups, something Chase had never been able to do.

He figured they were lying to him about his dad. That prosecutor with the lipstick and the big breasts, she probably wasn't even a prosecutor, an actor maybe, like him. God, he shouldn't have lost his cool, asked for a lawyer. Helene was getting him a good one, she said, but he should have just kept things going, called that woman's bluff.

They brought him a sandwich to eat, but he couldn't get more than a mouthful down. He kept having these odd feelings for the kids. He saw that weird black kid alone somehow and wondered how the hell he'd survive. He suspected his dad had taken the kids to the woods somewhere, and if he really was dead, or maybe hurt or something, how was that black kid going to make it? And the second girl he picked up. She was a whiner. She probably drove his Dad crazy. She—

Why was he thinking about the kids? He had to think about Jennifer. And Hector. He had to do a good job here for them. Wasn't that what his father had said in the beginning?

"This is a family project, Chase," his father had told him. "Someday you'll be able to tell your kids what a great thing we done. Income redistribution. No muss, no fuss. Relieve the rich of a few of their extra bucks. That's the heart of it, and the beauty of it is we're doing it together, father and son."

Chase paced the little room they were keeping him in. Lack of concrete facts chewed away at him now. Where was his father? Where were the kids? Everything had been fine when they were in touch. But this was so vague, so gut-grabbing. He sure hoped the lawyer knew what the fuck was going on.

But he didn't. Chase could see that as soon as he walked in the door. They had gotten him off the golf course. His name was Andy Bingham. He was about Chase's age, a hotshot who had won a high-profile defense of some politician who had beaten up his mistress.

"Chase, I never ask my clients whether they are guilty or innocent of the charges against them," he began after introducing himself. "I leave it to their discretion whether to tell me or not. But this is a little different—your case, that is."

"How so?"

"Well, this is an ongoing crime. This isn't something that happened yesterday and is over. This is ongoing. Those four kids are still missing." He waited.

"I don't know where those kids are," Chase said.

"Okay. You want to leave it at that. We can do an arraignment, say nothing. I'm fine with that."

"But I want those kids back." Chase said this before thinking, yet it was his deepest wish right now.

"We all do. Do you have information that would help get them back?"

"No. I mean. I just . . ."

"Do you think those kids are with your father?"

"They say he's dead."

"Right. That's what they told me too."

"You believe 'em?" Chase couldn't hide his vulnerability.

Bingham had pretty much sized up what he had in front of him now. Under some circumstances he would have told his client to zip it, not say another word to anyone, buy some time to figure out how to do damage control, game the system in his client's favor. But Bingham had seen the pictures of the kids, he had heard from the prosecutor that they suspected something had happened to the kidnapper and the kids were on their own in the wilderness, and he didn't want to do normal in this case.

"I do. I think he's probably dead. I'm sorry. Do you know where he took the kids?"

"No. No, goddammit. He wouldn't tell me so I couldn't tell. Shit. Why'd he do that?" Tears spilled over Chase's eyelids as he said this. He began to shake, giving himself up to the grief he had withheld for hours.

Bingham knew he could steer Chase toward a confession, but he also knew the confession wasn't going to help find the kids. He was half sorry now he'd rushed in to meet with Chase. He'd left his game at the twelfth green, three under par.

• • •

Detective Martin was still at the house when he got a cell phone call, took out his notepad, started making some notes, grunting one word questions, and then hung up. David and Lena knew it had something to do with the case. He shook his head.

"Well, the good news. The guy's confessing."

"The bad news?" David asked.

"He doesn't know where the kids are."

"How can that be?" Lena asked.

"Part of their operation, I guess. This Chase guy handed the kids off to the father. He took 'em somewhere and didn't tell the kid so he wouldn't be able to spill the beans."

"Fuck." David stood up from the kitchen table. "He didn't even have a clue, an area, something like that?"

"No better'n what the FBI came up with." Martin was searching for something positive. "They tell me it's a relatively small area for a search like this."

Lena didn't believe this in the least. The news had hit her hard. All the hope she'd put in the ransom, the fact of some communication with the kidnappers, was gone now. Sarah was as far away now as she'd been Saturday afternoon. Lena was drained and sickened and Martin could see it.

"I'm sorry," he said. Then it seemed like he wanted out fast. "I'm supposed to check some stuff over where they got the van impounded. You all right here, Lena?"

"Yes."

"And you're still going up there tomorrow?" he asked David.

"Damn right. Fuck. Did he say who's behind this whole thing?"

Martin looked at his notes. "Nope. He doesn't know. They set it up like a terrorist operation, cells and all."

"This sounds too organized. I don't think we were the targets. I think John Walker was. This sounds like somebody trying to get to Citibank or something. I think we just got caught up in something bigger."

"You may have something there," Martin said. "I really gotta go."

• • •

After Martin left, David picked up the remote and flicked on the TV. He found a live report from the Adirondacks. The reporter said a large manhunt was to start the next day, then corrected himself and said it was a rescue operation, not a manhunt. "Maybe a kidhunt would be a better description," he added, almost offhandedly. David flicked off the TV and went downstairs without a word.

A few minutes later the phone rang and Lena heard her mother on the line. Lena looked at the clock and realized it was four in the morning in Sweden.

"Dad just left for the airport. He's taking an early flight to Montreal," Sally said.

"What? No."

"We tried to stop him, Lena. Sylvie was here until late in the evening. He's got an old army buddy there who says he can get him across the border safely. I don't think I've ever seen him this worked up."

Lena filled Sally in on the new developments and the fact that David was getting ready to go join in the search as well.

"I have a number for Dad's friend in Montreal," Sally said after hearing this. "You can talk to him there. I think he arrives about five o'clock your time tomorrow. Maybe you can talk some sense into him. Maybe just flying there will be enough."

"And maybe they'll have found Sarah by then."

"Lord, I hope so, honey. I can't imagine what you're going through."

Lena stopped, not thinking so much as just letting the conversation breathe. Then she surprised herself.

"Mom?"

"What?"

"I'm pregnant."

Lena let the announcement sink in. Sally waited to make sure she had heard correctly.

"Why, well . . . when?"

"When? I don't know. I found out yesterday. I haven't told David."

"Is it his baby?"

"Mom!"

"Sorry, but you're not telling him. I live in Sweden, remember?"

"Yes, it's his baby."

"Then why aren't you telling him, why haven't you told him?"

"Truth?"

"Of course."

"We've been on the outs. Things have not been good. We were trying to have another, you know that, but we'd sort of given up. I just don't know how I feel about it. And with Sarah . . ."

Tears came now and Sally could hear them.

"Ah, Lena, I wish I was there. Do you want me to come over?"

"No, I'm okay."

David came upstairs and mouthed a "Who's that?" Lena mouthed back, "Mom." Then she spoke to her mother.

"Give me the number, Mom. I'll see if I can reach Dad."

She took down the number and listened when Sally said she was happy for Lena, for the pregnancy. Lena only grunted her responses with David still in the room, and then the two hung up.

"Dad's on his way to Montreal. He's got some guy going to sneak him across the border."

David had the childish feeling that Richard was stealing his thunder, but he shook that off and expressed concern for his father-in-law. "Serious jail time for what, one more pair of eyes up in the mountains?" But as he said this, he realized that he himself was only going to be one more pair of eyes in the mountains, and even though he wasn't facing any jail time, his trek north seemed to be just as quixotic. He went back downstairs.

Lena listened to David's tread going down to the basement. She thought about the call from her mother, about telling Sally she was pregnant. And then a sweeping, black thought nearly knocked her to the floor. This embryo, this new baby, was compensation for the loss of Sarah. Lose one. Get a new one. The irrationality of this thought was apparent instantly, but the force of the horrible equation was gripping, almost physical. Lena struggled to stay afloat, to reach the dry land of rationality where randomness and coincidence were seen for what they were, not for some playfulness and retribution by the gods. But the thought mushroomed and engulfed her. The next few hours were the bleakest she had ever known. She was going to lose Sarah. She had already lost Sarah. And the new baby's arrival was both the proof of that and the payback. The blackness deepened when she had the nearly insane thought that she could abort and get Sarah back that way. She flailed around the house barely aware of where she was.

Finally all she could do was check the computer for an email, and when there wasn't one and the fact that there wasn't one only pushed her further toward hysteria, she tore off her clothes and got under the sheets. David came in the room and started to get undressed only minutes later.

"I'm all set. Gonna leave early," he said, and went in the bathroom. Lena was churning. When David returned and slid under the covers, she turned to him and spat out her words.

"David, we're going to have another baby."

David thought, because of the force with which she spoke, that Lena was hoping to will another child into existence. "When this is over, we can try, do anything—"

"No, I'm pregnant. Now."

David looked deeply into Lena's wild eyes, trying to match the news with the fierce delivery. He stuttered a "Really?" and Lena nodded, tears coming. "When did you—?"

"Yesterday. Remember I was sick?"

"Holy shit." And then, as Lena had, he struggled to remember the last time they had made love. Lena could see this.

"That morning, when Sarah interrupted us."

David remembered. It had been a turning point for him. He had woken before Lena, his sleep roiled by his guilt and doubt surrounding the affair with Tricia. Lena had looked radiant next to him and he had felt a deep renewal of his love for her.

"That was beautiful," he said. Lena rejected this with a shake of the head, her eyes going cold again.

"It's because we're losing Sarah," Lena got out in choking bursts, a hard cry hitting her full force. "I know it. Sarah's gone forever and we get this new one."

"Lena." David reached for her, but she pulled back.

"No. Listen to me. Think about it."

David moved swiftly to Lena's side of the bed, grabbed both her shoulders, and wouldn't let her go. "Stop. Stop. Lena, no. That's crazy."

"It's not crazy. Why else would a baby come now?"

"Because we made love and it took." He grabbed her harder, wanting to shake the nonsense from her brain. "Look at me, Lena. It's new life. It's not Sarah. It has nothing to do with Sarah. Sarah is going to come back to us. I promise. This baby is just a baby on its own. Our baby."

"But—"

"Our baby, Lena. Yours and mine and Sarah's."

He looked at her with such resolve and passion that Lena couldn't help but leave the captivity of the black thought and swim up to him, to his eyes, to his arms. Relieved, she pulled him to her and kissed him as the tears still gushed. They said everything that needed to be said now with their bodies. They were beyond reason and love, loss and sorrow, and held each other as tight as they could. They were connected, once again, and a while later, when they fell asleep in the embrace of exhaustion, deep uncertainty, and indescribable joy, it was as if in the middle of the night, dawn had broken in the bedroom.

# Thirty

A strong wind had blown through the clearing for half the night and the noises it made in the trees, on the window panes, had kept the kids awake and alert long after their starved bodies had given out. They lay on their cold mattresses shivering, ears perked, taking turns at the window looking for bear.

When the wind stopped and the clouds opened to a nearly full moon, Sarah, at the window, realized that they were going to have to try to get back down to the road when daylight came. There was no food left. The computer didn't work. Yes, there were dangers in the woods, but hadn't they walked to the shack without even seeing a bear? Why couldn't they walk back and not see one?

Direction was the big problem. Which way to go? There was simply no way to figure out which one of the paths out of the clearing had been the one they had come in on. Mr. Everett had made sure of that with his blindfolds and his turning them around. He had made the whole last part of the hike like a game of pin the tail on the donkey.

Suddenly Sarah sat up. The thought of pin the tail on the donkey held some meaning for her, something important, but she didn't know what. She had only played the game twice, maybe three times, but she was very, very good at it. All the other kids cheated or had to be told "hotter, hotter, hotter" over and over. But Sarah simply *knew* where the target was, even though all she was seeing was the black of the blindfold. Now, looking out the window at the moonlit clearing, the daunting choice of which path to take home suddenly shrank to nothing. Swelling with confidence, she crawled over to where Linda was lying, still sniveling.

"Linda, Linda. I've got it. It's like pin the tail on the donkey. I can find the way out."

Linda didn't know what she was talking about. Sarah went back to the window. She would lead them, she knew now. If they balked, she would just forge on ahead herself. Her stomach grumbled and she burped a little nothing burp. But hunger wasn't the problem it had been only fifteen minutes earlier. Sarah had faith now.

When she woke, Lena had the sudden feeling that she didn't want David to leave her alone. As they kissed and unwound arms and legs, she nearly asked him to stay, to keep her from any more wild craziness like the night before. She imagined news of the worst kind coming while David was away and she didn't know how she would deal with it by herself. She even fretted that David himself would be in danger, would be like a rescuer swimming out to a drowning victim only to drown himself.

But David's smiling confidence made her keep her thoughts to herself. He ran his hand over Lena's stomach and down through her pubic hair.

"Are you all right?" he asked, as if he sensed something.

Lena took his hand and guided it downward, his fingers opening her. He kissed her breast. They stayed like this for long minutes, neither wanting to take the lovemaking further, neither wanting to leave the peace of their connection.

After a cup of coffee David wrote down the phone number of his contact in the Adirondacks, Les Malone, the founder of a hunting club who had organized his members for a search team. Lena went into the bathroom when she felt sick, but she didn't throw up. They said goodbye in the living room with a strong hug and an earthy kiss. There was little they could say. David parted Lena's robe and again rubbed her stomach.

"At least I'm not leaving you alone," he said. Lena fought tears.

"Be careful," she said. And he was gone.

Lena watched him back the car out through the news vans as he left. She felt an unexpected weight bearing down on her, a clutch in her stomach that wasn't morning sickness. Both David and Sarah were gone now. Why hadn't she gone? What could she do in the house? She went to the TV and turned it on, not for information, but for comfort, for a connection to the world.

About an hour and a half later Lena was in the kitchen trying to get a bowl of cereal down and heard the name "Rostenkowski" coming from the TV. She went quickly into the living room. On the screen she saw the front of the Rostenkowskis' house, seen through a long lens, and EMT workers rolling a gurney from the house into an ambulance in early morning light. Over this she heard a female reporter saying, " . . . taken to Pelham Memorial in critical condition. We have no more information at this time." The TV then cut to two local anchors in the studio who were soberly winding up the story.

"The pressures on those families," said the blond woman with the too-glossy lipstick. Her fellow anchor, a man who looked like he could be her father, agreed with a nod and a shuffling of his papers and then announced what the stories would be after the break.

Lena forgot that with their new DVR setup she could have rewound the story and seen it in its entirety. She went to the phone and dialed the Rostenkowskis. No one answered and she didn't want to leave a message. She decided to go directly to Pelham Memorial. She was certain Janet had had some sort of collapse, maybe a heart attack even.

Getting behind the wheel, opening the garage door, and backing down the driveway all felt like strange operations, even though it had only been a few days since she'd driven to the grocery store on Friday night. When she reached the end of the driveway a sheriff's officer directed her back through the reporters but couldn't keep them from crowding the car. Lena, still in the dark about what was going on, rolled down the window and let the blast of questions hit her. Then she singled out one of the reporters, a middle-aged man thrusting a minirecorder toward her, and asked her own question.

"What's happened to the Rostenkowskis? I didn't get the news."

"The husband," he shouted back. "Tried to commit suicide, they think."

Lena stared at him before she rolled up the window and sealed herself off from the onslaught. As the sheriff's officer directed her ahead, she tried to imagine Phil with a gun in his hand or with razor blades poised over his wrists, but the images didn't seem to have any reality. Then she thought of Linda somewhere out in the world being left in the lurch by her father's actions. Suicide, Lena would have admitted to anyone, was something for which she had very little sympathy. Maybe it was the unusually high number of times she had encountered its aftermath among friends in grade school in Sweden. Maybe it was a physician's pique at a potential patient who, by killing himself, in effect refused treatment. Whatever, she had trouble tolerating the people who chose the self-destructive route over some attempt, any attempt, to rectify their problems.

Walking into the hospital was more comforting than Lena could have imagined. This was the known world, a place where people solved problems. The astringent smells enveloped her and spoke of certainties. Unlike the nebulous tangle of fears and suppositions of the past few days, this was solid ground, home, a place to get things done and move forward.

She went first to the ER and found that Phil had already been stabilized and sent to a room. The ER doctor, an Indian woman whose name Lena didn't get and couldn't read on her pin, recognized Lena but said nothing other than to answer Lena's questions about the case. Phil had overdosed on sleeping pills at least, maybe some barbiturates as well, and had been found by his wife early in the morning. A stomach pump performed in the ER had been "minimally successful," meaning he had digested much of the overdose. Antidotes had kept him from death, but he was now in a relatively deep coma. The next twenty-four to thirty-six hours would reveal if he were going to pull out of the coma and whether there had been significant permanent brain damage.

"Barbiturates?" Lena asked. "Who prescribes barbiturates these days?" The young doctor shook her head.

Riding the elevator to Phil's floor, Lena remembered a doctor on rounds once talking about a male patient who had attempted suicide by sleeping pills, saying it was unusual for males to use that method, that males tended to either shoot themselves or jump off a building. Maybe this wasn't a suicide at all, just an accident.

Phil was in a private room, and Lena could see only the son, Paul, there with him at first. Lena barely knew Paul other than from the times he had come to the house to pick Linda up. But seeing her, Paul went to Lena quickly and hugged her. Lena held the hug, even though it was awkward. As she was doing so, she realized there were other people in the room, sitting in chairs against the wall. She turned to see Sheila Walker and another woman she didn't know. Sheila acknowledged her with a nod.

"I'm so sorry, Paul," Lena said as Paul finally pulled away.

"Mom screamed and I came down and saw him. I had to call nine-one-one. Is he going to be all right? They won't tell us much."

Lena didn't want to answer this question and so made a show of seeing Sheila and the other woman. She introduced herself and found out that the other woman was Phil's sister, Ellen, who lived in the Bronx. Sheila told Lena that she had been called because she was a part-time chaplain at the hospital. She said she had called Phil's priest, and in saying this she was asking a question similar to Paul's: was the priest necessary, were last rites needed? Lena now knew the room expected a medical judgment from her.

"I'm not that familiar with the case, and I really don't know this medicine. But, uh, he looks . . ."

Lena moved toward the bed. Phil was serene in the coma, an oxygen mask covering most of his features, his thick hair matted and unkempt. Lena looked for the classic signs of stroke—facial disfiguration, curled fingers—but saw none. Perhaps he had escaped some of the worst side effects of such an overdose, or perhaps he was simply slipping away by imperceptible increments. One of the first suprising things about medicine Lena had learned was that there was a point at which you had done everything you could for a patient and then you just had to sit back and watch nature either become a collaborator or duck and run.

"His vitals are normal, and he seems stabilized. I think those are good signs," she offered finally.

"I heard you're supposed to talk to somebody in a coma 'cause they can hear you," Ellen said, moving closer to the bed, running her fingers through her brother's hair.

"Yes, I think that's a good idea." Then Lena realized Janet wasn't there. He turned to Paul. "Where's your mother?"

"She's home. She said she couldn't take it."

"By herself?"

"I think so."

Lena suddenly felt a deep sympathy for Janet. Normally Lena might have been critical, seeing Janet's absence as abandonment and worse, leaving her what, sixteen-year-old son to carry the load. But Lena went in a different direction. She knew how the abduction and its horrors had caused her to think irrationally, do things she wouldn't do under less stressful conditions, and she imagined how much more difficult it would be if something like a suicide attempt were added to what they were already going through. Janet's fragile nature, Lena thought, had simply been unable to deal with the enormity of the crisis.

"I think somebody should be with her," Sheila said, and Lena was hoping Sheila would volunteer to make the visit. But she didn't and the room turned to Lena. Lena addressed Paul.

"Why don't I take you back home and we'll see what we can do to help your Mom."

Paul responded quickly. "I'd rather stay here with Dad." He said it so fast it was clear that he had thought about being with his mother and really didn't want to do that.

In the hallway outside Phil's room Lena ran into Detective Martin.

"How does it look?" he asked, nodding toward Phil's door. Lena was about to answer when a young priest passed them, knocked on the door, and went in. Martin continued. "Last rites?"

"I guess so. It doesn't look good."

"I'm a bettin' man. Can you give me odds?"

"No. I'm a doctor. I never bet against Mother Nature."

"Good idea. He seem suicidal to you?"

"No, but not many suicides do, do they?"

"Guess you're right."

Lena knew she should be going, but she didn't want to leave Martin. He had been the first. He had come into her house with news and knowledge and . . . what? Faith. He had been her faith. He was still. The FBI, Witherspoon, they were technicians. Martin was a lifeline.

"Any news?" she asked.

"No. Your husband left?"

"Yes."

Martin couldn't hide his pessimism about the search but he softened his real opinion. "They got their work cut out for them. But I'm sure they'll find the kids."

Sheila Walker came out of the room and Lena could see the priest preparing for what she assumed were the last rites.

"I would have expected his wife to do this, not him," Sheila said. "She seemed more, uh, on the edge."

"Maybe it's worse when it doesn't show," Lena responded.

"I'm going to have to leave," Sheila said. "I don't know how I'm going to do it, but I have to plan my mother's eightieth birthday. She has Alzheimer's. She doesn't even know Franklin is missing." She tried a brief smile. Lena was touched.

"I'll walk out with you." Lena turned to Martin, shaking his hand again, getting another welcome bath in the blue eyes. "I'm going to see if I can help Janet."

"She's not in there?"

Lena shook her head no. Martin scowled.

In the elevator Sheila surprised Lena with a confession of sorts.

"I admit I don't know much about such things, but I did a little research this morning, Google Earth, some accounts, stuff like that. It's like ants in the Sahara. I don't think they're going to find the kids."

Lena reacted to this blast of pessimism. "I have to . . . I mean, David's up there and . . . I'm sorry. I can't give up hope."

"I wouldn't want you to. And I know that such doom and gloom is just as unfaithful as hope and fear. But a mother knows, don't you think? Down here." She pressed her stomach. "There's no arguing with that feeling, is there? No sugarcoating."

Lena fought any such feelings in herself. The elevator doors opened. The bustling life in the lobby suddenly seemed dangerous to her. "I hope . . . ," she started, but Sheila stopped her, turned, and opened her arms. Lena saw tears in her eyes.

"I'm sorry. You don't know me. I can be blunt. I apologize."

Their hug, Lena found, was surprisingly warm.

Lena went past a uniformed sheriff's deputy sitting on a lawn chair in the Rostenkowski driveway, nodded to him, then knocked on the Rostenkowski door several times before trying the doorknob, pushing the door open, and calling in for Janet. She was all the way into the living room before Janet heard her and came from a back bedroom. Janet seemed dazed, flustered, but not as dragged out and weepy as she had been the last time Lena had seen her.

"Oh, hi," she said.

"Janet, I'm sorry."

Janet seemed to take a second to figure out if Lena was talking about the suicide attempt or coming in the house without being let in. "Oh, thank you. I . . ." Then something broke and a cry that sounded like a cough at first burst from her lips. Lena went to her but didn't give her a hug. Janet didn't seem to want one. She just wanted to try to choke off the strange noise and awkward moment.

Without saying anything, Janet went in the bathroom and got some Kleenex. When she came out she was composed, but something was off. She gave Lena a long, searching look.

"Would you like some coffee?" she said, still in the stare.

"Only if you've got it made. I don't want to—"

Janet didn't wait for Lena to finish. She headed to the kitchen; Lena followed. Janet dumped the coffee filter and started to make a new pot. Lena could see that protesting this would do no good. The indecisive Janet of the past few days was gone. The Janet bustling around the kitchen was oddly directed, almost zombielike, but not distracted.

"What do you think his chances are?" she said after a while.

"I don't know, Janet. It's not my area. It depends on a lot of things."

"Like what?"

"I really can't say. How long before he was found. How—"

"We figure he was there almost three hours. I think I fell asleep about two and woke up just before five. He wasn't in bed with me and I went to look for him. He'd been sleeping on the couch."

"Well, that's a long time, but . . . maybe not that long. If he had a full stomach . . ." Lena could hear herself go deeper into a prognosis than she wanted to. But Janet wasn't the blubbering near widow Lena had expected and the conversation was almost clinical.

The coffee began to percolate, and Janet caught Lena with that stare again. Lena felt she was being examined somehow, judged, evaluated. Finally Janet motioned for Lena to follow and left the kitchen. Lena did follow and when she caught up with Janet, Janet was standing at the door to a study near the bedrooms.

"Look at this," Janet said, hugging herself and stepping aside so Lena could come to the doorway.

The study was a shambles. Paper was strewn everywhere, desk drawers were flung open or thrown on the floor. Framed pictures were off the wall and tossed on a couch, some with their glass broken. Lena could only link this scene to a burglary. Janet said nothing.

"He did this?" Lena got out finally.

"No, I did."

Janet said nothing more, and Lena didn't know what question to ask. But the silence went on too long.

"You were mad at him?" Lena finally asked.

"Sort of." There was a resignation now in Janet's voice. From the kitchen they could hear the coffeepot gasping the last of the drips. Janet started to walk that way. "I forget. Do you take cream and sugar?"

"Just milk." Lena gave another look to the storm-tossed room and then followed.

As if she hadn't just shown her a scene of devastation, Janet went about getting coffee on the table. Lena suddenly realized that what she was witnessing was a case of shock. She was surprised she hadn't thought of that before. Of course she'd seen this many times in her professional life, husbands and wives wandering down hospital corridors in the moments after a death, seemingly calm and directed, but then collapsed by one slight hole poked in the bubble that was their grief. Lena was now aware of the fragility she was facing and prepared herself for Janet's possible crumbling. They sat.

"I was really looking for something specific." Janet said this as if continuing a sentence and Lena had to race to catch up, to remember what had been said last. Janet helped. "It wasn't so much that I was mad at him; I was mad that he had done what he'd done without giving me the information."

"I don't understand."

"You will. Give me time."

Janet began to breathe heavily and Lena couldn't tell whether she was about to cry or scream, or perhaps both. After a long while, however, she did neither. She stared down at the table.

"It all began when I had my accident and we didn't have adequate coverage. You know this. I've told you."

"Yes," Lena answered, though she didn't know what the "it" was. She assumed the suicide attempt was the end point.

"From there on it never stopped. Day in and day out after the pain in my leg and my hand finally went away, the bills kept coming. And then the collectors. And then the deals and the monthly payments. I would be in the middle of a class, trying to teach a lesson, and all I could hear was this pounding in my head about what we owed, how we were going to make the payments. And nobody wanted to listen to us. Nobody cared. We had been the victims and nobody cared. Do you know what that's like?"

An impossible question. Lena only nodded. It wasn't as if she hadn't heard milder versions of this for years from Janet.

"And then Paul got closer and closer to college and the pressure built even more. We had our jobs but that was it. We weren't going to get much more income and the bills were draining everything we had. How could we possibly pay for college?"

"I know," Lena said, expecting to commiserate.

"No, you don't. For chrissakes, don't say you know. You're a doctor. Say you understand but don't say you know."

There was real sting in this. Lena only nodded in reply. Janet continued.

"So when Phil saw the ad online for a grant, what could we do?"

"Grant?" Lena asked, wondering what all this had to do with the wrecked office down the hall.

"From foreigners. They said they wanted to help financially distressed people like us. They were very professional. Phil only dealt with them online. The scheme was complicated but it was always nonviolent."

The hair stood up on the back of Lena's neck. Gone were the thoughts of shock and shock-induced incoherence.

"Phil didn't even tell me what they were talking about until they had the whole thing planned."

"What thing planned?"

"What do you think?"

"What are you saying, Janet? Just tell me!"

Janet teared up but her words were still tough. "They said they'd done it dozens of times. There was no investment, nothing up front. What would you have done?"

"I don't know! I don't know what you're talking about!"

"Yes, you do! For chrissakes, Lena, wise up! We put the thing in play. It was our idea! And we get the cash. You couldn't see that?"

Lena could only see a murderous rage boil behind her eyelids, and she had all she could do to keep from leaping down Janet's throat and tearing that evil heart out of her chest. She didn't need details now. She could fill in the blanks. The Rostenkowskis were the elusive third party behind the whole scheme, the ones who had set it in motion. She knew this was something she could never, ever forgive them for, but in the same instant she knew, from the cold, almost deranged way in which Janet had revealed it, that now she, Lena, had to take all her hatred and deep desire for revenge and stuff those in order to get through this woman to Sarah.

"You set the whole thing up?"

"No, he did."

"I mean, you started it? It was your idea?"

"Some of it. It was only supposed to be one kid. But he made it four and—"

"Which kid? Which was the one?"

"Sarah."

Lena wanted to strike out and crush this horror in front of her. She had never felt such pure desire for destruction in her life. But she braked against the urge, knowing that destroying this evil would not bring Sarah back.

"Where are the kids?"

"I don't know."

"Oh, yes, you do, you goddamn—It's your daughter. You've got to know. Where are the kids?"

Janet gestured toward the study. "They're in there. Don't you get it?"

For a brief second Lena thought the kids had been hidden in the Rostenkowski house all along. But then she realized that Janet meant that she had torn apart the study because she herself didn't know where they were, because Phil had tried to kill himself with the connection to the kids hidden in his study, or perhaps just his brain.

"Phil knew and you didn't?"

"Yes. Yes."

"You're not afraid I'm going to call the FBI, Witherspoon?"

Janet's blank stare was all the answer Lena needed. Lena reeled back through the past few days, through Janet's reactions to the events, and realized why they had seemed either over-the-top, irrational beyond the irrationality of the crisis, or oddly out of sync with the norm: Janet was seeing the whole event through a different lens. And when the emails from the kids came, then the arrest of Chase, and the kidnappers' scheme seemed to be unraveling, Janet and Phil had almost disappeared. Now that made perfect sense.

"I don't care what anyone knows now," Janet said finally.

"Does Phil know where they are?"

"No, but he knows who he talked to. He said he tried to get in touch with him again, but the lines of communication were cut once we got the money."

Lena suddenly had the sense she might be in a dream. How far back did the dream stretch? Was she napping on the couch after Sarah left for camp and all this, all that had happened was an extended nightmare of a nap dream? Please let that be true. No one in the real world lets their own daughter be kidnapped without full knowledge of where the kidnappers will take her. Only in a dream could someone be that wildly out of touch with human fallibility and mistakes.

"I don't believe this is true," Lena said, trying to wake herself.

Janet didn't respond. She got up from the kitchen table and wandered back to the study. Lena found her there a minute later, slumped down in the piles of paper, listlessly pawing through them, disconnected and withdrawn, a mental patient in a dayroom. The image drew Lena back from the spiked realm of revenge and started her thinking about what was possible now. She found herself at the throat of the scheme, a place she had imagined all along as the source of information about Sarah. But what could she do to dig out the hidden facts? She didn't know. She couldn't think straight enough to weigh the pros and cons. She had the subconscious sense that to take Janet's confession to the authorities now would not further the cause and might even be a step backward. She didn't know if she could keep all this ugly revelation to herself. But, she thought, that might have to be her heroics in the battle to get Sarah back in her arms.

Janet stood and was starting to leave the room. "There's nothing in here."

"When did Phil try to get back in touch with the kidnappers?"

"He was never in touch with the kidnappers just—"

"I mean him, or them, the middlemen. When did he try to get back in touch with them?"

"Yesterday."

"And what happened?"

"Nothing worked. The phone. The email. We didn't even know what country they came from. Phil said they could hardly write an English sentence."

"How did you get your money?"

"It's in an account and don't talk to me about the money." This was said with a firm growl, as if Lena were somehow being insensitive for bringing up the subject.

"I'll talk about anything I want," Lena shot back. "Fucking money!"

"That's right, fucking money! Where were you when we needed help?"

Lena realized this was going around in circles. She worried Janet was on the verge of some sort of break with reality.

"If the information's not here, we need to see Phil," Lena said, stopping Janet at the door, trying to look her in the eye.

"No, I can't."

"You have to. You being there, talking to him might bring him out of the coma."

"I can't talk to him," Janet hissed. "He doesn't want me to talk to him. He didn't want to talk last night. He—"

"We can get him out of it," Lena shot back, matching Janet's bite.

"What?"

"We can use drugs. It's not permanent but we can get brief flashes, communicate." Lena wasn't quite sure about this, but she was getting desperate.

"Well, you go. I can't."

"Do I have to tell the police and have them make you?"

"I don't care. Tell them. I'm not going."

Lena suppressed the urge to grab Janet by the hair and haul her out of the house.

"It's your daughter, Janet."

"I know and I want her back as much as you do."

"No, you don't!" Lena shoved Janet back hard against the door jamb. Janet's eyes went wide with surprise. "Don't you ever say that again! You love yourself. You couldn't possibly have loved Linda and done this to her. You're a monster who won't even go to the hospital to try to save her daughter!"

Janet's eyes were truly nonresponsive now, Lena thought. Trouble. Lena knew arguing was out of the question. She took Janet firmly by the elbow and steered her toward the living room, the front door.

"Do you need your purse?"

Janet said nothing. Lena half pushed her, opening the front door, realizing that she would have to navigate the press outside. The sheriff's deputy leaped up from the lawn chair and came to help. He asked questions with a look toward Lena.

"Help me get her in the car," Lena said, then changed her mind. "No. I can manage her. Keep those press guys back."

The officer turned and went quickly down the driveway, arms out wide, yelling at the now-mobilized cameramen.

"I can't talk to him," Janet mumbled as they moved toward Lena's car. Lena said nothing, praying she could just get Janet in the car before something spooked her. When they neared the passenger door, Lena looked out at the press. A photograph of that look would, almost instantly, become an icon of the kidnapping; one parent victim helping another, a doctor able to care for a distraught friend, all the pathos of the tragedy in one image. That was the interpretation until the truth came out. And then anyone with a knowing eye could see that Lena and Janet were doing a perp walk of sorts, and that Lena wanted desperately to scream to the cameramen and the world that Janet and Phil were the evil heart of the whole sordid scheme.

Lena got Janet in the car and, circling it to her side, prayed she was doing the right thing.

# Thirty-one

Detective Martin had been alerted to Lena's arrival at the hospital and met her and Janet at the elevator. His face was drawn tight in a way Lena hadn't seen before, and she wondered if he knew what the Rostenkowskis had done. He went right to Janet.

"Mrs. Rostenkowski. I'm sorry this happened."

Janet, who had said nothing in the ride to the hospital, only nodded. Lena realized Martin didn't know what she knew.

"Any change?" Janet asked.

"No. Your son and Mr. Rostenkowski's sister are still talking to him, but no response."

Lena had forgotten about Paul's being there. She looked at Janet and could feel her tense at the mention of her son.

"Janet. Why don't you stay with Detective Martin? I'll see what the situation is."

Janet didn't have to be persuaded. She slumped into a plastic chair in the hallway. Detective Martin gave Lena a questioning look, but Lena ignored this and went into the room.

Ellen and Paul were pretty much where Lena had left them. They looked relieved to see her.

"Nothing's working," Ellen said, Paul nodding behind her. "Did you see Janet?"

"Yes. I brought her back with me."

"Oh."

Paul stiffened visibly at this, his eyes blinking. Lena could tell he didn't want to see his mother. She wondered if maybe he knew the truth, if maybe in the minutes after they had found Phil, before the EMTs came, a traumatized Janet had told all. Then, as Lena moved toward the bed, a dark thought. What if Paul had known all along? What if he was part of the scheme? Paul eyed her with innocent, almost frightened eyes. He doesn't know, Lena concluded, realizing her level of trust in humanity had nose-dived since J.D. showed up in her driveway.

"I think it would be best if you two went to the waiting room at the other end of the hall. Maybe something will happen if Janet can be in here by herself," she said finally.

They both complied willingly. Lena took a moment to be alone with Phil. She looked at his oxygen-mask-covered features, the olive skin, the bony cheeks, the thick dark hair, and she let her hatred flow.

"I hope you can hear me, you son of a bitch. And I hope you pull out of this goddamned coma so you can live the rest of your life paying for what you did. You're a fucking coward. If you've got any information about this shit, you cough it up now. I'm going to bring your goddamned wife in. And I'm going to want to hear everything you know."

She found herself shaking Phil's arm violently and then came back to her senses. She turned and went to get Janet.

Martin could see how rattled Lena was. He stood and asked if she was all right. Lena said she was. Excusing himself from Janet, he pulled Lena down the hall and said he wanted a word with her. Lena was certain now that he knew something.

"I'm no doctor," he began in a whisper, "but that woman's not well.

She wouldn't even look at her son when he came out. I don't know if it's a good idea for her to go in there."

"She has to. It's our only hope," Lena blurted out before thinking, then reddened.

"Our only hope?"

"Of saving him."

"Really?"

Lena didn't want to get trapped. She just wanted to get Janet in the room with Phil. She pulled rank. "Trust me on this. Yes. I've seen it work before."

Janet was in the room for a good half a minute before she let her eyes rest on her husband. The look she gave him was hard to read. There was something approaching melancholy that came through, a sad-eyed droop of a look that spoke of loss and remorse.

"Speak to him," Lena commanded. "Get close and speak to him."

Janet was startled by the tone, by the command. "How?"

"Like you always do. Ask him how to get in touch with the kid . . . the whoever, whatever you called them."

Janet reddened at this and hesitated. "It's useless. I don't care what they say. He can't hear me."

"You don't know that. You have to try."

"He never heard me! How is he going to hear me now?"

"What do you mean he never heard you? You two—"

"I didn't want to do this! It was his idea! I tried to talk him out of it but he wouldn't listen!"

"I don't believe that."

"It's the truth. You think I wanted to have my own daughter kidnapped?"

"You stood there and watched her being taken away by J.D. You didn't try to stop him."

"I couldn't. Everything would have . . . there wouldn't have been any money then."

Lena saw Janet start to slip from reality again and realized that somehow the money was the trigger. She went to Janet and turned her toward Phil.

"You talk to him. Tell him you can't get the money."

"I can't."

"Now!"

Lena held firmly to Janet's shoulders to show she would not take no for an answer. Janet's chest heaved, tears came to her eyes, but after a minute of gathering herself, she spoke.

"Phil. We've got to find Linda. Phil?" She turned to Lena, who let go of Janet's shoulders. "This is—"

"Keep trying." Lena made a threatening move with her hands. Janet turned back.

"Phil, please. Don't leave me with this. Tell me how to find the facilitators."

Lena almost gasped at the word. The cold-bloodedness of what the Rostenkowskis had done was now magnified tenfold by the use of that clinical, sterile, horseshit word. Lena choked off a vomit.

Instead, she turned toward the door to leave, to get some air back in her lungs.

"Keep talking. I'll be right back."

In the hallway Lena again thought she might be sick, this queasiness feeling more like the morning sickness of the day before. But the nausea passed and she looked up to see Detective Martin staring at her.

"Don't worry. I'm okay," Lena said, taking a deep breath. Martin didn't acknowledge this and seemed far off. Then he blinked and nodded.

"What's going on in there?" he said, indicating the room.

"Janet's trying to get him to come to."

"She's not going to have much time."

"What do you mean?" Lena caught a whiff of disgust in Martin's voice.

"Witherspoon's coming over to talk to her."

"Talk to her?"

"She called me to say there was some new information. She's been talking to the Williamses and then the Walkers. And . . ." Martin stopped himself and seemed distant, calculating how much to tell Lena.

"And what?" Lena asked.

"It seems the hotshot computer security guys at Citibank picked up a connection between the computer used to send the ransom notes and the Rostenkowski computer."

"What?" Lena gave a decent performance of ignorance. "I mean, we were all connected when—"

"Before. Months before."

"What are you saying?"

"Just that there are questions. And with this suicide attempt . . ." Martin trailed off. Lena almost confessed that she knew all, but then she realized that Witherspoon would want to talk to her as well. She couldn't be caught up in that now. She had to get information from Phil.

She shook her head and let Martin know she wasn't going to question further. "No, there's some mistake." She didn't wait for a response and started to go into the room.

"You're not going to say anything to her, are you?"

"No."

Lena couldn't hold Martin's blue-eyed gaze. She had broken a promise to herself. She had lied again.

David took the Taconic Parkway to Albany, then the Northway to the Adirondacks. There hadn't been much traffic and he found himself pushing the speed limit envelope, hitting ninety at times, figuring he could talk a trooper out of a ticket just by telling him what his mission was. He had filled the empty hours with scenarios of success, his efforts paying off, Sarah flying into his arms. But when, following Malone's instructions and the Google map on the front seat, he exited the Northway and headed into the foothills, his optimism withered.

He had expected lines of cars, searchers like himself going his way. But there was little traffic. And the woods on either side of the two-lane road were thick and impenetrable, even in the bright early morning sun. When he crested a ridge and saw what looked to be an endless rolling landscape of forested hills and drumlins spread out on the aprons of distant, rugged peaks, he almost stopped and turned back. What was he thinking?

Meeting Malone forty minutes later didn't help. Instead of the seasoned local David had imagined, Malone, in his fifties, had delicate features, a weak handshake, and crisp Land's End clothing head to toe.

"Hey, you found us," Malone said as David pulled up in front of the house. He was standing in the driveway with about ten other men and one woman, none of whom inspired much confidence. As Malone introduced him around, David tried to shake off the effects of the road and the disappointment of his arrival. The last person introduced was a twentysomething boyish-looking man, dressed in a buttoned-down shirt and khakis, who could hardly hold David's gaze.

"This is Steve Popper. He's from the local paper, wondered if it would be all right if he went along with us." Malone made this a done deal. David didn't want a reporter with him, but he felt he had no choice. He was adrift on foreign soil. For better or worse, Malone was his guide.

Then the insistent drone of a single-engine aircraft filled the air and they all looked up to see the silhouette of the plane against the morning sky as it made an oblique path over the town. Before the rattle subsided, Malone shouted to David.

"Search plane!"

David kept his eye on it until it was out of sight. When he looked back down, Malone had spread a topographical map on the hood of a car and the others were gathering around it.

"We call this the 'fingers of the hand' approach," Malone said to David as the others moved so he could get closer. "Five different vehicles will take five different roads, up into the grid we're assigned, looking for any trails that come into the roads, and—"

"If there are any trails," one of the men said, obviously extending an earlier argument about the plan. Others joined in. David saw confusion around him now, uncertainty. He suddenly wanted to be in touch with Lena. He fished his cell phone out of his pocket, saw he had bars, moved away from the group, dialed Lena's number, and waited. As he did, he looked over at the reporter, Popper, who stared at him for a long time, then scribbled something in a notebook.

• • •

Sarah had dozed off just as the morning light was appearing in the east. When she woke, the other three kids had left the room and Sarah could hear them talking. It was almost fully light out now. Sarah felt something important had happened during the night, but at first she couldn't remember what that was. Then it hit her. Pin the tail on the donkey. She got up and went into the other room.

The kids there seemed dazed. Franklin was still trying to get the laptop running but the other two were just sitting, talking. After the reaction she'd gotten from Linda during the night about her pin-the-tail revelation, Sarah decided just to tell the group what she was going to do, not how she was going to do it.

"We can't stay here," she started, breaking into the conversation. "We need to try to get back to the road."

The others saw a forcefulness in this that they hadn't seen before.

"But we don't know which way," Linda said, maybe forgetting what Sarah had said a few hours earlier.

"What if we go the wrong way?" Tommy asked. "We could get even more lost."

"We won't," Sarah shot back. "We won't. I promise."

Franklin looked up at this. He knew there was no way Sarah could promise such a thing, and yet it was just the sort of talk he wanted to hear. It was grown-up talk. Grown-ups promised you things like that in order to help you overcome your fears. "I promise you you won't drown. Just swim to me. Come on." Franklin knew he couldn't make such a promise to the others. He knew the odds and he couldn't lie about them. But if Sarah was willing to make a promise like that, he was willing to follow her. And, he told himself, maybe, just maybe she really did know the way back.

"I'll go with you," he said.

"What about the bears?" Tommy asked. He had spent most of the night imagining his father coming into the clearing with his brother, the two of them smiling and wrapping Tommy in big hugs. For some reason, when he imagined this, both his father and Jack were carrying rifles, even though Tommy knew they weren't hunters. He guessed they had the rifles to shoot bear.

Sarah didn't answer this question. There wasn't anything she could say about that. She knew she could guide them home. She knew that. But if there were bears in the way . . . Well, she couldn't think about that. Hadn't the bears come to the clearing? They had. So staying where they were didn't make them any safer. That was her thought, but she didn't know how to say it, so she just kept quiet about the bears.

"I'm going," she said finally, and headed toward the door.

"Now?" Linda asked.

"Yes."

"You can't leave me, Sarah. We're supposed to stay together, remember?"

"That was at camp."

"This is camp!" Linda whined, caught between the horror of going back into the woods and the terror of having Sarah leave.

For days now none of them had believed that Mr. Everett was part of the camp staff. But Linda's shout made them all miss the time when they had clung to the hope that what they were going through was part of Camp Arno. That was so much better than thinking they were completely on their own. Sarah would have none of it, though.

"This is not camp. Come on." She walked through the door into the hot morning sunshine. The others followed.

Once they were all outside, Sarah was the focus of attention. Though she was biting her lip, she was projecting a new decisiveness, and in a short time the others circled around her waiting for a pronouncement. Her eyes swept the perimeter of the clearing. There was the path to the pond. She knew that wasn't the right way. There was the path they had taken on their hike with Mr. Everett. That could be the right way but she didn't think so. She could feel the kids watching her. Pin the tail on the donkey came to her but she didn't want to close her eyes. Her charges would think she was just guessing.

She made a slight clockwise turn and there, in front of her, was a portal of sorts. A pair of young birches, white trunks gleaming in the sunshine, separated by about five feet, arched at their tops and nearly joined. Through the spindly birches was an opening into the woods.

Sarah could almost imagine a fairy princess waving a wand and trailing stardust, beckoning, showing her the way.

"There, that's it." Her voice was strong. The kids looked in the direction she was facing. Franklin, now fully invested in Sarah's leadership, made the first indication he would follow, with Sarah striding ahead. Tommy and Linda followed, not because they believed in Sarah's leadership the way Franklin did but because they didn't want to be left behind. Then Tommy did have a thought.

"Shouldn't we take some stuff with us?"

"Like what?" Sarah challenged, continuing to walk.

"I don't know. Stuff we brought, clothes."

"It's not going to take us that long."

"We'll be at the road soon," Franklin added. He too now saw the birches as the only possible way to safety.

Tommy, who had stopped briefly to ask his question, caught up with the rest of them as they went between the two trees and headed down a sloping path that opened wider as it descended, almost as if the trees were parting to show them the way.

Sarah felt her confidence grow as they walked. She even closed her eyes a few times to reassure herself she had zeroed in on the right direction. She had her eyes briefly closed when Linda's screech stopped them all.

"What's that?"

Ten yards away they saw what at first appeared to be a pile of clothes, a pile that had the shape of a body. All four of the kids moved closer, and as they did, the benign pile of clothes became a horror of human remains. The female hiker's body and backpack had been mangled and shredded by a bear, probably the one who had prowled the clearing, and the scene of devastation was ghastly. Tommy dry-heaved and turned away. The others backed up, gasping.

"Who is that?" Linda asked.

No one responded, but Franklin gave voice to their fears. "Bears." They all suddenly felt as if an attack was inevitable, unavoidable.

"We better go back," Tommy said.

Linda and Franklin agreed, but Sarah froze, staring at the ripped bloody mass of clothes and equipment in front of them. When Tommy turned and hightailed it back to the clearing, Franklin was torn for a second, then joined him.

"Sarah! Come on!" Linda screeched before she ran back as well.

Sarah knew she would have to go back with the others, but she didn't move and found herself mesmerized by the body. She squatted, still staring. Mr. Everett's body had held a similar fascination for her, but she hadn't had time to just look. She had once overheard a conversation between her mother and father that she probably wasn't supposed to have heard. Lena had talked about a patient who had died that day and how she had spent a much longer time than usual looking at his dead body. "I realized he now knew more than I'll ever know on this earth," Lena had said, and since then Sarah had wanted to see a dead body.

After a few minutes she heard Linda calling to her from the cabin and she stood. She looked down the trail they had been about to take. That was the way home. Sarah knew it. She looked back at the body, the jumbled bloody mess, and it seemed to speak to her. "You're right, Sarah," it said. "That's the way."

A nurse was checking IV lines and straightening Phil's pillow, talking almost nonstop while Lena and Janet stepped back and waited for her to leave. Lena saw Phil's hand jump a little, knocking into the raised bed rail, and thought at first that it was the result of the whirlwind nurse's tugging. But then she saw the hand leap up again involuntarily and knew that it had been caused by some sort of brain firing.

"Keep talking to him," Lena said.

Janet stared down at the hand and watched as it once again flew up.

"Phil. Phil. Can you hear me?"

Lena turned away and checked her watch. She was worried Witherspoon would show up now. A man's voice in the room turned her head. No one had entered. She looked at Phil.

"Was that him?" Lena asked.

"Yes."

"What did he say?" Lena asked Janet.

"I don't know."

Lena moved toward them. Phil seemed the same but his jaw was working now, as if he were trying to loose himself from the oxygen mask. Lena leaned in and spoke loudly.

"Phil, can you hear me?"

Phil's right hand bobbed and fluttered, as if in response. Lena turned to Janet.

"Say something to him."

"Phil. Are you there?" There was no response.

"What did you ask him?"

"Nothing. I don't know."

Phil's mask-muffled voice sounded again. "Paul." The word, though garbled, was clear.

Lena was startled. She wanted to take the oxygen mask off but she worried that Phil might need it to keep breath coming. She turned to the nurse.

"Who's his attending?"

"Dr. Halperin. He's on the floor. I just saw him."

"Get him."

The nurse was about to do so when the door opened and Witherspoon came into the room. Lena's anger rose at the horrible timing of her arrival. She put on her best doctor's face.

"I'm sorry. We can't have anybody in here right now."

"I don't need to stay. I just need to talk to Mrs. Rostenkowski."

"Well, not now. She—"

"I'm afraid I have to speak with her now."

Lena wanted to haul Witherspoon out of the room, explain what she knew, and tell her that Janet was vital to a solution of the case. But her gut told her that would take them farther away from Phil and his fragile awakening. Then a white-coated, chipper sixty-year-old, Dr. Halperin, came into the room. Lena pounced on him.

"Are you Halperin?" He nodded yes. Lena continued, "We've had some response, hand movement and a couple of words. I think he's responding to his wife." Lena indicated Janet. "She'll need to stay here, won't she?" Lena eyed Witherspoon, who didn't seem to be deferring to Halperin.

Halperin picked up on the tensions in the room. He went to Phil's bedside and watched the twitching right hand for a minute. Then he opened Phil's eyelids, pulling out a little flashlight, shining it in the pupils.

"How does it look?" Lena asked, knowing she'd hate to be asked such a question in the middle of an exam. After a while Halperin turned to her, his downbeat look one Lena knew she had given patients many times in the past.

"I don't see much improvement. I'd be surprised if his speech is responding to external stimuli."

"His wife said something to him and he said his son's name in return."

"Dr. Trainor. Forgive me for saying this but I think you're letting some emotions overrule sound thinking here. I'm not saying the patient won't recover, maybe even recover fully. But there's been a lot of damage to his system, and if he makes it through the thirty-six-hour danger period, he's going to need a lot of therapy just to get simple words out, to sit, to walk."

"But exercising neural pathways is beneficial in the danger period, isn't it?"

"Don't get me wrong. It can't hurt for you and Mrs. Rostenkowski to be here. And miracles do happen. But miracles are by definition unpredictable. And as you're well aware, we like to deal in the predictable as much as we can."

He looked over Phil's chart and made some notes. Witherspoon waited confidently. Lena realized that if she protested too much now, she herself might be suspect. Janet looked at her as if to say the jig is up. Halperin finished.

"Sorry what I said about your emotions, Dr. Trainor. I know this is a horrible time for you. My sympathies."

Lena snapped. "Sympathies for what? My daughter's not dead. I don't need sympathy."

Halperin nodded his apology and left. Witherspoon waited a few seconds before speaking.

"Mrs. Rostenkowski. Will you come with me, please."

"Can she come back soon?" Lena pleaded, knowing she wasn't going to be coming back.

"Possibly."

Janet, flooded suddenly with emotion, went red in the face and emitted a squawking cry like the one she had let fly in her house. The room echoed with the noise. Janet turned toward Phil. Lena thought she was going to attack him. But Janet held herself in check and just boiled for a while until she turned and marched herself out the door. Witherspoon gave Lena a long, searching look before she followed.

Lena turned back to Phil. The twitching hand had stopped. He looked as unresponsive as a corpse. The futility of trying to find Sarah through this piece of meat struck Lena full face. She felt her path blocked and herself alone, stymied. What could she do? She was in a hospital. You solved problems in a hospital. Did she have to go back out in the world knowing she had hit a dead end, knowing there was nothing more she could do but wait? That seemed intolerable. Phil, serene on the sheets, mocked her plight as much as if he were awake and laughing out loud. She couldn't help herself. She went to his bedside and slapped him so hard across the face his oxygen mask went all askew. She left it that way and hurried out of the room past the flabbergasted nurse.

# Thirty-two

When Sarah got back to the cabin, she found the other three kids in something like a state of shock. Franklin was once again trying to resuscitate the laptop. Tommy was banging a piece of wood on the floor. And Linda, Sarah could see, was balled up on a mattress, in the other room, crying. Sarah went in to talk to Linda, but when she sat down on another mattress, she felt how heavy her own limbs were, how tired she was, and gravity seemed to have doubled, sending her down on her back staring at the rotted wood of the ceiling. She closed her eyes.

Linda was able to leave off crying, mumbled something to Sarah, and when she didn't get a response, felt her eyelids droop as well. The heat of the day drew both girls into hard sleep while the boys, in the other room, fidgeted.

Linda didn't know how long she had been dozing when she came to and lifted, almost magically, off the mattress. She got up and found there was no one else in the cabin. The laptop lay on the floor, Mr. Everett's backpack had its contents strewn around the cabin, and the cooler was tipped over, the water and ice spilling out. Dense clouds outside made the rooms almost too dark to see in.

Linda called out for the others, listened, heard nothing in return. She was afraid to go out, so she looked through the door and called again. The grasses in the clearing were bent by a stiff breeze. She went to one window, then another, looking for the kids. Her anxiety rose and then spiked when she realized she had to pee. Again she called for the others. Nothing. Unable to hold her pee she made a dash out the door for the outhouse. She was nearly at the door when she saw movement at the edge of the clearing, near the birch trees Sarah had marched them through.

"Sarah!" Linda called and, forgetting about the outhouse, took giant steps toward the movement.

Suddenly the movement in the distance was very close and Linda stopped. It took her a second to realize that the mass coming toward her was the supposedly dead hiker, a ragged, horrible, bloody thing lumbering under a twisted backpack frame, hunched, now only feet away. The woman's bruised face was moving, trying to say something.

Linda screamed at the top of her lungs. But she was transfixed and couldn't move. She tried to step back but her feet were planted in the clearing's soft earth. She screamed again.

Sarah came out of a deep fog to Linda's screaming. Linda was on the mattress beside her, still asleep, it seemed, but screaming. Franklin and Tommy were at the door gawking at Linda. Sarah shook her and Linda jumped at the touch, was awake in an instant. She didn't know where she was, still in the grip of the powerful dream. Then she stood up and looked out the window.

"It's alive."

"What?" Sarah asked. Tommy and Franklin turned quickly to look out the windows in the other room.

"The thing we saw. It's out there."

"You were dreaming," Franklin said, turning back but still wary about what might be outside the cabin.

Linda was about to protest, realized Franklin was right, and rather than be relieved, dissolved in tears again. "I'm never leaving this cabin."

Sarah shook her head, stood up, and headed for the door, pushing past Franklin and Tommy.

"No. We've got to go now, while it's light. I know the way. I'm sure of it."

"Don't leave!" Linda shrieked.

Sarah didn't respond. She kept going and the three left watched her stomp out into the clearing.

"We should stay here," Linda pleaded with the others. Franklin shook his head. Tommy said nothing and moved quickly to catch up with Sarah.

"She knows what she's doing," Franklin said to Linda.

"No, she doesn't. It's . . . maybe it's really alive."

Franklin had no response but he too headed for the door. As if pulled by the force of the others, Linda jumped off the mattress and followed.

Sarah made sure the body wasn't moving as she came down the incline toward it. She waited for the others to catch up with her, to make sure they didn't balk. Once again the body seemed to give her assurance. Tommy stared at it as he came up behind her, Franklin kept his eyes straight ahead, and Linda, trailing, tripping as she tried to catch up, was crying hard as she came to them.

On an impulse, Sarah walked over to the body and stood only a few feet away. Linda gasped. Franklin mumbled something inaudible. Sarah hardly looked at the horror in front of her. She was simply trying to show the others, maybe herself, that she wasn't afraid of the body, of what lay ahead. She turned. The path they were on dipped and disappeared a hundred yards ahead. The woods were not dense where they stood, but in the distance there appeared to be a wall of saplings, full-growth hardwoods, pine, and brush. Sarah took confident first steps toward this unknown. The three others followed. Tommy was the last to leave. He had to force himself to stop looking at the mangled corpse.

From a thousand feet up, the Adirondacks, even in the bland overhead sun of midday, were gorgeous. Seth Cooper, who had been flying helicopters over this region ever since he returned from Vietnam in the spring of 1970, still found the undulations, the glinting light off the high lakes, the rich texture of the foliage canopy arresting, sexy even. But on this day he forced himself to stay away from the poetic and keep his mind on the task at hand.

A young park ranger, Jennifer Simmons, was riding with him. She was a very pretty woman, probably in her late twenties, someone new to the force, a ranger Seth hadn't worked with before. She was all business.

"Did you see the video?" she asked, not taking her eyes off the landscape rolling under the helicopter.

"Yeah."

"I studied that sucker. The saplings, behind the kids, looked like they were wind-stunted, so I'm guessing it was taken at an elevation over, say, twelve hundred feet. That's why I chose this section of the grid."

Seth didn't have anything to say to this. Looking for four lost kids wasn't routine, but still it was just a search when you boiled it down. Lost grandmothers, families who wandered off the path, hunters even who got disoriented—all had to be searched for with the same eagle eyes. Jennifer, Seth thought, would keep him sharp on this mission.

They had been in the air for about thirty-five minutes and had made seven sweeps of their assigned area, covering about a third of their grid space. The woods beneath them were thick and could easily hide four nine- and ten-year-olds. Seth wondered if they were smart enough to stay in open areas, clearings, and not follow paths the trees covered. He was thinking this as a hillock of spruce and white pine rose slightly in front of them and he had to lift the helicopter to accommodate the rise. At the crest of the hillock bright sun jumped off a small, hidden pond and Seth looked away instinctively so he didn't get sun spots in his vision.

As he did, he caught sight of three crows lifting off the water, scared up by the rotors. Seth had no love for crows ever since one had nearly taken him out by getting tangled in his rudder on a takeoff fifteen years earlier. He watched the powerful scattering of the crows closely. Jennifer's shout surprised him.

"Body!"

She pointed down toward the lake. Seth looked, but all he saw was water and a ring of marsh around it. "There was a body on the dock on that lake," Jennifer yelled over the rotors, craning around to look back.

Seth banked left and caught sight of some sort of dilapidated structure tucked in a small clearing. He headed the helicopter back toward the pond, slowing to a near hover as he did. When the pond came in view again, the dock was plain to see, and as they got closer, Mr. Everett's sprawled body was clearly visible.

"Shit," Seth mumbled, checking his coordinates, getting ready to reach the control center.

"That might be the kidnapper," Jennifer said, training binoculars on the body.

"Or some fisherman who had a heart attack," Seth said, having had the experience once of finding a long-missing lawyer from New York while searching for a couple of teenage hikers who had been lost.

As he radioed in his information, Seth surveyed the area. It wasn't all that rugged, no high, long ridgelines. Route 49 was visible about five or six clicks away. Seth figured that if nobody was nearby, command might be able to hustle somebody out there by late afternoon.

But he also could see that searching for the kids from the air wasn't going to be easy. They were in the middle of hundreds of acres of old-growth maples and beech, thick woods that would be hard to scour. And he had a further thought that didn't sit well. This was perfect bear country.

"Jesus," Jennifer gasped, still looking through the binoculars.

"What?"

"Looks like the crows ate half his head."

"They'll do that," Seth said, taking the helicopter even lower.

After she left Phil's room, Lena saw that David had tried to call her and dialed his cell. As the phone was ringing, she remembered that all that had happened with Phil and Janet had happened after David left. She wondered if this was the right time to dump all news on him.

"Lena, hi," he answered and Lena could hear car noises in the background.

"Hi. Where are you?"

"I'm driving with Les Malone. What's up? Any news?"

"No. You?"

"There was something on the radio from the park rangers a few minutes ago but we couldn't figure it out. It was out of our grid."

"Out of your what?"

"Grid. The area we're covering."

Lena welcomed David's voice. Even through the weak cell phone connection she felt his strength, the old strength she had fallen in love with. "Can you talk?"

"What?"

"Can you . . ." But Lena didn't want to tell him about Phil if he could hardly hear her. "Call me when we can talk, okay?"

"We can talk now."

"No. It's important."

"Okay. I . . ." and his voice dropped out. When it came back, Lena cut him off.

"I can't hear you. Call back later. David? I love you."

She didn't know if he heard that. The line went dead.

David had been distracted during the last part of the conversation because Malone was getting a radio transmission and David was hearing words like "dead body." When he finally hung up, Malone was slowing the pickup and pulling to the side of the road.

"What was that?" David asked.

"A state copter spotted a dead body that might be the one your daughter referred to."

"Where?"

"I couldn't quite tell from the description. I think I got the coordinates, though. Let me see the topo."

David handed him the topographical map he had in his lap. Malone spent a long few minutes searching the map. As he did so, Popper, who was scribbling in his notebook in the back seat, leaned forward a little and spoke to David.

"May I ask, was that your wife on the phone?"

David turned and glared at him but didn't answer. He turned back and waited for Malone to finish.

"There it is. Yeah, it's a pond. They said it was this small pond and they found him on a dock. Jeez."

"What?"

"I don't think there are any foot groups near there. It's gonna take 'em a little while to get in and check it out."

"You mean the helicopter didn't—"

"Guess there was no place to put her down."

"What about the kids?"

"No sign yet."

"Can we get there?"

"Yeah, but they don't even know if it's anything to do with the kids."

"Well, how many dead bodies could there be?"

"More than you might imagine."

"Well, I'd like to go over there."

Malone looked over at David. "I realize that. There's others gonna make it up before we could even get to the area. Let's stick to our plan here an' if we hear anything, we can go over and help out."

David chafed. Again he felt himself stuck in his decision to go with Malone. Suddenly he didn't want anyone else to find Sarah. He knew this was irrational, but it was a powerful desire. He wanted Sarah to come into his arms first. He wanted her rescue to be complete, not by some stranger. She had been in the clutches of a stranger and even if the person who rescued her wasn't the monster who abducted her, he or she still wouldn't be David. The others might rescue her but David knew that he was the only one in these woods who could truly bring Sarah home.

Lena hung up from the truncated call with David feeling even more alone than she had when she phoned him. She didn't want to go home. Gone was the feeling that she had to be at her house to welcome Sarah home. Home was just a place surrounded by the press.

She remembered that her father was probably in Montreal now. Standing in the hallway outside Phil's room, she fished the number of Richard's Montreal friend out of her jeans and dialed it. No one answered and no answering machine or voicemail picked up. She hung up and stared at the sheriff's deputy chatting up a nurse at the nurses' station. She went to him.

"Where's Detective Martin?"

The deputy pointed to a little waiting nook at the end of the hall. Lena went there and found Martin, sitting in a chair, head back against the wall, mouth open, asleep. She didn't wake him. She paced for a minute, then sat down next to him. Questions piled up. How did she miss the Rostenkowskis' evil design? Why didn't she see through J.D.? How naïve was she to fall for all that? Guilt rode the questions' coattails. She reminded herself that our expectations blind us, but that didn't help much.

She looked over at Martin. His open-mouthed snooze looked like the rictus of death, for Lena the image of failure. The hospital, with its beds and bodies, life and death, hummed around her mockingly now. You're useless. Your daughter is utterly lost and you can't do anything to find her. We're helping patients; we know what to do; what do you know? Martin snorted but didn't wake up. Lena couldn't stand the defeat stamped on his konked-out features anymore. She shook him hard to wake him and immediately regretted it. He was groggy and disoriented.

"What?"

Lena didn't know what to say. She heard a cell phone go off, thought it was hers, then realized, with relief, that it was his.

"You've got a call."

Martin fumbled for his phone, and as he did, his eyes danced once again, a resurrection. He looked at the caller ID, stood, and moved away from Lena. When she heard a cell phone ring again, she thought it was Martin's or an echo in her head. But after a couple of rings she realized it was hers. She saw the name Williams and she felt as if Mike or Po had known she needed them.

"Lena, are you at the hospital?" Mike started without introduction. There was an edge to his voice Lena hadn't heard before.

"Yes, I—"

"We just had a call from John Walker. Are they investigating the Rostenkowskis?"

"I think so. Witherspoon is questioning Janet now."

"Do you think . . . I mean, Jesus, could they have had something . . ."

"I think so." Lena hoped he would stop there.

"What do you know? Did you talk to her?"

Lena couldn't avoid the blunt question. She told him everything she knew, her time with Janet at the house, their attempt to get Phil to talk. When she finished, the line was filled with Mike's choppy breathing.

"You didn't have any idea they were involved? You couldn't see any changes in them?" This near accusation from the amiable Mike had real sting. Lena waited to reply.

"No," she answered finally. "I really didn't know them all that well."

Mike huffed. "Your kids played together. Jesus. How fucked up can this Janet be? Her own daughter and she doesn't know where she is?"

Lena was about to say she was sorry but thought better of it. Martin came to her waving his hand to get her attention.

"Who is it?" he mouthed.

"Mike Williams," she answered out loud.

"Tell him they spotted a body they think might be the father, Everett." Lena passed this on.

"I know," Mike shot back. "I've got a friend in the Adirondacks just called. They're sending in somebody by helicopter." He paused. "I gotta go. I'm getting too heated here. Jesus, I can't fucking believe this."

"I'm sorry," Lena said, against her better judgment.

Mike paused and let out a long sigh. "It's not your fault, Lena. I'm sorry I implied . . . I'm at my wits' end. They don't see the kids around where the dead body is. That probably means they tried to make it back on their own. I don't think Tommy can handle being out in the wilderness like that. I'm scared shitless."

They said a bit more and hung up, but it was that profession of fear that stuck with Lena. Mike had been her anchor and now he seemed adrift. Martin was on another phone call and Lena started walking aimlessly down the hallway. Sarah was a strong-willed, independent little girl, but that was in familiar surroundings. She was now just a fleck in some immense forest. How could she ever find her way out? How could David and the others ever find her?

The hospital's gleaming floors and fluorescent-lit walls suddenly became a barrier, a sanitized labyrinth walling Lena off from Sarah and the wilderness she was now wandering in. She had to get out. She began walking quickly toward the elevators when Martin's voice stopped her.

"Lena, wait." He came to her with a concerned look on his face. "Are you all right?"

"I've got to get home."

"I can't drive you. I'm supposed to stay here."

"I have my car."

"Did you get what I said earlier? They spotted a body by a pond and they've got hikers going in and they're going to drop somebody in by helicopter."

"But the kids aren't anywhere around," Lena said, hoping the tears that were forming in her eyes wouldn't come spilling out. She needed to get out of the building.

"Well," Martin started, then realized Lena was on some other tack. "You know they're questioning Mrs. Rost—"

"I know. And I know what she's going to tell them. And I know it's not going to bring the kids home. I've got to go. I can't stand this!"

"Wait a minute. You know? How did you know? Did she talk to you?"

"Yes."

"When?"

"When I went to her house."

"What did she say?"

"She said she and Phil were behind the whole scheme. They set it up. Through some middleman or something. I've got to go."

"Why didn't you tell me?"

"Because I thought she could help me get to Sarah. I thought she could get through to Phil. Don't make me explain. It only took me farther away. I can't even see Sarah anymore. Don't make me stay here!"

Martin obeyed, didn't ask any more questions, and before she knew it, Lena was in the parking lot of the hospital, fumbling with her keys, trying to get in her car. In her haste her cell phone popped out of her jeans pocket and clattered to the pavement. She scooped it up quickly and opened it to see if it was still working. She speed-dialed David's number and he picked up after the first ring.

"David," she said, not knowing why she called. She could hear car noise again in the background. "Where are you?"

"We're heading up toward . . . They found a body up . . ."

"I know about that. Are you going to go up there?"

"No. Others."

"David. I can't see Sarah anymore. I'm scared. I'm really scared."

"We're going to find her. They found a body."

"I know. That doesn't make any difference."

There was a long silence from David. When he came back on, he seemed distracted. "Lena, we're going to lose contact here soon. Is that what you wanted to tell me earlier?"

"No. I wanted to tell you the Rostenkowskis set up the whole thing."

"What whole thing?"

"The kidnapping."

David didn't respond to this but Lena could hear him talking to someone else. Then the line clicked off. Lena stood by her car and waited for David to come back, but he didn't. Even though the late afternoon was throwing up plenty of heat, she began to shiver. "Trauma," she said to herself, acknowledging for the first time that what she had experienced in the past few days was a traumatic event with all its bodily ramifications. Added to this was a growing horror that Sarah was slipping from her memory, from her tenuous grasp.

Nearly paralyzed with anxiety, Lena forced herself to get in her car and drive home. The world that had threatened to collapse ever since the Camp Arno counselor had walked from his van to her front porch was now actually cracking. She felt as if she could look in the rearview mirror and see the road behind her crumble. Lena forced herself to focus on the streets, the turns, but the nightmare of a receding, unreachable Sarah was in the front seat screeching at her. Throughout the drive she wondered if she was having a breakdown, if she should admit herself. But then she was on her street and through the media crush and past the sheriff's deputy and inside the front door and alone, shivering still, with Sarah now utterly lost to her. She stood there, too adrift to move, too horrified to cry.

David had left the phone call with Lena because as he and Malone and Popper were driving up a paved road toward the area where the dead body was found, two young teenagers, with bikes, had jumped out onto the road and flagged them down.

The teenagers were from a hamlet a few miles away and had joined the search when they heard about the helicopter's discovery. They had seen a team of park rangers at the trailhead to the blazed trail leading to the pond, but they knew of another, more southerly route that was not marked. They decided to see if there was anything on that trail.

"That's when we found the SUV," the taller of the two teens said as he and his friend guided David, Malone, and Popper up a grassy non-trail. A couple of minutes later they arrived at Mr. Everett's SUV, still hidden where he had left it.

"Jersey plates," David said as he went to the back and peered in. What he saw in the back hold made him gasp. There were the remnants of the kids' duffels, Sarah's prominent. He turned to Malone, who was coming up behind him. "This is it," he said, looking around to see which way the trail went. But they were surrounded by dense thickets. The shorter of the teenagers seemed to know what David was thinking.

"That way," he said, pointing. David still couldn't see a trail. They were all standing around not knowing exactly what to do. Then David remembered Lena had said the Rostenkowskis were responsible for the kidnapping. He shook his head, thinking to himself that he must have heard her wrong. There could never have been any connection between this SUV, those duffels, Linda's included, and that mousy teacher couple.

Malone used a cell phone to call in his information. Then he listened, said, "Got it," and hung up.

"The Navy Seal they dropped in reached the body. It's the right one." He was matter-of-fact, as if delivering a military communication.

"The kids?" David asked.

"No sign of them."

Malone's information about the Seal was actually not true. He had found plenty of signs of the kids once he left Everett's body and explored the shack. He radioed up that he could see kid clothes, a cooler, a backpack, a laptop, and recently used mattresses. With the helicopter still hovering above, he walked a perimeter looking for signs that would tell him the direction the kids had taken. His investigation was cut short when he heard noises in the woods in front of him. He thought at first he'd found the kids. But as the noises came closer, he realized he had just run into the park ranger rescue team reaching the clearing. They had spotted nothing on their way up, no sign of the kids and no sign either of a female hiker who had been reported missing.

# Thirty-three

About a mile after it left the clearing, the trail the kids were on petered out and they were looking down a long slope of strewn boulders.

"Is this the path?" Tommy asked, and Sarah said it had to be.

"I don't remember any rocks like this," Franklin added.

"We don't have to go back the way we came," Sarah said. Linda questioned this with a look, but she was too tired, hungry, and bothered by the no-see-ums that had been buzzing them for a while to argue.

They were halfway down the boulder field when Franklin slipped, turned his ankle, and wedged his leg up to his knee between two large granite rocks. The other kids got him out, but his ankle pulsed with pain when he tried to walk. They sat down to rest in a patch of sunshine coming through the dense leaves above.

"How long is it going to take?" Tommy asked.

"I don't know," Sarah answered. "But we'll get there." Sarah was trying as best she could to sound adult. Just below her consciousness was the running question, "What would Mommy do/say?" She drew strength from simply trying to imitate her mother. The rest of the kids drew strength from her. Their organization was a house of cards, but it was all they had. Sarah was sure that if they had stayed in the clearing, they might never be found.

Linda heard the noise first and jumped. The others heard it almost immediately after Linda and whipped their heads quickly toward the sound. Cracking the stillness of the woods, the heavy flap of a helicopter's rotors was on top of them before they could even react. Through the tree-tops they could see a black shadow rush over their heads, the ear-splitting noise pounding in their chests.

And then it was gone. They made feeble attempts to call to the swooping machine, but to no avail.

"Maybe that's for us," Franklin said. "Maybe they're coming to pick us up."

"It's too big," Tommy said. "Where would they land it?"

"They don't have to land it." Franklin was getting excited. "They drop a rope down and pull you up."

The kids were quiet, listening for more sounds from the helicopter, but the woods were still again. Then they heard the faint staccato of the rotors far off and Sarah began looking for an open area. She spotted one about a hundred yards away, back up the boulder spill.

"Come on!" she yelled, and all but Franklin, whose ankle was still in pain, followed her. They stopped once on the ascent to listen. The chop was getting closer. They had almost made it to the sunny open area when the helicopter barreled overheard and then was quickly gone. This time, though they waited what must have been ten or fifteen minutes, the helicopter stayed gone.

Slowly the kids went back down to be with Franklin. It was only when they left the open area that Sarah realized the sun was getting lower in the sky, slicing through the leaves instead of raining down on them.

"Can you walk?" Sarah asked of Franklin. He had been testing his ankle while the others were up in the open area. He nodded yes.

"Which way?" Linda asked. "It's going to get dark soon."

Sarah didn't really know which way to go now. She knew going back up the hill would be like turning around. She couldn't see a well-defined trail straight in front of them. Something about a patch of spread-out saplings looked promising though, and she made her decision immediately.

"That way."

"There's no path there," Tommy said.

"No, but that's the right direction." She didn't wait for a debate. She started off for the saplings and one by one the others followed.

To David's chagrin, after they got word that the rescue team, following a route close to the one the kidnapper must have taken from the SUV, had made it to the cabin, Malone insisted that they go back to his house for the night. Malone said he would make sure David was out in the search party before daylight, and that a good night's sleep would be best. David didn't want to move from the spot they were in, didn't care about sleeping at all, and wanted to be in the woods should Sarah and the kids happen to wander out their way.

But he wasn't in charge, and before the sun even went down, they were on their way back to Northville. They stopped for gas and Popper went in to take a pee. David, in the front seat, glanced around and saw some computer printouts folded and tucked into Popper's notebook. He peeked at one, saw that it had something to do with searches in the Adirondacks, and pulled the pages out to look at them.

The information was the result of background searches Popper had done. All were accounts of rescue efforts in the vicinity, going back to the late 1800s. There were a number of success stories, many were filled with heroics of one sort or another, but one, which Popper had highlighted, involved a ten-year-old boy who, in 1973, had gotten separated from his family on a hike and had become lost. Authorities were alerted quite soon after the family had missed their son, and the area in which the family was hiking had been scoured thoroughly for days, weeks. But the boy never turned up. Four years later his remains were found by hikers only a quarter of a mile from where he had gone missing. No one had ever been able to explain how such an intensive and focused search, one which must have combed the very area in which his remains were found, could have missed the boy.

Popper returned as David was finishing the article. David, who had become increasingly agitated reading the story, wheeled on Popper. "Why did you highlight this one? Huh?" Popper, taken by surprise, had no answer. "You think we're going to miss those kids? Do you?"

Malone got back in the cab as David finished this. Popper was still too taken aback to answer. David flung the papers back at him, turned to the front, and spit out, "We're going to find those kids."

When they first heard the humming sound, far off, Sarah thought it was a highway. She had a friend who lived near the Hutch, and when they played in the girl's back yard, they could hear a steady hum from that roadway. Sarah now was sure they were getting near such a road and her only worry was whether cars whizzing past would stop for them.

But as the sound got louder, it sounded less and less like a highway.

"River," Tommy said.

They walked another fifty yards and then, through a thicket of dense brush, they saw the white foam of a small, fast-running stream. The four kids stood looking at this barrier. Sarah was crestfallen, having expected relief, knowing she had led them all here. They were in a small depression caused by the river, and the sun was already gone in this valley. Deerflies had been buzzing the kids for the past half hour and Linda, their main target, was blotchy with bites. Had the river noise not been so loud, they could have heard the grumbling of their own stomachs. Franklin's ankle was now puffy and his movement slow and hampered.

But none of them were crying. None of them had reached a paralyzing level of despair. Three of them were still believers in Sarah, despite the dead end they seemed to have reached. Sarah felt this and looked around at their possibilities. They had in fact been on something of a trail for a while. It wasn't blazed, but there was a rut of sorts to follow. Now that trail branched, with one leg going upstream, one down, and a third following an incline away from the water. She knew she would have to choose one of these routes. But she didn't feel as if she could do it just then.

"Let's rest," she said, and the others found rocks and exposed roots to sit on.

They had been sitting like this for only a few minutes when a loud thump behind them turned their heads. They could see nothing, but the thump sounded again, this time from a slightly different direction, one farther upstream. Then they heard the scrape of leaves and underbrush and suddenly the regal head of a white-tailed deer, chewing vigorously, lifted from the foliage. It was a young buck with deep black eyes. It stopped chewing and stared at the kids, who were frozen on their seats.

Then with a sudden fury that made Linda rise and stumble back, the deer leaped toward the river, its hooves sounding on the soft ground; it seemed for a second to be heading right toward the kids, then it veered and bolted away through the bushes near the water. Tommy gasped. Franklin, who had moved quickly when he thought they were being attacked, hobbled painfully on his swollen ankle.

When Sarah's heartbeat returned to normal, she took control again.

"Let's move over there," she said, pointing to something of a natural lean-to made by two half-fallen tree trunks. The light was falling fast now. Sarah didn't know which way was the right way out. But whatever way they chose might take them longer than she had expected. She didn't want to be completely lost when night came. The others obeyed and soon they were huddled under the trunks. They listened for more deer, but none came. The white noise of the river continued, and as the dead-tired kids dropped off one by one, the only other sound that could be heard was Tommy mumbling what he remembered of the rosary.

# Thirty-four

Lena didn't know how long she had been standing near the front door. Being inside the house had stemmed her panic somewhat, though Sarah was no closer to her than she had been in the hospital. Lena tried to absorb the optimism of Martin and David about the body that had been found, but she couldn't. What law of physics or optics or geometry was it that said the closer you got to something, the farther away it seemed?

Lena went into Sarah's room hoping to have the real Sarah come to her there, among her possessions and posters and smells. But the room didn't yield any depth; all was surface, an extension of a Facebook page without the true substance of the girl Lena had given birth to.

Then Lena had the horrible thought that she was being prepared for something, that this lack of a full memory of Sarah was a precursor to loss, a way the body and mind armed itself for the horrendous shock of total absence from an other. This, Lena thought, might be the complete opposite of faith, or it might be an indication of some very deep-seated synchronicity.

Then she remembered the windows of the phony Camp Arno van

as J.D. backed out of the driveway. There were reflections blocking her view of Sarah. She had waved anyway. She was certain of that now. She could almost see her own hand in the foreground of her memory. For a long minute she tried to stay on the shores of rationality, away from the black churning waters of superstition. But finally the forces of irrationality were too much. Lena felt a hard cry well up from her stomach and just let it come. She wailed Sarah's name over and over, but the cry wasn't about words or thoughts, it was about the body at last reacting to the assault it had suffered. She cried until she thought she was going to throw up. She cried until her body shook violently and she had to sit on Sarah's bed. She cried until she could cry no more. And as she was heading to the bathroom for tissue, David called.

"Can you hear me okay?" he began.

"Yes." Lena's response was barely audible.

"You okay?"

"I've been crying."

"I saw Sarah's duffel."

"What?"

"They found the car, an SUV; the kids' stuff was inside. I couldn't touch it because of fingerprints but . . ."

Lena wanted desperately for this to be a sign of hope, but she found herself sinking deeper into despair.

"So she hasn't got any clothes with her?"

"I don't know. There were only two duffels. Maybe they—"

"I'm really scared, David. She can't make it out of the woods by herself."

"We'll find her. There are a lot of people coming up here now."

"What if they walk the wrong way, the kids? What if they just wander?"

"Lena . . ."

"I can't see her anymore. She's not with me. Do you understand what I'm saying?"

"Honey, we're going to find her. This is . . . this is a high-tech operation up here."

David didn't believe that but he could hear Lena slipping.

"High-tech? Don't we have to find her in our hearts first?"

David didn't reply right away. "That doesn't sound like Dr. Trainor."

"I know, but it's right, isn't it? She's lost in the woods and, and I can't really see her."

"Go in her room, honey. Look at a picture."

"I already did that. Nothing came."

David thought about the boy in the article Popper had highlighted, how he had been right under the noses of the searchers but had not been found. He fought off that fear.

"We love her, Lena. Isn't that the best way to see her?"

"I . . . I don't know," Lena said. That word, *love*—always problematic, always ill-defined and amorphous, bandied about without any real understanding—maybe that was, after all, the depth Lena sought. Unlike an image of Sarah, or words to describe her essence, the love she felt wasn't a thing or an idea. It was vital, dynamic tissue that bound them all without the least effort. It was timeless, existing before Sarah was born and destined to exist long after all of them were dead. "Yes," Lena decided. "It's enough."

David said he would be getting up before dawn. He said the area was being mobbed with searchers and news media. Not mentioning the haunting article about the boy, he professed unbridled optimism that they would find the kids.

Lena forced herself to echo the optimism. "We're going to have to think about the aftereffects, what Sarah's going to need when she gets home."

"I know," David said. "But she's tough."

"I wonder if that's a good thing."

David wanted to tell Lena to stop being so negative, but he didn't want to argue, didn't want to become a flashpoint for Lena's anxiety and insecurity. He took another tack.

"Lena, one thing at least is going to be changed for her when she gets home."

"What?"

"Us."

"Yes."

"I know she's felt the tension. But that's over for now, isn't it?"

"Yes. And another thing."

"What?"

"The new one," Lena said softly.

"You know I woke up this morning and didn't know if I dreamed you saying you were pregnant or if you really said it."

"I really said it."

"I know."

They celebrated the pregnancy in silence for a moment, then David, wiping away tears, said he had to go, to get some sleep.

Lena sighed. "I don't think I'll be able to sleep. I wish now I was up there with you."

"Just be with Sarah, Lena. Lead her to me."

The few tears Lena had left spilled over her eyelids then. They mumbled "I love you's" and hung up. David's request, that Lena be the guide, now raised a lumpy fear in Lena's chest. She went in the bedroom and lay down on the bed, staring at the ceiling, wondering where such a power was going to come from.

The landline phone ringing woke her from a doze an hour later. Disoriented, she didn't recognize her father's voice at first.

"Hey, honey, it's me."

"Who?"

"Dad."

"Where are you?"

"Can't tell you but I'll be there with the searchers tomorrow. Is David there now?"

"Yes."

"Give me his cell number, will you? I'll see if we can hook up. But I don't know. I'm going to have to be pretty anonymous."

Lena had to get her own cell to give him the number. After she'd done so, Richard was all business.

"I still sound American, don't I?"

"Yes, Dad."

"Once we get the kids, I'm gonna have to go back the way I came. Won't be able to be part of anything or come down to see you. Sorry, honey."

"Dad, thanks."

"No thanks involved. You give my Sarahbell a big hug for me, okay? I love you. Bye."

Lena was fully awake now. She turned off the bedroom light as she headed for the kitchen. But she stopped when she saw a stretched rectangle of moonlight on the bedroom floor. In her mind she took the oddly angled shape and made the corners square, the sides equal, something she had done since she was a kid. And when she'd righted the patch of moonlight, a piece of her faith returned. She would find a way.

The kids slept fitfully, leaning on each other and the logs that surrounded them. A heavy crashing sound woke them deep in the night. Tommy calmed them by being absolutely certain it was another deer.

Mosquitoes buzzed them out of the dark, but when Sarah woke in the first very faint light of dawn, they were gone. A fine, misty rain probably kept them away. Under the logs the kids could hardly feel the rain, but when Sarah unfolded her legs, lifted Linda's head off her shoulder, and poked her own head out, it felt like she was under the mist sprinkler in her back yard.

She looked again at the three trails leading from where they were. A little bubble of panic floated up from her stomach. She didn't feel sure of any of them. How was she to lead?

David had slept on a daybed in Malone's attic and was the first one up in the house. He heard the rustling of a soft rain on the leaves in the trees outside the attic window and wondered if weather would hamper the rescue effort. In the dark he made his way downstairs and turned on the coffee machine, which Malone's wife had set up the night before. He went out on the porch and saw the main street of Northville clogged with news vans and cars idling with their headlights on. Unlike the press outside their house, this gathering felt like a swell of support and it brought tears to his eyes.

He went back in the house and fiddled with the GPS device a friend of Malone's had lent him. He was nervous about his assignment. Others had assured him that he would not be out of the sight of other rescuers, but they had told him what to do in the event he "wandered." Fears that he himself might get lost compounded the fears he had for Sarah and the other kids. Those four nine- and ten-year-olds had no team with them, no GPS devices, no maps, no guidance, and no experience. Only by the dumbest of luck would they get out of the woods by themselves. They couldn't make it on their own. They would definitely have to be found.

Lena was surprised to see that there was news in other parts of the world. She had turned on the television and dialed up CNN expecting full-time on-the-spot coverage of the search for the kids, even though it was six o'clock in the morning and she knew the rescue effort wouldn't start in earnest until seven or so. When a long piece on renewed efforts to start a Middle East peace summit began the hour's newscast, and that was followed by problems with a dam project in China, and *that* was followed by some celebrity nonsense outside a Hollywood club the night before, Lena almost threw a book at the TV. But the teaser for the next segment had a clip of David and promised an interview with the "father of one of the little kidnap victims."

Lena stared at the screen through a soap commercial and a car commercial. The David she had seen in the clip seemed like someone other than her husband. The lens had distorted him; the fact that he was on TV had distanced him from the man she had talked to only hours ago. Maybe she shouldn't watch. She needed to be closer to David, closer to Sarah. Why was she concentrating on this silver car swooping around some apocalyptic landscape?

Then there was the anchor again and the screen was ablaze with words and information. And suddenly a female reporter stood on the main street of Northville, in the near dark, with frenzied activity behind her, yammering on about the plight of the "brave little boys and girls" who had been forced to endure a nightmare and now were wandering in these "almost impenetrable Adirondack woods." The dark vision of this made Lena seethe, and she missed most of the woman's interview with some park ranger. Then David's face popped up. He was inside a house. He was looking at the reporter off camera. He was dry-eyed and sound-bite friendly.

"We're going to find them. I don't have any doubt about that." He listened to a question and said something further but the reporter was talking over what David had said and then the newscast cut back to her live. The quick in and out threw Lena for a loop, and she didn't hear anything the woman said. Then the anchor was back on and another story was beginning. Lena punched the remote and the TV went dead.

When all the kids were awake, they still huddled under the log because of the continuing rain. Linda's face was a mess of bug bites. Franklin stared out at the middle distance, seemingly lost to himself, rubbing his ankle. Tommy was animated but his thought, which he shared, didn't help.

"Mr. Everett must have had some friends. Maybe they're coming here looking for him, right?"

None of the kids answered, but Sarah, in particular, absorbed this and sighed. Another hurdle. She was already anxious about what to do and when, and she didn't need any thoughts about Mr. Everett's friends. She jumped out of the shelter.

"Come on. We've got to go."

"Now?" Franklin asked.

"We can't just stay here."

Linda was uncurling from her sitting position. "Which way?"

"That way," Sarah said, pointing to the branch of the trail that led up the incline, away from the river. She made her decision without thinking. Thinking was bad. Thinking didn't help.

"Are you sure?" Tommy asked. Sarah didn't respond. She started out in the direction she had selected. The path was muddy and the spritzing rain made it difficult to see. She wanted to cry. But she didn't. She swung her arms wildly as if to ward off anything that might get in her way. The sight of her striding so purposefully made the others feel she really did know what she was doing. They followed and Linda, thinking Sarah was swinging her arms for some reason, did the same.

There were video cameras and still photographers waiting for David when he pulled up to his assigned section of the search area in Malone's pickup truck. A couple of reporters tried to get him to say something, but he just walked behind Malone to the trailhead. State troopers kept the press from following and soon David, along with about fifteen others, some carrying rifles, huddled about a quarter of a mile into the woods. The leaf canopy there was thick and the rain was minimal, though the ground was muddy. David's porous running shoes looked inadequate for the work ahead.

But his real worry was the rifles. He pulled Malone aside and asked about this.

"Why do they have to have guns?"

"We all should have 'em."

"Why? Everett's dead."

"Bears aren't." Malone said this not wanting to elaborate. David suddenly had to imagine coming on the kids just as a bear was about to attack them. He felt completely out of place then. He tried to remember what they had said the night before about dealing with bears. You don't run. He remembered that much. Do you look them in the eye? Do you flap your arms?

The park ranger in charge then spoke loudly.

"I want you all to line up by the numbers you've been given, then we're going to go north-northwest, approximately fifty-eight degrees, single file, and set up quarter-mile spacing. When the last of the line is set, I'll blow this foghorn. When you hear that, begin walking toward the headings you've been given. If you see anything, holler as loud as you can. Got it?"

"What's the second number they give us?" one man asked.

"That's your stopping point. That's where we intersect with the other grid. When you get there, just turn around, retrace your steps, and come back here. That'll be it for your day."

David adjusted the cheap poncho he had bought in Northville the night before. He pulled the GPS device out and the piece of paper with his instructions on it. He saw others doing the same. Then they began to line up and walk in the direction the park ranger had said they should. There was a lot of talk along the line about the accuracy of the devices they were using. David punched in fifty-eight degrees in his, but had he followed it, he would have veered away from the line by forty-five degrees. He realized quickly that the search for Sarah was not built on precision. All these well-intentioned souls were going to be zigzagging through the grid they were meant to cover. One of those errant zigs or zags could miss the kids easily. He thought about the conversation with Lena. He did want her to guide him now. These machines, he knew, were not going to do the trick.

His cell phone rang. He didn't recognize the number but answered.

"David. It's Richard." It took David a little while to realize it was his father-in-law calling.

"Richard. Hi. Where are you?"

"I'm, uh, in the Adirondacks, with a search party, in upstate New York."

"What? You?"

"Yes. Don't want to say any more. Do you know what grid you're in?"

David wondered briefly if this were a joke, but Richard's voice was distinctive and this was definitely Richard. David looked down at his instruction sheet. "Forty-nine south."

"Ah, we're way over on the other side of the ridge, twenty north. That's good, I guess."

"Uh, yeah. Why?"

"One of us is going to find her. I gotta go. You give her a big hug for me if you're the one finds her, okay?"

"Yeah."

"David, you all right?"

"Yeah, fine. Just surprised, I guess."

"Couldn't give you any warning. You got my cell. Let me know if you hear anything. I'll do the same." And he hung up.

David had been standing by himself for a while as the line spread out. Now he could see no one to his left or his right. A little wind had picked up and the fine rain swirled. He could see his instructions were starting to run on the paper, so he memorized them and put the paper under his poncho. Then the foghorn sounded, far away it seemed, and he started to walk in the direction the GPS indicated. There was no trail but there was no knotty underbrush either. He was in the middle of a pine stand and the floor of needles was relatively dry. He lifted his head and then swiveled it left and right. You couldn't miss four kids in these woods, he thought. He looked far to his right. He thought he saw movement there, but he wasn't sure. That would be the searcher to his right anyway. Or would it? Why weren't the searchers wearing chartreuse or something? Assurance and doubt alternated as he went down a small embankment and up the other side. He checked his GPS directions again and they said he should go a bit to the left. That didn't feel right, didn't feel like he would be making a straight line. But finally he followed the direction. For now at least, he'd have to trust the machine.

After the kids had been walking for an hour or so, Franklin asked if they could stop. They had been climbing another boulder field and his ankle was swollen and throbbing. It was while they were sitting, all of them really in need of a rest, that they heard what sounded at first like an elephant far, far in the distance. Tommy actually asked out loud if that was an elephant, but then quickly withdrew the question. None of the kids, however, knew what it was. It didn't sound again.

As they were trying to puzzle this out, a crow flapped overhead and its presence sent several small birds fluttering around, chattering their warnings. The crow reminded the kids of Mr. Everett and their uneasiness was evident. Franklin, in fact, stood despite his bad ankle and said they should move on.

Sarah started up the boulder field again, but her anxiety built with every round stone she moved to. She was not at all sure now of their direction. When they reached the top, she hoped she would have some sense of the right way to go, but she couldn't count on it, didn't trust herself now. She had never been the sort of girl to run to her parents at the first sign of trouble. She only went to them if it was absolutely necessary, if she had come to the end of her own independent road. Now, she began to think, she was about to reach that end. But where were Mom and Dad?

# Thirty-five

Skeleton news crews hung out in front of the Williams, Walker, and Trainor households in the morning. There were no news vans at all in front of the Rostenkowskis. Word of Janet Rostenkowski's arrest had been leaked and action on that front had switched to the federal building in White Plains after Paul Rostenkowski, led by two uncles, left early in the morning.

Mike Williams had started to go to work, but he didn't get out of the garage before he realized he wouldn't be able to get anything done thinking about the search. He briefly thought about heading north but settled for staying in the house and keeping in close contact with his friend in the Adirondacks who had the police scanner.

John Walker actually did go in to work, but only because it was absolutely necessary. He had to sign papers in an international, time-sensitive closing and had to be on site to do so. A company car picked him up at eight and was ready to whisk him home as soon as the closing was finished. Sheila stayed home and spent the morning with five of her congregants. It was Sheila who suggested they do a Bible study, but that soon became more of a support and prayer group when one of the women said she just wanted to reach out and bring Franklin back home.

For Lena there could be no deeper hell than having to just sit and wait for news of the search. She did field one urgent work call, an emergency consultation that was needed before a tricky lung surgery was performed. When she hung up, she felt the void again and briefly thought about calling work, maybe attending to other cases, just to keep the emptiness at bay. But she knew that all her cases were covered in what was supposed to be her vacation, and she realized she might be doing her patients a disserviçe trying to work only to distract herself.

She finally allowed herself to take a shower, checking computer news outlets first and putting the mobile phone in the bathroom with her. The cascade of water felt good, but she didn't want to linger, didn't want to feel comfort when there had been no resolution. Yet the thrum of water held her briefly, and it was in those brief seconds that something changed. She couldn't say what it was. As she got out and was starting to dry herself, the image of a fanlike lawn sprinkler sweeping back and forth caught her. That, she knew, had something to do with what she had felt in the shower.

Then a rush of related images: Sarah and some friends running wildly, laughing through that sprinkler; Sarah and those same friends being called away from the sprinkler; the back yard at the friend's house decorated for a birthday party; and finally Sarah, in a still-wet bathing suit, having a blindfold put over her eyes, being spun around.

Lena recoiled from this last. It was too much like the image of a kidnapping. She opened the medicine cabinet and watched her own image slide away, only to return when she retrieved her skin cream and shut the cabinet door. Seeing her own wet hair in the mirror, she let go of her resistance and let the birthday party scene return.

Sarah, now blindfolded, had been spun around several times, was shushing all the kids and parents, telling them she didn't want them to say anything. The parents looked at Lena and gave her a "typical Sarah" look. Then they all watched as Sarah started off, veering left, away from the garage. The kids had all they could do to keep from saying anything.

Then, Lena remembered, staring at herself in the mirror now, a miracle had happened. Lena had simply told Sarah, without saying a word, which way to go. This telling had been stronger than mere thought. It had been stronger even than some corny telekinesis. It had been at its root the powerful mother-daughter connection Lena had felt when bloody little fifteen-second-old Sarah had been laid in her arms. There was no difference between the two of them, they were one, and Sarah responded as if Lena had screamed in her ear. She moved toward the donkey, veered again, responded again when Lena used the power she had discovered, and after a couple more of these course corrections, put the tail within inches of the donkey's rump.

Lena didn't give this memory a second thought. She closed her eyes and let the towel that had been wrapped around her torso fall to the ground. Standing there naked she hardly breathed, she didn't think, her existence as a separate body, one apart from the world, from Sarah, drifted away. This time she wasn't aware of saying anything to Sarah, telling her which way to move. But she knew in the deepest part of her being that she was guiding her daughter, showing her the way.

The phone rang and its clanging ripped Lena from the melded existence she had been in, forcing her to use thoughts. She tried to stay where she was, but then she wondered if the call might have some connection to the feeling. She picked up the handset and saw it was David.

"News?" she asked in a rush. David's voice was crackly.

"No. I'm halfway up my route. This is really hard, Lena. They could be between me and the next guy and I wouldn't know it."

Lena hung up without a word. She stood still again, the drying water goose-bumping her skin. She didn't know if she could will the feeling of oneness she had had. She reeled back through the birthday party images, but that was too mechanical an approach. She was in a panic to return to that essence. She knew only grace could give her that blessing. Faith, she needed faith. She let thoughts tumble and drift away. Come, Sarah. Be with me. Be with me.

Franklin was the last one to get to the top of the boulder field, and when he did, he sank down and put his head in his hands. There was nothing there. No paths, no trails, just woods and underbrush. Sarah, standing, looking at this, realizing the others were watching her, couldn't conceal her own anguish.

"Which way?" Linda asked, her voice cracking and feeble. The others, starved, aching, and exhausted, waited for some sign of assurance.

Sarah could feel she was on the edge of tears. Now, she knew, was the time to turn to her parents, to feel her father's arms lift her, to smother herself in her mother's soft skirt. But Sarah and the other kids were farther away than the road they had come in on, far away from Camp Arno, wherever that was, far, far away from her bedroom. They were nowhere.

She felt dizzy, as if she were going to fall back down the boulder field. But she couldn't fall, couldn't sit, not now. The others could but she couldn't. She fought the dizziness and held on. She stabilized herself and suddenly remembered what had given her her courage back in the clearing—pin the tail on the donkey. She had won that game. She had done that herself. She hadn't known really which way to go, but she had gone the right way and she had won.

Sarah closed her eyes. The blackness now was a comfort beyond comfort, as if she were being wrapped in assurance and peace. She felt herself turn left a quarter turn. She opened her eyes. She was still looking at the same woods, but they looked radically different now. It was as if a ribbon of blacktop stretched out in front of her, winding between the trees, skirting the underbrush. The certainty of it was overwhelming. She practically shouted her response to Linda's long-ago question.

"This way!"

David was checking the GPS device when the unmistakable sound of movement to his right startled him.

"Hello!"

The movement stopped and a voice responded. "Hello." Then there was more rustling, and the thin, bearded man in all-weather gear who had been in front of David in the line appeared through the underbrush. Both men were disappointed to see each other.

After a few minutes of figuring, they realized that either David or Carl (he only gave his first name) had drifted from the straight line they were supposed to walk. That meant that one of them had failed to cover the ground they were assigned and could possibly have missed the kids.

Water had pooled on the upturned brim of Carl's hat, and when he dropped his head, the water dripped off.

"I guess we better split up, take her to the top an' maybe cover what we lost on the way down." Carl then turned unceremoniously and walked back in the direction he'd come from, leaving David to figure out which way to go. Lena's call, with its abrupt ending, had been tough. And now this. He looked down at the GPS device and had the urge to throw it as far into the woods as he could. He looked back down at the route he'd taken to the spot in which he was now standing.

As if it were a wind sweeping through the trees, a confidence surrounded him. To hell with the numbers. He knew where he'd come from. He knew Sarah was somewhere in these woods. He'd forge ahead and let his instincts take over. He wasn't going to get lost. If he wandered, he'd just bump into Carl or one of the others. Richard was out here somewhere. Hadn't he said one of them would find Sarah? David made a little course correction in order to avoid a marshy patch near what looked like a natural spring and began to lengthen his stride. As he did so, he could hear Lena's voice, not in some mystical way, not even saying anything in particular, but just the music, the sounds she made when she talked to him. It wasn't guidance, but they were together. He could feel that completely.

Lena had dressed after her shower, but that had taken a long time. She would pull on a piece of clothing and then sit for long stretches, doing nothing, seeing nothing. When she finally was dressed, she stayed in the bedroom, staring at a blank screen on the computer. And while there was no overt action in this, Lena experienced a presence, a fullness that she didn't want to lose. The phone rang twice more, but she let it go, reasoning that if it was good news, she'd get it sooner or later; if it was bad news, she didn't want to hear it. Right now, she realized, "the best thing I can do is nothing." When she came up with that phrase, she felt silly at first, as if this were some variation on the Hippocratic oath's "First do no harm." But the nothing she was talking about was really everything, the void being more like a vacuum that nature abhorred and filled to the brim with Sarah. Gone was the question of who her daughter was. Gone were any questions at all as long as Lena could just empty herself and let Sarah rush in.

As the hours passed, the intensity grew. Lena had moved from the bedroom, spent at least forty-five minutes making a piece of toast, surprising herself when, sitting at the kitchen table, an hour passed in what she would have guessed was five minutes. Had she not been so certain of the connection to Sarah, Lena would have thought she had become unmoored, disconnected from reality. And maybe, Lena thought briefly, this was the inner experience of madness or schizophrenia, the bounty and wellness she felt inside looking to the outside world like loony irrationality. But if that were the case, if the loss of her daughter had sent her into some realm of mental illness, Lena didn't care. She and Sarah were together. Wherever that placed her on some scale of mental health didn't matter. The ground of her reality was this feeling she now had, one she increasingly was able to stay in, one that grew stronger and seemed more and more potent with every hour. And as the feeling ballooned out, it had less and less to do with results, with guiding her daughter as you might guide a remote-controlled model airplane. Sarah, to Lena, was already home.

Tommy saw him first. He was at the front of the group because Sarah had stopped to prod Franklin. Franklin's ankle had been bothering him, but more than that, he had lost faith in Sarah's ability to get them out of the woods. Sarah, whose certainty about the correctness of their direction had grown almost exponentially in the past hour, didn't want to argue with Franklin. She just wanted to keep them all moving. She knew she was right. Tommy's little cry from up front whipped her head around.

Tommy crouched quickly and the others, including Sarah, did the same. Sarah was certain that a bear was up ahead. She moved very slowly, past a cowering Linda, and reached Tommy. He pointed. Far in the distance Sarah could see a man making his way through a stand of saplings, slashing at them, clomping up a small incline, swearing to himself, it seemed. Even from a distance Tommy and Sarah could see his foul temper, one very much like that of Mr. Everett. The comparison didn't help their judgment.

"He's looking for us?" Tommy asked. Sarah, whose confidence in the path they were to take was secure, didn't, however, have a clue how to interpret this man. In her mind she hadn't imagined any saviors but her parents. Her mother had been such an incredibly strong presence in the last hour that she was certain they were heading toward her. Anybody else they might encounter in the woods was potentially dangerous. Tommy's earlier question about whether Mr. Everett's friends might be coming to get them had been imprinted on her thinking and it surfaced now.

"What's he carrying?" Sarah asked. Tommy rose up slightly for a better look.

"A gun."

That did it for Sarah. Franklin and Linda were now with them. Franklin whispered, "What is it?" and Sarah pulled him close.

"Quiet," she hissed low. "It's one of Mr. Everett's friends." Linda whimpered. All four plastered themselves to the ground. They heard the snap of branches in the distance and tried to gauge whether the snaps were coming closer. But after a while, the snaps silenced altogether, Tommy rose enough to see ahead, and he told the others that Mr. Everett's friend was gone.

Sarah decided they had to wait longer because the direction she knew they had to take was one Mr. Everett's friend had just crossed. As they waited, Sarah realized the rain had let up some. She could hardly feel it now. Though she never could have articulated it, she took this as a sign of some sort, an affirmation. They were on the right path, they had done the right thing in avoiding Mr. Everett's friend. She could feel her mother. And the rain had stopped. They were going to make it.

• • •

David reached the top of a ridgeline and figured that should be his turning-around point. He took out the GPS device reluctantly, and the reading told him he had gone as far as he was supposed to. But he didn't want to go back down the way he had come. He wanted to keep going. Sarah was out there somewhere, not behind him. He couldn't have missed her. He trudged on another five or six hundred yards and then saw the terrain sloping precipitously away from him. He turned back. As he crested the ridge again, he saw movement to his right and quickly realized it was probably Malone, who had been behind him in the line, heading back down the way they had come.

If he was that close to Malone, he realized, either Malone had drifted toward him, or Carl, earlier, had been the one to go off course. Whichever, his own alleyway of searching had been narrowed. He decided to go back down and keep to his left, in Carl's direction, to cover any ground Carl might have missed.

David had a sandwich lunch with him but he hadn't stopped to eat. The rain was letting up and he decided he could walk and eat at the same time. As the clouds lifted, he realized that the sun was getting lower in the sky and that he had been walking a much longer time than he imagined. He checked his watch. It was three twenty. It had taken him some five hours to cover his territory. He would have to hurry down to make it back by dark.

About fifteen minutes later David came to a small brook, didn't bother to look for an easy crossing, tried to traverse it by the small slick stones sticking out of the water, slipped, and went down. He scrambled to his feet and made it to the other side. His left half was soaked, as were his shoes. He decided there was nothing he could do and continued on. But after a few yards he realized that he hadn't crossed that brook on the way up and the woods in front of him didn't look familiar.

He pulled out the GPS but the reading he got didn't mean much to him. He punched in the starting coordinates, but they pointed him in the direction he had just come from, the other side of the brook. He stood for a long while looking from the GPS device to the brook to the unfamiliar woods ahead.

And then he laughed. He was lost. He was in the middle of the

Adirondacks looking for his lost daughter, and he himself was lost. He laughed at the absurdity of it all. The incongruous reaction relieved the pressure but didn't last long. Which way would lead him out of the woods? Which way would lead him to Sarah? He panicked to think that he might find Sarah only to be lost with her. He checked his cell phone and saw no bars, no coverage.

A long-forgotten adage about following a river when you're lost came to him. He decided to walk along his side of the brook for a while. He wouldn't be retracing his steps and he wouldn't be heading into the other unknown woods. Walking with his clammy left pant leg was dispriting, but he had made a decision and he felt better as he continued. His movement, the rustle of the leaves he was pushing aside, the crack of sticks under his feet, broke the silence of the woods around him.

And then he wondered why he had been quiet all this time. Did the rangers forget to tell the searchers something? Shouldn't they be shouting the kids' names as they walked? If you missed seeing them, they might hear you.

"Sarah!" he called out, a little embarrassed at first by the sound of his voice in the aural emptiness of the woods around him. But he got over his self-consciousness quickly.

"Sarah!" Soon he was shouting at the top of his voice, using all the kids' names, stopping only when an incline forced him to take more breaths. Why hadn't they told him to do this? Was there a reason? Was he scaring up some animal with his shouts? He didn't care. The shouting felt right, help banish his insecurity about where he was, where he was heading, and it might just be the thing that brought Sarah to him.

"Sarah!"

When Lena heard the doorbell ring, she was deep inside herself, lost to the world. On her way to the front door she regained some of her touch with reality, but not all. Detective Martin seemed to realize this when she opened the door to him.

"Am I disturbing you?" he asked, moving back a half step.

"No, I was just . . ." Then Lena came fully back and realized he might be bringing news. "Come in. What is it?"

Martin didn't step forward. "I have some news about the Rostenkowskis."

"What?"

"He died fifteen minutes ago. The press won't know for another hour or so."

Lena saw Phil's face as she slapped him on the hospital bed. She struggled to put this out of her mind, to feel nothing. She had to get back to Sarah. "I . . . I'm sorry. I can't . . ."

"And I don't know if they're going to charge her, the wife."

"What?"

"Witherspoon says she doesn't believe her. Says she's nuts, making up stuff out of grief."

"No. She told me. She wasn't making stuff up."

Martin sighed. "I know. You're going to have to get involved."

"Okay, but not now. I need to be alone."

"I'm afraid I have to bring you with me."

"No. I need to connect with Sarah. I need to get to her."

Martin stood his ground and Lena realized she sounded half-cracked.

"Please," she said. "Later. What difference does it make? She doesn't know where the kids are."

"I know. But I have orders." His eyes were still soft but he was firm.

"Fuck your orders! It's Sarah's life!"

She slammed the door shut and stood stock-still. She fully expected Martin to open the door, but when he didn't, she spent agonizing minutes trying to return to the place she had been, the nothing that led to everything. She closed her eyes.

As she did, the image of Sarah playing pin the tail on the donkey came to her again and with it a peace. Sarah was still there, with her, still listening or moving with her mother. Lena didn't dare move.

• • •

They were in a small hollow and the light there was low in the early evening. Franklin had been crying for a half an hour now, the pain of his ankle and his despair leading him to shed any embarrassment. Linda had been badgering Sarah for long stretches about the direction they were taking. But Sarah had been certain, and because she wouldn't let up, wouldn't even engage their concerns, they followed her.

Suddenly Tommy, uncharacteristically, told Franklin to shut up. Franklin did for a second, and Tommy told them all to listen. All they heard was the silence of the woods, a slight soughing in the branches above.

"What is it?" Sarah asked finally.

Tommy didn't have time to answer before they all heard a very faint, far-off human voice shouting what sounded like "Linda!" Linda gasped.

Franklin lifted his voice and shouted in return, "Hey!" Sarah jumped on him immediately.

"Quiet. What if that's Mr. Everett's friend?"

The shout in the distance came again. "Sarah!" Sarah's heart beat fast now, the desire for this to be her father warring with her instinct to be cautious.

"We can go see," Tommy said, his own hopes evident. Another "Sarah!" sounded and the kids turned their heads slightly to face the direction of the sound. The shouts were getting fainter.

"That's not the right direction," Sarah said. "He's out there. We've gotta go here."

"No," Franklin wailed. "We need to go see." He started in the direction of the voice, but no one else followed. He stopped. Sarah bit her lip for a long minute, closed her eyes again, and suddenly it was as if her decision had been made for her. She opened her eyes and headed in their original direction. Linda and Tommy were now between Sarah, striding off in one direction and Franklin, stopped on his way toward the voice. Tommy first, then Linda followed Sarah. When the three of them were so far away from Franklin that he could hardly see them in the falling light, he gave in and hobbled after, tears streaming.

"Wait! Wait for me!"

• • •

The brook had ended in a swampy muck and David had had to skirt the sucking earth by going at least a quarter of a mile to his right around it. His voice was giving out but he continued to shout the kids' names. When he reached some higher and drier terrain, he suddenly began to recognize some of the landmarks he'd memorized on his way up the hill. Then, as if he were following street signs, the route back to his starting place became clear, the turns at this rock or that fallen tree trunk evident. He stopped yelling the kids' names then, knowing he'd already covered this territory. After fifteen or twenty minutes of easy walking, he heard voices and then saw a clutch of rescuers gathered near where they had gathered at the beginning of the day. The sight was not a welcome one for David. Had there been four kids with them, he would have run to the scene. As it was, he didn't want to even join the group. But Malone saw him and turned.

"Hey, we were worried about you." The five or six others in the group and the park ranger turned to David now. "You get lost?"

For some reason, David felt like punching Malone for the question. "A little." He turned to the park ranger and took his anger out on him. "Why weren't we calling out the kids' names?"

"Good question," the ranger started, with a smile. He was a very young redhead with freckles and an ill-fitting Smokey the Bear hat. "Sorry we didn't cover that. Rescue teams used to do that, and you see it in movies and such, but it's a bad tactic to use for lost kids. For lost adults, yes. Lost kids will sometimes get even more disoriented by hearing their names being called or will think they're going to be scolded or will simply not understand what's happening. It's much better just to sight them."

Bullshit, David thought, but he held his tongue. The ranger turned back to what he and the group were doing when David had come upon them. He had a topographical map and he was trying to draw on the map the route every rescuer took. David opened his cell phone, saw that he had bars, walked away from the group, and dialed home.

Lena was exhausted. She opened her eyes and realized that she had been sitting in the same position for a long time. The light in the living room was very low. Her exhaustion came from the intensity of her concentration. Yet she didn't feel bodily tired the way you might if you'd just run a marathon. Nor did she feel the weight of thought. She was hollowed and the room she was in floated all around her. Sarah occupied every molecule in her sight and sense now. Her presence had grown stronger and Lena knew, absolutely knew her daughter was close and getting closer.

The jangle of the telephone made Lena gasp. But again she didn't want to be shaken and she let it ring. When the answering machine picked up and she heard David's voice, coming from the kitchen, she couldn't, however, ignore what he was saying.

"Lena, it's me. We're giving up for the day. I—"

Lena raced to the kitchen to pick up the phone.

Sarah stopped and the three kids behind her stopped as well. The woods in front of them were taking on a bluish hue in the fading light. Sarah closed her eyes, hoping for the return of the internal compass that had guided her this far, but the blackness was just blackness, and she quickly snapped open her eyes, afraid.

"We can't go any farther tonight," she said, as much to herself as to the others.

Linda whimpered. Tommy stared ahead as if he might be able to see something. Franklin balled his fist.

"We can't stay out here another night," he wailed. "We can't."

But the others realized they had no choice. It would soon be too dark to walk. Sarah looked around for a place for them to shelter. But this time there were no natural lean-tos.

A thump and breaking branches behind them caused Linda to shriek and the others to jump and turn. The sounds increased but they could see nothing. Then, as quickly as they had come, the sounds went away, leaving the kids with their imaginations and a long night ahead of them. Now Sarah felt as if she might cry. This was all too much for her. She had truly reached the end. She wanted her mom and dad.

Now.

• • •

Lena reached the handset on the kitchen table and punched the talk button.

"David. I'm here."

"Hi."

"What did you say?"

"They've given up for the night. We're going in."

"No, you can't. It's not dark yet."

"It is here. Almost. We all walked our routes. Nobody—"

"David, don't. I know she's near you."

"How do you know that?"

"I can feel it. I just can. Don't go in yet."

"There's nowhere to go, Lena. We've covered everything near here."

"She can't stay out there another night."

"We'll start first thing in the morning."

"No, David. Please. Don't do it."

David realized then that Lena had turned some sort of corner, that the debilitating tension of the past few days had finally caught up with her, that she had, perhaps, snapped. He figured a small lie was better than any sort of attempt to reason.

"Okay," he said. "I'll keep searching."

"Yes. Thank you. She's close. I swear. I feel it. She's here now, with me, with both of us. Just reach out. Go."

Even through the tinny sound of the cell David could feel the pathos of this, the desperation, the nonsense. "Okay. I'll call you later."

"Thank you. Thank you."

David hung up and was about to pocket his cell when it rang. He didn't recognize the number.

"Hello."

"It's Richard. No luck over there, I take it."

"Right."

"I'm going to come your way. If we can find somewhere to be alone, I'd like to see you," Richard said, decidedly more downbeat than he had been in the morning.

"I just talked to Lena. She's . . . she's . . ."

"What?"

"I don't know. Maybe it would help if you talked to her. She was almost hysterical."

"Lena?"

"I know. She's not herself."

"I gotta catch a ride here. Hope I see you."

Richard hung up and David folded his cell. The group of rescuers was already starting back for the road and he followed. The defeat in the scene in front of him was evident, and yet some of the rescuers were laughing softly about something or other. The woods pressed in on David now, laughing as well, mocking him for not being able to find his daughter among their trees and underbrush. Lena's insistence pushed against this mockery and it seemed to David as if he were in the middle of some crazy battle between a distraught mother and the implacable forces of nature. With every step toward the road, the pressure of this defeat and violation bore down on him.

Had all this been his own fault? His stupid relationship with Tricia that got him fired, that took him away from Sarah's departure? He boiled in anger at himself. Sure there were the kidnappers and the Rostenkowskis and whoever else, but wasn't it his failures that had caught Sarah in this trap? He couldn't stand another failure now in the woods. Those people ahead of him could walk away laughing, but with every step he was taking out of the woods, he was walking away from Sarah, compounding his failure and guilt.

Then he snapped.

He wheeled suddenly and without a moment's thought began running back in the direction he had come from.

"Sarah!" he screamed as he ran. The rescuers turned quickly, saw a deranged father hurling himself back into the woods, and followed to help, to bring him to his senses.

David tripped on a root, rolled, got up, and kept running, kept screaming.

"Sarah! It's me! Dad!"

Still running, he stopped screaming briefly to listen. He went blindly into the underbrush, bulled his way through, and kept running, his face and arms a mass of scrapes now, his cheap poncho torn to shreds.

An incline took his breath away and he could only scream weakly, then not at all as he reached the top. But then at the top he thought he heard a faint sound ahead of him. Was he imagining it? He stopped and tried to listen but the sound of his own hard breathing was all he could hear. He gathered his breath and screamed again.

"Sarah!"

It was weak and small and far away, but what came back was a voice, a human voice, Sarah's voice.

"Daddy!"

David heard the rescuers calling behind him, their shouting jamming his hearing. He plunged ahead in the near darkness. When he stopped again, Sarah's voice sounded, louder now, a little to the left. He screamed again, heard her respond, and turned toward her voice.

Now even as he ran he could hear his daughter. He was getting closer; she was joined in the shouting by other small voices. They were all there.

Sarah saw him before he saw her. His yellow poncho was a beacon in the blue wood. She ran toward him, yelling at the top of her lungs, the others racing behind her.

"Daddy!"

They met in a crush of a hug, Sarah enfolded in the scraps of the poncho until David lifted her and hugged her as hard as he could. Linda followed, gripping his leg. Tommy and Franklin held back but inched forward as Sarah's tears and David's became tears of joy. The rescuers following stopped when they saw David and Sarah twirl in happiness. "I couldn't believe my eyes," one of them would later tell a reporter. "That father. How he found his girl. I don't know how he did it, but damn, there it was."

Lena had left the call with David and collapsed on the couch. He hadn't sounded sincere when he said he would continue searching, but she had to believe him. She could no longer feel Sarah the way she had all day. She had been sent back to her normal bodily self, and she buried her face in the soft fabric of the pillows. But she didn't cry. She saw Sheila in front of her congregation professing the power of faith, real faith. And Lena dug into her own soul and her own faith and trusted David and trusted Sarah.

And just before there was a knock on the door, just before she heard the shoving reporters breaking protocol and surging toward the house, she knew. She knew that David had told the truth, that he had searched and that he and Sarah had found each other. When she opened the front door and stepped into the thrust microphones and the glaring lights, she didn't have to be told the news. But she asked anyway.

"What? What is it?"

"They found the kids!" a reporter shouted.

A wave of screamed questions broke over her but they were all gibberish. She buried her face in her hands. Time and space didn't exist. She was standing where she had stood when the counselor got out of the van and walked toward the house. He was gone now. The nightmare was over. The world had mended. The days that had felt like eons had passed and suddenly David and Sarah were with her then in a way they had never been before. The new life inside her nuzzled up to join them all. There was nothing more to hope for.

They were together.

# Epilogue

Sarah was supposed to meet the others outside the club at ten thirty, but none of them were there when she arrived. She was tired of texting people to find out how close they were to a rendezvous, and so she decided to just wait. She had had a beer after her last class and she was in good spirits. The night was warm. She would just watch the street life.

The girl was about Sarah's age, though she was so heavily made up it was hard to tell how old she was. She was with a group of retro goths, all dressed in black, pierced, a real mess, Sarah thought. But the girl looked familiar in some way. Sarah stared, and as the girl passed, she must have felt the stare and turned briefly toward Sarah before moving ahead. Then she stopped, turned back, left her group, and came to Sarah.

"Sarah?"

"Yes." Sarah looked closely. "Linda?"

They stood looking at each other for long, awkward seconds. It had been ten years since they said a tearful goodbye as Sarah's father delivered Linda to her aunt's house in the Bronx. Neither knew then exactly why Linda wasn't going to her own house in Pelham. When, several hours later, Sarah had found out from her mother about Mr. and Mrs. Rostenkowski's role in the kidnapping, Sarah's young mind wouldn't let her separate the parents from the child. She screamed that she never wanted to see Linda again.

"You're in the city?" Linda asked nervously, glancing at her friends, not able to look Sarah in the eye.

"I'm at Columbia. You?"

Linda started to answer but found her words choked off. Tears brimmed quickly and sent rivulets of black mascara down her cheeks. She blinked and shook her head.

"I'm going to go back to school sometime. I've . . . I've got some problems to straighten out."

Linda's friends called. She turned to them, turned back. The tears still flowed. She rushed her words.

"I'm sorry," Linda said, her eyes pleading and sincere. "I've wanted to say that to you for so long. I'm sorry."

"It wasn't your fault."

Sarah hadn't gotten this out before Linda shook her head violently, wheeled, took big clomping steps back to her friends, hooked arms with one of the boys, and pushed them all down the street. The boy turned and gave Sarah a confused look as they walked away.

When Linda was out of sight, the street bustled again for Sarah and she wondered if she really had seen Linda or if she had seen some imagined ghost. Over the years much of what had happened back then returned to her more as dream than reality. The days in the woods lost specificity and became a mishmash of heat, trees, a bear, marshy smells, the sight of decomposed bodies. Her father had taken her camping a few times—partly as therapy, she now realized—but those days in the woods were vastly different from the ones with Mr. Everett and the kids.

The rescue played like a dream for Sarah as well. After the joy of seeing her father in his ripped poncho, there was the surreal crush of the press, pushing and shoving microphones in her face. And then out of this scrum, a heavily disguised man came to her, and instead of pushing him away, her father let the man hug her. He called her his Sarahbell and said he loved her. He sounded a lot like her grandfather in Sweden. When she learned later that he was indeed her grandfather, the knowledge took none of the surreality from the moment.

When she got back to her house, to her mother, to her room and her things, life started to become real again. For days she wouldn't let her mother out of her sight and her mother held her as much as she wanted. Then one night her grandfather came to the house, without his disguise, and it was his full, strong hug that told Sarah the real world hadn't spun off into space after all.

Sarah's initial anger toward Linda had subsided when her mother told her that Mrs. Rostenkowski had been declared unfit to stand trial for her part in the kidnapping and had been committed to a mental institution. Linda, Sarah learned, was sent to live with her aunt in the Bronx. Sarah, who by that time was back in school, back with the friends she and Linda had shared, sympathized with Linda and defended her to others, though she never felt like getting in touch with her.

Nor did she feel she wanted to get in touch with Tommy or Franklin. Her mother and father had kept up with the other parents, and so she knew that Franklin was a year ahead of her, a junior at Cal Tech, and Tommy was some sort of all-state in football but had turned down college scholarships in order to travel in Latin America. Sarah tried to imagine them all together again, what they might say to each other, but she just couldn't see that happening.

It wasn't until she was in her last year in high school that Sarah, at the urging of a very sensitive writing teacher, researched what had come to be known as the "camp kidnaps." Reading about her nine-year-old self was like reading about a stranger. The man who had called himself J.D. had done his time and was seen in one picture looking much older, bearded, his head hung, unrecognizable to Sarah. The ransom money had been returned to the parents after the State Department had intervened on their behalf. Five years after the kidnapping a Bulgarian sex-trade ring was broken and in their computer records was found evidence of their role as middlemen in the "camp kidnaps" scheme.

Sarah was going to write a paper about these facts, but they didn't seem to have much to do with her. Instead she wrote about the birth of her brother.

She had heard the story so often from Lena that it was easy to write the paper. Michael had been born during a snowstorm. Lena and David had had trouble getting to the hospital because the roads were so choked. Sarah had been with them, in the back seat. When they finally made it to the emergency room door, Lena had turned to Sarah with tears in her eyes, smiled as bravely as she could between contractions, and said, "I'll see you later." Sarah had nodded to this, but she hadn't waved goodbye. She knew better than that.

Out of Sarah's sight, Lena had balked as they neared the birthing rooms. Almost hysterical, she had shouted that she didn't want the baby out in the world, that he was safe where he was. David had talked her down from this perch and the delivery had gone smoothly after that. Sarah had been let in to her mother's room only minutes after the birth. The little flesh ball that was Michael opened his eyes when she came near, and Sarah leaned her face near his and waved a little greeting. "Hi, Michael. We'll take care of you," she said, without really thinking. And when she looked up, she saw her parents dissolved in tears.

But after writing that paper, Sarah had put thoughts of the "camp kidnaps" and their aftermath out of her head.

Linda's appearance on the sidewalk in front of the club, if indeed she was real, had made the feelings of that traumatic event long ago immediate. The helplessness, the fear, the separation from the world and her parents all bubbled up again. Sarah was about to call her mother, to hear Lena's reassuring voice, when she remembered Lena was at a conference on the West Coast. The unearthed feelings made Sarah wonder again, as she had often, how her mother had found such strength in the aftermath of what had happened. In the months after the kidnapping, Lena left her practice to devote all her time to Sarah. Sarah had been helped enormously by her mother's strong, clear attitude toward the tragedy: it occurred; we can't do anything to change that; we can't let it shape our lives forever. David found he needed work structure and had easily landed a job with a startup in White Plains. Lena and David had been visibly, palpably in love then. The horror of the abduction had given way to a cocoon of warmth and security.

But Sarah now knew there were still vestiges of the tragedy in her life. Not as apparent as Linda's perhaps, but real and tenacious. Trust. That was still the hurdle, Sarah thought, as she saw her friends come down the block toward her, laughing about something. She had survived, she had absorbed her mother's strength, but the world, her world at least, was full of J.D.s. She never could fully give herself over to others. These people coming now, good friends—could she one day let them deeply into her life, tell them what had happened to her? Could she fall in love the way her parents were in love? She didn't know. The future was like the deep woods. She closed her eyes. She'd find her way.

# Acknowledgments

The idea for this book had come years ago but it had been shelved. Then Mary Hedahl one night on the back porch said, "What about that camp story?" Thanks for that. I would like to thank Graham Greene for pioneering (at least as far as I know) the method by which this novel was written. My sister Linda Esposito, my first reader back when we were kids, was the first reader of this book and was enormously helpful and supportive. A bow of thanks to Lynn Schnurnberger for looking out for a fellow writer and for rigging the bid. A one-word (and she knows what it is) shout-out to Penn Whaling for her work on my behalf. And thanks to Amy Schiffman for her helpful suggestions.

Trish Grader championed the book and saw that it found a very good home. Sulay Hernandez took it under her editorial wing and gave it fine loving care.

And many thanks to Ann Rittenberg for donating her time and expertise to support a worthy cause, for her early editorial suggestions, for her patience with a newbie, for making no promises and keeping them all just the same, and for being a spirited friend throughout.